The Whisper of a Saint

Richard Dietrich Maddox

Copyrighted Material

Dedicated to

Tina and Stuart

A GIFT

As a way of saying "thank you" to my readers, I
recorded a video entitled

"*The One True Path to Happiness,*" which you can get
access to on my website.

To receive your FREE download, go to:

http://richardmaddox.com

My sincere goal is to help all my readers find the Bliss
of Enlightenment, in this very challenging age of ours.

First Appearance

Theo Reyesin had first seen the man during childhood. The boy had been playing in his grandmother's garden, had been, in fact, holding a free-flowing conversation with his imaginary friend, Jocko, when he noticed the old fellow floating in the air above the strawberry plants. The fact that the man was suspended in midair did not bother the child, but his *appearance* did arouse his curiosity. For one thing, he wore a beard. It was white, about the size of a sponge, and seemed to the daydreamer to be a shred of cloud that had fallen from the sky and landed below the man's jaw. And his eyes appeared to have been broken off from some bright star and set, like jewels, into their sockets.

The old man wore strange clothes, too: a sort of bedsheet that wrapped his body up as though he were pretending to be a ghost. Theo stopped and stared at him and the man smiled, in a very winning way. They carried on a short conversation, in the same manner Theo communicated with Jocko: through clearly enunciated thoughts. The man told the boy that he knew him and watched over him, and that he would continue to do so in the future. And Theo thanked him for being so kind and wondered how he managed to float in the air as he did. To this question, the response was merely a broader smile. Then the man began to dissolve; that was the only way to describe it: his image grew vaguer, before resolving into thousands of tiny light points, and then finally disappearing from view.

After the garden encounter, Theo did not see the man again for several years. But, one day, as he was lying in the spring grass at school during recess, while he was examining the clouds overhead, in which he saw springing lions, and a girl's head, and a dragon preparing to devour a snowball, Theo felt a light tug on his attention. Turning his head to the right, he observed the old man in the sheet. This time the visitor sat on the ground, with his legs crossed, apparently in complete comfort on the moist grass.

1

But something was different about him this time. His smile spread broad and his eyes gleamed with an affection such as Theo had never before encountered. Theo sat up and felt, for some unknown reason, that he should bow his head. When he lifted it, the man began to communicate, again without recourse to words. "I am your friend. I have been keeping an eye on you. You are going along well. See how happy you are when you are by yourself, just being quiet and observing nature? Continue in this way. I will come to see you again."

Theo found himself unable to form a thought. Had he been capable of doing so, he would have spoken-thought "Thank you for caring about me." But his mind rested empty, and all he could do was beam at his wonderful visitor.

Once more, as before, the image of the man softened and faded; it began to sparkle, as if made up of minute flashbulbs, before finally disappearing completely.

Theo had reached the age when one is capable of reflecting on things a bit. "Who is this man who has come to me twice in this strange way? How can he just appear and disappear as he does? Why does he dress so strangely?" For none of these questions did the boy have reasonable answers.

He thought about asking someone, his teacher, or his father, his minister at church, or some older boy, but realized, through intuition, that the effort would surely end in failure. Who could possibly explain what was certainly inexplicable? Better to keep this experience quiet and ponder on it.

Theo asked himself if he might have fallen asleep and dreamt about the old man. But he knew that he hadn't. One moment he had been staring at those unusual cloud shapes, and the next, at the bearded old man. He wondered if the man might be a magician, capable of projecting his image across space. And this seemed as likely as any other explanation he could muster.

2

The third time Theo encountered the old man was during his training to become a spiritual teacher. It happened during a period of intense meditations, when the students had been instructed to spend three hours a day with their eyes closed. At the end of one especially deep meditation, he had opened his only to see the same bearded man seated nearby, next to an enlarged photograph of Theo's own Master. Oh, such love poured out from the eyes and mouth and tilt of the head and lean of this man's "body"! It struck Theo in this way: all the compassion in the world was now concentrated on him; all the tenderness in the universe was now spread over him, like a warm blanket over a shivering infant. A flood of the most intense bliss imaginable surged through Theo's soul, rendering it content to a degree he had never conceived possible.

He sat there gazing at the man. No thoughts came, for his mind seemed to have been forgotten, back somewhere else at some other time. All Theo could do was wonder at this image of Absolutely Perfect Love, and bask in It, and savor It.

The thoughts of the holy man sounded clearly in Theo's consciousness. "This is the last time I will visit you. There will come a time when you will seek me out. But I shall continue to be aware of you until that day arrives. Trust your instincts and continue on the path you have chosen."

Pressing his palms together, Theo fell down in prostration at the feet of his saintly visitor. When he lifted his head, the man was gone. But, in the place where he had appeared, having roughly the shape of a human body, a silvery-white shape glowed. And, within that shape, small waves of what Theo could only describe as mirror glints flowed smoothly in every direction, giving off warmth and contentment as they moved.

3

Into the World

Theo Reyesin instructed people in meditation techniques for a number of years. His own meditations became gradually deeper over time. He married and eventually, succumbing to the attractions of the material world, sought out and landed a job in the business world.

His responsibilities took him all over the United States. Rising before dawn, he hurried to the airport, landed in a distant city, held meetings with his prospects, and, finally, collapsed exhausted in a hotel-room bed. But no matter how tired he was, the young man always remembered to meditate in both the morning and evening. In fact, he could not have even imagined heading out into the world or off into sleep without having first bathed his soul in inner silence.

The stress of trying to close difficult deals, of constantly rushing from one place to another, made him miserable. Oddly enough, he had never really cared much about money. So he found himself regularly wondering why he put his body and mind through all the travail. But the answer quickly came: He had a family now and a home and all the expenses involved in supporting both. So he lowered his head and kept charging forward, growing progressively more fatigued and sick at heart as the years passed.

From time to time, in the middle of a long airplane flight or before attempting to fall asleep in a strange hotel bed, Theo's thoughts would revert to that holy man who had three times appeared before him, manifesting out of the ether. He could still, after all these years, see those forever eyes that had spoken of heavens and paradises beyond one's wildest imaginings. He could still feel the tender love that poured forth from the visitor, causing his host to feel wrapped safely in the arms of the very universe.

Theo had studied Eastern Religions in college and come to learn a fair amount about Indian spiritual traditions. These studies, and his fascination with the idea of human enlightenment, had led him into the meditation movement where he had spent several years of his life. And even after starting his career in business, the young man had continued to read extensively in the field of Indian sacred texts and commentaries. He now understood that, like his own Master, who had dropped his body some years before, the visitant who had come to him was certainly an enlightened Saint.

What he had not yet figured out was the purpose of the holy man's visits. He had foretold that Theo would eventually come to him. But how, the daydreamer wondered, would such a trip ever occur? His schedule was so busy that he barely found time to eat. His yearly vacations of one week were constantly interrupted by urgent phone calls from his staff or conference calls arranged by the CEO. No, there was certainly no chance that he would be able to take a long trip to visit a holy man. And, besides, how would he ever find him? He didn't know the saint's name or even the region where he lived. He seemed, of course, to be Indian, but even that was up for question. Theo could not understand how the prediction would come true. But he knew without a doubt that the saint would not have spoken the foretelling words if they had not been certain to reach fruition.

Years Roll On

Successes piled up for Theo as he mastered his craft. He carried what he called his "bag of tricks" with him as he moved from one company to another. By dint of both success and failure, he had learned precisely what moves to make at which times in order to complete a large deal. The companies he worked for flourished. He earned a reputation as the man who could launch any company on the path to prosperity.

But awards and accolades and large checks had come to mean very little to Theo Reyesin. The energy consumed by sixty-hour weeks and eighty-percent travel had fatigued him to the extent the English appropriately called "bone weariness." By the time he made it home late on Friday evenings, he could barely make it to the sofa before collapsing, a heap of listless inertia.

Wishing to be a good father, he attended his son's baseball games and encouraged his daughter on the basketball court. But he could not summon the energy to accompany his wife to parties or dress up and take her out to dinner. He needed every hour of the short weekend to recharge himself for the shock of the 5:30 am alarm on Monday morning.

His body had begun to feel as if it had fought through a long and arduous war. The fatigue in the man's muscles carried an actual weight, which constantly pulled his body downward, toward rest, relaxation, and sleep. Theo had been blessed with inordinate natural energy, so he was able to power through this profound tiredness, but always at the price of adding to its cumulative load. The businessman's mind, too, had paid a price for all its red-zone RPMs, all its efforts to achieve creative invention while struggling to remain awake. Whenever he finally found a bed or a sofa to collapse onto, Theo would lie there catatonic, his brain resembling a heavy gray stone.

He took solace from the fact that his family thrived. His son had attained Eagle Scout status and his daughter played oppressive defense on her school's basketball team. Their mother coordinated the household staff, shuttled them to parties, games, and sleepovers, and celebrated birthdays with her lady friends from the neighborhood. At least, the man thought, all "this" has purchased a pleasant lifestyle for my family.

But then another Monday arrived and the dire routine began once more. Worse than the pressure of producing sales for a company whose product only half worked, whose salespeople required personal assistance all over the country, was the internal politicking. Theo had always been an idealist: in his view, everyone in the company was on the same team, striving for the same goal of producing revenue by closing sales. But experience had taught him that such idealism was misplaced. Other departments had their own priorities. When Theo's prospects demanded a new feature in the product, for instance, the engineering team might tell him that such work was "not interesting" to them. At which juncture he would have to argue the point as to whether the engineers existed to amuse themselves or to build products companies wanted to buy.

Or, Theo would phone the CEO from the road, at the end of a 16-hour day, and ask how the support team was doing at Stravinsky Enterprises, a company then testing the product prior to purchase and encountering difficulties in its trial. He would be told that support had decided the issues could be resolved over the phone, that they didn't need to fly out to Stravinsky. Now Theo's closing strategy had been based on a certain expert engineer from his company bonding with his counterpart at Stravinsky. Without that manager's nod of approval, the deal would never come off. But now the two men would never meet. And the deal would be lost.

Occasionally, the political infighting was to the knives. Theo learned that the Vice President of Marketing had taken the CEO out

7

to lunch and proposed that he, the VPM, take over Sales, arguing that Theo was a great "hands-on peddler," but not an executive capable of taking the company to the next level of success.

The man attempting to outflank Theo never once had to take a redeye flight; he left the office at six every day, and had dinner at home every night. While Theo was working his way to premature collapse, his opponent was busy wheedling at headquarters to remove him from his job.

So pressure came from every direction: prospects refused to buy unless the product was changed, but the company refused to change it; prospects had limited budgets, but the CEO refused authorization to discount the price of the software; salespeople promised the closure of deals, but never delivered them; the heads of other departments failed to provide the support Sales needed to meet its quotas. Theo began to feel like one of those movie heroes surrounded by enemy soldiers sniping at him from every side.

The prospect's proposal required international product support. How was he to make Hong and Ari in technical support assume the dimensions of a vast, dispersed team of experts based in cities spanning the globe? The prospect asked to speak with five customers in her own line of business. How was Theo to get around the problem that his company had only five customers *in toto*? Customers sought credit terms which the Chief Financial Officer refused to approve. Sales representatives demanded Theo's presence in Chicago and New York at the same hour of the same day. And, at every turn, the pressure of the quarterly sales quota loomed like the glinting blade of a guillotine. How could he possibly achieve his number?

The Breaking Point

The breaking point came when Theo got fired from his job by a CEO who had always claimed to believe in him as "the finest sales guy I have ever known."

Theo had pulled off a near miracle: convincing a prestigious Wall Street firm to buy his small company's product, when larger, more established competitors seemed to offer a far safer proposition. He had even had to persuade the buyers to structure their own website differently than they had expected to, in order to accommodate the new software. But when the installers went onsite to bring the application up, it failed to function. The software revealed bugs no one had previously known to exist. The engineers worked late into the night, receiving "code patches" from their fellow developers in an attempt to right the ship. In the end, they failed, and the customer rejected the software and refused to pay the vendor's invoice.

The Vice President of Engineering convinced the CEO that Theo had promised performance from the software that it had never been designed to deliver. Normally an honest fellow, he now felt his position threatened if he let it be known that the product simply did not work in a real-life installation. Complicating the politics was the fact that a Board Member of Theo's company had initially referred him to the prospect, who was a personal friend. The Board Member, personally embarrassed, demanded that the CEO take action. And Theo paid the price.

He had been fired before, so this was not a devastatingly new turn of events. Startups regularly brought in new sales executives as they upgraded their CEOs. And Theo was a fierce warrior for his cause, which sometimes rubbed his peers and bosses the wrong way. But something about the nature of this dismissal shook him deeply. He had been blamed for a failure entirely out of his own control. And he had won the deal against incredibly steep odds. Fairness said he should have been called "hero," but reality named him "villain."

9

Something inside him snapped. He knew that he had had enough of all this, and told his wife that he would like to retire early and pursue spiritual interests. The couple had plenty of money and a house worth several million dollars. Their children were close to college age. They could easily sell the house, move into something smaller, and, by cutting back expenses, continue to live a comfortable life.

But his wife refused to countenance such a change. "You can easily get another job. You always have. So you got fired. Big deal. Update your resume and call the headhunters." Her response finally convinced him of what he had suspected for many years: she loved him as much for the money he provided as for any inherent qualities he possessed. She failed to empathize in the least with his "last straw" exasperation. He should "just get over it."

These words, laden as they were with self-interest, barren as they were of even a suspicion of empathy, caused his snapped fiber to completely break away and fall to the ground. Theo knew that an era in his life had just ended.

Alone Again

Theo moved out of the family home and into an apartment overlooking the Pacific Ocean. Behind him lay the long years of stress and struggle in a business world whose sole goal had never really meant anything to him. In the past lay his marriage, his status in the world, and all his emblems of success.

He still saw his children every weekend, but, otherwise, virtually every tie to his former life had been severed. He was alone, unemployed, and living on a modest income. He knew no one in the eccentric beach community where he had taken up residence.

Other men passed through the clichéd "mid-life crisis" in the sunken seat of a cherry-red Corvette, or in the company of a cherry-lipped blonde several decades more youthful than they. But Theo broke from his previous life with precisely the opposite intention: to ignore material concerns and cultivate his own quiet company.

He would meditate in the morning and then take a walk along the ocean-view pathway. The salt air cleansed his inner being. The reach and breadth of the ocean reminded him of matters grand and everlasting. The recurrence of the waves, their plashing, first hard and loud, and then soft and whispering, lulled his soul like a mother's lullaby. Thousands of minute mirrors signaled urgent messages to whoever might be watching. Comforters of lilac-colored ice plant draped dun cliff faces, not quite reaching to the places occupied by sharp boulders silvered by the morning sun. Sea lions yelped their peculiar clown-horn barks; gulls circled and swooped; uncanny brown pelicans grew majestic as, wings outspread, they rode the thermal updrafts.

Small coves, whose pellucid green water revealed every detail of their bottoms, seemed about to yield up, at any moment, a lovely mermaid, her locks dripping, her tail slowly waving in contentment. Theo would round a curve and encounter a Monterey pine or cypress, hiding in its branches a cacophony of invisible birds. He would stand, stunned, as pools of sea water, caught atop rocky outcroppings, got transformed by sunlight into quicksilver shields, electroluminescent eels, and Zeusian breastplates.

The ocean had fascinated him since he had first encountered it as a child. It spoke to his soul of eternal recurrence, unfathomable depth, and continual change. Now, in this new period of his life, the ocean cleansed him and gave him hope that miracles might still be possible.

Later in the day, Theo would wander the streets of the bizarre town, observing its colorful denizens: the "crazy hat" woman, a homeless virago, with a vocabulary that would have been competitive in any fish market, whose crumpled and stained Stetson bore at least a hundred pins celebrating everything from the 4H to the Water Ballet Junior Olympics; Hercule, a former bouncer from a sleazy dive in Marseilles, who, in a single day, had been diagnosed with cancer, falsely arrested for murder, and abandoned by his wife for his best friend; and Daisy, a transvestite fond of the Gatsby-era look, who would regularly promenade down the main street in long pearls, spangled, sheathing dress, and prim toque hat.

Theo would buy a coffee and sit outside the cafe to observe the passing parade of human phenomena. Reeking beggars would argue to the point of fisticuffs over a discarded butt. Giggling teenage girls would break into shrieks over photos and subtly flash their charms. Aged hippies decked out in floppy, flapped REI hats, colorful beads, and tie-dyed t-shirts slowly made their way into the bookstore or the music shop. All of this wild visual stimulation had the effect of pushing Theo further and further back into his own soul. It was as if all the emotion and desire, all the noise and color, reminded him of exactly what he *didn't* want in his life. The morning oceanscape indicated the future, while the afternoon townscape pointed toward the lost past.

Theo settled into a sort of decompression state, in which he began to gradually slough off the uncountable layers of fatigue, stress, and worry that had accumulated in his body, mind, and heart over the course of years. Simple absences of certain stimuli made him supremely happy: the cell phone not constantly ringing, the email inbox small, no one knocking on his door with an emergency requiring immediate attention. He had been used to experiencing every minute of the working day under the fire of enemy cannon. Here was the CEO telling him that unless they closed the Ford deal, the company could not make payroll; then came the phone call from the sales representative who had broken his leg and could not make the next day's crucial meeting. Could Theo take a redeye and his place at the table? Then the call-waiting signal. On the other end of the line was a prospect demanding an immediate fix to a bug or else "everything is off." There was the rush to the airport, the race across the concourse with the heavy computer case banging against his shoulder, the canceled flight putting the meeting at risk. A phone call from the CEO wondering if he could explain to the Board why sales were not growing faster; another call from a salesperson regretting the loss of an important deal.

No matter how tough one considers himself to be; no matter how much energy one has at his command; there ends up being a limit, a tolerance that no human being can safely exceed. And Theo had exceeded his. So now, having dropped the burden, he could afford to sit on a cafe chair, languorous, and simply smile.

Going Deeper

Theo mused that he had now entered what the Indians called the *vanaprastha* stage of his life, the period in which, in the Vedic system, a householder moves to the forest and detaches himself from the cares of everyday life. The setting might not be sylvan—his apartment featured only a wispy *ficus benjamina*—but Theo felt that it qualified, nevertheless. He had certainly separated himself not only from all affairs of business, but also his home and wife. Living alone, he turned ever more inward, hardly conversing with anyone throughout the day, listening mainly to his own thoughts or the reverberant sounds of silence.

His meditations took him progressively deeper into the boundless ocean of Being. The walks along the Pacific allowed the man to maintain some of his meditative quietude while his eyes remained open. The repetitive exhalations of the ocean releasing itself against the shore served as a sort of mantra lulling him into tranquility, as his feet carried him forward. Even the interior of the apartment took on a cavelike quality. After years of listening to urgent voices in offices and the high-pitched voices of children in his home, the silence of the small place seemed almost tangible. Since he had no visitors, no words were ever spoken in the apartment. It served him as a sanctuary, a retreat, a hospice: it was there that he could begin the process of sloughing off the scurf that all those years of competing and struggling had accumulated in his body and soul.

For the first time in decades, Theo enjoyed an experience he had known often as a young child and several times at college. The experience consisted in a feeling of his head expanding outward, as if it were an inflating bubble, to encompass a large area outside his frame. This expansion was accompanied by an extreme lightness of body and a radiation of blissful contentment.

Now, Theo had nearly forgotten that he had ever even had such experiences. He associated them, now that he reflected, with a time when he was about four years old. He recalled lying on his bed, staring at the white-plastered ceiling, feeling disconnected; then, suddenly, the inflation would occur. And, at that moment, all *was* right with the world. The unhappiness of his mother disappeared. The anger of his father vanished. The torments of his brother evaporated. All that remained was JOY: joy such as he had never known; joy for which one would trade everything one possessed.

And now, one day, as Theo reclined on his old torn sofa, his book temporarily put aside, that same feeling returned. He began to smile in an entirely new way. He smiled so broadly that his cheeks started to sting. And he floated there, in perfect peace, blissful, forgetful of time and place, and utterly free of thoughts.

This experience had served Theo as a guidepost during the years he spent at college studying mysticism and Eastern philosophies, and over the course of the time he invested in becoming a spiritual teacher and training hundreds of beginners in meditation techniques. His meditations were rarely flashy or profound, but he kept in mind those stray experiences of sheer bliss, and they indicated to him the state he hoped eventually to reach.

As he examined this newest delightful moment, Theo realized that inherent in it was a childlike wonderment, an innocence of not expecting anything, of accepting the "now" exactly as it presented itself. He saw that his mind had stopped functioning during the experience. The joy of the moment overpowered all normal brain functions. No sense of passing time disturbed the experience. No reflection that it was "he" who was enjoying it intruded upon the profound stillness.

He believed that this was "transcendence," as the spiritual literature described and as his own meditation Master had talked about it. But it was not the transcendence of meditation, when the eyes were closed, but the transcendence of the waking state, with the eyes wide open.

Human Enlightenment was, he believed, the only goal of life truly worth pursuing. Other lesser ones resulted in momentary pleasure or

15

satisfaction, but they were accomplishments of the body or mind and pertained only to the ego. Human beings were meant to aspire to Perfect Bliss, which could only result from attaining Enlightenment. People were souls, not merely bodies. They were, ultimately, solely Consciousness, Unitary Consciousness that underlay everyone and everything. To rediscover one's identity as that Consciousness was the purpose of life.

Such Enlightenment, embodied by his own Master and others he had read about, brought Eternal Peace and Bliss. It united what was wrongly conceived of as a separate individual with the Consciousness that is the basis of all beings and things. Theo thought that the Enlightened resembled all-wise children. They showed the innocence of the very young child and the wisdom of the greatest thinker. Nothing in the external world affected them. In fact, for them, no "external" world even existed: all was wrapped up in the Infinite Consciousness that they realized themselves to Be.

Theo knew how very far he was from attaining his goal of Enlightenment. Humbled by his awareness of his many faults and weaknesses, he never indulged in fantasies of attaining that state. But he did take this new experience of "expansion" as an indication of progress. At least he was recovering from all that weight of amassed tiredness. It was good that he had succeeded in freeing his mind from worries to the extent that he could once more float free as he had as a young boy. Every step taken was a step forward on the long journey.

A Visitor

On one especially resplendent morning, Theo sat in his favorite hiding place at the beach, marveling at the scene by which he had been swallowed up like a speck of dust within a cosmos. He sat in the entrance of a cave carved out of a cliffside by the skilled sculpting action of ceaseless waves. They had scooped out an oversized snail shell from the yellow-gray siltstones and blue-gray sandstones that made up the cliff, which rose at a forty-five-degree angle from the beach. The cave opened like the bell of a huge tuba, and then wound round itself, in smaller and smaller passages, before finally closing at the back. The walls of the cave were alive with what Theo's imagination recognized as seals, sea lions, dragons, sharks, mermaids, and spirits of the deep, all seemingly melted into the rough stone by some coastal Vulcan in a past long forgotten.

Long locks of mermaid hair streamed down the moist stone walls. Mouths a meter wide opened to whisper important secrets to the visitor. Faces of generals, like those carved in ancient Greece, with beards whose every strand could be clearly made out, loomed over the interloper, apparently wondering why he had come. A sheen of water silvered the nearly vertical slabs on Theo's either side.

The man sat facing the ocean, the Pacific on that day living up to its name. But the color of the water had no name. Its ever-so-slightly green-tinted blue had never been painted on canvas, but existed only on the impeccable palette of Nature. In fact, it was not so much a color as a feeling: one of purity, hope, and grand possibility. As Theo stared at the water, he understood not only that everything in the world was perfect, but also that behind its perfection lay the Eternal Source that rendered it so.

Light-pink, lilac, and soft-white rabbits, fish, and foxes pretended to be clouds. Thousands of stunningly bright flashes irradiated the water close in. Gently smoothed undulations, resembling the backs of porpoises, spread out school-like in the offing. The sun broke from behind a fox and scorched the water with a horizontal pillar of flaming, incandescent light that might have been the torso of Apollo, his head being the sun.

Nature now exerted her delicate transformational power on the man. He evanesced like the foam on the beach before him. Devoid of thought, he sat enthralled by the spectacle of nature simply being her exquisite self. The deep sighs of the tide lulled him; the tender, lovable blue-green of the water transfixed him; the silently stretching sky-animals amused him. Better by far than those of the finest symphony were these elements orchestrated. More perfectly than those of the most masterful painting were its hues and tones blended. No humans were in the vicinity to break the perfect spell the scene had woven around its observer.

Theo became aware of a powerful energy behind him in the cave. He turned, first his head and then his body, to see what it was. There, in the dim light at the back of the first coil of the cave, sat the Saint. He looked exactly as he always had. The white beard had grown no longer. The eyes still shone like stars, and still sent out the overpowering love and affection that Theo had noted the last time he had seen the holy man. He still wore his white cloth and sat with his legs crossed as he was wont to do.

As the two looked deeply into each other's eyes, Theo lost sight of the form of the man. In its place, he perceived a continuously swelling eddy of tenderly golden light. The light slowly rotated clockwise, expanding its range with every turn. But this golden light possessed unique properties: it bathed him in solace; it warmed him from the inside out; and it had the effect of setting bells tinkling in his soul.

As each wave of the golden light washed over him, Theo felt purer and brighter. It seemed as if the light were literally bathing his soul, freshening it, restoring its long-lost pristinity. No thoughts were exchanged with the Saint. Theo simply sat motionless, fully joyful under the soft radiation of the light.

After he knew not how much time had passed, Theo saw, once more, the physical form of the Saint. And then the thought transmissions began. "Now you will come to me," the holy man said.

"But how will I come? And where will I find you?" asked Theo.

"You needn't concern yourself with the details. All will be taken care of. It is time that you come, and time that you learn. There is much to be mastered while you still occupy this body that you take to be yours."

Theo wanted to ask more questions, but an almost physical restraint, something like a hand laid on his shoulder, held him back. The Saint smiled and nodded, and then began to dissolve into the millions of minute light points that Theo remembered from earlier encounters.

Once the visitor had disappeared, Theo felt that the cave had been sanctified. If one took the atmosphere of a medieval cathedral for a comparison, that in the cave now pulsed with a thousand times its sacred energy. Invisible light glowed from the wet stones; the bearded generals beamed; the mermaids wriggled contentedly; the spirits of the deep bowed their heads; even the seals, sea lions, dragons, and sharks shone with otherworldly luminance. The Saint had blessed the space by his mere presence.

That night, as he lay in bed contemplating the encounter, Theo's mind kept revolving questions: how *would* he know where to look for the Saint? how *would* he recognize the appropriate time to search him out? On a practical level, the one on which his mind was accustomed to working, such a trip made no sense at all. Had he explained his plans to his ex-wife, for instance, she would have laughed him out of the room, just prior to denouncing him for never *once* in his life acting like a normal human being.

And, logically, her objections would have carried weight. "You see Ms. Psychotherapist, I'm planning a trip to I don't know where, at a

19

time I don't know when, in order to see a man whose name I don't know, who has several times magically appeared before me before disappearing in a shower of silvery points of light." He could readily imagine the good doctor's response.

But no one other than himself could possibly appreciate the reality of the holy man. Even without a physical form, the visitor was a hundred times more real than anyone Theo had ever met, other than his meditation Master, of course. And he had only ever encountered him once, for a matter of seconds. Though the Saint had communicated, over the many years of their interactions, no more than a dozen sentences, and had communicated them telepathically, his words carried more weight than any that Theo had ever heard.

Germination

Theo had always been one who thrived on routine. Since his days in school, he had structured his time methodically, finding great satisfaction in knowing when and where he would be at certain hours of the day. Others might have considered him eccentric, for he created hundreds of little rituals for daily life, which governed how he shaved in the morning, exercised in the evening, and even how he prepared to fall asleep.

The business world had, of course, presented a major challenge to this tendency of his to turn the randomness of life into a pattern of order, but, even amidst the hectic pace and constant change of startup life, he had always managed to preserve most of his important habits. For something deep within him required ritual and routine; ceremonious predictability satisfied him.

Theo's recent life by the ocean, devoid as it was of responsibility to others and subservience to superiors, allowed him to fully indulge this character trait. He had succeeded in turning his everyday life into a secular liturgy. Every day followed a precise pattern: his morning toilet, meditations, exercise, meals, walks, and evening entertainment traced exact routes. By living in this way, the man freed himself from the care and worry normally associated with simple physical existence. He ate food that his body easily digested. His exercise routine kept him in shape and allowed him to sleep well. Twice-daily meditations centered him. He had never been happier in his life than he was living in that small apartment on the shore of the magical sea.

But now came this urgent call from the highest spiritual plane. An enlightened Master—for as such Theo knew him to be—beckoned him to some faraway place for some unknown mission. How was he, a man fifty years old, who blossomed in a parterre called routine, going to drop everything and set out in pursuit of someone whose name he did not know, whose residence he could not even imagine? Just the thought of all the upset such a trip would cause in his manner of living disturbed Theo deeply. Thoughts of mail holds, broken leases, waiting on airline-reservation lines, immunization shots, and explanations to his family: all overwhelmed him.

Rationality began to try to talk him out of even considering such a foolish pilgrimage. He didn't know with certainty what country to fly into. Well, that wasn't quite correct; obviously, the Saint was from India. Okay, well India is an immense country populated by 1.25 billion people. He would be looking for a needle in a haystack! Well, holy men tended to stay in certain parts of that country; it might be possible to find him by going to those areas. How? Without a name, without even a photo? Ha, ha! All this was the product of a midlife crisis, a spiritual boondoggle. Might as well buy yourself a red sports car. That would be less expensive in the end.

Theo argued with his inner doubt, telling it that he might get an artist to sketch a likeness of the Saint, which he could show people in India as he searched for him. But inner contempt scorned this absurd device. But then Theo played his ace: I won't even need to! "All will be taken care of." Those were the words the Saint had used. If Theo really *was* meant to meet the holy man in the flesh, nature would support him in his search. He would be guided by higher powers. The Saint would call him to his location by sending out signals unmistakable in their clarity. To this, the inner doubter remained silent.

Once he had secured a tentative hold on the possibility that he could actually *find* the Saint by recourse to the guidance of destiny, Theo started to explore the bigger question: why was he even *meant* to meet the holy man? Possibly, he reasoned, the Saint was his guru from a previous lifetime, who had watched over him in this one and was now summoning him back to his feet. Or maybe the Saint had somehow "noticed" him in his vast field of vision, seen that he was a seeker lacking a personal guide, and, out of compassion, beckoned him to his side.

Theo mused over the repeated appearances the holy soul had made over the course of passing years. He had seen the man first as a young child, then as a slightly older one, then as a young man, and now as a middle-aged one. These visitations had served to inspire Theo in his pursuit of the Holy Grail of enlightenment. They had inspired him by proving that what others would have called "miracles" could actually occur. But, he now reasoned, they must also have been meant to give credibility to the Saint's final call to him. Theo could not write off the sea-cave visit as a fluke or hallucination, for it had been preceded by three other quite similar appearances.

People fall all along the spectrum of trusting their intuition: the least spiritual among them believe only in rationality; if logical reasons cannot be produced for taking a course of action, then they simply refuse to take it. Those who have spent some time learning about themselves, either in psychological terms or in spiritual endeavors, reside in the mid-range of the spectrum: they will pay some attention to a whisper from their deeper sense, but subject it to custodial screening by good old common sense. At the far end of the range lie those people whose extensive spiritual explorations have granted them full faith in their intuitions. These are the few trusting souls who, even in the face of overwhelming objections to the contrary, are able to follow the lead of the very subtlest of hints emanating from their soul's adytum deep within. Theo numbered himself among these latter faithful.

In his way of conceiving the situation, the Saint's appearances could only possibly mean one thing: there really *was* a holy man on the other side of the world, whom Theo urgently needed to find. Who cared if most people were too mired in conventional thought to put any credence in "visions"? Why even consider the opinions of those who would decry his germinal plan as "magical thinking"? Theo had never been graced with visions of angels or upsurges of kundalini energy; his spiritual development had been a relatively dull road trip toward a destination not even visible on the horizon. But he *had* experienced the Saint, and the fact that the holy man's visitations were his only unusual spiritual experiences lent them greater weight than they would otherwise have possessed.

And what did he have to lose, after all? He had completed his education, succeeded in his career, and raised his family. These societally approved milestones lay in his past. What else might occupy his future, if not this journey to meet the Saint? Theo played devil's advocate with himself: "Say I go to India, spend months searching for this holy man, but never manage to find him. How much worse off am I? Yes, I will have spent some money, of which I now have no excess to spare. Maybe I will develop intestinal disorders and suffer the consequences. Certainly, I will have wasted some time. But so what? India has always fascinated me, and I will get a chance to see and explore it. I will probably enjoy some mild adventures and encounter some fascinating people. The risks are minimal, after all.

"But think of the upside! If I do succeed in locating the Saint, and do spend time with him, my spiritual journey could be immeasurably shortened. The texts say that the company of Saints is the quickest route to enlightenment. Who can possibly tell what progress my soul would make were I to hear the words of wisdom from a real jivanmukti, from one who is enlightened and in the flesh? Yes, without a doubt the risk/reward ratio skews one-sidedly toward reward."

And so, Theo began to grow comfortable with the idea that he would actually set out on this voyage, which, to the practical-minded, would have seemed as fantastic as one of Sinbad's. He researched the best times of year to travel in India, basing his investigation on the likelihood that he would find the Saint in the Himalayas. Oh, saints had resided in the South and elsewhere in this vast country, but Theo's instincts told him that *his* holy man would be found in the pure air of the North, in the vicinity of the holiest Hindu pilgrimage sites: Badrinath, Kedarnath, Gangotri, and Yamunotri. The seeker dug into

24

flight schedules and train timetables, bus routes and trekking paths. He read blogs about the challenges and dangers of traveling in the high mountains. He even built a spreadsheet detailing the costs that such a trip would entail.

The initial plan that Theo came up with was to fly from San Francisco to New Delhi, then take a bus to Nainital, a town in the state of Uttarakhand, in the foothills of the Himalayas. His research had taught him that the forests of this region had been, over the centuries, home to many saints, and that Neem Karoli Baba had established an ashram in the area in the 1960s. From Nainital, Theo would make his way to Haridwar, one of the seven places holiest to Hindus. Legend had it that the celestial bird Garuda had accidentally spilled a drop of amrita, the nectar of immortality, on Haridwar. The town was the site of the great spiritual festival Kumbha Mela, held there every twelfth year. At Haridwar, the Ganges first entered the plains of Northern India; the river's waters here were considered especially sacred.

From Haridwar, Theo contemplated traveling to Rishikesh, either by taxi or, if he felt especially energetic, by foot. Rishikesh, where Theo's own Master had spent time, was considered one of India's holiest cities. Holy men and women had lived, meditated, and gained enlightenment there for millennia. Hindus regarded Rishikesh as an important pilgrimage destination. Intuition told Theo that if he did not find his Saint there, he would, at minimum, gain clues as to his whereabouts.

Rishikesh would lead the pilgrim to Uttarkashi, another place renowned in spiritual literature. Its name meant "Kashi of the North," for it was viewed as the sister of India's holiest city, Varanasi. The small town gave birth to two of the country's great rivers: the Ganges and the Yamuna. It was the home of the Yamunotri Temple, one of Hinduism's holiest sites.

The final destination sketched out by Theo was Gangotri, the place where, according to the holy books, the River Ganga descended from the locks of Shiva. Gangotri sat at an elevation of 10,200 feet. Theo hoped that if earlier-visited locales had not proved to be the residence of his Saint, he would certainly find him here, at an ultimately sacred site, in the heights of the holy Himalayas.

Once he had this itinerary planned out, doubts began to assail Theo. What evidence, he asked himself, did he possess that established the Saint's location on the way toward or in Gangotri? He could equally well sit, for instance, in the jungles of southern India, near the holy mountain Arunachala, in the state of Tamil Nadu. Or the holy man might live in a hut near Shirdi in the western state of Maharashtra. Theo really hadn't a clue where to find the great one whom he sought. Why all this confidence to plan a specific journey, when all was supposition?

But Theo recognized this voice: it was the voice of doubt and ignorance, the carping of a captious skeptic that had formerly played a major role in his inner workings. This voice was a vestige of his less-evolved mind. Its harsh tones had been taught by surroundings echoing with the dismissive laughter of derision and disparagement. Time and growth had faded out this coarse vocalist, and nowadays he rarely heard it. It most often sounded its raspy cackle when Theo contemplated putting full trust in his intuition. Faith is the sworn enemy of doubt, so the cynic that a harsh childhood had nourished in his soul always made a stand when credulity threatened to carry the day.

Theo threw off his doubt. Of course he had no evidence pointing in one direction or another. This entire pilgrimage was taking shape in that vaporous kiln called "hope." But intuition served as the best guide one could have. Especially with matters nebulous and incredible, one could really *only* trust one's intuition. What role could reason play when the very impetus of the trip consisted in a series of spiritual materializations, which most people would have called hallucinations? No, rationality had its place where issues were practical and concrete, but it offered little help with challenges such as those now faced by Theo: finding a needle-sized Saint in a haystack a million miles square.

A beautiful heuristic would guide his pilgrimage. A methodology as fine and delicate as the goal of the journey would determine its course. Theo decided that he would trust entirely to the barely audible whisper of intuition that came to him from a source deep within. He would allow serendipity to be his cicerone. Reason would take a back seat to instinct. Logic would be supplanted by destiny. The Saint would, he realized, be quietly beckoning him to his presence, if he only silenced his mind sufficiently to hear him.

Theo would do whatever seemed natural. If waiting struck him as appropriate, he would wait. If walking felt preferable to riding, he would employ his feet. If someone offered help, and the offer sounded beneficial, he would accept it. At every step of the journey, he would trust nature to guide and protect him. Forces larger than logic were at work in this search, and Theo chose to surrender himself to those forces rather than resist them.

Plans

Theo decided that he would set out on his long venture in April. Research had taught him that the weather in the lower Himalayas was best from April to June. By April, the snows would have melted and the daily temperatures might reach the 70s or 80s. If one waited until later in the summer, the monsoons would literally wash one's feet off the muddy trails up the mountains.

He informed his family of his plans, and their reactions were predictable. The children considered it a great adventure; his mother worried that he would break his leg and be stranded with goatherds in a filthy hut; and his ex-wife told him bluntly that he was out of his mind. "Don't you realize how dangerous this could be at your age? There won't be any decent medical care there when you need it. Think of your kids! They still need you around, you know."

At least he had gotten over the worst of it. Now, before he left, he would have to suffer the continual chastisement of his ex and the regularly expressed hand-wringing of his mother. But their nags and worries would decrease in severity the more he reassured the ladies. Yes, he would take out medical insurance for the trip. No, he would not take any needless risks. Yes, he would avoid unclean water. No, he would not try to climb the highest mountain that presented itself.

Theo bought an airline ticket and took a full dose of vaccination shots. He had never imagined India to be so potentially dangerous until he suffered through the punctures of those darts whose liquids would protect him from typhoid, Japanese encephalitis, hepatitis A, hepatitis B, rabies, polio, measles, mumps, and rubella. At a travel store, he found a money belt, sleeping bag, hiking boots, water-purification tablets, and backpack. He already owned a warm cap, sandals, gloves, and good sunglasses.

Theo ran scenarios in his mind to make sure he was bringing all he might need. For wet weather, he had a good raincoat. For cold nights, he packed a fleece jacket. To protect his feet, he would carry boots, running shoes, and sandals. To preserve visual memories, he had a digital camera and extra batteries. He dug out an old first-aid kit for use in any medical emergencies that might arise. To protect his skin, he took sunscreen. In case he got lost, he would carry a compass. He printed out maps of every area he planned to visit. He figured that anything else he might possibly need could be purchased in India.

By the time he had assembled all this gear, it covered his living room floor. Again and again he would try to imagine an urgent need that he would have to meet, and then determine if his equipment would allow him to do so. Theo foresaw slipping into a river, as he crossed it, and submerging his pack. This possibility prompted him to add large ziplock bags to his storehouse. He could use two of them to protect his camera, money, and other water-averse items. He then extended this scenario forward, seeing himself in dripping clothes at the doorway of a hut. His pack had, therefore, to contain a fully redundant suit of warm clothes that would keep him cozy while he dried out the wet garments.

With the worried voice of his mom in his head, the man pictured all sorts of possible injury: a twisted ankle, a strange outbreak of rash, severe sunburn, Delhi belly, and sundry other nastinesses. Checking over his first-aid kit, he confirmed the presence of Ace bandages, antifungal cream, calamine lotion, and rehydration packets. He also found Band-Aids, cortisone cream, insect repellant, tweezers, aspirin, and an instant-cold pack.

Thinking of the need to keep warm in the wild, Theo packed a trio of portable lighters. Wondering if he might need to check out a distant path, he pulled his compact binoculars out of storage. Slowly but surely, he assembled everything reasonable precaution suggested he bring.

Research had informed him that his pack ought not to weigh more than forty pounds, so Theo stuffed all his gear into it and set it on the scales. The verdict: forty-four. He would just have to put up with the four extra pounds.

Now he began to explore the details of his travels toward Gangotri. Walking to Rishikesh from Haridwar, a distance of some twenty miles, was easily within his capacity. But getting from the former town to Uttarkashi was another matter entirely. Ninety miles separated the two places. Now this was the stage of the trip where Theo would certainly have preferred to travel with his legs; the scenery would be gorgeous and the spiritual vibrations progressively richer with every mile covered. But, besides the distance, there was also the matter of elevation. Rishikesh sat at 1800 feet, which was nothing; but the route to Uttarkashi rose continually, and the town itself lay at 4400 feet. So the trek would be uphill and the air would steadily thin as he made his way. His health was good, and he exercised daily, so he didn't doubt his conditioning. But ninety miles was still ninety miles.

Theo thought about breaking this leg of the pilgrimage into five days. Certainly, he could manage eighteen miles a day. With that idea, he tentatively settled on walking from Rishikesh to Uttarkashi.

The last segment of the trip—assuming he had not found the Saint before then—presented the ultimate challenge. Sixty miles of mountain road lay between Uttarkashi and Gangotri. More importantly, the latter stood at 11,000 feet. The air at that height would contain only two-thirds the oxygen found at sea level. Assuming that he continued on foot, Theo would have to be steadily climbing hills, for long distances, with only thin air to breathe.

He looked into the subject of altitude sickness, and concluded that he should soon be able to overcome any of its symptoms if he did not go any higher in the mountains. Ten or eleven thousand feet seemed to be the limit of safe ascension for a novice climber like himself. Yet a walk of sixty miles through ever-less-oxygenated air! That would be a challenge of the highest order. He would soon see how fit he really was.

Once Theo had all his equipment aggregated, once he had run through all the challenging scenarios he could imagine, he turned his attention to what really mattered: the purpose of the pilgrimage. There was no way to be sure that he would meet the Saint on the path he had laid out. One could not even say that it was likely he would. The entire plan had its source and foundation in intuition. But Theo believed that if he found himself off course, some serendipitous event would bring him back on it. The holy man would beckon him with telepathic radar signals and employ strangers and events to steer and, if need be, push the visitor onto the optimal trail. Since he knew that he was *meant* to meet the Saint, Theo thought that everything that happened on his trip would conduce to this end.

He tried to imagine the moment when he would meet the Saint. It might be in a cave in the area of Gangotri. Theo might round a turn on a sliver of a mountain path and see the holy man standing in the sunlight at the entrance of his cave-home. Or maybe the two would come together by a susurrant and silvered stream, the Saint bathed in his own and a sun-lent aura. It seemed unlikely, and somehow inappropriate, that they would meet in the presence of other people. They never had before. No, Theo did not see himself bumping into the white-robed figure in a crowded market or the courtyard of a populous ashram. The two of them were certainly destined to make their first physical acquaintance in a beautiful natural scene, where they could fully take each other in under a cloak of maximum privacy.

Oddly, though, whenever Theo began to picture his first encounter with the holy man, his normally vivid imagination failed him. No matter how hard he tried, the seeker found it impossible to "see" the Saint as he had witnessed him in the four visitations. He could manage to form a vague outline of a white-robed form in the nebulous distance, but not once could he call to mind the actual face, those piece-of-star eyes and that smile embodying pure love, he had seen in his previous meetings.

31

He wondered about this difficulty. Maybe such a being could only appear of his own accord, could not, in other words, ever be "summoned," even into imagination. Or, possibly, whatever Theo was meant to learn in his next contact with the holy man could only be communicated via personal interaction. Whatever the reason, the result was the same: try as he would, Theo never succeeded in visualizing the Saint at the moment of their meeting in India.

Unable to envisage this fateful juncture, Theo turned his attention instead to its possible purpose. The guru had been encouraging him since childhood, and had certainly planned this meeting for decades. Based on the reading he had done, Theo considered it quite likely that he had been a disciple of the Saint's in an earlier lifetime. The seeker's studies had taught him that gurus watched out for the welfare of their spiritual charges in time spans crossing physical lifetimes. It seemed most unlikely that this enlightened Being had taken up the boy's cause without having had previous contact with him.

Accepting all that, Theo applied himself to analyzing the probable reasons for his being summoned to India. Most likely, he thought, the teacher would instruct him in some spiritual knowledge vital to his personal evolution. This instruction would be of a sort requiring personal contact with the Master. Theo considered, but only for a moment, the chance that the Saint would ask him to perform some service in the West, undertake a course of lectures or something. No, that was unlikely. Theo's acquired humility now prevented him from conceiving himself sufficiently advanced to presume to instruct others in matters where he was still only a novice. Maybe the holy man had a karmic connection to Theo, which required him to push him forward spiritually while he still occupied his present body. The Enlightened, the seeker knew, as a result of prarabdha karma, remained in their physical bodies even after attaining Realization. This karma is that destined to be experienced in the present body. Enlightenment destroys other stored karmas, and prevents new ones from accumulating, but the Realized must take delivery of these karmas that resemble arrows already launched. They in no way restrict Enlightenment, but they do bring up issues related to the physical body, personal encounters, and the like. So the seeker asked himself if, possibly, the guru had taken an interest in him in the previous lifetime and now fulfilled this responsibility in the present one.

Setting Out

His children were busy working, so Theo took a cab to the airport. Prior to locking the door of his apartment, he had triple-checked his backpack and pockets. All the clothing, devices, and medical supplies for the trek were packed. He had his boarding pass and his passport in his pocket. In his wallet was cash sufficient for ready conversion to rupees once he arrived in New Delhi. He left his key ring in the apartment, fearing that he might lose it on the long trip. The extra apartment key he stashed in his travel-belt wallet. No, he couldn't think of anything he was forgetting. Of course, he *had* forgotten something; he knew that for a certainty. A day would come, on a dark night in some lonely mountain nook, when he would slap his thigh and exclaim, "How did I ever manage to forget *that*?"

But, at this point, all seemed in order. Always one to expect chaos in travel matters, Theo left the apartment three hours before his scheduled departure. The trip to the airport would take half an hour. Security check-in should consume no more than an hour. That should, he thought, leave him with a solid ninety minutes leeway. Flights usually pre-boarded thirty minutes before takeoff, so he should be waiting when that process began. The reason for the extra time-padding was an allowance for highway delays on the way to the airport, longer-than-expected security lines, and some unexpected problem with his ticket or passport. Theo always felt comfortable trading off a bit of wasted time in the boarding area for the miserable stress of worrying about a missed flight.

Luck supported the traveler, however, and he took off only twenty minutes late, curiously aware of the people occupying the seats around him. At least half the passengers were Indians, returning, he imagined, to visit relatives or take care of family business. They were a noisy and gregarious lot. Many of the women wore the salwar kameez, trousers matched with a tunic top, or a conservative sari. Some of the men sported kurta tops and pajama-type trousers. Probably a quarter of the passengers looked like business people setting off to inspect the customer-service operation of an Indian outsource vendor or consummate a deal to import apparel from that nation's clothing manufacturers. The last quarter of the plane was filled with tourists: Millennials who reminded Theo of a new generation of 60s wanderers; older couples with *National Geographic* subscriber written all over their tan-colored, multi-pocketed travel vests and khaki boonie hats; middle-aged Connecticut-suburb types out to expand their cultural horizon and increase their storehouse of cocktail-party vignettes.

Theo had done a great deal of flying during his business career, so he knew what he was now in for. He had a window seat, so he was not in danger of losing a kneecap to the sharp corners of the beverage cart; he had a thousand-page spiritual text, in which he could lose himself for hours at a time; and he had noise-reduction headphones, so the engine roar would not deafen him before the end of the flight. A middle-aged tourist couple occupied the seats next to him. And they proved ideal neighbors, keeping thoroughly to themselves.

Flying was a physical challenge for sure. One could never manage to quite stretch out one's legs. Getting past two seats to the aisle to find the bathroom was a challenge. The food was just passable. The seat must have been designed by an accountant focused on maximum number of bodies per square foot of cabin space. No matter how Theo squirmed, no matter what he tucked behind the small of his back, he could never attain lumbar support. And sleeping, which would have come in handy as a timewaster on a 16-plus-hour flight, was rendered impossible by the configurations of the window and the edge of the seat. He formerly could manage it with a pillow, but pillows had by now gone the way of blankets, free peanuts, and carrier pigeons.

Nevertheless, Theo made it to New Delhi, and after disembarking from the plane, worked his way, with thrilled anticipation, into the airport. The airport had that universally homogeneous character of airports in major cities around the world. Duty-free shoppes (British spelling prevailed here) had no nationality; conveyor belts spoke no language; and ticket counters lacked ethnicity. But there were statues of elephants in the center of a concourse and gigantic mudra fingers poking out of walls fifty feet above the ground.

Seeing the hordes of travelers gathered around the luggage carousels, Theo was glad that he had stowed his backpack in the overhead compartment. He exchanged some money and headed out to the street. Knowing what to expect, he was not surprised by the fetid smog. It was so filthy that he could actually see dark particles floating in the air. One both smelled and tasted this foul air. He thought that the sooner he escaped this huge city, the better.

Theo took the orange line Metro to Connaught Place, where he held a reservation for the bus to Nainital. He had five hours to wait, so he set out to explore the area. It reminded him of Bath, England: a circular series of two-story buildings, fronted by light-gray Doric colonnades, housed shops on the ground floors and corporate offices above. The streets were crazily busy and cacophonous: minicabs painted in brilliant red and yellow honked their clown horns incessantly; bicycles loaded with goods darted between Opels, Hyundais, Tatas, and Renaults. Motor scooters beeped duck-like as they slithered in between the larger vehicles. Passengers did their best to avoid injury as they made their way across busy intersections.

After wandering around for an hour or so, Theo consulted an Englishman on the street and found himself directed to the Mother India restaurant. This subterranean eatery was decorated in yellows and oranges and brightly lit. Its floor comprised hundreds of orange, amber, and brown circles of tile set adjacent one to the other. A sealed-off fireplace supported, on its mantel, a brass clock, a white-framed mirror, a statue of Lakshmi, and an assortment of Victorian knickknacks. A floor-to-ceiling column was inlaid with photographs of Indian saints, goddesses, and film stars.

The tall and mustached server greeted his guest with a broad smile and understanding gesture. He instantly knew him for a tourist; but, Theo surmised, would likely have been surprised had he been informed of the diner's ultimate destination. With Arjun's assistance, Theo selected, for an appetizer, jimikand ki galouti, delicious and tender yam kebabs, and for an entree, angeethi ka bhuna bharta, eggplant prepared with onion and tomato masala. The food, rich and spicy, proved delicious, and the diner lingered over his meal, going through several bottles of Pellegrino in an attempt to cool down his internal organs. A glance at his watch, a waterproof, multi-featured model he had bought just for this trip, told him it was time to make his way to the bus stop.

The bus, a sleek Volvo, turned out to be more contemporary and well-maintained than Theo had imagined it would be. He arrived half an hour before the scheduled departure, but the bus itself did not appear for another hour. It seemed obvious that their departure would be substantially delayed. The driver, from whom he bought his ticket, was a turbaned Sikh whose mischievous eyes and smile seemed to infer some perverse motive on the traveler's part for wanting to travel to Nainital.

"Are you sure my stuff will be safe down there?" Theo asked the burly fellow, as he tossed the heavy backpack into the luggage storage at the bottom of the bus.

"Quite safe, sir."

"But you make several stops along the route, right?" The man was breathing heavily as he worked to load some heavy suitcases from other passengers. Having done so, he straightened up, wiped his brow with his forearm, and replied.

"Yes, but I myself take the bags off. So there is no way a mistake can be made."

Theo lightly touched the man's muscled shoulder. "I appreciate that. You see, I am going on a long pilgrimage and everything I need to survive is in that backpack. I'm a bit overprotective, like a new mother." The driver smiled broadly, showing the gap between his two main upper incisors. He was about to speak when an overwrought elderly lady engaged him in a rapid-fire exchange carried on in Hindi. Apparently, from what Theo could gather, it had to do with the separation of some bags in the storage compartment. She finally went away dissatisfied.

"A pilgrimage? You don't look like a Hindu to me," the driver said laughing.

"It's a spiritual trip, not really religious, but a pilgrimage nevertheless." For some reason, this explanation completely won the driver over to his new passenger's side.

"Don't worry. I never lose bags. The company is very concerned about that. Sometimes there is confusion. Bags look alike. But yours is not like the others. I will watch out for it, and it will be there for you when we get to Nainital."

"Thank you so much, my friend. I appreciate your help." Theo climbed into the bus and found one of the few remaining seats far in the back, on the aisle. The window seats were occupied by view-hungry tourists and a few children struggling to stay awake at the sides of their parents. The window-people *thought* that they would be aware of the landscape they drove through, but, as the trip was to be completed during the night, there would be little to see, and most of them would be asleep the whole time anyway.

The bus ended up starting two hours late. Many of the passengers didn't notice, of course, as they were leaning back, bent or twisted, snoring or stertorously breathing, utterly oblivious to the passage of time. The more energetic travelers complained to one another about the delay, compared expectations of Nainital, and inquired about their neighbor's hotel plans. Theo sat quietly, musing about what lay ahead of him. He mentally ran through his itinerary for the hundredth time: Nainital, then Haridwar, then Rishikesh, then Uttarkashi, and, finally, Gangotri. Where on that path, he wondered, would he find his Saint?

The streets of Delhi had given him a glimpse of the immensity of the nation's population. One and a third billion people! How would he ever find the guru amongst so many, many souls? But his concern lasted only for a moment, before giving way to the certitude that his feet would be guided by the radar of an Enlightened Master. Theo felt confident that he had structured his trip the way he had as a result of the Saint's wise control. For he had not struggled to come up with the plan; it had sprung up of its own accord. What struck him now was the necessity of not asserting any sort of personal bias into the pilgrimage. His instincts told him to simply flow with the currents as they washed him forward, from one place to the next.

At last the bus engine roared to grinding life, the interior lights dimmed, and the vehicle edged out into the night traffic of New Delhi. Corners of columned buildings were spotlit to render their upper stretches turquoise and their windows electric blue. Distant streetlight bulbs glowed golden like luminous balls kicked heavenward. Fountains jetted up at irregular heights like variously statured family members. Trees, stalking monsters, brooded in shadow beside light-patched roadways. And, all around the bus, vehicles of every size and shape maneuvered and darted, paused and raced. Taxis blared their horns at mosquito scooters. Vans edged dangerously close to two friends astride a motorcycle. Trucks, as they struggled to pick up speed, expelled nauseating tailpipe emissions. Pedestrians gathered in groups before daring to negotiate a busy intersection. Lights, noises, and smells fought and writhed and strained like souls caught in the toils of some vast, dark demon's net. Theo wondered how the bus would ever make it out of the city.

Theo had learned from the driver that their route would pass through Moradabad, Rampur, Bilaspur, Rudrapur, and Haldwani and, if there were no problems on the roadways, consume eight and a half hours. They had departed Connaught Place at 11:30 p.m. and thus could be expected in Nainital by eight in the morning, barring complications.

The pilgrim had slept on the airplane and his body clock told him that it was the middle of the day, so he felt no sleepiness at all. As the Volvo made its way out of Delhi and onto National Highway 9, Theo strained his eyes to see whatever he could in the darkness. For several minutes at a time, he could only make out dark swaths of trees and upthrustings of power lines and telephone poles. But then, suddenly, a huge bright red-and-yellow arch announced, of all things, a McDonald's restaurant. That company's kitsch design and unhealthy food had, unfortunately, both made their way around the world.

Short billboards, really placards more than anything else, lined the road. Low, scrubby bushes, interrupted occasionally by feathery, taller growths, rose up behind the raw dirt at the edge of the highway. A rough shack appeared, followed by a garishly painted store, whose fascia featured alternating squares of green and yellow, and whose facade was spotlighted as it paraded itself before the world. Theo saw a petrol station open for the night, and its lighting revealed scattered piles of rubbish at the highway's edge.

Theo was surprised to see that scooters, and even the occasional rickshaw, continued to travel on the berm of the highway, even at this late hour. Low concrete barriers stood in front of fields, serving no apparent purpose. As the bus entered the outskirts of Moradabad, he could discern banners strung across the road and handmade signs advertising an event or a political candidate. Some of the scattered buildings stood only one-story high; others, rose three, and featured a balcony on the highest level. Vehicles of many types. sizes, and colors were parked helter-skelter in front of and along the sides of buildings. A rusted minivan, its side-message plumping auto parts, had for its neighbor an antique motorbike. A miniature truck, whose sides were covered in canvas, looked ready to T-bone a sedan whose tires were buried in mud three inches deep.

Theo finally did fall asleep for some time, wakening after the bus hit a large pothole in the road. He stood up and walked toward the front, where he engaged the driver, whose name he found to be Binder, in conversation. "Where are we now, Binder?"

"Outside Rampur."

Theo could see that the bus had entered the outskirts of a larger town that he could faintly discern on the horizon. It was just after four a.m. The sun had not yet risen, but the sky in the east had lightened, as if the retinue of Ushas, the Indian goddess of dawn, had lit its first torches to welcome the brilliant one onto the scene.

"What's Rampur like?"

Binder had to raise his voice to be heard above the straining of the engine, working to ascend a hill. "It's mostly Muslims here. Lots of history. Very many beautiful buildings built by the Mogul Khans. They used to have cotton and sugar factories, but many of them are no longer in operation."

Theo also spoke louder: "A large town?"

Binder shook his turban vigorously. "Not too big. Maybe a few hundred thousand is all."

Dawn approached quickly now. A cottony haze filled the air, muting the light of the sun as it floated up above an unseen horizon. Palm trees with spiked fronds and deciduous ones with clumpy crowns got transformed into glowing chunks of fire-hot lava, the unity of their structures broken up into discrete parts by the backlighting rays. The scumbled pale yellows and faint oranges in the sky reminded Theo of Turner's "Dawn after the Wreck."

Then the bus rounded a corner of the road and the full glory of sunrise met them head on. To their left stood a hill whose jagged top contours resembled a charcoal silhouette. A lone, massive evergreen tree loomed over the hilltop and seemed to say, "Behold! I offer you magic!"

The molten white sun was halfway over the cusp of the hill. Just where it touched the hill, the ground was painted the purest of primary yellows. Sunbeams dug channels down the side of the slope. A large arc of primrose shone above the rising star, and a thinner concentric band of Venetian pink, in turn, vaulted it. And on top of all these colors, the sky gradually, ever so delicately, resolved into, first, lavender, then pastel, then vivid violet. It was as if an extremely subtle rainbow, using only a few of its colors, had expanded immensely to cover an entire sector of the sky.

Neither man spoke, awed as they were by this stunning display of natural beauty.

But the scenery quickly changed as the hand of humanity showed itself. All along the sides of the road squatted tiny huts: one with a stack of automobile tires piled high by its entrance, another fronted by a ramshackle cart carrying a few spotted melons and a weary-looking youth. An old bicycle leaned against a telephone pole whose wooden fibers had peeled under the assault of the sun. A handwritten sign advertised some product for sale. Flaccid canvas tunnels broke off from the shacks and led out toward the street. Refuse littered the sandy ground. Rampur, the Rampur finished by the hand of man, did not make a very good impression.

Soon, however, the bus reached the central portion of the town. It passed a gorgeous mosque featuring four Bordeaux-red minarets tipped in gold and two onion-shaped domes, from which elaborate whirligigs seemed to sprout. Atop the paneled walls of the mosque stretched an intricate parapet formed of semicircular archlets topped by finials. It was easy for Theo to trace the Mogul influence on the architecture of the mosque and several palaces that the bus now passed by. India, it seemed, alternated ravishing beauty with disgusting squalor. At one moment, its visitor was enthralled by a dawn for the ages or a mosque materializing straight out of a fairyland, and at the next, he had to turn his head away from the sight of a rotting animal carcass.

Some of the passengers had now begun to awaken, stretching, clearing their throats, blowing their noses, and making muted comments to their spouses and companions. The bus was equipped with window shades, so several people pulled them down and adjusted themselves with the hope of falling back to sleep.

As the bus moved steadily forward, Theo waited for what he knew to be the next town it would pass through, Bilaspur. Consulting his pocket guide, he learned that Bilaspur was a very small town with little claim to renown. Apparently, it was home to many Muslims and a good-sized minority of Sikhs. "Lots of Sikhs in Bilaspur, right, Binder?"

The driver bent his head backward so as to be heard. "A few thousand, I think. Many different castes there. It's a farming town. We only go through it because the road is better there than the other way."

In short order, they were in and through Bilaspur. From the little he saw, Theo considered it very much like the outlying areas of Rampur. Billboards bombarded the eye with bright cerise and staring yellow messages. A small one, advertising an MBA course, hung from a power line in the middle of an intersection. Most of the messages were written in foreign languages, which Theo could not decipher, but he caught the word "TOURIST" on several of them. Clearly, they had entered a district that made a fair amount of its money off visiting Indians and foreigners.

The road leading from Rampur to Rudrapur seemed to deteriorate with every kilometer traveled. The bus slowed to its lowest gear as it negotiated potholes six inches deep and whole sections of pavement that had disintegrated into particles in whose loose sand the tires could not get a grip. But Theo's eyes, and now those of the other passengers, who had all finally woken up, paid little attention to the road surface, for the scenery showed very pretty indeed. Just ahead of them now, emerging from a dense growth of weeds and shrubs, a massive oak tree bent at a sixty-degree angle over the road. Eerily, the biggest boughs of this tree closely imitated the forms of grotesque humans, and the arms and hands of each of these forms pointed straight out toward the bus. The tree limbs might have been specters from some Gothic romance, clinging to the trunk as if it were a ship's mast, and cackling at the passing humans who little knew what lay ahead of them.

But a hundred yards further down the road, the close dark quality of the bordering trees yielded to an open, sunny, airy feeling. Two graceful, maidenly poplars, apparently best friends out to take the air, stretched tall and straight and a little big haughty, ignoring the bus as it groaned past them. Friendlier but equally youthful elms bent curiously toward the windows of the passing vehicle. Rough cinnamon-barked acacias, under the influence of a mild breeze, waved their feathery leaves at the travelers. The scene was one to charm and delight the receptive viewer.

Rudrapur proved to be a bustling and prosperous city of some 150,000 inhabitants. The government had established an Integrated Industrial State here, which had led to the establishment of dozens of major manufacturing facilities. Power, automobile, motor, and tractor companies had factories in Rudrapur. As the bus passed through the city, its buildings gleamed clean and white. Theo did not see the piles of trash he had observed in Rampur. Computer stores advertised the latest models of laptops. The windows of cell phone shops were postered with images of iPhones. The billboards that had defaced the other towns through which the bus had passed were not to be seen. The signs were less obtrusive and more tasteful. One could tell that the population here enjoyed a more prosperous lifestyle than that of Moradabad and Rampur.

The road began to climb as the travelers left Rudrapur for Haldwani. The latter city, the third most populous in all of Uttarakhand with 230,000 residents, sat at 1400 feet. The city bordered the Gaula River, silvery-blue with a graveled bottom, down to whose very banks, from the adjacent hills, stretched thick growths of trees. Haldwani served as a depot for market goods intended for the hills rising ever higher toward the lower Himalayas.

The bus slowed to pass over a steel bridge spanning a deep canyon. In the soft morning light the plant growth below the bridge showed the color and texture of peat moss. The trees climbing up the banks above the bridge, protected as they were from the sunshine by a rim of encircling hills, shone with the soft coolness of Constable's foliage in the "Cornfield." The hills themselves, set back one from another, and enveloped in luminous mist, seemed to be in the process of manifesting out of nothingness. For the first time since arriving in India, Theo felt the ancient spell of Bharata begin to exert itself on his soul. These woods and hills, these deeper and lighter colors, these shadows and muted lights spoke to him of profound mystery. There were only the first hints now, but these hints foreshadowed greater mysteries to come.

Like Rudrapur, Haldwani was cleaner, better paved, and obviously more prosperous than the other towns they had passed through after leaving Delhi. Whereas the smaller towns had been populated mostly by lower-income Indians, Haldwani was filled with members of the middle class. These people zipping by on scooters, in miniature cars and vinyl-topped cabs, must have been warehouse foremen, shipping managers, and shop owners.

Theo had an opportunity to study the city as Binder patiently negotiated his big vehicle through the modest-sized streets. The bus resembled an elephant attempting to move forward without accidentally squashing a darting squirrel or meandering chicken. Every ten seconds, a motor scooter would dart in front of it or a pedestrian would rush by it heedless of the danger represented by the huge tires. Far less honking shattered the air here than it had in Delhi. People moved, but they did not move with the urgency of the great city, nor did they exhibit the impatience and short tempers of many of the metropolis's residents.

They passed a row of small shops of the typical Indian sort: a mesh gate lifted up to reveal a dark interior filled with shelves stocked with propane stoves, small pumps, electric motors, drills, and tools. The next store over advertised oxygen tanks, gas pipes, v-belts, welding machines, and electrodes. Clearly, this section of the city catered to people involved in river transport and depot maintenance. Theo imagined the sort of conversations that must have taken place between the pullover-wearing proprietor and a couple of warehousemen in stained overalls, as they discussed the repair of a critical welding machine.

Finally, the bus pulled up to the Haldwani station. Eight others of various models stood in the asphalted yard. One, painted pistachio green, had a ladder leading up from its back bumper to its roof. All of the vehicles had destination signs upfront in Hindi. Several were spotted with mud, as though they had just emerged from a jungle trail. The station itself consisted of three small wooden buildings topped with Coca Cola advertisements. Gray-and-brown awnings protected their entryways from the sun.

Binder announced to the passengers that they would have a thirty-minute layover here at Haldwani, before continuing on to Nainital. Five or six passengers were getting off, to be replaced by an equal number headed to Nainital.

Theo sought out the restroom, which he found to be pleasantly modern, no worse certainly than most of the ones to be found in small town Greyhound stations in America. The place was not overly clean, but the plumbing worked and water flowed from the sink fixtures.

Having some time to spare, the pilgrim wandered through the station's shack-like structures. Two clerks in jeans and striped cotton shirts stamped tickets and separated greasy rupee notes. A concessionaire sold bottles of soda pop and fruit juice, packets of sweets and nuts, potato crisps, cookies, and dried fruit. Another vendor offered bars of sandal-scented soap, candles, sacks of rice, brightly-hued socks, and boxes of laundry powder. An Indian wife, engaged in a discussion with her spouse, vigorously shook her head in that peculiarly Indian way, which involved tilting the head from one shoulder to another. Apparently she did not approve of the price he was about to pay for some snacks. She pointed to a bag she carried on her shoulder, and must have been telling him what American mothers had so often told *their* husbands, "I brought food from home. It will suit us just fine. Who would ever pay *those* prices?" A college-age couple, obviously sweethearts still in their early dreamy days, held hands and constantly caught each other's glance, smiling in slight embarrassment afterwards. Two mothers tried to ride herd on their wild youngsters, worried that they would dart in front of a bus and be killed or permanently maimed. One of the women, as could readily be seen even by someone unfamiliar with her language, was scolding her husband for not taking a firm hand with their boy. But the man was holding a lively conversation with another fellow, and merely waved his arm, as if to say, "Boys will be boys."

Binder had some difficulty assembling his passengers for departure, but finally managed to gather the final wayward and playful children onto the bus. As the vehicle climbed the road up to the famous Nainital (which, the driver informed Theo, was one of the government's favorite children, and which, therefore, boasted a fine road of approach), the pilgrim immediately understood what all the fuss in the tourist brochures was about. The two-lane road was, indeed, of the best quality they had driven on since leaving Delhi, smoothly paved, its dividing line cleanly painted. But no one paid any attention to the highway, for, on both side of the bus, the entire world had turned green.

Hillsides rose straight up from the roadway, covered, in every square inch, by virid growth. The road angled steeply, the bus straining to make progress against the clawing forces of gravity. A stone bridge traced a smooth curve as it passed above a ribbon of stream five hundred feet below. A yew tree, with a diameter of two men's encircled arms, drooped its heavy, shaggy limbs of cones and needles over the roof of the bus. Deciduous trees marched up the sides of cliffs leaning forward, as if on a mission to attack the travelers. Families of parent and children trees clustered in curiosity as the lumbering vehicle passed them by. Clusters of gray boulders seemed ready to drop down on the bus like projectiles launched by hidden forest warriors. Several trees stood at least one hundred and fifty feet tall. One straight tree had been deprived of all its branches and stood denuded and embarrassed. Thick clumps of shrubs protruded from the hillside like oversized heads of broccoli.

The government had stuck cuboids of concrete and cute little wooden fences at the back of the road berm. Theo had to silently laugh, imagining the possibility of either of these small barriers preventing a ten-ton bus from dropping plump a thousand feet down into the waiting ravine.

Theo realized why everyone, including himself, had gotten spellbound by the scene through which they were passing. Civilization, which, in India especially, is almost always a close and pressing matter, had been left far behind. There were no billboards here, no political placards, no staring advertisements featuring comely young women. One saw no houses, no stores, no factories. Nature had swallowed the travelers whole, and they were delighting in the process of digestion.

The distance separating Haldwani and Nainital was only twenty miles, but the bus, constantly climbing as it had to, made slow progress. And, for once, everyone on it was glad that they moved so gradually. At one point the road curved and they all beheld a cluster of owl-colored foothills. The rightmost hill, shaded deeply on its left flank, had the shape of a prism. And, for the few seconds Theo had to examine it, came to resemble an androgynous god. His eyes were wide set, his nose delicately narrow, and his mouth pursed and small. He seemed to have taken refuge in the hill, to be both hiding and revealing himself. In a flash, the bus had passed out of sight of the god.

When they entered the town, there were small concrete houses, multi-story hotels with semicircular, arched windows, shops fronted by colorful awnings, a public fountain in the shape of a lion's head, trucks loaded with asphalt, tourist cars piled with possessions, orange 55-gallon drums clustered in a road niche, a public notice board papered with brochures, and then, flashing upon their eyes, without warning, stunningly: THE LAKE!

Nainital Lake sparkled in the morning sun like a royal-blue sapphire set in a recess of faint gold and verdigrised copper hills. Sloops whose triangular sails were striped in orange, yellow, and white passed silently over its surface. Oarsmen rowed couples seated on benches over the faintly ruffled waters. Long canoes, paddled by smiling young men, made slow progress close to shore. A bevy of swans, some with their long necks shot straight down into the water and their white tails wagging, floated silently in the shallows.

Even the children on the bus had grown quiet under the influence of this remarkably beautiful scene. It might have been Theo's imagination, but, as he looked out the window at the passersby, the tourists and locals going about their business, they all seemed to partake of the aura of magic wafting out from the sapphirine waters. Pedestrians walked slowly and with light steps. Cars and trucks waited their turns and avoided their horns. Shopkeepers refrained from hawking their goods. Nainital Lake was spreading its gentle influence out over the proximate humans.

On His Own

Binder backed the big bus into an open space at what was really more of a bus stand than a bus station. A row of four buses were parked below what appeared to be a college. The college, built as it was of hodgepodge brickwork, with arcuated windows framed in creamy stone, adorned as it was with a pyramidal, terracotta-colored tower, might have been a German provincial church from the 18th century. A pedestrian, dressed for rain and walking his large dogs, turned to stare at the bus. Several scooter riders, whose vehicles were parked across the street, unflinchingly gawked at the new arrivals.

Binder climbed down the steps, stretched as far as his arms could reach, and proceeded to unload the luggage. Theo waited while the other passengers disembarked. He contemplated the next stage in his pilgrimage to the Saint. He had decided to hire a car or taxi to travel from Nainital to Haridwar. He might have taken a train or ridden another bus, but preferred to be as private as possible as he drew (he hoped) ever closer to the holy man. The driver might prove to a chatty fellow, but that chance had to be taken.

"See! I have not given away your pilgrim's clothes," Binder smiled, handing the other man his backpack.

"I never doubted!" replied the American. After the families and children and honeymooners and tourists had gathered all their luggage, Theo remained to speak further with the driver. "You were a good driver and an informative one," he said.

"Oh, you pick up information here and there, driving the same route all the time. Where from here?"

""Haridwar."

"Two hundred and fifty kilometers."

"Three hours?"

50

Binder guffawed. "More like six hours. The road is bad. Lots of construction going on."

"I was thinking of renting a car and driver."

"You could do that. A bus would be cheaper."

"I feel like a little privacy."

"Your driver may be a monkey person."

"Can you give me some information, Binder? Where would I hire the car and how much should I pay?"

"A taxi is cheaper. Or do you prefer private car?"

"A taxi would be fine."

"Get one down there at the corner. You should pay 5,000 rupees, no more. Make sure the driver has been to Haridwar many times."

"Will he speak English?"

"Probably a little. But someone around there will help if you need it. Make sure he has done this before."

"Thank you, Binder. I hope you and your family will be blessed." The two men smiled and took each other in for a moment before parting.

Theo managed the transaction with surprising ease. Ashok, a spindly, clean-shaven man of about twenty-five, had, indeed, driven to Haridwar several times over the past year. He initially asked for 6,000 rupees, but sheepishly accepted 5,000 when his would-be passenger counter-offered.

The taxi was a Tata Indigo SW station wagon. Sky blue in color, the car was shorter than American station wagons, but looked solid enough and fully capable of the trip. In fact, it still carried splotches of mud from its last journey, for which Ashok politely apologized. He spoke good English, having, as he said, studied it up through lower secondary school. His goal was to master computer programming, but he drove taxis in order to save up money for his education in that field. As Theo listened to the chatty fellow, he began to wonder if Binder had correctly prophesied a "monkey" driver.

"When do you think we'll get to Haridwar?" Theo asked.

Ashok glanced at his complicated Japanese watch and tilted his head sideways several times before answering. "I think maybe by five o'clock. Would you want lunch on the way?"

"Is there a good place you know of?"

"Oh, yes, Gulmohar Palace! Excellent food. Low prices, too." Ashok recommended the place with the enthusiasm of a proprietor. Theo wondered whether the place might, indeed, be owned by a relative or good friend of the driver's.

"Sounds good. Shall we be off? I only have this backpack."

"Going trekking?"

"A sort of pilgrimage." For some reason, Theo did not feel like going into detail about the reason for his journey. He wanted to hold it close to his heart. The closer he came to the Saint, the more precious the meeting seemed to him.

Once on the highway, Theo learned that he would actually be doing some backtracking. The quickest way to Haridwar was to get back on National Highway 74 and pass once again through Rudrapur. Ashok informed him that they would then travel through Kashipur, Nagina, and Najibabad before arriving at the sacred city of Haridwar.

"Do you know what the town's name means, sir?"

"No, I don't."

"Gateway to Lord Vishnu. Pilgrims, and you said you were on a pilgrimage, often start their trips to Badrinath from Haridwar. So the name makes sense, right?"

"Yes, it does."

"Do you know why the town is holy, sir?"

"Please tell me." And Theo heard again about the drops of the immortal liquor amrita, which Garuda, that apparently clumsy celestial bird, spilled on Haridwar, far back in the time beyond time. Whenever Theo began to settle himself comfortably to take in the landscape, Ashok offered up another morsel of his local knowledge. But his passenger was not annoyed. Something in the man's innocent desire to be of service pleased him, no matter that he would have preferred to remain alone with his thoughts.

"Every twelve years, Haridwar is the site of the great Kumbha Mela festival. Millions of Hindus gather there, sir, to bathe in the Ganges. They hope to purify themselves so that they can attain jivanmukti."

"Yes, enlightenment."

"Ah, you know about that! Yes, but you and I know that enlightenment requires more than just taking a bath. American tourists are very clean, but I have never met one who was enlightened." Ashok turned to face his passenger in the back seat and smiled, proud of his joke.

"I'm sure it does."

"Everyone comes to Kumbha Mela, sir. Even the sadhus who avoid people throughout the year come to the festival. There are huts and tents as far as you can see. And many times there are great tragedies. People panic and get trampled underfoot. Very sad."

"So I have heard."

"Many of the holy men are pretenders, of course. They only want the bhiksha and alms they get. But there are genuine saints, too. People talk about seeing miracles performed by a man sitting under a pipal tree. One passenger told me he had seen, with his own eyes, a fakir completely disappear." Ashok snapped his finger. "Just like that. One minute he was leaning against a banyan tree and the next, poof, he was not there anymore. What do you think?" Again, the driver turned his head to see his passenger's reaction.

"Quite possible, I'm sure."

Maybe Ashok thought that these answers were too succinct, but, for whatever reason, he now turned his attention back to driving, and Theo had time to examine the landscape through which they were passing.

They were now approaching Kashipur, and the scenery reminded the American of what he had twice seen traveling through Rudrapur. Trees of average height hugged the sides of the roadway. Occasional small hoardings advertised automobiles or face lotions. Close to the city, piles of refuse, potato-chip packets, soda bottles, and sandwich papers, lay scattered in the dirt of pull-off areas. Small clusters of bicyclists and scooter riders gathered in these places, chatting, eating, and drinking. At one point the trees gave way to large fields planted with low crops of dense green color. "What crop is that, Ashok?"

"Paddy, sir. Remember when we passed the river? These farmers irrigate their crops by carrying off water from the Darkeswar, that's its name, and using it on their fields. They grow wheat here too."

"Oh, thanks."

Before long, Ashok announced with fanfare their approach to Dhampur and lunch. "I think you will like this restaurant, sir. I may have made a mistake, though. It is a *vegetarian* restaurant..."

"Great, I'm vegetarian."

Ashok seemed to literally shake off his worries on this score. "Oh, good. The food is very fine. Prices not too bad. I think you will like it."

"I'm sure I will. You will join me, of course."

"Very kind of you, sir. Thank you."

They pulled up to what did, indeed, resemble a colonial-period palace. A tall portico featuring four Corinthian columns served as the entrance to the place, and a colonnade with smaller columns of the same style, surmounted by a shallow, arced entablature, ran to its left. A large fresco of two stylized Indian lovers from some ancient era decorated the right side of the building's front wall. Young palm trees surrounded the parking area and drooped their fronds refreshingly near the entryway doors.

Ashok was greeted in a friendly manner by the hostess who quickly seated the two men at a small table. Both the table and its chairs were covered in shiny red cloth. The dining room was huge; it might have served, and probably did serve, as a dance floor for gala events. The few dozens of diners looked like afterthoughts in this large space, as though they had been sprinkled here and there just to allow the "restaurant" to prove its bona fides.

After cooling off from the heat of the car with large glasses of mango nectar, the men ordered lunch. Theo loved Indian cuisine, but, of late, had found the restaurant variety too rich and fattening for his tastes. So he made a mental note to restrain himself. He ended up settling for a vegetable biryani and dal makhani, while the driver ordered saag paneer and raisin naan. The aromas rising from dishes being served a few tables over whetted the men's appetite.

As they headed out after lunch, both driver and passenger felt the effects of the rich food. Ashok had brought a flask of tea with him and asked the American if he wished to partake. "No, thanks, Ashok. Caffeine and I have been estranged for years now."

Ashok was not certain of the precise meaning of this remark, but realized that the gentleman in the backseat did not want any tea. Theo put the windows down so that the fresh air blowing in might help him stay alert. But the cabbie had already been wonderfully restored by the strong black tea. "Did you know that Nagina, which we are just now approaching, was involved in the rebellion against the British, sir?"

"Tell me more."

"I am no historian, sir, but I do know that the nabob fought the British here during the Rebellion of 1857. He lost, of course. It was not a major part of the uprising, but I thought you might be interested."

"Do Indians consider that rebellion the first move in their efforts to attain independence, Ashok?"

"We are taught that, yes. The British were the ones who wrote history, but they only presented their version of the rebellion, sir. They wiped out whole villages, women and children, as you know."

"Horrible."

The taxi was now approaching Nagina. A vista opened up revealing gently rising hills, lush fields, and, in the distance, the burnt sienna outlines of the area's buildings.

As they exited the town, Ashok remarked that "Nagina is famous for its wood carving, sir. They have been doing it for 500 years. All kinds of interesting objects they make here."

"I imagine they're very beautiful. I appreciate the skill of Indian craftspeople."

Thirty minutes later the travelers hit the outskirts of Najibabad. Theo hurriedly rolled up the windows. A stench like that of rotten eggs spoiled the air. Fogs of dust and pollution swirled up from the roadway and the adjacent fields. Ashok turned to his passenger. "They have paper mills here, sir. We will be beyond the town in a few minutes."

"I clearly remember that smell from my childhood, Ashok. My grandmother lived in a town whose only industry was the paper mill. The sulfurous smell of that factory is something I can never get out of my nose, no matter how long I live." The driver laughed.

Hoping to put his passenger in a better mood, he mentioned that "Najibabad has a beautiful old fort, built in the 1700s by the nabob who founded the city. It is Mogul architecture, sir, very beautiful. Tourists come here a lot to see it."

"It sounds lovely."

"Lots of white stone arches and carvings in the actual stone of the walls. The Moguls were great artists."

"I understand that they were."

Theo glanced at his watch and noted that they appeared to be right on schedule. Haridwar lay 30 miles to the north, so, given their relatively slow speed, they should arrive there in an hour or so. He closed his eyes and passed into a revery in which he saw the outline of the Saint, clad all in white, at a near distance. The scene had that peculiar vagueness of dreams, but he could tell that the holy man was standing on rocky soil in a mountainous area. His back was turned to Theo. Theo moved his legs but, for some reason, according to the weird logic of reveries, could not get any closer to the man he wanted to meet above all others. He sensed that the Saint knew of his presence, but the Enlightened One kept his back turned.

A jolt awakened Theo from his musing, and he opened his eyes to take in a wonderful scene. Everything outside the taxi was vividly green. Grass grew along the verges of the road; bushes surmounted the grasses; and trees towered over the bushes. Theo felt as if he had been plunged right into the center of a wonderful world of viridity. The greenness that overwhelmed him didn't vary its tone in the slightest degree. A consistent hue of English ivy enveloped him, not only enveloped him, but penetrated his deepest being. He seemed to have been swallowed whole by one gigantic verdant mouth. The softness of the greenery tickled him, like feathers on his tender spots. The lushness of the green enwrapped him, like a Pashmina blanket cuddling his limbs. And the omnipresence of the green protected him, as if it had caused the dirt and clamor of the outside world to thoroughly disappear. The trees bent over the roadway in a charming attitude of protectiveness. They breathed Silence and instilled Silence into him. All this greenery worked like an immense eraser, removing from the earth every indication of man's paltry struggles, and announcing to the seeker that the mysteries of the forest, the secret of the mountains were his to be discovered.

Haridwar well deserved its ancient reputation as one of the seven holiest cities in India. The Ganges entered the plains just above the city, and was channeled off into subsidiary streams separated one from the other by small islands called aits. The city was nestled under the protective embrace of the Shivalik Hills, the outliers of the grand Himalayas. It is a glittering gem lying at the bottom of a basket of circumambient hilly greenery.

Haridwar is arched and beamed and suspension bridges in silver and coral and vermillion. It is sacred ghats backdropped by pastel-pink turreted temples. It is shoreside towers rising crisply delineated in strawberry and white. Haridwar is an ancient stone structure with the color and appearance of a weathered oyster shell standing mid-channel in an arm of Mother Ganges. It is a lone temple rising as if freshly born from a hilltop of faintly pink sandstone apparently dripping with the blood of terracotta.

As the taxi slowly made its way through the crowded streets, Theo marveled at this spiritual center called Haridwar. They passed a lone aghori sage whose hair was piled atop his head like a pillbox hat and ran down his sides to below his waist in braided strands. The man wore long necklaces of colorful beads, one that included a three-inch animal tooth; and he carried a kamandalu or watering pot. The sage's forehead and the side of his cheeks were painted white, and a crimson insignia, like a namaste hand gesture, flamed from the center of his brow. He wore an ochre robe over which he had thrown a blanket of Parma violet.

Of course there were also the streets with their shops as one saw in every Indian town, but Theo sensed something different about the ones in Haridwar. The streets were clean. The building facades had been painted in attractive colors: burnt orange, melon, woodland pink, and nasturtium rose. High, semicircularly arched windows adorned the buildings. Window boxes gaily decorated with flowers enlivened small balconies. Colorful awnings, with hues of tangerine and royal blue and stripings of cafe-au-lait and ecru, protected proffered arrangements of flowers, incense, beads, and perfumed oils.

A row of antique-looking carriages, pulled by single horses, stood off to the side of the road. One horse had a black feedbag attached to its muzzle. A couple of pedicabs, one advertising the local gondola service, kept on the lookout for passengers. Suddenly, Ashok stopped the car, and Theo followed his line of sight. Coming down a side road, in a naked parade, marched a group of sadhus wearing only loincloths. The men, whose skin color graded from black bean to dark taupe to raw umber, sported leis of orange marigolds around their necks. One had the hair of a Rastafarian; another, the slightly shaggy cut of a 70s disco dancer. One fellow showed a bald head and a face encircled by a forked growth of yellow-white beard. A couple of the paraders were emaciated, and several looked like they had only recently left their business suits behind.

Ashok began to laugh. Again, Theo looked where the driver looked. It proved to be one of those moments of synchronicity that serve to prove nature's piquant sense of humor: right above the naked men sat a hoarding diptych advertising men's underwear. On one panel, a muscled man posed in only boxers, and, in the other, in only briefs.

Theo observed all sorts of religious types in the streets of Haridwar: old men, using canes, wrapped in saffron cloth from head to foot; a squat ascetic, whose entire body was coated in gray ash, who wore a pomegranate-hued Speedo and a court jester's cap; and a stitchless, uncircumcised ecstatic tossing his five-foot-long braids as though they were slender branches dancing in the wind. There were holy men carrying umbrellas and ones with spectacles. Astonishingly, Theo noticed, in an alleyway, an ashen sadhu lying on a pile of thorns, his danda, or staff, held above his chest like an arrow that had pierced it through.

Ashok pulled to the side of the road and asked his passenger where he would like to be dropped off. Theo hadn't even considered the question. It brought him face to face with the realization that he had not yet decided how he would make his way to Rishikesh. Yes, he had contemplated trekking the thirteen miles that separated that city from Haridwar. But he had also thought about taking a taxi. Now that Ashok posed the question, Theo had to make up his mind. "I am thinking about walking to Rishikesh. What do you think?" He expected the driver to strongly recommend taking a cab, and offer his as the one to take, but the taxi man surprised him.

"Less than 25 kilometers, I think." He looked at Theo's body and made a quick assessment of its fitness. "You could certainly do it. But it's getting late. I would recommend staying in a hotel for the night and then setting out in the morning."

"Yes, that makes sense. Then I could experience Haridwar at night. I've seen photos; it's lovely at night. Do you know of a good hotel, Ashok?"

"I suggest the Haveli Hari Ganga, sir. It is on the Ganges. The rooms and the food are both very fine."

"Expensive?"

Ashok shook his head. "Not so bad. If you are going on a pilgrimage, you might want one night in a nice place before you set out for the mountains, yes?"

"That's probably true," Theo laughed.

"But you cannot reach the hotel by car, sir. You will need to walk or take a rickshaw. I can arrange a rickshaw if that would be useful."

"Oh, don't bother, my friend. I need to start getting used to finding my own way around India. Might as well begin tonight."

Theo paid Ashok his fare and added a generous tip. They shook hands. The driver clearly wanted to say something more.

"Did I forget anything?" Theo asked.

"I was just wondering where you were going on your pilgrimage, sir. If I'm not being too nosy."

Theo laughed, looked up at the early evening sky and around at the subdued pedestrians making their way down the narrow road. "Not at all. I am going to meet a man who I'm not sure exists, in a place I have no idea how to locate. How's that for a clear itinerary?"

Ashok looked momentarily puzzled. "Well, I hope you find him, sir. Good luck on your journey!"

"And you on yours, my friend. Are you going straight back? That's a lot of driving in one day."

"Much less traffic at night. You have to pay attention to the road, though. Sometimes animals cross it and there are bad accidents." Ashok climbed back into his taxi, turned it, and, waving, made his way back towards Nainital.

Before leaving, the driver had given his passenger a tourist map of the city and marked out the way to the hotel. Now, Theo thought that he would get a room there, deposit his bag, and then set out to explore the city by night.

He found the place without even needing to accost a stranger for assistance. He passed through a narrow portico, lined with clay-potted plants, half of whose breadth was taken up by several parked and logoed pedicabs. The entrance to the hotel was primrose yellow and black. The transom was painted with a semicircular motto in Hindi, which Theo could not understand. The jambs of the doorway glistened in deepest black. A completely black lantern—whose opaque

61

paint rendered it useless for such an object's normal purpose— hung on the right side of the entrance.

The staff proved gracious and accommodating. After a short walk down a hallway whose checkerboard floor stones were of apricot and ebony, whose walls were graced with elaborate battle scenes from the *Mahabharata*, Theo entered a bedroom delightful to behold. Every decoration in it rang with Indian authenticity. The bed scarf, which looked to the inexpert like a tie that might have been worn by a giant, was made of a heavy brocade in beige and nutmeg; the pillows were crimson satin and chocolate cotton; the mirror above the desk looked to be hand-carved; the tabouret had been crafted from native wood; and the print hanging in the alcove portrayed a gathering of holy men on the banks of the Ganges.

Theo washed his face, using the aromatic sandalwood soap he found on the sink, changed shirts, and headed out to explore Haridwar.

It was now twilight and the city had just begun to sparkle in its evening dress. For Haridwar resembled a very lovely, but proper, righteous lady, who, despite her religion, cannot restrain the charms she presents when going out at night. When the sun sank, the city's bridge lights glinted on the Ganges' blue waters like diamantine strings; spotlights illumined the cupolas of her temples so that they came to resemble fairy-fashioned broaches from *A Thousand and One Nights*; towers rose erect in salvia red and linen white like the figure of the elegant dame herself; a fire pot set in the middle of the river sent out concentric waves of aureate shimmer like the yellow-gold hooped rings dangling from her ears.

The narrow streets curved smoothly, with nothing voluptuous about them, much like the person of the handsome woman. The city sparkled brilliantly, in certain places, like the twin crystals of her eyes, and cast demure shadows, in others, like the recesses of her dimpled cheeks. Haridwar clad itself in the amber of her bracelet and its riverine breezes hinted at wonderful mysteries like the emanations from her soul.

Theo walked and walked and walked some more. He said nothing to anyone, bought nothing, stopped for nothing. With easy steps, he simply wandered around and through the magic that was Haridwar.

As he ambled, the pilgrim began to think about the Saint. For now he must be approaching him, closing in on his white-dhoti'd form. His intuition told him that the holy man would not be found in Haridwar. But Rishikesh was not far away. And Rishikesh was renowned as a home for saints. Maybe there the two would finally meet in the flesh. Or would he need to continue his travels? Move on to Uttarkashi, even on to Gangotri? So far he had only enjoyed that one revery of the Saint, in which he had seen him from behind, standing on rocky soil, in a mountainous area. Yes, undoubtedly, the Saint would be found in the Himalayas, away from crowds of people, away even from pestering seekers who wished to become disciples. The Saint would live in the clear, pure air of the high mountains, above the world, halfway to heaven.

Afoot in the Himalayas

Theo vaguely inquired with people at the hotel about the presence in Haridwar of the Saint he was seeking. Their looks of surprise hinted at veritable astonishment. The pilgrim could almost read their thoughts: "Did this man come all the way from America to find a yogi whose name he doesn't even know?" Of course, the staff responded to his queries with perfect politeness.

"You don't know his name, sir? But do you possibly have a *photograph* of him? Do you know if he is associated with a certain temple or ashram?" When the people at the Haveli Hari Ganga heard that he knew and had nothing more specific about the holy man, they were very sorry that they could not be of further assistance. What they did not say, but what Theo clearly "heard" them thinking was, "This gentleman must be slightly crazy." How in the world, they wondered, could an American find a specific guru, amongst the thousands in wide India, going on next to no information?

In their doubting, these modern Indians proved that they had less connection to the ancient teachings of Sanatana Dharma than even this Western foreigner. For Theo took it completely on faith that he *would* find the holy man. He had not explained his visions to the counter staff and hotel manager from whom he had sought advice, believing, rightfully, that they would have then *certainly* written him off as a kook, but he himself placed complete credence in these paranormal experiences.

Although his instincts told him that the Saint was not in Haridwar, Theo chose to spend another day there just in case. After rising early, he took to the streets and, as he had done before, wandered through them for hours on end. He walked by the river, observing the Hindus bathing in the sacred waters of the Ganges. Naked holy men splashed with the gay abandon of children. Clusters of embarrassed women carefully sunk themselves, inch by painful inch, into the cold water. Aides handed important men flowers to launch upon the wavelets.

Kids raced up and down the steps of the ghat, playing games as children always do. Merchants in huts set back from the steps offered for sale flowers, towels, statuettes of Hindu deities, strings of rudraksha beads, and packages of incense.

And Theo walked through the streets, ignoring the beckoning shopkeepers and their wares, always on the lookout for that one, unique, supremely delightful face with the bright-star eyes and the mouth that poured forth affectionate love. His gaze passed over businessmen intent on conversation, over women eagerly sharing stories, over impatient youngsters, tormenting each other behind mother's back. It passed over barely dressed sadhus and ochre-robed temple priests and disciples wrapped all in white. Most of the faces looked very ordinary to Theo. Even the supposed "religious" men did not reveal to him countenances bathed in Peace. Although he kept walking, so long that his legs grew sore, the seeker finally understood that the Saint would not be found in Haridwar.

After that day spent searching Haridwar for a holy man he did not actually expect to find, Theo made up his mind to leave, on foot, for Rishikesh the next day. Thirteen miles didn't sound that bad. But he would make some inquiries about the difficulty of the trek.

Theo was advised not to walk on the main highway leading to Rishikesh. That route would be dirty and dusty. Too much road traffic passed over NH 34. The hotel manager told him to go, instead, to Chilla, and then on to Rishikesh. During the day, the man said, wild animals would not be a problem. The wildest creatures he should expect to encounter were some unkempt sadhus, the dapper fellow joked.

The following day, the pilgrim left the hotel, pack on his back, and crossed the Ganges over to Chilla. He walked at the side of the Chilla Dam-Rishikesh Road, feeling, at last, as though he were making a serious physical effort to reach his teacher.

What made his route interesting was its following the path of the watercourse from the Dam. The road itself was narrow, bordered on one side by bushes and trees, but the jade waters of the diverted Ganges kept it company as all three moved toward Rishikesh.

Theo chose to extend his trek slightly by passing through the Rajaji National Park. The park was home to elephants and tigers, but Theo did not expect to encounter either. In fact, he would only pass through the edge of the park before heading back north to Rishikesh. And what a delight the park proved to be! The section he walked through was jungle pierced by the dried-out bed of a river, covered by thousands of rounded white and brown stones, some as big as grapefruits, others as small as acorns. In the monsoon season, these rivers would, he knew, come to raging life, sweeping the unsuspecting trekker to a painful and inglorious death.

At one point the small trail opened up into a single-lane path rolled smooth from the finest of small stones. A chill and comforting breeze passed through the trees along the roadside, some of them elms and chestnuts eight feet in diameter. Bright sunlight illuminated the boles of the trees, so that they glowed in immateriality. The shadowed portion of the road ahead had a soft powder-blue color. The canopies of the tallest trees glared in richest green. And the flat stones on the verge of the road, caught in full sunshine, seemed nothing more substantial than landed light.

Theo's attention was drawn by a somewhat muted klak-klak-klak-klak sound coming from a nearby tree. Instinctively, he stopped, and looked over to where the noise had sounded, scanning the area carefully. The most interesting bird he had ever beheld clung to the trunk of what looked like a poplar. Its scarlet crest stood out like a racing yacht's bright sail. Black-and-white stripes, amusingly reminiscent of a convict's uniform from an old movie, ran down the side of its head. The bird's back and rump feathers had the color of rust and its tail ones were entirely black. As the creature turned toward

66

Theo, he could see that its breast decoration, all black and white, comprised dozens of little nugget shapes, which resembled dried-out corn kernels.

The bird stopped making noise the moment Theo located it. In fact, it turned its head toward the observer and held his attention. It seemed to wish to "say" something to the man. After a short period of silent communication, the amazing bird nodded its head sharply three times. Its beak pointed in the direction the pilgrim was walking. Taking this as affirmation that he was on the right path, Theo thrice nodded back, made a namaste hand gesture, and carefully walked on.

The manager of the hotel had led him to believe that he would likely run into other trekkers, but, up to this point, Theo had seen or heard no one. After another half hour's walk, he came to the dam and, after that, to the canal again. He passed over a small bridge underneath which whirled and swirled the foamed and honey-colored waters of the canal.

Following the canal road in its straight-as-a-measure run, Theo checked his watch. He had been on foot for nearly three hours and had calculated that the entire trip to Rishikesh should take him no more than four. But he realized that he had lingered.

He looked to his left, through a sparse grove of slender trees, and made out a cluster of three small huts. The huts had pyramidal thatched roofs and low, roughly hewn timber walls. He imagined that they were the homes of either park rangers or farmers granted the right to plant crops here on the outer edge of the public land. What must it be like, he asked himself, to live in such a hut, in such a park, in such a country? He could hardly even imagine.

Soon he came to a group of hills whose contours formed perfect demispheres. Like breasts rising from mother earth (and she must be a very nurturing one indeed, given their number), the hills made him wish he possessed the hands of a giant, that he might gently palpate them. On one of these hills grew scores of saplings, slender as ten-year-old girls, and twisting and turning as actively as those maidens did at play.

The soil here was grayish-pink and delicately shadowed by the thin leafage of the youthful trees. This leafage showed the color of shamrocks lower down, and gradually lightened to absinthe and finally to citron in the canopy.

The young trees, so fragile and delicate, the mounded earth, so maternal and nurturing, the fresh greens of the foliage all around him, caused the pilgrim, for some inexplicable reason, to fall to his knees. He knelt before this scene as if it were an altar; and he felt holier than he had ever felt in any religious edifice. The faintest of faint whispers, wafting from the grove on the breath of the breeze, informed him that a new life awaited him, that, just as these gracile saplings had risen in grace from the fertile earth, he, too, would emerge fresh and clean from the soil that awaited him.

Before another half hour had passed, Theo found himself by the Ganges, at the entrance to the Ram Jhula, an iron suspension bridge spanning the river. The twin towers at his end of the bridge reminded the man of oil derricks or, alternately, of constructions he had fashioned as a boy from his erector-set parts. The bridge was six feet wide and here, for the first time since entering the forest, Theo saw other people. Probably fifty of them walked, at various distances from him, on the bridge's surface. Only two people, twentyish men in colorful shirts and jeans came towards him, the rest were heading southwest towards Rishikesh.

The bridge possessed the delicate strength one associates with a well-built spider web. It seemed so slight, its cables, so thin, that Theo found it hard to believe the construction would actually support the weight of all these pedestrians.

He had taken his time on the day's journey, stopping to marvel at the dry river bed, to talk to the bird, and to admire the grove of saplings. The afternoon was now coming to a close, and evening

68

approached. The Ganges showed only the slightest ruffling. And its hue, in the chastened light of earliest evening, was a caressing grayish glaucous. a sort of toned-down aquamarine, something like a patina green. What one called it did not matter; the color embraced the eye of the observer, hinting at tasteful gowns and understated stones, of ancient gardens and feminine softness.

And the tempered rays rendered the houses and other buildings on the far side of the river powdery white, and barely blue and palest yellow. As Theo contemplated the scene before him, his focus attenuated, a familiar stillness permeated his body and mind. A sort of frozen-awareness trance came over him, as it had on many occasions in his life. The silvery cables and towers of the bridge, the lithographic, postcard quality of the pruinose buildings on the far side of the river, the modern-architectural-glass look of the aqua Ganges, all combined to form what seemed like only a snapshot of a pseudo-reality, nothing more. There were no *real* buildings, river, and bridge; there was simply an illusion of one: a sort of mirage, such as thirsty desert travelers imagine to be an actual oasis. Everything that his eyes beheld struck Theo as imaginary. It was as if he had stepped outside the world to which human beings give their unquestioned allegiance and seen it from a remove, seen it as a fiction, a construct, a flimsy postcard that no more contained a "real" world than the card did a real scene.

After some time, the spell passed and everything resumed its normal look and feel. The traveler made his way across the bridge and oriented himself toward Rishikesh. He had to travel about two miles to the southeast to reach the holy town.

The name of the city derived from the apparition of Lord Vishnu to the rishi Raibhya. Theo knew, from his research, that the word "Rishikesh" meant "Lord of the senses." The rishi had mastered his senses, been visited by the god, and thus named the city. Three famous temples founded by Adi Shankara, the saint most responsible

69

for the establishment of advaita Vedanta, the teaching of the non-dual nature of Being, were located in Rishikesh: Shatrughna Mandir Bharat Mandir, and Lakshman Mandir. The city is so holy that no meat or alcohol is allowed in its precincts.

Rishikesh turned out to be a far bigger city than Theo had imagined. With a population exceeding 100,000 souls, the holy city spread out, up, down, on both sides of, and away from the river. The Shivalik Hills rose high all around it. Great gray blocks of the schist and gneiss of which the hills are composed had rolled down to the very beaches of the Ganges. Immense boulders of slate, slashed deeply here and there, striped with white veins, climbed straight up from the edges of the water. Thick woods covered the hillside, rising steeply from the riverbanks. Temples and ashrams, some white, some pink, some coral-and-pearl, built atop squared foundation rocks, presided gracefully over the ever-flowing waters of the holiest of Indian rivers. In places, boulders the size of small automobiles made access to the water difficult.

As Theo wandered along the riverside, just after he passed under the Lakshman Jhula Bridge, he came to the Tera Manzil Temple, a magnificent thirteen-storey structure dedicated to the worship of all the various Hindu gods and goddesses. He had to step as close to the Ganges as possible, and completely crane his neck, to take in the pinnacle of this wonderful edifice. The ground storey comprised a series of closed-off pink rooms that looked like garages. Three tiers of latticed rectangular windows, separated at each level by a decorated persimmon-colored frieze, formed the next higher floors. Then came three progressively narrower storeys (forming in outline something like the deck of a Mississippi River paddleboat), interspersed with pointed arches, and featuring copper-hued friezes. Four melon-painted pyramidal turrets, topped with vertebraed finials, rose from both the first and third of these levels, the latter of which ended in a tower. This ultimate tower of the temple consisted of six square platforms, all of which contained, on each side, the same pointed arches seen on the

70

storeys immediately below them. The turret atop the thirteenth level perfectly replicated those of the sixth and seventh storeys.

Walking away from the riverbank and into town, Theo found himself among the same sort of small shops he had seen all through his travels in India so far. One difference lay in the names of the shops and their offerings. He noticed Wahe Guru Traders, for instance. And he saw that much of what was being advertised for sale had to do with either religion or trekking. Some stores sold boots and footwear, walking sticks and compasses; others tempted passersby with framed photographs of famous saints, packages of locally produced incense, and strands of beads blessed by the monks of a local ashram. A book store spread holy texts on tables by the store entryway. Jewelers displayed ruby earrings, gold bracelets, and heavy necklaces under the protective cover of glass cases. Beautiful silk saris fluttered in the breeze outside a clothing shop. And tourists were encouraged to buy cameras, memory cards, disposable phones, and postcards covered with the beauties of Rishikesh.

But the town failed to capture Theo's interest. He felt strongly drawn to the river and the temples adorning its banks like extravagant, filigreed charms dangling from a silver bracelet. There was definitely something spiritually purifying in the very air of this part of Rishikesh. Saints had sat here cross-legged, immersed in the Ocean of Bliss that was their natural home. Teachers had instructed students here: students who had gone on to become great gurus in their own right. Yes, there *were* tourists busy taking photographs and discussing where to have lunch, but the underlying current of Rishikesh, which Theo was surprised to find himself tuning in to, vibrated pure and potent.

Rishikesh is often referred to as the "Abode of Gods." Sri Shankara's spiritual influence, though first brought here in the distant 8th century, had permeated the very stones of the place. It was here that Maharishi Mahesh Yogi had instructed the Beatles in the technique of Transcendental Meditation. It was here that holy men

71

and women and Hindu devotees had come on pilgrimage for centuries past. Both Swami Rama Tirtha and Sivananda Saraswati had lived, meditated, and taught here. And history has lost track of the rishis and other Enlightened Beings who had graced the banks of the Ganges in this place where the city of Rishikesh later formed.

As Theo sat on a rock overlooking the Ganges, he noticed the bridge and the temples, the glinting water and one of the most amazing birds he had ever seen. On a boulder ten yards from him sat what he later identified as a tern. This bird had the body of a seagull and a smooth coral beak. What rendered it stunning, however, was the black hangman's hood that covered its entire head and neck. As he stared at the tern, Theo smiled. It might, he thought, have been a Christian tourist visiting a mosque, who must drape her head in black cloth so as not to offend convention.

Soon Theo's thoughts focused on his search. He decided that here, in Rishikesh, he would make his first serious effort to locate the Saint. What could he do? He could visit temples and ashrams and approach holy men that he encountered, seeking at every place, and from each person who might have knowledge, the location of the Saint for the gift of whose presence he had traveled half way around the world.

Making Inquiries

Theo was sitting cross-legged at a slightly lower level than the monk on the dais. The dark-bearded monk wore a saffron dhoti and the friendliest of smiles. "You don't know this holy man's name?"

"No, Guruji. He has appeared to me in visions throughout my life, and has prompted me to follow him to India. So here I am."

The plump cheeks of the monk swelled out even more than usual as he leaned back to enjoy a long, contagious laugh. Now his hand began to play with his rudraksha beads as he stared up toward the gaily painted ceiling. "If he has *led* you here, what makes you think that he will abandon you now that you *are* here?"

"I didn't mean that, Guruji. I just thought that it might be part of his plan for me to consult wise men like yourself in my efforts to find him."

"How did you describe him?"

"He looks something like Ramana Maharishi, at least based on the photos I've seen of him. But his beard is longer and his eyebrows are thicker. His nose is fairly broad. His eyes are," he was going to say, "like pieces of star," but chose not to, "very brilliant and piercing."

"And your intuition tells you..."

"That he might be above Gangotri. My plan was to travel that far and see what happened there."

The monk shrugged his shoulders and gave the pilgrim a quizzical look.

"You mean why then am I seeking information about him here? I guess you're right. I should have just trusted my instincts. But I know that Rishikesh is a city famous for wise men," Theo looked at the monk meaningfully, "so I thought that there might be a chance to find him here."

Again, the monk fingered his mala, this time looking to his right at a large framed picture of an ancient rishi. "Trust your inner voice. The holy man will not lead you astray. If you feel called to spend time in Rishikesh, by all means do so. But the beacon guiding you to your teacher will not stop flashing. Pay attention to it and your desire to meet the Saint will be fulfilled."

"Thank you, Guruji." Theo pressed his palms together in the namaste gesture and bowed his head before the monk. He then quietly backed out of the room.

The monk had reaffirmed what he already knew. The Saint was not likely to be found here in this populous city. Theo had always pictured him—indeed, the holy man had so appeared in his taxi cab revery—in an isolated spot in the Himalayas. Far up into the sacred mountains was where the seeker ought to wend his way.

But the monk had correctly inferred Theo's desire to spend a short amount of time here in Rishikesh. Time spent here, he reasoned, functioned as a sort of spiritual training camp for the highland climb he must undertake in order to join the Saint. In Rishikesh, he would bask in the subtle energies left here, as their spiritual heritage, by hundreds of Enlightened Beings. In Rishikesh, he could begin to drop the burdensome baggage of the material world, which he had for so long carried on his shoulders. In Rishikesh, he might acclimate himself to the higher frequency of the masters who still, albeit in very small numbers, resided in the ashrams and temples that surrounded him on every side.

Theo found a room in a hotel called the Ganga Kinare, located right on the river. The place was affordable and clean, and its location, perfect.

The next day, as he enjoyed breakfast on a deck overlooking the Ganges, Theo marveled at the scene presented to his eyes. Here, as on the road leading into Nainital, the world had turned completely green. The Ganges, barely riffled here and there with the smallest of

74

waves, shone the color of an aventurine gemstone. The low bushes on the far bank of the river resembled the darkest shade of broccoli. The taller trees backdropping the shrubs were colored like privet hedges. The Shivalik Hills, dusted and faded by the matutinal mists, showed that hue called Spanish green. The silent beauty of the morning, this morning clad all in green, passed into Theo like a blessing. The soft air lulled his nerves. The barely audible flow of the river water lullabied his heart. The gradual transitions of the shades of green tranquilized his eyes. He began to lose contact with his body. That sense, which one always has, of being right *in* one's body, dissolved. Numbness froze him. He might have been mirroring glass, for he reflected the scene before him and did nothing more. An echo of silence—as absurd as that phrase sounds—reverberated in his innermost ear. The peaceful flow of the river carried him away from the deck where he sat, and away from all thoughts and concerns he might previously have known. Some ancient spell wrapped his soul in the softest of cashmere shawls, warming it, comforting it, and setting it at rest.

When the waiter appeared, Theo had no idea how long he had been "gone." Had his life depended on it, he could not have said if the dreaminess had lasted one minute or thirty. As it was, he found it difficult first to understand what the server was saying, and then to respond to his question. "Would there be anything else, sir?" The man looked at him quizzically, and Theo knew he must have had to repeat his query.

"Oh, sorry, I was just daydreaming. No, can you put it on my room bill, please?"

"Certainly, and the number is?"

"Room 108." The man hesitated, and Theo realized he had not yet signed the check. He added a gratuity and, after a pause necessary to remember it, signed his name.

"Thank you, sir." And the waiter disappeared.

75

After breakfast, Theo went for a very long walk along the river, coming finally to a small town called Muni-Ki-Reti, "the sand of the sages," a holy spot where saints had meditated over the ages. He passed clusters of tourists and one very thoughtful Brahmin, head bowed, hands clasped behind his white kurta. Then he came to a pile of large rocks on which he noticed a seated yogi. At first, Theo hesitated about approaching the man. He might, the pilgrim thought, be swimming deep in meditation, and not want to be disturbed. But the seeker remembered the purpose of his trip and took slow steps toward the white-dhoti-clad figure. When he was directly at the Indian's side, about five yards away from him, the man spoke. "You are searching for someone, whom you know, and yet you do not know, whom you have seen, but yet have not seen."

Palms pressed together, Theo approached the rock on which the speaker sat. "Yes, Guruji. Yes, I am. Can you guide me?"

Theo was now close enough to observe the yogi closely. His black hair, swept back behind his ears, reached his shoulders. His thick mustache extended out to the sides until it merged with his salt-and-pepper beard. Stripes of pearly paste ran across his thrice-furrowed brow. A flattish nose spread out above thick orchid-pink lips.

"He has been guiding you all along. Didn't you understand that?"

Theo remembered his revery in the taxi and the bird in the tree on the way to Rishikesh. "Yes, I understand he was guiding me all along." The seeker had the odd experience of finding the other man's words on his own lips, as if they had passed through his ears and then come into and out of his mouth.

"And you realize he is not here."

"No, not here."

The yogi now opened his eyes and very slowly turned his head to face Theo. His eyes were barely open slits, but the bits Theo could see radiated maternal tenderness. The Indian's voice now softened.

76

"Why do you question his guidance? Has he not brought you all this long way?"

Theo had to make a distinct effort not to repeat these words as well. "You are right, Guruji, I should just listen to my intuition."

The man smiled. "It is not *your* intuition. It is the voice of your master calling you. Sometimes it will call you with a vision; sometimes it will call you from a tree. If necessary, even the river itself might speak to you."

"It is hard to forget that the logical mind does not always need to be in control."

"Think of the lunacy of the wide world and consider where the *logical* mind has gotten it. Truth comes from a much deeper place than the monkey mind, which runs after every banana and nut."

Theo wanted to ask the yogi how he had known the specifics of his journey, his vision, and his bird-guidance. But he felt that he should not pry into the man's secrets. Obviously, this adept had developed wonderful powers of second sight, and the source of and route to his knowledge ought to be allowed to remain private. Theo considered him a messenger from the Saint, another signpost on his journey. "I will continue on to Uttarkashi and Gangotri, as I had planned."

The yogi had now turned his head back toward the river and once again closed his eyes. His last statement was, "Let the guru guide you. Following him, you will never be led astray."

If Theo had held even the slightest doubt that he should proceed on to Gangotri, he let go of it now. As he stood looking out over the Ganges, into whose parrot-green flow a group of rocks, of diminishing size, which resembled a creep of tortoises, crawled out, the seeker considered the amazing ways in which the holy man kept guiding him. Theo knew from experience that the Saint could appear in a vision, so the taxi revery was unsurprising. But exactly how did he inspire a forest bird to point the way? How precisely did he communicate, via telepathy, with a lone riverside yogi, knowing that Theo's steps that morning would take him past the man? These questions were beyond the pilgrim's ken.

Now he asked himself whether any reason remained to linger in Rishikesh. Why should he sightsee and marvel at religious devotees here, while the Saint, the sole object of his trip, now the main purpose of his life, waited for him, walking lightly, somewhere higher up, up there in the Himalayas?

That night, Theo sat at the dining table in the hotel's restaurant and closely examined his map. All along, he had been worried about the leg of the trip from Rishikesh to Uttarkashi. Ninety miles on foot was a challenge for a man of his age, no matter how good his physical condition, especially when the ever-thinner atmosphere en route got factored in. The plan he had devised involved five days of trekking, eighteen miles a day.

As he sipped his chamomile tea, Theo mused. He worked out daily and considered himself fit. Walking was walking. How hard could it be? He had spent time in Denver, where the air was thinner than it would be in Uttarkashi. Certainly, he had noticed its lack of oxygen, but it hadn't proved an obstacle to his daily exercise regimen. No, he could certainly manage this long walk, broken up as it would be over five days.

A Change of Plans

As he was leaving the restaurant, Theo accidentally bumped into someone and turned to apologize. He found himself nose to forehead with an Englishman who appeared to have just risen straight from the pages of a Trollope novel, as *The Warden*'s cleric, Septimus Harding. The short man shared with Harding the small mouth, gray mutton-chop whiskers, and benignly mild persona. If he had been holding a cello in his free hand, the one not patting Theo's upper arm, the gentleman would have proven himself to be a time traveler.

"I'm so sorry. I've always been clumsy," the pilgrim said.

"No, no, entirely my fault. You see, I *don't* see, that is not very *well* these days. With age, the eyes deteriorate."

Theo ended up sitting down with Mr. Amblin Mollifer and having an entertaining chat. "So your family lived here, back in the Empire days?"

"Yes, yes, my grandfather was a Provincial Governor during the days of the first rebellion. We have some old letters of his from those days. Very difficult times, very difficult, indeed."

It turned out that Amblin, as he insisted on being called, was headed to a place called Jyotirmath, which Theo recognized as the site of one of the four cardinal monasteries founded by Shankara to perpetuate the teaching of Vedanta. It was here, he knew, that the great saint Brahmananda Saraswati had held the position of Shankaracharya in the middle of the 20th century.

"I thought a retreat would do me good, young man. At my age, you know, one's thoughts turn more and more to what comes next."

Theo chuckled aloud. "I haven't been called 'young' for many years. I think you *do* need to get those eyes checked out."

Amblin smiled his gentle smile. "All relative, all relative. I must have thirty years on you, so 'young' it is."

Theo suddenly got the idea of traveling with Amblin to Jyotirmath. The "idea" was more like a direct and irresistible demand, and in it he heard the call of the Saint. Seconds after conceiving the idea, Amblin made the offer it involved. "Why not postpone your hike to Uttarkashi and come with me to Jyotirmath? It's a tiny little place, stuck right in the mountains, elevation about 6,000 feet, if memory serves me well."

"You know, I would be delighted!" And, just like that, the Indian itinerary, which had stayed fixed since before he left America, changed. He would go to Jyotirmath. Maybe, he thought, it was within the walls of some small temple there that he would finally meet the holy man. No matter what the purpose of this diversion from his plans, Theo could not possibly question its necessity. The thought had come with the clarity of struck crystal and its fulfillment had followed instantaneously.

Once on the road, Theo got so involved in his conversation with the charming Englishman that he only occasionally stopped listening or talking to pay attention to the surroundings. He caught glimpses of the most primitive roadside huts imaginable: jerry-built lean-tos fashioned from corrugated iron roofs supported by bent and weather wooden posts. But behind these flimsy structures, rising like a silent commentary on the difference between the skills of human beings and those of nature, were the sentinels of the magnificent Garhwal Himalayas. Mountains the color of old chocolate soared sheer from the side of the road. More distant peaks gleamed heavenly white, as if they had been coated with immaculate clouds, which, in turn, had been infused with scorching sunlight. Portions of the topography rounded like soft feminine shoulders; others spiked like urban skyscrapers. A river of white flowing down the flank of a mountain was juxtaposed with speckled patches of barren greenish-gray. At roadside level, brilliant oblongs, like golf-course greens, were bordered by thick growths of bushes and trees of a darker shade. And the entire scene was swallowed up by an immense evergreen bowl that completely surrounded it.

For the first time since arriving in India, Theo felt as though he were close to the magical, mystical Himalayas. These were not they; these were the outliers, the advance guard sent ahead to spy on interlopers entering the sacred zones. But these small mountains functioned like the faint salt smell of the air one notices while still miles away from the ocean itself. They whispered about the awe-inspiring magnificence that lay ahead. They hinted at the glory of the great peaks. And something deep inside Theo thrilled at the very hint of what was to come.

Amblin offered his guest lunch, which they ate out of a wicker basket while lolling on a hill fifty yards away from the road. The Englishman being a vegetarian like Theo, the food was welcomed by him. As they stared in awe at the rocky marvels surrounding them, the two absentmindedly chewed their rice and beans and tore off pieces of and ate their buttered naan.

They had been traveling now for about five hours and were outside Gopeshwar, about forty miles from Jyotirmath. "See up there?" Amblin asked.

"Beautiful. Words don't do it justice."

The older man smiled gently. That tallest peak is Chandrashila; it means "moon rock." Thirteen thousand feet high. They say Lord Rama meditated there after defeating the demon Ravana. Evening had begun to fall. The triangular peak showed large upright deltas of golden ochre. The flanks of the mountain were banded with well-smoothed snakes of snow. But the low light from the sun softened this snow, so that it reminded the viewer of strips of giving foam.

Amblin continued, pointing his finger slightly lower. "Just below it, maybe a thousand feet lower, is Tungnath, the highest Shiva temple in the world. Said to be at least a thousand years old. It's connected to the Pandavas..."

"From the *Mahabharata*?"

"The same. There's a whole story about them seeking Shiva up there. Anyway, it's a major pilgrimage spot for Hindus, especially those who worship Lord Shiva."

Theo turned his head slightly to a vista where the sun still shone bright. Here the mountains had the irregular contours of a thick chunk of chocolate that has been gnawed on by a greedy child. Strangely, the snowy contours threatened, at any moment, to disappear completely, as if they had been only a trick of magic, and could come into or go out of existence with the snap of a thaumaturgist's fingers. The pilgrim could not turn away from this spectacle. His intellect told him that these were solid stone mountains, the most concrete of concrete realities. But his senses showed him that they were, on the contrary, the stuff of mist and fog, of cloud and vapor; they trembled on the verge of disappearance at every instant.

"We'd better push forward, my friend. Evening's coming on apace, and we don't want still to be driving on these mountain roads once darkness sets in."

And as they continued their journey, Theo appreciated the driver's words. The roads leading into Jyotirmath were built into the sides of the mountains, which seemed clearly not to want them there. In relative dimensions, the narrow road might have been the faintest wrinkle on the vast hide of a huge elephant. Theo first thought that the road resembled a snake, but then, on reconsideration, concluded that no snake could possibly twist and contort itself in the manner that this strip of rutted asphalt did. Sometimes the car appeared to be going *back* exactly the same way it had come *forward*. They were looping their way toward the holy town. And, all the time, evening came on fast.

The lower hills, untouched by snow, now sprouted whole new series of masses, fashioned from shadow: the impressions of those across the valley. So there would be a trapezoidal stone face, like the side of a human habitation, with the color of butterscotch, tipped by "eaves" in mossy green; but directly beneath this structure stretched a continuous line of ever-taller peaks colored solidly in the black ink of shadow. Thick masses of cumulus rose behind the highest peaks as if with the hope of covering them in blankets for nightly sleep.

Theo looked over at Amblin. The old man never showed signs of stress, but he was clearly intent on reaching town before the sun fell below the mountains. But the travelers were very close now.

The passenger looked up once more at Chandrashila. The clouds behind it had stretched straight out, as though they refused to interfere in one's perception of the eminence. And that eminence was as beautiful as anything Theo had ever in his life seen. The setting sun shone full on the face of the rock. The mountain looked like a gigantic nugget of copper heated to the point where it glowed incandescent. Near its top, 24-karat gold splashed out from the hot copper. Everything below Chandrashila lay dark and shadowy. Only the peak itself burst forth in the coruscating fulgor of melting metal. The clouded backdrop of burnt orange perfectly set off the colors of the mountain. So unusual and entrancingly beautiful did it seem that Theo thought it must belong to some other planet, some distant orb out there in vast space, where exotic atmospheres and special star configurations made such phenomena possible. This mountain, he mused, did not belong on earth. It ought to exist as a reward hard to deserve in some god-populated heaven on another spiritual plane.

"Made it!" Amblin's shoulders relaxed and he leaned his head back in satisfaction. "I got trapped on a road like that once in my life, and vowed that it would never happen again."

Theo looked over at his companion and smiled a smile that originated in part from his happiness with the man, but in larger part from the spell of the mountain vision he had just been granted. Poor Amblin, he thought, must have missed the whole thing, having to keep his eyes on the road. 'And your hands on the wheel / Keep your snoopy eyes on the road ahead.' The seeker's mood was so joyous that the lyrics from this childhood song spontaneously popped into mind.

The light had faded so much that Theo could only get an idea of Jyotirmath as a hodgepodge of small houses set against one another at weird angles, of covered wells and a winding road. Amblin pulled the car up to a hotel painted all in white. They checked in and, skipping dinner, immediately retired. The combination of the long trip and the thin air had thoroughly worn them out. The attenuated air of 6,100 feet made breathing more of a conscious matter, and fatigued the body greatly.

After breakfast the next day, the Englishman took his new friend to the Narasimha Temple, founded by Shankara himself, which, the pilgrim was informed, contained a cave where the saint had practiced "tapas," austerities designed to purify their practitioner. Narasimha was an avatar of Vishnu, a major Hindu deity. The temple, Amblin explained, was about 1,200 years old.

The temple featured brilliantly colored decorations and statuary. Everywhere one looked, sky-blues competed with ochres and raspberries. Paintings of bearded and benevolent-looking Shankarachryas hung from walls and ceilings. They came to a small idol of Lord Narasimha. "The locals believe that the right hand of this idol gets smaller every day. On the day it breaks completely, they say, the mountains will suffer a great landslide, closing off the route to the sacred Badrinath temple. Geologists confirm that the area here is quite prone to such slides."

The two men descended to the cave where Shankara had once engaged in deep meditation. And there was no gainsaying the atmosphere of that small space. Theo involuntarily closed his eyes and found that the interior of his head immediately lit up, as if a fire were burning within his skull. He remained motionless until Amblin spoke again. "See, these are the four disciples of Shankara and the great saint himself." Theo could barely bring himself to open his eyes, but he finally managed to. The air in the cave was densely packed with what he could only conceive of as intense vibrations of joy. Layer upon layer upon layer of Silence composed that air, every layer being richly impregnated with perfect happiness.

The friends walked around the town for a while, noticing the brown-and-white walls along the road, which reminded them of giraffe skin; noticing the rusted iron roofs and the clothes hung out to dry; and noticing the 2400-year-old, fenced-off banyan tree, said to bring its visitors good luck. But, most of all, their attention kept moving up, above the town, to the sweep of grand mountains that protected it. In the morning light, the ones free of snow looked to Theo like immense arrowheads, ready to be mounted on a shaft for some mighty god's powerful bow. He felt sorry for these smoke-brown and ivy-green younger siblings; they so obviously yearned to be their taller brothers and sisters, whose peaks tickled the cerulean, whose perfect white flanks gleamed immaculate.

The mountains rendered the mundane life of the town inconsiderable. No, Theo mused, that wasn't fair. The holy men and women seeking enlightenment in the purlieus of Jyotirmath were certainly involved in something more important than being a mountain. But how many such people actually lived here? All around Amblin and him were tourists taking selfies, tourists hanging from tree limbs for the amusement of their friends, and tourists pretending to push one another off the side of a cliff. Hotels wanted to rent rooms. Restaurants wished to sell meals. Even the temple staffs seemed more interested in offering tours for tips and guidebooks for a price than they were in high advaita knowledge. So, yes, on third thought, the mountains did put the petty concerns of human beings into pathetic perspective. The giant peaks were silent. They touched the heavens. They glowed and sparkled and radiated pure light. They spoke more eloquently of spiritual grandeur than all the memorized prayers of the Hindus visiting the holy temples. God lived up there, in the soaring heights, Theo felt sure of it.

Over lunch in a roadside restaurant, Theo asked Amblin how long he planned to stay in Jyotirmath. "I'm leaving it open-ended, maybe a month, maybe a year. I've felt drawn to this spot for a long time. I'm a seeker like yourself. This place feels holy to me."

"It certainly does," responded Theo, turning his head to look once again up at the stunning peaks.

"And how about you? Will you stay with me here?"

"As you know, I'd originally planned to go directly to Uttarkashi from Rishikesh. But the Valley of Flowers is fascinating to me. I may explore it before heading back toward Uttarkashi."

"That's quite a distance."

"A hundred and eighty miles. Yes, quite a ways. I don't think of trekking that far, of course. But maybe I'll meet another fine gentleman like Amblin Mollifer, who will give me a lift."

Amblin's face took on a dreamy look. He was staring at his glass of water, slowly turning it from side to side, as if he were looking for an answer in its misted, jiggling contents. "The Valley of Flowers....I've often wondered about that place myself. Probably read the same descriptions you have in those wonderful books written by sadhu wanderers. I'm sure you'll have some wonderful experiences there."

The Valley of the Flowers

The friends parted the following morning, promising to keep in touch, if not on the material, at least on the spiritual, level. Theo had spent the previous night carefully going through his backpack, making sure that everything that he believed to be in it was, indeed, in it, and verifying the condition of all his trekking apparatus.

After saying goodbye to Amblin, he set off on the ten-mile walk to the Valley of Flowers. It was a most remarkable place, from everything that he had read, a high-altitude Himalayan valley extremely rich in flora and fauna, home to hundreds of threatened plant, and more than a dozen endangered mammal, species. Set at 10,000 feet above sea level, the Valley stretched from subalpine to lower and upper alpine zones. In it could be found streams, meadows, river beds, plateaus, cliffs, stone deserts, and caves. But, of course, what it was most famous for was its flowers: botanists had recorded over 600 species of flowering plants in the Valley.

Having been told that he needed to acquire a permit, Theo stopped at Ghangaria and received it. He then continued on toward the Valley of Flowers.

As he entered the area, Theo noticed the moist coolness of the air, no doubt one of the reasons for the profusion of flowers here. The space through which he walked lay in shadow. A stream, all afoam and churning, raced beneath the path. The banks of the stream consisted of thick piles of rocks and stones, which must have fallen from the cliffs above them. The declivities just above the stream, which dropped down from the path on which Theo walked, bore a pelt of extremely thick, dark green plants. Not a single square inch of these drops but was covered in greenery.

Theo, who was breathing hard now in the thin air, came to the highest point of the pathway and broke out of its shadow. Before him stretched one of those delectable panoramas that nature, in her kindest moments, offers up to favored human beings. Everything in front of him was brightly illuminated by the morning sun. Torn wisps of pure-white cloud hung in space directly over his head. A thick knot of trees adorned the lower portion of the valley before him. Above the trees, the mountainside rose at a sixty-degree angle. He noticed sharp-edged rock formations, dusty-gray monoliths, cement-gray plinths, rises reminiscent of serried haystacks, steps fit for the boots of giants, and landing strips shaped like carrier decks. But what made all this rock so fascinating were its colors: the entire scene was a variation of yellowish green. Theo saw artichoke green in the landing strip, and eucalyptus green on the monoliths. The sharp-edged rocks had the color of watermelon rind, and the haystacks that of absinthe liqueur. Long slopes like ski runs showed a predominance of yellow over green, looking like unripe limes.

As Theo stared ahead of him, he again had that strange feeling that none of this was at all real. These mountainsides belonged in a Maxfield Parrish painting or in a film about Shangri-La. In no way did they fit in the terrestrial zone with which the pilgrim was familiar.

As he moved slowly forward, feeling more like a weightless spirit than a physical body, the seeker caught his first whiffs of the Valley's scents. The perfumes of wildflowers, wild rose bushes, and wild strawberries wafted up and into his nostrils. Having always been highly susceptible to fragrance, he stopped walking and closed his eyes, so that he could put all of his attention on these delightful natural aromas. Theo felt as if he were approaching the person of the most beautiful woman imaginable, whose skin emitted this variegated perfume.

Once he managed to reopen his eyes, the trekker noted the patches of flowers and bushes whose olfactory gift he had just received, and sent out to them a silent "thank you."

One group of flowers especially drew his attention. They rose up about a foot high from the midst of an outcropping of ash-white stone. Their mauve blooms opened up like butterfly wings. Their stalks grew

88

thick, almost like cane, and their long, lanceolate leaves were divided down the middle by a vein the color of Bordeaux wine.

As he walked on, Theo came to a small cluster of Himalayan bellflowers. He recalled their scientific name, "campanula," and, at the same moment, a classroom scene from high school, in which his hoary old Latin professor, Mr. Levens, explained the derivation of a "campanologist" or bell-ringer. This word led him, in turn, to the memory of the San Francisco cable-car drivers' bell-ringing contests.

The pale-violet bells had the texture and pronounced ribbing of onion skin. Something about the deeply notched flowers reminded him of jellyfish: these violet beauties might be easily imagined floating lazily in an oceanic atmosphere of heavenly mist. Theo's eyes wandered to the right, where they found a butterfly clinging to the top of an unflowered stalk. The lepidopteron showed a sidelong eye as big as its head, twin black antennae weirdly akin to television rabbit ears, legs and feelers aplenty, and a fine geometric color pattern of cream, russet, coal black, and robin's-egg blue.

After walking for another half hour or so, Theo heard that most delightful of sounds, flowing water. He turned a corner on the path and saw, above a bend in the small river, in the middle of a semicircle of dark cliffside, a gushing waterfall. The white, racing water shot down about a hundred feet, in three distinct streams. He could feel the chill mist of the water on his face. Where it met the ground, a spread of flat gray stones, the water shot out sideways, before flowing at a slower pace into the river.

Theo stopped to watch the waterfall for some time. There was something about the incessant flow of water that had always tranquilized and even mesmerized him, and he now once again fell subject to its spell.

When he finally managed to move on, the pilgrim followed some twists and turns on the path before coming face to face with a group of most unusual flowers. He recognized them from the brochure he had studied before coming to the valley. They were honeysuckles; but *such* honeysuckles as he had never previously seen. The flowers stood three feet high and their apple-red stems were at least an inch in diameter. What made them so unusual was that the actual flowers were presented in individual cups, as if as offerings. Each honeysuckle possessed five or six of these cups, out of which peeked eight or ten azalea-pink flowers. The image presented by these honeysuckles was that of a tiered series of nests containing fledgling birds, which just happened to be flowers rather than aves.

After refreshing himself with some water taken from the stream running along the pathway, Theo continued forward. He reached a confluence of hillsides completely covered, in all directions, for a distance of at least a quarter mile, with pale orange, lemon-yellow, lavender-blue, and bright tangerine-hued flowers. The perfume of these flowers overpowered him. Their combined scents enwrapped him like an aromatic cloak. Their aromas hung so heavy in the air that they felt almost tangible, as if he might grab hold of them and rub them into his skin.

These perfumes literally intoxicated the pilgrim. He lost the ability to think and to move. He could not even remember his own name! For the fragrant power that they wielded, these acres of flowers might have been opium poppies that had somehow magically released their potent contents to the wind. All that Theo could do was smile. He stood transfixed, his eyes on the multicolored scene in front of him. All thoughts, all memories had disappeared. There was only this single moment, this forever of now, this fantastic beauty, and this inebriating redolence.

Had Theo been able to form thoughts, he would have described the vista as follows: hills on either side of the path were woven, like the yarns of a wonderful afghan, with streams of bright flowers. Closest to him ran a band of faint-orange poppies; adjacent to the orange ones stretched a belt of lavender ones; below these, in a small pool, swirled purplish flowers of some unknown variety; and in the far distance, at the top of a hill, shone a grouping of tangerine-hued blooms.

On the opposite hillside, the colors were fewer but even brighter. Long, glowing flows of primary yellow, which looked like lava made of butter, spilled down the face of the hill. Occasionally interspersed with these cinquefoils were irregularly shaped growths of the lavender poppies seen on the other side. And, in the farthest visible distance, dark, Parma-violet colored poppies merged with mates growing up from the bottom of the opposite hill, below the tangerine-hued blooms previously mentioned.

The hills seemed to have become gigantic flower vases spilling over their sides charming soft textures and enchanting bright colors. Not an inch of raw soil could be seen. Every spot on the landscape was covered with a cornucopia of blooms.

After an indeterminate time, Theo shuffled forward, drunk with the thick perfume in the air, which seemed to have been breathed out by a massive pair of bellows. His feet moved unsteadily beneath him, and his head swam in a buzz of pleasant confusion.

At one spot he stopped, drawn by a flower just to his left. He sat down on the path and stared hard at the geranium. One bloom dominated his attention. Its five petals had the shape of guitar picks. Each of them still held on to their morning dots of variably sized dewdrops. The stamen formed a cerise pentacle. Flamingo-pink pigment had flowed from the outer portions of the petals toward the center of the flower. Cyclamen-pink veins ran straight to near the edges of the petals before branching.

The seeker stared and stared at this single bloom, regardless of all else, lost in spacelessness devoid of time.

Feeling himself about to doze off, Theo resisted the urge and, exerting all his will power, managed to rise to his feet. Mechanically, like someone lost in a great desert, who moves simply to be moving, without goal or plan, he walked on.

The flower-vase valley ended, and he soon came to a rough terrain whose small outcroppings were sharp-edged and dangerous to a trekker. Now that the air was no longer saturated with floral perfume, his head began to clear. The land here reminded him of the Ireland he had observed in films: not a flat piece of ground to be seen; everything was rough-spined hillocks, unclimbable cliffs, and rocks and boulders strewn like dice from some god's immense cup.

But once he climbed over a mound about ten feet high, Theo saw a delightful rapids cutting diagonally across the landscape. The bed of this stream contained nothing but rocks, so the rushing water could only foam and seethe. It splashed atop a boulder, bent round a middle-sized rock, sped straight over smaller stones, and poured down smooth over a declivity of schist. In the few places where the bigger rocks were absent, the water, clearly thrilled by its newfound freedom, exploded in a frenzy of fuzzy white exuberance. Whereas the olfactory sense had dominated him in the flower-vase valley, now his aural awareness did. The thrilling sound that is fast-rushing water lulled the pilgrim. It possessed an underlying steadiness of "whoosh," but then played variations over that sound, little high-pitched squeals, occasional excited pants, and even, once in a while, a low guffaw.

Putting His Feet to Work

Theo exited the park and found a place to pitch his tent. For the first time since entering India, he felt that he was truly deserving of the name pilgrim, for he was now alone, in the Himalayas, and single-mindedly seeking the Saint.

And, though the night proved cold, Theo slept well, indeed. The perfumes of the myriad flowers appeared to have somehow cleansed and refreshed his inner being, and he woke full of hope and possibilities. Near the bank of a small stream he sat to do his morning meditation. The moment he shut his eyes, his consciousness sank deep, his everyday mind disappeared, and he enjoyed a space of perfect peace and joy.

It took him two weeks to trek from the Valley of Flowers to Gangotri. Getting a ride on the highway would have been faster and easier, but that was not the route he preferred to take. No, he wished, at this point in his pilgrimage, to be alone and with nature.

Theo knew the mythology associated with Gangotri. Here, according to Hindu lore, the river Goddess Ganga dropped from the unfurled locks of Shiva. Gangotri was one of four pilgrimage sites on the "four small abodes" route in the Himalayas. It was a tiny town that formed the source of the mighty Ganges River, known at this place as the Bhagirathi.

When Theo first observed it in the far distance, Gangotri appeared to be no more than a sprinkling of small buildings set in a vast formation of mountains. Lilliputians must have lived here, at the feet of the Brobdingnagian peaks. Gangotri itself sat at 10,000 feet above sea level, but the peaks surrounding it soared to heights above 15,000. They loomed, dark and shadowed, right over the tiny town. And, in the distance, white-capped and -flanked mountains rose as high as four miles.

Theo spent little time in the town, stopping only to visit the temple, a domed white-stone building attractive to Hindu pilgrims. Instead, he went in search of Gomukh, the glacial source of the Ganges, ten miles distance from the town.

Gomukh was the terminus of the Gangotri glacier, and was backgrounded by the razor-edged Bhagirathi peaks. Theo arrived at night and pitched his tent at the best spot he could find, the flat top of a boulder twenty feet square. The effort that he had to make to breathe fully convinced him of the elevation of this place.

When he awoke the next morning, it looked as though the night had carried him to a distant planet. The morning light showed the rock formations in front of him in striking chiaroscuro. They looked like the work of a master ink drawer. To his immediate right, a declivity of loose rock threatened to fall to pieces at any moment. Further left, closely pressed serrations of silvery-gray rock resembled, in shape, piano keys. Straight before him rested a hollow in the semicircular rock formation. At one moment, it looked to Theo like a giant stone throne and, at the next, like a beshadowed god with his arms flung out in welcome. On the left were platforms of huge boulders set out as though in expectation of the arrival of equally large visitors.

After completing his morning meditation, the seeker wandered down among the boulders to what was known as the "mouth of a cow," a half-circle-shaped opening at the bottom of the stone throne. Out of this opening, the melted glacier waters flowed, growing stronger and more voluminous, becoming the mighty Ganges as they moved southeast, before finally emptying into the Bay of Bengal.

Breathing with effort, Theo descended to a vantage point above the snout, whence he made out two other people: one a half-naked sadhu, performing a morning ritual, and the other a twentyish trekker, delighting in matching his skills of balance against the rock formations. Their relative proportion, compared to the rocky surroundings, was

94

that of two bees playing about on the hide of a brontosaurus. Theo was only fifty yards from these people, but he could have easily missed them amongst all the gargantuan slabs, plinths, balls, and pyramids of rock. What had impressed Theo from a great distance, when he first beheld this place, now astonished him up close. He mused that the origin of a river as important as the Ganges deserved a source as impressive as Gomukh,

The water that emerged from the great cave, having only recently lost its icy solidity, sparkled white. The light-gray color of the rocks at the edge of the stream blended smoothly with this whiteness of the water itself. But the light of the sun shone so brightly that Theo could not be sure what that color would be later in the day, when the friendly star's angle dimmed its beam.

Theo climbed back up to his rock and sat down to observe the scene. He might have come to the very end of the earth. The otherworldly appearance of Gomukh, its utter isolation, and its dramatic features spoke of a grand culmination. But the Saint was not here! The pilgrim had not planned his trip further than Gomukh. It had always struck him that the source of the holy Mother Ganges ought, fittingly, to be the place where he met the Being who would nurture his Enlightenment. But he was nowhere to be seen.

And Theo had not had another "sign" from him since the conversation with the yogi on the "sand of the sages." He recalled speaking with the saffron-dhoti'd monk in Rishikesh and telling him that he expected to find the Saint "above" Gangotri. Yes, Gangotri had always stuck in his mind as the end point of his pilgrimage, but the pilgrim had nevertheless envisioned the holy man as being alone, up high in the mountains. Now, Gomukh *was* high, 14,000 feet high. And he remembered his research indicating that 11,000 feet was the safe limit for a novice climber. But maybe the Saint awaited him at a point still higher up. Not much higher, he hoped, or his lungs would not be able to stand it.

Theo stayed three days in Gomukh, primarily to acclimate his lungs to the thin air of the high mountains. On the second day, he approached the sadhu he had seen on his first morning there. The sadhu, who was entirely uncovered above the waist, and wore only an orange loincloth below it, possessed limited English.

"Namaste, sadhuji!"

The yogi had been busy filling his kamandalu with water from the stream. He met the visitor's eye, but continued to fill his can.

"I am searching for a holy man. He is older than me, and has a white beard, sort of like a sponge. And his eyes are like pieces of star, very bright and clear."

The yogi shook his head, denying knowledge of such a man.

"I came from America looking for him. I have only seen him in visions. He told me to come. And I always thought I would find him near Gomukh."

Having filled the kamandalu, the sadhu now squatted on his haunches, examining the speaker more carefully. "Few come here."

Theo smiled, encouraged that the recluse had spoken. "But have you ever seen an older holy man, with a white beard, near here?"

"I live closer to Gangotri. Only come here a few times a year. Never saw such a sadhu. Not here, not in Gangotri."

Crestfallen, Theo couldn't keep himself from frowning. But then he remembered his manners. "Well, sorry to have troubled you. And thank you for letting me know." He placed his palms together, bowed slightly, and walked away.

Where Might He Be?

As Theo sat in front of a low fire he had built on his rocky home, as he contemplated the glowing sticks of wood, the bed of lava-colored embers on which these sticks rested, and the dancing spirits of ivory and jonquil-yellow that shivered and shot into the cold night air, he contemplated what he thought would be one of the most momentous decisions of his life. He knew, of course, how he would decide the matter: he would go off, up higher in the mountains, in pursuit of the Saint. But he realized that the dangers of such a lone quest were anything but small. The nights would be frigid; the climbing, arduous; the air, thin; and his middle-aged body, severely put to the test.

Knowing that he would go, he asked himself, as he stirred the fire, causing sudden flames to emerge where none had been before, how exactly he would proceed. The holy man no longer sent him signals. Had matters gone as they ought to have, the half-clad yogi would have informed him that he had, indeed, seen a lone saint at a location not far from here. But, instead, he had shaken his head in denial and claimed ignorance of such a man. Now Theo had nothing whatsoever to guide him on his forward journey. He felt abandoned by the very being who had called him here, to Holy India.

But, despite his reservations, the next morning, his fourth day at Gangotri, Theo packed up his equipment and tent and began to walk up into the higher mountains.

The flora differed at these high elevations. He saw far fewer flowers, mainly a sort of yellow daisy with spear-shaped leaves, a fumitory with purplish flowers and thick but flexible stems, and pale violet locoweed, whose spatulate leaves he most often saw growing around dried-out bushes.

But late in the afternoon of that first day after leaving Gangotri, Theo was thrilled to come across a thick spread of rhododendrons. He had seen nothing but rocks and boulders for some time; then he

97

looked up and beheld the cyclamen-pink flowers growing low to the ground and over a space about a hundred feet square. The flowers seemed like sunrise at midnight. Their colorful joy brought life and hope to the deadness of the surrounding rocks. Theo felt his spirits lift.

He wasn't pursuing any special direction now, for he had absolutely no idea where the Saint might be found. He had decided to trust completely in destiny and the holy man himself to guide his feet where they ought to go.

That first night he camped in a small cave he had managed to find. It sheltered beneath an overhang of rock fifty feet high. He carefully examined the cave for signs of unwelcome life, but found it empty and dry and, all-in-all, perfectly suited to his needs. A foray in the neighborhood led him to a small grove of poplars from which he took the wood for a fire. He was amazed and pleased to see a pair of sky-blue pheasants with brown tails meandering through some thick bushes near his stand of poplars. So, fauna as well as flora, he thought, even at this great height.

That night, Theo left his cave and found a smooth spot on which to sit and watch the night sky. For years, he had been an amateur student of astronomy, and he knew the constellations well. The mountains above and around him glowed sulphur blue, their shadowed portions resembling great slabs of coal. And above him glinted a veritable snowstorm of stars, more than he had ever imagined it possible to see. The sky was smoke blue at its lightest and in most places, but darkened to Prussian blue near the edges of visibility. The stars were so closely set that they reminded him of those myriad, infinitesimal sparks he sometimes saw, throughout his life, when gazing at the sun or the moon. It did not look as if a single additional star could be squeezed into this sky. When Theo recalled that some of these stars were 100 times more massive than the sun, and when he recollected that the average distance between them was 30 trillion miles, his mind boggled. Each tiny speck he now looked at was immense and vastly distant from its nearest neighbor. And, yet, the entire sky was cluttered with them.

He found the constellation Hydra, a long staggering snake-like shape that was the largest of the modern constellations. It lay below the ecliptic, and none of its stars gleamed very bright. On the ecliptic itself shone Orion, the hunter, a constellation seen by people all over the world. Theo easily made out the reddish star Betelgeuse and its equally bright bluish-white partner, Rigel. That very visible constellation, the Pleiades, or Seven Sisters, beaconed with its hot, blue stars on the western horizon. Southeast of Orion, Theo noticed Canis Major and, in it, one of the sky's brightest stars, Sirius.

In the far north, he identified the Dragon constellation and to the northwest, the Great Bear, with its familiar astral arrangement known as the Big Dipper. Near the Great Bear, Theo located the brightest visible star, Arcturus, known as the Guardian of the Bear because of its proximity to Ursa Major.

Theo had lived alone for most of his life, and, even during the times when he had physically been in the company of others, he had *been* alone, self-contained, for as long as he could remember. So sitting here by himself, near the top of the world, under an apparently infinite starscape, surrounded by cold, gigantic monuments of rock, did not bring on any thoughts of isolation. On the contrary, he felt closer to the world than he ever had. The sheer vastness of the sky and the Himalayas rendered the difference between the worlds of matter and spirit negligible. One's body seemed so very, very small here that it hardly existed at all. It was one's spirit that expanded up into those glorious heavens and out and over those blue and black giants of rock.

Half expectantly, Theo waited that night for a message from the Saint. But nothing came. There was only the great sky and the grand mountains, the faint whistle of the wind, and a silence so profound that it threatened to swallow him whole.

The next day he headed off further up the mountain. He noticed, growing out of one steep slope, a stand of juniper bushes loaded with blue-colored berries. To his right rose a nearly vertical wall of purple granite. Once, he had to hold his foot in the air before landing it in order to avoid stepping on a gray lizard immobilized on the ground. And as he sat for a break, wiping his brow with his sleeve, Theo looked over at a nearby bush and saw an extraordinary butterfly: black and yellow in coloration, with dentilated markings and an all-of-a-piece body, the creature possessed a swallowtail.

Oddly, however, it never moved. As he stared at it, Theo began to conceive the idea that it was pointing him in a direction, for its head and wings formed the sort of caret shape used for signposts. But, on second thought, the pilgrim believed that he was imagining it all. He stood up, stretched, drank another sip of water, and proceeded in the direction he had been going all along, the opposite of the way the butterfly had pointed.

An hour later, Theo came close to disaster. As he was mindlessly walking through a narrow col, over the talus that regularly sent some additional stone skittering down to the path, he heard a deep rumbling sound, as if a Cyclops were clearing his throat. In an instant, rocks began to crash down the mountainside just ahead of him. It all happened in slow motion: he saw one particular rock, about the size of a car tire, rotating on its edge straight down the face of the mountain. It plunged over the cliff and down into a deep gulf. Other rocks hopped and jumped, animal-like, before smashing hard into the path. First one rock would come by itself, and then three or four would follow in a group. After a few seconds, regaining his wits, Theo turned his head to take in the situation behind him. The mountainside there showed no activity. He quickly turned around, and hiked back toward the place where he had seen the butterfly.

At first he was stunned. The butterfly was still there, in the exact same spot! Now he *knew* that it had meant to send him in a different direction, and he vowed to pay attention to all such future signs.

The place to which the bumblebee-colored insect directed Theo proved difficult of access. There was no real path; one had to pick one's way over rocks and low bushes, making slow progress indeed. Despite his recent internal vow, the seeker several times asked himself if this could *possibly* be the way.

Keeping him company as he carefully climbed and stepped were a pair of turtledoves with taupe breasts, orchid-pink beaks, and fox-colored back feathers, who kept singing the same four-beat song, with two long notes at the beginning and end and two short ones in the middle.

After passing a pair of tamarisk trees, short—bushy things with gray-green leaves—Theo heard a faint series of sounds. Stopping to listen, he located the sounds in a tamarisk fifty yards to his right. The calls were those of an alpine thrush. They reminded him of the squeaking of an unoiled pulley, or of a monkey's mutterings turned to the lowest possible volume. But though such unflattering similes came to mind, Theo enjoyed the thrush's song. It possessed a delightful, airy, triangle-like quality, and the more he listened to it, the more his pleasure grew.

The afternoon was near its close. Theo looked around for a place he might camp. But no good site showed itself. So he pushed on for another tiresome hundred yards, before coming to a small clearing that struck him as so out of place in its topographical context as to be considered a miracle. For the place was flat and almost completely free of stones. Behind it soared a sharp-surfaced crag; below it lay a stony draw; and on either side of it sat boulders, rocks, and sinewy bushes. But he was not going to argue with a smiling destiny, so he simply pitched his camp.

In the midst of unpacking his gear, the sun began to set. Theo stopped what he was doing and moved to a hummock overlooking the draw. The sinking sun had painted a wide swath of the mountains before him in deepest rose. The huge piles of cumulus set behind the tallest visible peak showed the shape of cotton candy and the color of a pink sapphire. The rim of the sinking star burnt a candescent arc on the far horizon. Then the colors deepened to ruby and orange, and the mountains turned black, and their faces curved like mighty Hawaiian waves preparing to crash into an unsuspecting shore. Finally, one lone cloud hung high, cream and tangerine, and the sky itself assumed a solemn purple hue, and one lone peak stood out against it, nothing but a molten shimmer of flowing lava light. And it all ended.

Still Alone

The next morning, Theo found a lookout that commanded many miles of his surroundings. Far in the distance, he noticed a quicksilver-colored thread winding its way to lower elevations, and he knew it to be the Ganges. On either side of the silver thread miniature cliffs dropped down steeply to meet it. These cliffs were completely covered with greenery the color of fir trees. The observer realized that they were, in actuality, declivities a thousand feet high. But the distance separating him from them rendered them toylike.

After eating some dried fruit and sipping some water, the pilgrim packed up his gear and continued on. Forward progress was made difficult by the absence of any path: he had to climb, clamber, and scuttle over or through boulders five feet tall, wiry locoweeds, and thick grasses that rose waist high.

After two hours of hard trekking, he left the alpine area through which he had been traveling and entered a nival zone seemingly devoid of plant life. Now, stretching out before him for several miles was a glacier backdropped by a massif consisting of a peak with twin, pointed ears and slightly lower mountains that cascaded down closer to where he stood. Directly in front of Theo rose a partially snow-covered mountain that looked like the big peak's smaller brother.

The glacier, which gave Theo the odd impression of flowing water (so wavy was its surface, so riverlike, its course), ended at the side of the brother mountain. Thousands of pieces of scree, smoothly polished gray stones, lay flat, like ill-fashioned flooring, directly in front of the spot where Theo stood.

A butterfly-blue sky, faintly streaked here and there by filaments of cirrus cloud; towering mountains almost completely draped in snow; a frozen white river of glacier; a mostly gray smaller mountain formation; and a wide scattering of stones: such was the scene presented to the pilgrim.

He wondered how he had ever come to be here. The Saint seemed so very far away. He felt as though he stood at the very top of the world, at an infinite distance from other human beings. "He can't possibly be here." Theo looked all around. "No one could survive for long in such desolation. Nothing but rock and snow and more rock, for as far as I can see. How could I possibly find him now?" And he sank down onto a rock, bent his head, and lost himself in depression.

Theo's unhappiness was magnified by the physical strain created by his surroundings. Although he had begun to adjust a bit to the lack of oxygen at these elevations, it still caused him to feel slightly "needy" in the lungs. And the temperatures here were lower and more uncomfortable than they had been further down the mountain. It must have been in the mid-forties now, he reasoned, but at night the thermometer would certainly drop to twenty. He had the clothing necessary to keep himself warm, but the mist that sometimes blew past him still managed to sting his face.

Seeking to avoid depression, the pilgrim searched the area carefully and succeeded in finding a shallow cave, which was really more of a simple recess in the side of a rocky wall, where he could spend the night. His tent did not fit into the available space, but he managed to jerry-rig a flap at the opening of the space capable of keeping out the night winds.

Hoping to take his mind off his worries, Theo climbed up one of the smaller prominences of the brother mountain and looked about. Where he had before seen the Ganges, there was now only a thread of white fog. The cooling air must have caused thick mist to rise over the river.

As he watched the scene, the fog visible so very far below him began to spread out from the river. This cottony envelopment of the valley happened within a matter of ten minutes or so. Soon, it appeared as if the sky had dropped huge piles of cumulus down onto the earth. Discrete iceberg shapes of cloud settled into the recesses formed by the contours of the mountains. Gradually, these swellings lost their individuality and began to merge, one with another. Soon, he could see only a vast lake of lightly rippled white, tinged faint purple where the cloud-borders had formerly been.

The fog began to crawl up the sides of the mountains, licking up in tongue shapes, here and there. Less dense patches floated up the flanks of the rock, looking like waterfalls or ghosts splayed out in abandon. The cottony softness of the white fog utterly blotted out the sharp, hard outlines of the gray prominences of quartz, granite, and gneiss. Mother Nature had tucked in her stony child, laid a comforting blanket atop his ungainly limbs, and sent him off to sleep.

Theo was not so lucky; he hardly slept that night. The moist winds found seams between the tent fabric and the rock and slid in to freeze him. He wore a shirt, sweater, and parka, two pairs of woolen socks, and moon boots, and zipped himself into a mummy sleeping bag, but none of these preparations mattered. The rock inside his alcove seemed to receive the cold from outside and multiply it, radiating frigid air straight into his enwrapped body. He couldn't understand how the wind managed to penetrate the sleeping bag, but it did, nevertheless.

He would doze off for a few moments, seeing images of monstrous snowmen threateningly marching towards him, and then he would regain consciousness in crystalline lucidity. His body yearned to sleep and continued to drag his mind down into it, but the cold would not allow his brain to relax. Popping in and out of sleep every few minutes made for a torturous night.

With the first morning light, he rose and tried to stretch his aching limbs. Every movement he made revealed the awkwardness that comes with fatigue. He pulled at his boot, but his hand kept slipping off it. He tried to fold up the sleeping bag, but couldn't succeed in getting it rolled properly. His brain felt like a dead mass, a metallic solid incapable of mental functioning.

Theo was going to look for wood when he noticed that the sun was about to rise. The celestial conductor had motioned for the tuning-up to stop, and had raised his baton in preparation for the first orchestral notes.

The sun first appeared on the horizon as a white-hot lens-shape, framed above and below by semicircles of lemon yellow. These half circles formed what *looked* like a complete sun, but was actually only an illusion of one. So the impression on the viewer was of a rounded yellow sun pierced through its middle by a bent laser beam. Banding the lower half of this "sun" was a thicker arc of deepest rose, which thoroughly washed away any contours of the mountains over which it spread. An immense cloud formation above the scene, reminiscent of a breaching Leviathan (but one imagined by J.M.W. Turner), was painted in madder red.

As the sun mounted up onto its firmamental ledge, Theo could hear the orchestra's timpani pounding away for all they were worth. And the strings were building the tension of the moment with all their combined skill. Halfway up, the star looked like a celestial igloo. Three quarters of the way, it brightened to ivory and wrapped itself in a yellow cape. Once it sat fully on the horizon, the sun was completely encircled by a primary-yellow disk, so that Apollo himself resembled the missing center of a cosmic 45 rpm record.

The sky had been transformed to magical wonders by the changing light. The perfect image of a horse pranced directly in front of Theo. She seemed to be racing away from the smoky conflagration of orange and black directly behind her. A welkin scepter, its handle steel gray and its tip, raspberry, threatened the advancing flames. Delicate island chains on the low horizon bore peppermint hues. And rolling away from under Theo's feet, utterly blotting out the intervening mountains, was a vast stretch of mushroom fields, sprouting fungiform growths large and small, ranging in color from darkest indigo to grayish

106

lavender. And, in the center of this fantastic panorama, was visible the very smallest cutout of baby-blue sky.

Theo turned away from the sunrise reinvigorated. His brain no longer ached, inert; rather, it was enlivened. His body lost its fatigue and felt charged with energy. It was as though the beauty and grandeur of the matutinal display had filled up his internal fuel tank.

When he turned away from the cliff on which he stood, Theo looked down the hill that approached the field of talus from the opposite side. A light mist made it hard to see clearly. But he continued to stare. For about a hundred yards away, he could have sworn that he made out the figure of a smallish man swathed all in white. Straining his eyes, he bore into the image. It blended into the mist and appeared to share its insubstantial nature. But it was *not* mist, for it moved steadily down the hill, away from the plateau on which Theo had camped. Soon the figure was lost to sight.

The seeker felt certain that the Saint had come to him to show him the way. Theo's mouth stretched into a smile and his eyes twinkled and his soul felt cleansed by the apparition (for so it seemed) of the holy man. And he was thankful that the Saint was showing him to a lower elevation. They would meet, then, at a height more conducive to comfortable conversation. Theo felt no regrets about leaving the desolation and cold winds of his present locale. He immediately began to pack up his gear.

Closing In

Theo moved downhill faster than he ought to have done. Conditions were dangerous: the ground was slick, the rocks sharp, and the wild herbs and shrubs thick and prickly. No path existed, so he had to climb over every obstacle that presented itself, sometimes having to come treacherously close to the edge of a steep drop-off. But the sight of the Saint, or his doppelganger, had inspired the pilgrim. His spirits had been low after so much time without a clear message from the holy man. Now that he had seen him, he wished to close the distance between them as quickly as possible.

After several hours of hiking, having reentered the alpine zone, he welcomed the sight of trees and flowers. Three squat oaks clustered on a level piece of land off to his right. A row of spruce trees on his left lined what had now become the thinnest of trails. Silvery-green Himalayan mint, adorned with tiny flamingo-hued flowers, scented the air. Lovely white marguerites, with honey-colored centers, filled a small clearing a dozen yards off the path.

The thinnest of mists hung in patches, appearing over there and then disappearing over here. As the mist moved, Theo got the impression of a foggy window having been cleaned to reveal, where there had just been only the vaguest outline of a spruce tree, a clearly delineated one. At times the mist would hover over a portion of an object, rendering half of a fern-clad hill invisible and the other half perfectly clear.

The seeker had expected to catch up with the goal of his voyage on this path, and so had hurried to make good time. But hour after hour passed, and still he did not see the familiar white-robed figure. As evening came on, Theo decided to look for a campsite and wait until the next day to continue his pursuit.

By now the energy of the sunrise experience and the excitement of seeing the apparition of the Saint had both worn off, and Theo was left with the extreme fatigue he expected to feel after a sleepless night at such heights. Tiredness came over him like a sack of bricks dumped into his backpack. His legs refused his brain's signals to move. His arms performed actions at a third their normal speed. His head felt as though it had been injected with a stupefacient gas.

How, he wondered, would he ever manage to find a safe spot to sleep, when he was half asleep already? Then his eye glanced up and noticed a circling eagle. He recognized it as a golden eagle, a bird reverenced in traditional lore for its remarkable hunting abilities. The fine bird was circling smoothly and quietly only a hundred feet over his head. Its wings spread at least four feet across. And it had its eye on Theo.

As he observed the eagle, the pilgrim felt dizzy. In fact, he worried lest he should lose consciousness completely and tumble over the side of the sheer cliff at the edge of the pathway. The eagle stopped circling and descended to no more than twenty feet over Theo's head. Then it began to lazily flap its wings, moving forward parallel to the path. And the stumbling man followed it in a trance of complete fatigue.

Fifty yards along, the eagle came to a rest on an outjutting piece of rock that overlooked miles and miles of lowlands. When Theo finally caught up with his aquiline guide, he was so tired that he could only drop in a heap to the ground. His head fell forward and he dozed for some time. When he finally opened his eyes, darkness was settling on the mountain. His awareness of the danger of his situation stimulated his mind, and he looked around.

The eagle no longer sat sentinel on the projecting rock. But Theo noticed that one of its feathers had fallen on the left-hand side of the path. The tip of the feather lay at the outer edge of a growth of the strangest looking cacti the man had ever come across. Summoning his willpower, Theo stood up and looked over the top of the cacti. Thank god! A small cave lay behind them!

Making a great effort to gather his wits and energy, Theo paused to examine these cacti. Their stalk was about three feet high, but it was what grew out of that stalk that amazed him. Dozens of celery-green "snakes" spilled down the side of each cactus. These furry feelers, denser at the top of each plant, extended about eighteen inches in length and curled up at their ends. They truly looked like alien creatures dreamed up in a Hollywood studio.

But the pilgrim was too tired to contemplate the cacti for long. He found a way around them, entered, and shone his light on the walls and floor of the cave, looking for lizards, pheasants, goats, or, heaven forbid, pit vipers. His luck with caves continued. This one, also, proved free of inhabitants. Too tired to erect his tent, Theo simply climbed into his sleeping bag and immediately fell deep asleep.

He didn't wake until late in the morning. The long sleep thoroughly refreshed him, body, mind, and soul, and he felt like the proverbial new man. Not having the tent to pack, the seeker found himself back on the path in short order.

As he walked, noticing with delight the pink and white daisies adorning the trail, Theo considered the eagle and its feather. Here again, he decided, was the sign of the Saint. For the trekker had been on the verge of exhaustion when that circling eagle had straightened its path and landed to show him the cave. And without its feather pointing to a small opening at the side of the cacti, he would never have even become aware of the cave, so perfectly was it concealed by the exotic cacti.

Theo also thought about the complete absence of people since he had ascended above Gangotri. These mountains were never widely traveled, of course, but there ought to have been at least a *few* pilgrims or sadhus making their ways along their paths. But he had never come across a single soul. The only human figure he had seen was that of the Saint, and even that, he believed, was not the actual man.

He asked himself where the Saint was leading him. And he searched his memory for the details of the vision he had experienced in the back seat of Ashok's taxi on the way to Haridwar. The holy man had been standing on rocky soil in the mountains; that was all Theo could remember. Well, there was plenty of both where he walked right now. Maybe the Saint would appear around the next corner.

Theo could see the thread of the Ganges far below him once again. As he watched the river, its thick cloak of fog began to dissipate, until, after only a short period of time, it had totally disappeared. But the moisture must have hurried uphill, for suddenly the pilgrim found himself in a downpour. No trees nearby, no cave to be seen, he simply accepted the rain, and allowed it to soak through the clothing to his skin, whence it ran off down his limbs in ticklish streams.

Theo stood still and reached his arms up toward the sky, welcoming this aspersion from the heavens as the purificatory blessing he knew it was meant to be. Suddenly, lightning blazed, first across and then down from the sky. Large, crashing masses of brilliance inflamed a full third of the heavens. White phosphorus arcs outlined peaks in the distance. Then at least twenty blinding and dazzling bolts, which formed colossal heads and outlines of bodies, lit up the space between the firmament and the ground. The major ones looked like energetic arteries and the smaller ones like capillaries. Being all fulgurant together, these greater and lesser radiances formed a network overlaying the Danish-blue sky. Their thunder nearly shook Theo off the precipice by which he stood, so much did it make him jump.

For one long moment, the seeker beheld the outline of the Saint in this lightning. Its shape corresponded perfectly to the back of his robe. And his profile and beard shone in coruscant white.

Within fifteen minutes, the spectacle was over. Theo decided to keep walking, not wanting to let the Saint lose him, even though he knew the holy man would do no such thing. In his mind, ignorance kept conflicting with wisdom. The temperature was reasonable and the sun had come out. He would dry as he moved.

First, the fog had lifted. Then, the purifying rain had doused him clean. Then mind-boggling amounts of lightning had stunned him and the world around him. And, finally, the Saint had appeared as lightning in the sky. Theo saw all these events as omens and metaphors. The mists of his ignorance would soon dissipate. He needed to be pure before meeting the holy man, whose Being would flash with untold brilliance and power.

Theo now passed through some pleasing scenery, which contrasted with that of the higher altitudes as a homey cottage does with a Gothic castle. Below him lay twin gorges of grayish olive green. The hills leading down to them shone rich with papaya- and corn-colored marigolds and daisies in yellow, pink, and white. Brown mint covered wide patches of ground and scented the air like a vat of freshly brewed tea. Creepers and lichens wound spirally over the short fir trees, and birds of various sizes and colors flapped, darted, and dived in search of prey.

The thought passed through the seeker's mind that he was closing in on an earthly paradise.

The Encounter

For some reason, Theo chose that evening to travel later than he normally did. He felt himself on the trail of the Saint and wished to make rapid progress toward him. So, as twilight set in, the pilgrim continued to trek on. But he got caught by the sudden onset of darkness. One minute it had been twilight, and the next, it was black night. As ill luck would have it, he was walking through a stretch of thick woods, where the ground was uneven, and the poor excuse for a path often encumbered by vines and fallen branches. One could easily twist an ankle or break a leg here, he thought. And how many people might come along to find him if he did? Humanity's age-old fears of darkness descended on him. Areas like this were known to be populated by vipers. He remembered reading that tahrs, goat relatives with 18-inch horns, as well as aggressive black bears dwelled in forests such as this one. As if to confirm his fears, the deep and eerie cry of some wild beast sounded in the air.

Well, he had gotten himself in a fix this time! One of the first rules of camping in such areas was not to do so without first thoroughly checking out the area for snakes. But Theo couldn't see ten feet in front of him. And the bushes, grasses, weeds, and fallen tree limbs all around him served as perfect hiding places for vipers. The night had stolen his sense of direction, so he didn't even know how to keep moving in the line he had been moving up till now. What a mess!

He was certain now that he heard a slithering sound in the thick grass beneath his feet. The eerie cry sounded once again, this time much closer than it had been the first. Theo closed his eyes and silently implored the Saint for assistance.

A sudden brightening on his closed lids, something like what one feels while lying on the beach when the sun emerges from behind a cloud, caused the pilgrim to open his eyes.

No more than twenty yards away, a Being of Light, who looked like a young man of thirty years or so, hovered beside a spruce tree. Theo stared at this amazing apparition. Its features and form were blurred, so that the main impression one got was of Light, the purest of fine, white Light. And the "body" of the Being broke up into ever fainter points of Light in the area around it. Theo experienced a perfect sense of protection as he gazed upon this wondrous Being.

The form turned and the seeker realized that he was meant to follow it. So he did. Without even considering where he placed his feet, Theo walked unharmed past sharp stones, fallen branches, and knee-high stumps. It was as though he were being guided by an invisible hand past all dangers that lay in his way.

After walking for an indeterminate amount of time, they came to a glade whose ground was dotted with herbs whose upright, many-petaled cerise flowers for some reason reminded Theo of corn on the cob. He had no idea what they were, but suddenly, out of nowhere, their name popped into his mind: fleeceflowers!

The Being of Light floated about three feet off the ground at the far end of the glade. Theo nodded and then bowed to the Being. But when he straightened up, it had vanished.

Although he realized that he ought to erect his tent, a sense of protection, which lingered in the Being's wake, assured him that he wouldn't need it. And, anyway, how could he have set it up, now that darkness had settled on him? So he once again had recourse to his mummy sleeping bag. The thought had come of food, but he felt not the slightest bit of hunger. And he couldn't wait to zip himself in, so that he could start to contemplate the marvelous experience through which he had just passed.

Had the Saint sent a helper to him? Had the Being really been one of the Himalayan Masters he had read about, who lived incorporeally and for unbelievably long times? Could it have been an angel? But it had no wings, so, if celestial lore was to be trusted, it could not have

114

been. Theo remembered that the Sanskrit word "deva" or "god" had the etymological meaning of "bright being." So it was certainly a deva! Then he began to think practically: how had the Being succeeded in leading him around all those numerous obstacles, which could easily have twisted or broken his ankle or shattered his knee, when Its back was to him the whole time? Theo fell asleep contemplating these various mysteries.

He awoke in Eden. The fleeceflowers dotted the low groundcover like tiny temples of color in the otherwise even green. Short to moderately tall spruces and firs encircled him. Lichens spiraled up the side of the trees like boas round a lady's neck. The early morning light chastened the green hues of the trees and bushes at their feet, bringing in yellow subtones and fuzzing the distinctness of object shapes.

The air was as fresh as an infant's breath, laden with moisture, and vivifying in the extreme. Soft and melodious bird calls sounded, though their makers remained invisible. Theo felt as if he were the only man in the world, and that he had gone to sleep only to wake up in paradise. Although he had lived alone for a very long time, Theo found his present locale so reminiscent of the Garden of Eden that he would have been only slightly surprised to turn around and find a charming naked woman approaching him, bitten apple in hand.

The unique beauty of this Himalayan bower was such that it rose to the level of the surreal: it looked like something a supremely talented fantasy painter or Hollywood artist had produced in order to effectively convey the mystery of the innocence of first creation. The contrast between all these ever-so-delicate shades of green and the black boles of the trees showed consummate genius. The way the fleeceflowers and marguerites played off their cherry and lemon hues against the viridity of the ground cover likewise revealed supreme artistry. This glade appeared to be insusceptible to influence from the contaminating external world. It was set off, guarded by some sort of invisible protective barrier, from all threats from outside its small

115

domain. Here, in ancient days, a guru might have sat teaching his disciples, Theo mused. Here a god might have manifested to an Enlightened Being, bearing heavenly gifts in recognition of her sacred wisdom.

As he lay, innocent as Adam, in his heavenly Himalayan oasis, Theo recurred to the Being who had led him here. This is truly a land of miracles, he thought. Saints appear, devas materialize, the future is seen as clearly as the present. How anyone could ever doubt the advanced spirituality of Mother India was completely beyond him.

As pleasant as this wooded nook was, the seeker felt the pull of the Saint tugging him up out of the comfort of repose. So he stood up and, with many a look around, with the hope of remembering the stunning beauty of this place, he finally left it.

As he stepped out through the spruces to a small trail running along a cliff's edge, Theo glanced up and saw a rainbow such as he had never before in his life beheld. What he stared at was not a rain "bow" at all, but, rather, straight, wide, parallel stripings of color painted across the western sky. Each observed hue covered about 10 degrees of arc. Violet gave way to blue; blue to aquamarine; aquamarine to green; green to yellow; and yellow to orange. The colors shone as bright and pure as sunlight refractions from a prism. The aquamarine band especially interested the pilgrim. Usually, one barely noticed it in a rainbow. Typically, it was the thinnest of arcs. But here, now, the Turkish-stone pigment dominated the palette. Together, the huge colored arcs completely blotted out a mountain on the far side of the valley below him. And the yellow hue spilled over onto the toothed peaks below it, giving them the appearance of antique ivory carvings.

Miracle was following miracle. The Being leads him to a veritable Eden. He emerges from Eden to a sky dazzling in color. The thought came to Theo that he must be getting close to the Saint now. For all these marvels felt like portents.

He trekked on for another mile or so before feeling an unusual sensation. His mind went completely numb; as if supercooled by some invisible cryogenic apparatus. His body lost all sense of itself; none of his extremities sent signals back to his brain. In fact, he lost all awareness that he even *had* a body. And, wonderfully, his whole soul was suddenly saturated in indescribably delicious bliss.

Lifting his head, he saw the exact scene he had envisioned on the cab ride. Only fifty yards ahead of him shone the bright white back of the Saint. He stood on rocky soil, and he appeared to be gazing peacefully at the vista of mountains spread before him. Theo tried to move toward the holy man, but, just as in his vision, his body refused to respond to its brain's commands.

After a time, he regained bodily control, and slowly walked toward the Saint. Once within ten feet, he sank to his knees, pressed his palms together in namaste, and pressed his forehead into the dusty earth.

"You have come to me. I hope that your journey was not too difficult." The sweetness, delicacy, and charm of the voice was impossible to describe in words. Theo slowly raised himself up, not immediately looking at the Master, but giving himself some time to adjust to his overpowering presence. "You have seen many beautiful things, I know."

Now Theo did dare to gaze upon the object of his long search. The Saint looked precisely as he had in all the visions. Most notable were his eyes, still reminiscent of pieces of stars in their clarity and effulgence. He sat on a large rock, hands pressed together, his fingers toying with a wild, white Himalayan rose.

The Saint did not feel to Theo as though he belonged in the terrestrial world, but to a higher one. A steady stream of tranquility and peace flowed out from him and spread into and over his guest. His aura chased all thoughts, ideas, and concerns from the seeker's mind. All that he could do was kneel in wonderment. The holy man must have connected his mind with his disciple's, for the latter now experienced great exaltation and a sense of weightlessness.

"You are probably wondering why I have maintained contact with you over the years and why I have called you to my side."

"Yes, Master, I *have* wondered about all that."

"You were with me before, many times in fact. And I have kept my eye on you, even though you lived in a distant land. Do you know that you have been a serious seeker for many lifetimes?"

"No, I did not."

"You have studied the holy texts and you have performed the sacred rituals. You have meditated in groups and by yourself. In your last life, you were one of my close disciples."

Theo bowed his head and pressed his palms together. "I am honored to know that."

"And keeping good company is one of the most powerful tools for spiritual evolution. I thought that your coming to India would benefit you greatly."

"And it has already, although I know that the true benefits will begin only now that I have found you, Guruji."

They stood up and began to walk around the area that surrounded what Theo now saw to be a spacious cave. No words were exchanged, but the experience thrilled the seeker to his core. An electric energy passed from the Saint's body into his own, enlivening and thrilling it. Every object that Theo looked at appeared utterly fresh, as if he were seeing a tree and a stone and a flower for the first time. As one walked beside the Master, one had the sense of existing in a timeless place that lay outside of conventional space. Everything swelled to awesome importance. The tiniest creatures and bits of grass gained glorious status, now that they were witnessed in the context of expanded awareness.

118

Theo got the impression that the Saint, without having to speak, was teaching him many lessons. At this point, the seeker did not fully comprehend the content of these lessons, but he realized full well that he was being shown how to look at the world in an entirely new way.

After some time, they entered the cave and sat down. In its center was the dhoori, a fire pit that Theo knew was never to be extinguished. The only other light in the cave was provided by four-inch-long sticks of dhoop, bundles of aromatic herbs, which had been stuck in crevices in the sides of the cave. The dhoop provided both illumination and scent. The cave extended about twenty feet back and ten feet to the sides. Its floor was earthen, but the soil had been ground smooth, probably by generations of sadhus who had resided here.

The only objects the pilgrim noticed were a framed photograph of a holy man, a water can, and several blankets. If the Saint did, indeed, live in this cave, it was certainly the most primitive residence Theo had ever come across.

But the lack of decoration in the outer was rendered inconsequential by the brilliance of the inner space spreading out in waves of bliss from the small body of the Saint. Theo failed to find words for what he was experiencing. The spiritual vibrations emanating from the holy man acted on him like an intoxicant; but an intoxicant of the soul rather than the body. His spirit became obvious and central: it pushed his body out of the picture. It pulsed in joyous beats, extending out from where his physical form used to be, shining, glowing, and suffusing peace.

"Guru comes from "gu," meaning darkness and "ru," meaning light. Guru dispels the darkness of ignorance. "Deva" means "bright being." You may have met a deva recently, yes?" And he smiled broadly, knowingly. "My Master," here he pointed a finger at the photograph, "was called "Gurudeva" because his brilliance eliminated any darkness around him. The guru's only purpose is to selflessly guide souls to Enlightenment."

"And you will guide me!" Theo exclaimed.

The Saint stroked the flower that he held between thumb and forefinger. "Yes" was all he said.

"You have meditated regularly for a long time now?"

"Yes, Guruji, for many years, twice daily."

"Good, good, that is very good. And you find your meditations getting more and more quiet?"

"Yes, there are long periods of inner silence and great happiness. Sometimes I get distracted, but I soon settle down again."

"There are six requirements for Enlightenment: quietude of mind, control over the senses, forbearance, that is, tolerance of discomfort, desisting from sensual pleasure and attachment to possessions, the ability to put things in proper context, and the desire for liberation. Truly, these resolve into purity, one-pointedness, and the control of mind."

"I am slightly confused, Master."

"When you are settled deep in your meditation, you discover your true nature: Pure Consciousness. That Consciousness is truly all there Is. Everything else that one perceives is actually nothing but Pure Consciousness. Now you ask: why don't we all *see* people and objects as such. And that is the trick played by maya, the supreme illusionist.

"You see, the world of names and forms is artificially created by ignorance of Reality. Think of the ocean with its waves and foam. We give a swelling piece of water the name "wave," and then think of it as something other than "ocean." But, in truth, it is *only* the ocean. The same applies to the foam. Or think of a golden necklace. A woman calls it "necklace," and sees it as such, but is it not really just "gold"?"

"In other words, people miss the big picture by focusing on the small details."

"You could say that. Or think of a mirage in the desert. The thirsty traveler rushes towards it to sate his thirst. He is convinced that an oasis is within reach. But the water is nothing more than an illusion. There is only the air on which the image appears, as if real.

"When you dream at night, you are fully convinced that the world in which you wander is real. The food in the dream satisfies you. The textures in the dream register on your dream fingers. But all your experiences in the dream are produced out of whole cloth by your mind, which borrows events and impressions from your waking life. When you awaken in the morning, you tell yourself that those dreams were false. But you are only doing so from the position of a new state of consciousness: the waking state. Enlightenment is to waking state as waking state is to dreams."

"But we all see the same world when we are awake."

"My Master taught that we do not. He showed us that an Enlightened Being sees nothing but Pure Consciousness. Think of attending a movie show. The film is projected onto the white screen. One sees a great deal of exciting drama; people race around here and there doing all sorts of activities. But no one is really doing anything on that white screen: a beam of light is projecting impressions onto it, but the white screen remains unaffected.

"My Master saw the white screen behind the film. Enlightenment means knowing that all people, creatures, and objects are truly nothing other than Pure Consciousness. The wave is only the ocean. The necklace is only the gold. Since you have meditated so long, I feel sure that you have begun to see this."

Theo bowed his head in humility. "I can't say that I do see it very clearly, Master. But I have at least begun to appreciate the underlying essence of my fellow human beings and nature itself."

"Understand this: the teaching does not deny that the material world exists; it certainly does. We feel the warmth of this fire and the

121

solidity of the ground on which we sit. But the holy texts tell us that the 'reality' of the world is relative; it depends on the state of consciousness of the perceiver. For example, it does not exist at all when you are asleep. And when someone like my Master looks at it, the world shines solely as Pure Consciousness."

"But, if I may, he must have *seen* objects, in order to navigate through the world."

The Saint bent his head to the side and chuckled, in such a winning way that he caused Theo to join him in laughter. "No, the world does not become invisible to such a great soul, but he *witnesses* the Reality behind its superficial images. When he looked at a suffering man who brought his problems before him for resolution, the Master did not see a body and an associated ego, he saw the radiant light of Being, which was the man's true essence."

The Saint passed into silence, his eyes closed. Theo followed his example, enjoying, for the first time ever, an absolutely undisturbed meditation. Thoughts simply did not come to interrupt his oceanic sitting. For so he thought of it when he considered the meditation after the fact: it had been like sinking to the bottom of the sea and resting there in perfect tranquility, not a sound, not a sight to unfocus his awareness.

A thought eventually came, informing him of the need to open his eyes. When he did so, he was astonished to see the Saint enveloped in a dazzlingly bright aura: pure white light extended to a distance of three feet all around his body. And it merged *with* his body, lighting it up as well. Something told Theo to go outside, so he quietly found the entrance and walked through it. On the ground sat an earthenware pitcher and a small bowl. Automatically, he picked both up and took them in. One contained fresh goat's milk and the other, salted gram, otherwise known as chickpeas. They must have been left by some well-wisher who knew that the Saint inhabited this cave.

Together they ate this simple meal, which the pilgrim enjoyed more than any he had ever before eaten. Then, while the Saint continued to sit cross-legged, eyes closed, the disciple lay down on one of the blankets and fell asleep.

The First Day

At sunrise they left the cave, the disciple following in the steps of the Master. A great marshmallow of cloud the color of orange sherbet rested on the crest of a nearby ridge. A flamingo-pink filament of cloud formed a heart shape next to it. The sun's light transformed the entire side of the mountain in front of them into immense bricks still hot from the oven. The Saint sat down on a rock and the seeker, at his feet.

"The sun never varies in its brilliance. But a cloud may come and appear to lessen its light. A person might suffer from an eye disease which distorts or blurs that light. In the same way, the Absolute is always the same, always Being, Consciousness, and Bliss. You ask, 'Why, then, doesn't everyone see it?' And the answer is that clouds and diseases of the eye are the nature of spiritual ignorance.

"So long as one believes that he is a body, mind, and ego, then the clouds remain thick, blotting out the sun of Pure Consciousness. But one is *not* such things. After all, you say 'my body, my mind'; who is it saying 'my'?"

For a while they sat in silence, enjoying the beauties of the rising sun and the vibrant animal and vegetable life of morning. Finally, Theo spoke. "But it is so difficult, Master, to get rid of this sense of being a body and a mind."

"Yet everyone cares most about himself and seeks constantly to find perpetual happiness. If you bring these two together, you see that one's search for happiness is really a search for his true Self. So the motivation is there in everyone. Remember that you *are* whatever you know yourself to be. If you see yourself as a body, then you *are* a body. You say it is difficult to change. To change, two things are important: first, non-attachment and second, constant awareness of Absolute Reality.

124

"Attachment to the world means bondage, and detachment from it means liberation. Desire is the mother of all misery. The world of desires is like a bowl of endlessly self-filling food: one eats and eats until ready to burst, but there is still more in the bowl. Sense cravings draw the mind to the external world, away from Peace. And worldly objects, being transient, can never be the source of permanent happiness. Modern people are prisoners of their own possessions. Possessing more than necessary only creates obstacles for one's progress."

"But modern people don't want to be indifferent to life, Master."

"Non-attachment does not mean indifference. Love for all, for people, animals, plants, stars leads to freedom. One can love deeply without experiencing attachment."

"The holy books say that all this," and the seeker waved his hand toward the mountain and sun, "is maya, an illusion. Where does maya come from?"

"Maya is rooted in attachment. Ultimately, it is the play of the Absolute. All that one needs to know is that the stronger one's sense of attachment, the more real maya seems. You have certainly had the experience of meditating and coming out of the Silence to view the world. Did it look the same?"

"No, Guruji."

"It did not, because you were less attached to it than you were before meditating. It may have seemed to you a bit vague or insubstantial, yes? These experiences are glimpses of what Enlightenment brings: the realization that the entire, apparently self-sustaining world is truly nothing but Pure Consciousness. The more one meditates, the more one knows the Absolute. And, recall, constant awareness of the Absolute is the second of the keys to change."

125

After they reentered the cave, the Saint suggested that his disciple might wish to meditate; so they both closed their eyes. Instantly, Theo sank to the depths of his Consciousness. An almost unbearable surge of bliss flooded his soul. After some time spent in Absolute Stillness, he became aware of celestial ladies whose beauty radiated contentment, vast golden temples shimmering in otherworldly light, rivers of heavenly blue, mountains fashioned from starlight, and bands of glinting mystical sands. Then came astral beings, who hovered around him, human-like forms of white, gold, and silver, who smiled and bowed, pressed their palms together and spread their hands in welcome. When the astral beings disappeared, the disciple beheld visions of ancient rishis, the wise souls who had first cognized the Vedas. These were Saints of incomparable brilliance, whose presence induced feelings of the deepest reverence.

The oddest thing was that when Theo opened his eyes again, after a period of time about whose length he conceived nothing at all, the internal peace and joy carried over. The Saint still sat in his place with his eyes closed; the cave remained the same bare, rocky grotto; but the atmosphere the disciple perceived was greatly enriched and enlivened. Minute, infinitesimal particles of light sparkled in the semi-darkness. A sense of unreality belonged to the few material objects that sat in the space. An invisible but nearly tangible grandeur permeated the air. One had the sense that any sort of miracle, even the most incomprehensible, could instantly occur.

When the Saint finally opened his eyes, he gave Theo a knowing look containing a hint of mischief. "Meditation was good?"

The pilgrim smiled till his lips seemed to meet his ears. "Very good, indeed, Master."

"You might look at these." The holy man handed two books to Theo. He had no idea where they had come from, as he had not seen them in the cave before now. One was *Yoga Vashistha* and the other, the *Brahma Sutras*. Theo took the thick books and wondered if he

126

should just begin at page one. But intuition told him to simply open one of the books and see what words presented themselves.

Theo knew as soon as he turned the first page that the Saint intended him to land on a certain paragraph containing a specific piece of knowledge. Nothing that occurred within the precincts of the holy man was random. Destiny hung heavy in his atmosphere. The disciple opened one of the books and scanned a portion of it.

"This world appearance is a confusion, even as the blueness of the sky is an optical illusion. I think it is better not to let the mind dwell on it, but to ignore it. Neither freedom from sorrow nor realization of one's true nature is possible as long as the conviction does not arise in one that the world appearance is unreal."

The words corresponded perfectly with what the Saint had been explaining before their meditation: that behind the appearance of the world lies its Reality: Pure Consciousness.

"But, Master, how can I ignore the world when I have to live in it every day?"

The holy man tapped his flower against the palm of his free hand. "What Valmiki means in that passage" (Theo smiled, realizing that the Saint knew precisely which passage he had just read silently to himself),"is that one should not *dwell* on the world appearance. No need to get attached to all that is going on. No need to take on a role in the play. See your work; do your work; but stay out of the misery."

"I have read deeply in the holy texts, Guruji, but inspiring as they are, they only take me so far."

"Yes, only direct knowledge of the Absolute is valuable. Memorized facts are not. Philosophers can debate all day and never take a single step closer to Enlightenment. But you can see the value of the texts. You read that freedom from sorrow can only arise in one for whom the world appearance is unreal. This knowledge, recorded by a great Rishi, confirms your experience coming out of meditation,

127

when the world looked vaguer to you. Knowledge and experience go hand in hand: knowledge shows you *what* to experience and explains what you *do* experience.

"You asked about living in the world. Remember that it is not action itself that one needs to renounce, but attachment to the fruits of action. Karma will propel one forward into activity; such is the way evolution happens. Go ahead and act. But refrain from becoming attached to the results of your actions. You attain freedom by conquering your desires, not by running away from your duties."

"Desires are for the fruits of action?"

"Yes, in one's subtle body are impressions of past experiences. The strongest of these form one's tendencies in life. One has a memory of pleasure enjoyed in a certain way, so one has an urge, a desire, to know that pleasure again. The desire motivates action, and the action creates more karma and further impressions. The cycle of ignorance thus perpetuates itself.

"How can one ever attain peace when one constantly desires something he does not have? By definition, this is a recipe for misery. The desire/attachment cycle must be broken. And it can only be broken by developing non-attachment. And one does this by meditating."

A Visit

Later that morning, the Saint walked out of the cave, followed by his new, or, rather, rediscovered disciple. They climbed and climbed until they reached the transalpine zone, of which Theo carried shivery memories. He was prepared, though, as his Master had advised him to dress warmly. He himself wore nothing more than his dhoti.

After several hours of climbing, they arrived at a place whose rocky walls glinted like mother-of-pearl. These walls curved in smooth arcs, as though they had been shaped by a craftsperson out of clay. Some of them looked like immense skulls, and shadowed recesses might have been taken for mouth and nose openings or eye sockets. Smatterings of snow dotted the rocks.

On one large boulder sat a naked holy man. The Saint walked straight up to him and pressed his hands together in greeting. Theo waited at a polite distance.

The naked man did not turn, but did speak: "I have been awaiting your arrival. You honor me."

"The honor is certainly mine, Anandaji. We have not visited for some time."

"And you bring a disciple?"

The Saint motioned to Theo, who now came forward, bowing and pressing his palms together respectfully. The naked holy man spoke, "You teacher is a knower of Truth. Much good work you have done in the past to be able to join him here in the sacred Himalayas." Theo remained silent. "You are wondering why I do not get cold sitting out here like this. One who knows his true Self not to be this bodily cover can wrap a veil around it, so that neither heat nor cold is a bother. Such a veil protects this body now."

Probably out of concern for Theo, the naked saint climbed down from his rock and led the way along an incline that eventually brought them to a dark, squared entrance, like that of a mineshaft, from which opened a spacious cavern. Like that of the Saint, this rocky home offered few amenities. The dhoori burned, the dhoop provided a touch of light and a lovely scent, but there were no signs of food nor any blankets that Theo could see.

"Anandaji has lit the dhoori in our honor," the Saint said. "He himself does not eat, and does not require a fire to keep himself warm. He is self-sufficient."

Theo examined their host. He was of indeterminate age. Very old, of course, but bordering on *ancient*, the visitor thought. His body completely lacked fat. His skin had the shiny look of an onion peel, and the antique quality of a sheet of Egyptian papyrus. His beard, thin and snow white, extended down to his navel. But the man's eyes! His gaze was nearly impossible to meet, so piercing and powerful were those eyes! It seemed to Theo as if all his spiritual power, which was obviously vast, had gotten concentrated in those eyes, whose amber color was that of a tiger's.

For a few minutes, no one spoke. Anandaji sat cross-legged, expressionless as a statue, his tigrine eyes staring into Infinity. "You received your invitation in a cave by the sea. And then were surprised when your host dissolved into a million bits of light."

Theo realized that the naked recluse was referring to that time in the beach cave when the Saint had appeared in its far recesses and called him to India. But how could this venerable man know about that? And, instantly, the response came.

"What you call the past and the future is all bundled up together in the present. All is here and all is now. The inner Self knows All."

"I wonder how that works," thought Theo.

"Remember what your Master has said about real knowledge: that is the knowledge of the Absolute. Discover who you really are, and you

130

will no longer have this question. But you *will* have access to everything from what you call the past and future."

Theo was stunned. Anandaji had answered both his unspoken questions immediately, and had even referred to the remarks the Saint had made that morning. How did he do it?

"Thoughts are subtle vibrations moving in the air. If you become very quiet yourself, you will begin to notice them. There is no trick about it. Abilities that appear miraculous to you, because science cannot explain them, are simply beyond the present thresholds of your instruments. Spiritual knowledge is just as precise as scientific knowledge, and," for the first time he showed the tiniest inkling of a smile, "infinitely more useful."

"Would you like to see?" Moving as quickly as the tiger from which he had taken his eyes, Anandaji tapped Theo's chest with his fist. The effect was instantaneous. The pilgrim's buttocks seemed to take root not simply in the dirt of the cave floor, but in the center of the earth itself. His body emptied out, so that it seemed a mere paper container. He experienced complete Oneness with his surroundings, spreading out into the stone walls, the fire, and the two Saints. His "eyes" now enjoyed 360-degree vision: he noticed the V-shaped hollow in the cave wall behind him. An exquisite, divine perfume pervaded his awareness. Everything began to vibrate, faster and faster, before dissolving into an ocean of the tenderest Light. Now there was Light; now there were objects; and now Light once again. The Bliss that filled his soul expanded outward to take in the entire universe. Nothing existed but This!

When Theo finally regained his normal awareness, he found himself seated in his Master's cave. Night had fallen and the fire was crackling pleasantly a few feet in front of him. Try as he would, he could remember nothing after that tap on the chest. Somehow he had gotten home without his brain having reengaged its gears.

131

The Saint beamed at him. "I think you liked Anandaji," he said enthusiastically.

"I don't remember much."

"Sometimes spiritual experience can be a bit too strong for the unprepared body."

"Could you make me Enlightened right now, Guruji, so that I could have that Bliss forever?" Theo bent forward in eagerness, longing to return to that timeless Peace.

"If I did, it would be like stopping a vehicle racing at a hundred miles an hour by running it into a wall. You see how your brain failed to adjust to Anandaji's little love tap? If you were to be given the full experience of Enlightenment right now, it might kill your body."

"In other words, I'm not ready yet?"

The Saint played for some seconds with the rudraksha beads dangling from his neck. "One must gradually work his way toward the final experience. You have already done much; but some work remains. That is why I called you here."

Theo had the idea to fetch the bowl of chickpeas and pitcher of goat's milk. Once again, a thoughtful disciple had left them for the Saint. The two enjoyed a light repast, and then Theo, for some reason utterly fatigued, dropped off into deepest sleep.

Who Was He?

Theo slept late and, when he rose, found the Saint out sitting on his favorite rock. The long sleep had refreshed the pilgrim, and the gorgeous view of the jutting, snow-mantled peaks sparkled with the vibration of Pure Consciousness.

"The mountains teach us that Silence and Presence is what we must aspire to."

"They are so very beautiful, Guruji." Several minutes passed before Theo spoke again. "I wanted to ask you about Anandaji, if I might." The Saint nodded his acquiescence. "He looks very old."

"How old, would you guess?"

"A hundred?"

"Anandaji is 500 hundred years old. He was alive when the Protestant Reformation began."

"But how would anyone know?" Theo immediately regretted this remark, realizing that it cast doubt on the credibility of his Master.

"He has told a few others. And the Enlightened ones know these things because they are able to."

"And the human body can survive that long?"

"You noticed that he does not eat. Anandaji draws his nourishment from the raw elements themselves. He has mastered the fifth chakra, which controls the ether. He lives on the ether itself. And you saw that he is unaffected by the weather. Realized ones like him produce heat from within and do not require external fires. The normal human lifespan is limited by ignorance: the ego demands unhealthy food and drink; sleep is insufficient; exercise is limited. The chaos of the soul leads to disintegration of the body. A pure soul like Anandaji develops a highly efficient body. He has no more need of it. There is no work left for him to do. But something in his prarabdha karma keeps him in the flesh."

"Prarabdha karma: that is the karma that is already active and continues even in the Enlightened, right, Master?"

"Yes, it is the karma responsible for the present body. Enlightenment destroys sanchita karma, the accumulated karma from past lives that is not yet ripe. Since the Enlightened One no longer identifies as an individual body and soul, his agami karma, the effects of his present activities, produce no effect. But the prarabdha is that which has already become active. It is the arrow that has already left the bow. Even Anandaji must tolerate the effects of prarabdha."

"So a great saint could still suffer in the body."

"Yes, even a great One must put up with the changes in the bodily sheathe. He is not overshadowed by them, for He knows himself to be other than the body. But the changes still happen. When the prarabdha works itself out, He can drop the body or remain in it, as He pleases."

"But five hundred years!'"

"You doubt that it is possible. But there are mountain families who have visited him generation after generation in that same cave. On very rare occasions, he will tell a story from the old days. He was here when the British East India Company first secured a foothold in India."

"Amazing!"

The Saint got down from his rock and began to walk. Their way led them through some heavily shadowed woods before they eventually came out into a delightful small meadow, among whose slaty rocks were interspersed *fleeceflowers* and some pale yellow ones whose onion-shaped buds resembled poppies'.

"The people call them the Lotus of Brahma. When the flowers open, they resemble those in the paintings of Lord Brahma sitting on a lotus."

As they walked, taking in the visual and olfactory pleasures of this place, the two remained silent. Finally, the holy man spoke. "You are still wondering how Anandaji knew so much about you."

"Yes, Guruji. It couldn't have been my thoughts floating around, because I wasn't even thinking of the time you appeared to me in the sea cave."

They were now gazing out at the idyllic scene. A marvelous butterfly, whose wings were a miniature work of art colored in azure and ebony and decorated with oblongs of burgundy encircled with black, flew about directly before them. A snow partridge, camouflaged in a pattern of brown, gray, and white, pecked at the ground and then stopped and directed her full attention at the Saint, almost as if she were awaiting some instruction from him. And now it came.

"When Anandaji looked at you, he did not see merely your physical shell. He observed your astral body, your causal body, and your samskaras. The cosmic eye within him noticed everything about you. What you think you are; where you have come from; and what your experiences have been along the way. Anything that is useful for him to know, so that he may uplift the environment, is made instantly available. That is how he saw the sea cave."

"When I think about you and Anandaji, Master, I feel that I am so far away from liberation that it is no use even *trying* to attain it." Theo felt ashamed of his weak words as soon as they were out of his mouth.

The Saint stared at the snow partridge as he spoke. "The greatest mistake one can make on the spiritual path is thinking himself weak and evil by nature. You are actually strong and good. Your thoughts and desires may sometimes be weak and evil, but they are not your true nature. Your true nature is Being, Consciousness, and Bliss. You and that bird and this butterfly and the sky and the stones are all nothing *but* Pure Consciousness."

"But when one is ignorant..."

"There is neither ignorance nor bondage nor liberation. All three words refer to a delusion: that you are a separate, struggling soul cut off from Purity. You are not that. You are only Purity. The ignorance can no more block Infinite Knowledge than those wispy clouds can blot out the sun. Remember the earlier teaching: you are whatever you believe yourself to be. Get rid of the idea that you are ignorant. Infinite Wisdom is yours for the taking."

They then began to walk back towards the cave. At a turn in the path, they came across the snow partridge. The bird squatted down in the grass and pressed its head fully into the ground. The butterfly with the gorgeous wings sat on a flower, its wings bent forward to provide the passing Saint with the full display of its beauty.

"These are two souls spending this lifetime in these bodies. Don't be deceived, however; they are genuine seekers and have been trying to discover their true identity through many incarnations."

Theo looked at the bird and the insect with new respect. He was going to ask his teacher why souls would take on such bodies, but decided to wait to see if he continued his remarks.

"The butterfly is very beautiful. Always remember that both beauty and ugliness are used by maya to entrap souls. Attraction and repulsion, desire and hatred all serve to build up the illusion of the external world. Desire and karma hold the physical, astral, and causal bodies together. Overcoming desire and hatred weakens this connection and allows the soul to settle down into the Peace of the Self."

A Surprise on the Trail

Darkness had descended by the time the two men began to make their way back toward the cave. Theo wondered how they would possibly be able to stay on what was really not even a *trail*, but his faith in the Saint caused him to push aside all doubts and worries that might normally have arisen. After about half an hour of walking, the quiet of the night was suddenly rent by a growl that penetrated the seeker's guts. The growl sounded like, and had the deep vibratory quality of, a large ship's diesel engine. And it overwhelmed Theo with an atavistic fear first learned in mankind's primitive hunter days.

He stopped in his tracks, but the Saint didn't seem fazed in the least, continuing forward as though he had not even heard the echoing growl. Theo considered proximity his safest bet, so hurried to catch up with his Master. They turned a corner on the trail and there it was! Standing directly in front of them was a tiger nearly as wide as the trail itself. The animal's eyes glowed like illuminated gems. In the moonlight, Theo could make out its long whiskers and thick nose.

The Saint stopped and looked benevolently on the magnificent creature. The tiger first sat down, then lay down, moving sideways a bit, leaving a narrow space on its right. As the partridge had done, the tiger bent its head down, so that its eyes no longer met those of the holy man. The latter then continued on his way, closely followed by his disciple.

Theo's mind was busy. Think of it! A tiger hunting in the night comes across two small men, whom he could easily have mastered. Instead, he sits down, then *lies* down, then, most unbelievable of all, *bows* his head! That's a completely vulnerable position, taking his eyes off a potential enemy. But all these scurrying thoughts suddenly vanished as Theo looked toward the Saint. He had gotten twenty yards distant, and the moonlight was not sufficiently strong to separate his form from that of the shrubby growth around the trail. But his body was outlined by a rim of soft white light that gently pulsed in the darkness. He's a living lighthouse, the seeker mused, guiding lost souls like mine to the only Goal worth finding.

Once they were back in the cave, Theo asked the saint a question. "Guruji, why didn't that tiger consider us dinner?"

The holy man chuckled, straightening his dhoti as he gently shook his head from side to side. "Remember Anandaji's remark about thoughts being vibrations, actual physical energies? All creatures are sensitive to such vibrations. Animals well know who is a threat to them and who is not. If you yourself are established in Peace, then Peace will vibrate out from you and positively affect your environment.

"Ego is the source of fear. If you conceive yourself to be a separate body in a world of bodies, then you are potentially in danger from others. If, on the contrary, you *know* yourself to be Pure Consciousness, which is Infinite and Eternal, Unified and Unchanging, then what is there to be afraid of? Nothing *exists* outside your Self. There is no 'other' of whom you need be afraid. If from ego comes fear, then from Oneness rises Peace."

"So the tiger somehow realized that, from your perspective, you were One with him?"

"Rather say it like this: the tiger has finely tuned instincts regarding danger. And he sensed no danger at all from us."

"Excuse me, though, Master, doesn't it have to be more than that? He was hunting for dinner and we were there to be eaten. He intentionally gave up a meal."

"Pure Consciousness exists in every creature and every object. In inert objects, It is deeply covered by ignorance. In living creatures, It is less obscured. Animals recognize their friends, and he knew us to be such."

Explanations

Theo woke the next day shivering. Snow had fallen during the night. Not just a bit of snow, but a blizzard. The pilgrim found himself inside his mummy sleeping bag. That was odd! He had gone to sleep with just a blanket covering his body. The Saint could not possibly have gotten him into this complexly zippered bag. How had it happened?

The storm was one of those freakish Himalayan outpourings in which fierce northeast winds from Tibet bury the heights of Uttarakhand in several feet of snow over a matter of hours. The opening of the cave was entirely sealed off by drifts. Theo knew that the narrow trails in the area were impassable. No right-thinking mountain man or woman would have dared to venture out into that storm.

Having already run through his own supplies of dried food, he prepared himself for a hungry day.

"I am afraid you will have to dig a tunnel out to retrieve our breakfast."

Theo looked at the Master with astonishment. "Guruji, no one could possibly have made it here through that storm, no matter how dedicated to your welfare they were."

The Saint had a playful look on his face. "Nevertheless, I am hungry, so you had best fetch our breakfast."

Theo got a tool out of his pack and began to excavate. After thirty minutes of sweaty work, he had succeeded in creating a tunnel big enough to allow for his passage. He crawled out, and, to his great astonishment, discovered the usual bowl of gram and pitcher of goat's milk! Their location under a projecting rock had kept them from being covered by snow, but Theo knew that he would have to thaw out both food and drink before breakfast could begin.

"I don't know how anyone could have gotten through that storm, Master. The drifts are five feet high in places. The trail is nowhere to be seen." He paused a moment. "Also not to be seen are any footprints." He looked at the Saint, whose face gave nothing away. "I guess they could have come hours ago and the prints would have been covered up by now. But wouldn't they have been risking their lives to attempt such a delivery?"

"The ways of nature are very complex. Best not to question too closely, but just accept her gifts as she brings them."

"Well, I will have to thaw the chickpeas and milk out on the fire. Unless, that is, we prefer to eat goat's milk ice cream." He smiled to himself as he carried the two containers to the fire. But he vociferated loudly when he uncovered the bowl and pitcher. The chickpeas radiated heat, as if they had just been ladled up from a hot stove. The milk was warm, as if it had come straight from the udders of a goat. The cave fire was unnecessary.

Theo looked at his Teacher in perplexity. But the Saint did not meet his inquiring look. "How could this be? There were no footprints. Such heat would have disappeared in a matter of minutes with these temperatures. How could this possibly be?"

Theo dawdled so long wondering about the miracle that he had to be chided. "If you wait any longer, it will actually *get* cold."

"Sorry, Master." Theo prepared the simple repast and handed a portion to his teacher. "I just can't figure out how it happened."

"My Master used to have a saying, "Take care of others, and nature will take care of you." He spoke no more during the meal, allowing the student to mull over that statement.

Finally, Theo could no longer contain his itching curiosity. "Master, did you use superpowers to bring us this food? I honestly don't see any other way it could have gotten here."

140

As the disciple, awaiting an answer, looked at his teacher, he was once more awed by the intense energy that radiated from the Saint. It was difficult to keep one's mind focused in the presence of this great soul, for from him emanated an overpowering aura of sublime Peace, profound Bliss, and comprehensive Knowledge. Theo would find himself slipping into a sort of trance as he gazed upon this Enlightened Being. His energy simply rolled over one's own weaker stuff and swallowed it up.

But sincerely wishing to learn about siddhis, the famous powers of the Realized, he shook himself and paid attention.

"You are fascinated by siddhis. But you know that true spirituality has nothing to do with them. You have read the sacred texts, and understand that those who seek such powers divert their attention from what really matters: Pure Consciousness. What does it matter if you can become as tiny as an atom or as large as a galaxy? These are children's games, unworthy of a genuine seeker. And what lies behind such desires? Ego! The yogi wishes to be recognized for having great powers, to become famous. And to what end? Such fame will only lead to more desires, more attachment, more ignorance, and more incarnations."

"But such powers defy the laws of science."

"Science knows natural laws, but subtler, spiritual laws also exist. Of these, science understands nothing."

"But how do such things work, Master?"

"'Rita' means natural righteousness, the laws of nature. 'Ritam-bhara pragya' is that state of the mind when it has settled down and is just at the edge of Pure Consciousness. At that time, the mind is in rhythm with the laws of the universe. On that level, the mind can only produce Truth. A thought initiated from ritam-bhara pragya is the subtlest seed of its object and, thus, can yield that object. Very simple really."

Theo had to laugh. Very simple indeed! To manifest objects out of whole cloth! To the Saint, such a deed seemed matter-of-fact.

The holy man continued. "Pure Consciousness is the ground state of the universe. Everything gross arises from It. Operating from the ritam level serves to stir Consciousness into manifestation. Think of it like this: the giant oak tree grows out of a tiny acorn. In that acorn lies the massive trunk and heavy branches that will come later. By holding the acorn, you hold the entire tree. Realizing that you are Pure Consciousness allows you to sit at that very fine level, just above transcendence, and play with the acorn.

"Now remember what I said about the uselessness of siddhis. It is a waste of our time even to be discussing them. No one has ever attained Enlightenment by pursuing special powers. Sometimes they come to a seeker unsought. In that case, it is best to accept but ignore them. They are there, but no need to focus on them. Do you see?"

"Yes, Guruji."

"In that event, they are a spontaneous result of one's evolution. So long as you do not give them undue importance, they will not set back your growth. But beware of becoming enamored of them. Many yogis have fallen off the path by doing just that."

Theo still felt the itch. "But the texts describe marvelous powers..."

"From the Absolute one can manifest anything: whole universes. One can transport himself anywhere, know anything, enter any body. But so what? Games for little ones. And *you* should be attending to matters far more important than games."

Sickness and Death

The snow kept them inside the cave for the next two days. After one day, Theo began to feel sick. His stomach seemed to want to eat itself. Pain tore at his guts as if a voracious serpent was determined to gnaw them to shreds. Every ounce of energy drained from his body. His forehead resembled the flat of an iron set to "high."

The Saint did not appear concerned about these symptoms, though they loomed large to their sufferer. He made sure Theo drank plenty of water, and lit some stems of herbs positioned so that their aroma wafted over the patient. Theo would have asked what was wrong with him, but could neither form thoughts nor get them words out of his mouth.

By the end of the second day, Theo had recovered sufficiently to sit up, nibble a bit of his gram, and sip a little of his goat's milk. Curious about why he had fallen sick in the presence of such a potent force of Wisdom, the disciple considered probing the matter, but his intuition told him to wait. For his part, the Saint simply avoided the topic entirely, saying, in fact, only a few words the entire evening.

The next morning, surprisingly, the holy man informed the recovering invalid that they were going to visit a friend. The weather had turned fine. Most of the snow had disappeared under the sunshine of the past two days. But water ran everywhere. Streams were swollen. And the mountainsides dripped like profusely sweating cheeks.

The effects of his illness had largely disappeared, but Theo remained listless and a vague sense of ill health pervaded his body. He assumed that he had picked up a gastrointestinal bug from the food or water, and that the symptoms would now taper off before leaving him completely.

After forty-five minutes of trekking, the two came to a hairpin curve, above which loomed an almost completely vertical rock face.

The Saint stopped, but Theo began to step forward. "Wait," the Master said.

A noise like the shaking of gigantic dice; a rattle like a snake's; then a loud cracking. Theo glanced up and saw that virtually all the rocks on the mountainside were in motion. A landslide was beginning right above their heads! He thought, "At least I will die in the presence of an Enlightened One." Several boulders were now only ten yards from the path on which they stood. They would both be crushed out of all recognition. Theo instinctively covered his head and closed his eyes.

But seconds passed and....nothing. He opened his eyes again and saw that the boulders and rocks had simply stopped in place on the face of the cliff. He could not believe what he was seeing, because it was an utter impossibility. How could a boulder that had to weigh five hundred pounds hang on a vertical wall without any means of attachment? The sight was literally stunning, something like seeing a racing locomotive stop instantaneously three feet in front of a wandering toddler.

The Saint did not seem at all fazed. He continued walking, so Theo followed him, several times glancing back over his shoulder at the rocks frozen in space.

After they had gone a hundred yards or so, the holy man said, "We'll go back a different way." As soon as he had finished speaking, a thunderous roar exploded. Theo could not see the spot where the landslide had fallen, but he pictured it in his mind, drawing on the impressions of the one he had already experienced. Dust and rocky particles would fill the air. Large boulders would have tumbled over the path into the valley floor. Mounds of smaller rocks would be massed at the base of the hill face. And the path would be invisible and impassable.

The trail was level now, so the seeker could allow himself to muse on what had just happened. Any scientist would have vouched for the miraculous nature of that event. Not even the most inveterate doubter of all things spiritual could have explained those boulders clinging impossibly to the side of a vertical rock wall. No, this had been a true and obvious miracle. The Saint had somehow willed the rocks to stay in place until they had passed, and then allowed them to find the natural routes dictated to them by gravity.

After another hour of hiking, the two men reached a small pond upon whose surface appeared the disk-like leaves and spiky pink flowers of lotuses. The water itself had a soothing grayish-blue color. On the bank, seated in the appropriate lotus position, was a recluse of very small stature, whose face fairly burst with joy. He had his eyes closed, so, Theo surmised, it must have been his meditation that was bringing him such happiness.

The Saint approached him and they greeted one another warmly. The pilgrim could see that his guru held this short Brahmin in high regard.

"So you have come as we planned. I am pleased. And this must be the newcomer you told me about."

Theo wondered how they had ever spoken. Certainly they had not seen each other in the time since he had found the Saint. Maybe the man referred to some earlier conversation.

"Yes, I thought it would do him good to see it."

"And how do you like this pond?"

"It's quite beautiful, Shivaji. The lotuses seem to be yearning for heaven. Hoping to rejoin their ancestor flowers, no doubt." And they chuckled together over this witticism.

Once inside Shivaji's shelter, which comprised a skeleton of timber pieces, into which had been pressed mud, and over which hung a tightly woven roof of fronds, they enjoyed hot herb tea and saffron rice balls.

"How do the fronds survive the winds and snows, Shivaji?"

"This place is a special nook with its own particular weather patterns. The configuration of the mountains here blocks the snows from reaching the pond and deflects the winds away from it. So this fragile hut withstands the worst Vayu can throw at it."

After the meal remains had been cleaned up, the Saint positioned Theo facing Shivaji, while he sat at his side. The dhoori's low flames warmed the space. The host turned to his friend. "It has been my very great honor to know you, Gurudeva. Your light will continue to shine for a time now. Blessings!"

The Saint did not speak, simply smiling and nodding his head to Shivaji, as if saying, "I return your compliments in full."

The host then closed his eyes and a solemn look shone on his face. The hut turned deathly silent. The fire died down. Shadows darkened the space. Theo could not keep himself from staring at Shivaji. Instinct told him that something extraordinary was about to occur. After some time, a faint rumbling sound was heard. And then....and then....and then the man's body began to dematerialize right before their eyes. First, his legs disappeared; then, a section of his torso; then, one arm; and then, another. Finally, only the recluse's head remained. With a final burst of brilliant light, it, too, was gone.

Where Shivaji had been, there was now nothing. No bones, no cinders, simply nothing. To say that Theo was astonished is to state the obvious. His mind stretched high and wide trying to make sense of the spectacle he had just witnessed. But it simply could not.

The Saint had his eyes closed and wore a faint smile on his face. He appeared completely relaxed about the entire situation, which, Theo quickly realized, he *would* be, as an Enlightened Master.

After about an hour, the guru opened his eyes and received the questions he knew would be coming. "Master, how did he do that?"

"It is a yogic technique. Nothing extraordinary."

Nothing extraordinary? The man dissolved right before our eyes!
146

"The yogi concentrates on his solar plexus, and generates a fire that moves through his body, consuming it as it goes."

"But there weren't any ashes!"

"The physical shell is made up of subtle elements. The 'fire' under discussion is not physical, but subtle. It resolves the gross flesh into its subtle elements, and allows those elements to go back into space."

"How utterly amazing!" Theo realized that he had gotten so excited that he was forgetting his manners. "Guruji," he appended.

"You are thinking about all this from a Western science point of view. As you have heard before, that science does not begin to understand the subtler one of spirituality."

"And now he is nothing but Pure Consciousness?"

"Yes. But who is to say whether he takes another body or not."

"You mean he might be born again."

"No, he might simply take another body. A yogi can enter into a corpse and reanimate it. Some yogis will leave their body, apparently dead, and then come back to it at a later time. All these things are possible."

"But why would he want to?"

"Sometimes a Realized One will assume a body in order to continue his teaching or look after a disciple who requires his assistance."

"As you have done for me. But luckily you were still in your body." The Saint paused a moment.

"It is not important to the Enlightened, having a body or not having one, but it can make things easier when passing on knowledge. You will admit that you had your doubts about me, since I did not appear to you in the flesh."

Theo had a sheepish look. "I did ask myself a few times if it might have all been a dream. But not too often. I usually just wondered who you were and why I had been lucky enough to be visited by you."

The teacher and his pupil slept in Shivaji's hut that night, and, in the morning, moved down to the pond, where they admired the lotuses. The flowers looked quite different in the early morning light than they had the previous afternoon. Their leaves shone vivid green under the young sun. The blooms revealed shades of pink ranging from faintest empurpled white, to cyclamen, to Persian rose. If flowers had voices and could speak of heaven, then these flowers did.

"Master, I was wondering why I got so sick and why you then brought me here to see Shivaji drop his body."

The Saint, as he often did, allowed the profound silence emanating from him to provide at least the first part of his answer. Theo understood by it that everything shown to him was intended to emphasize the all-importance of Being. After some time, however, the holy man did speak. "You had some quite serious karma around illness. Grave illness. In fact, during your time of suffering, a moment came when you ought to have left the body behind as a corpse."

"Why didn't I, then?"

"The guru can, at times like these, take on some of the student's burden."

"You mean that you became sick yourself on my behalf?"

The Saint did not answer this question. But Theo realized that he had, in fact, done so: he had transferred a portion of the painful karma to his own body, thereby preserving that of his disciple. Such is the love of a Master.

Thirty minutes or so passed in quiet contemplation of the flowers. "And why was it important that I see Shivaji in his last moments?"

The guru laughed. "His last moments? He would be surprised to hear that he no longer exists. Sickness and death are part and parcel of samsara. The life of ignorance is no *real* life at all. From the trauma of birth, to emotional loss, disease, pain, and death: such is bodily existence. You must understand that you are *not* the body. There was a Witness inside that suffering when you underwent it, yes? Shivaji could make a conscious decision to exit his physical shell, yes? One of the most difficult lessons for humans to learn is that they are something other than, something far more profound than, this little sack of bones and blood called a body.

"They call it 'my' body, but never stop to ask who is claiming it. Some might say 'mind,' but people also say 'my' mind. Behind the body, mind, and ego is the Witness of all that and everything else. The Witness that knows you slept deeply even though your mind and senses were not working at the time. The Witness that observes the antics of dreams and watches the mind go about its tricks and games. This Witness is Pure Consciousness, the Absolute, Brahman. It matters not what you call It, only that you Are It. You don't need to reach It or become It, because It is your essential nature. All you have to do is remember, realize who you truly are."

"But isn't that the problem, Master, that spiritual ignorance prevents one from just that realization?"

Again, the holy man remained silent for some time. Theo noticed a visible band of pure white light gently pulsing around his form. With each pulse, the disciple felt a soothing wave of joy wash over him.

"But you have heard clearly that bondage, ignorance, and liberation do not exist. There is only Pure Consciousness, an ocean of blazing, living Light, Rapture, and Love. Do not for a moment give in to the delusion that you are a body and a mind limited by ignorance. Focus your awareness, instead, on what you *truly* are: Infinite, Eternal Being. The Self is like a billionaire's bank account. You have forgotten your

149

great personal riches. Meditation is like finding the check book proving how wealthy you actually are."

"How sad it is to realize that human beings have this infinite wealth at their service, but choose to ignore it, don't even look for their checkbooks," Theo replied.

"They strive tirelessly to gather material wealth, but don't spend even a moment seeking to gain the Absolute, which provides everything they could ever possibly want. Desiring peace from worldly things is like looking for light in a dark cave. What lasting peace can come from something outside oneself, which is inherently subject to loss, change, or death at every moment?"

"What is peace, Guruji?"

"Peace is a state of stillness, a state of not desiring. When one is established in Pure Consciousness, the Everlasting Peace is Everywhere. United with the entire creation, nothing being separate from one's Self, what could possibly be desired? There is no 'other' to fear. There is no 'other' to desire. There is no greater Bliss. There is no greater Love. There is no greater Peace. Find the Absolute within yourself and rest there, contented."

The World Outside

They left Shivaji's oasis that day and took, perforce, a different trail back to the cave. This one passed through forest so thick that Theo began to imagine that he had entered into a verdant netherworld and would never again see the open sky.

Invisible birds serenaded them along the way. One heard long, drawn-out whistles and sharp, staccato chirps, three-beat songs of which the last was upslurred, and steady lower-pitch notes that progressively ascended. Cracklings of branches announced the presence of hidden mammals. Fainter disturbances of leaves hinted at rodents. The dense, virid woods was teeming with life.

The Saint appeared always to be at home, wherever he sat or walked. Theo wondered if he had ever used this path before. He could have, but it was out of the way and far less convenient than the one now buried under the landslide. But the disciple had the clear intuition that one could plump the Master down in the middle of a Saharan desert, and he would remain equally comfortable. The cosmos was his home, and he remained seated in the Absolute no matter where his body appeared to be.

On the long way back to the cave, they passed through the smallest of villages, consisting of but five houses, which were really no more than large huts topped with somewhat hardier roofs. As the Saint passed the third house, three men emerged from it and immediately sank to their knees, bowing their heads against the ground. One of them spoke excitedly, "Help us, Gurudeva!"

He stopped and silently inquired about their needs.

"We wish to light our lamps for Diwali, but no oil can be brought from the town because of the landslide."

"You have no oil at all?"

151

"None, Gurudeva, not even for our cooking, until the trail is cleared."

"Let me see." And the three men led him and Theo inside the nearest hut. Indeed, the oil bottle contained not a drop of the necessary liquid. "And other neighbors?"

"All in the same boat, Gurudeva. We had counted on a shipment coming the day of the accident."

"And these are your lamps?" The holy man inspected a row of twenty-five small lanterns. He picked up a pitcher from a nearby table.

"That is only water, sir."

"But you may be mistaken," the Saint replied. He then poured a pool of the pitcher's contents into each of the empty vessels. His glance then implied that they ought to light the lamps.

The second man, a short, rotund fellow with elflocks, immediately produced a packet of matches. At a sign from the Saint, he lit one of the lanterns. All three of the villagers jumped backwards at the sight of the steady flame rising from the liquid.

"And there is enough left in the pitcher to allow you to cook some food until the next shipment arrives," added the esteemed visitor.

Again, as one, the three sank down and prostrated before this holy soul who had, right before their eyes, performed a miracle. As Theo and his Master walked out the door, followed closely by the men, everyone else in the village, many of whom had been peering through the windows and had witnessed the miracle, gathered round the entrance, some bowing with hands pressed together, others seeking to touch the Saint's feet, and still others staring at him as if he were an apparition.

Theo did not dare speak until they had walked for some time. Then he gathered his courage. "Master, you have said that siddhis can distract one from the goal..." As he often did, Theo instantly regretted his words, for they implied that the Saint still had a 'goal' before him.

But the teacher was not offended. "Sometimes the environment requires some assistance. These good souls wished to celebrate the religious holiday in the only way they know how. Had they not been able to light their lamps, they would have felt as though they had committed a great sin. They were worried and miserable. The oil not only helped them to practice their religion, it inspired them with greater faith in the power of spirituality. All this is good, you would agree?"

"Oh, yes, oh, yes, certainly."

They walked for a while, and then Theo remembered a question he had tucked away but forgotten. "Guruji, you were talking about Anandaji's karma, and you mentioned that he did not identify as a body. That is still a bit unclear to me."

"To a Realized One like Anandaji, his body is unreal. What you might see in a dream and later label a figment: that is how such a One views his food-sheath. He also has no ahankara, no ego principle. You are clear on the teaching that the Enlightened know themselves to be nothing other than Pure Consciousness?" Theo nodded. "So, regarding karma: no karma can return to an ego and body that have ceased to exist. It would be like sending mail to someone who has moved and left no forwarding address. The mail will never arrive."

"Thank you. That makes sense now." Then, after a moment's reflection, he continued speaking. "But those villagers really ought not to have been attached to the lamp, right? Attachment, as you have told me, is the real problem."

"Yes, it is not the things of the world that are inherently troubling. It is one's attachment to them. Oil can come and go and should never overshadow one's experience of Pure Consciousness. But remember that 'individuals,' those who falsely believe themselves to be such, are in

153

various stages of ignorance. Some are so grotesquely lost that they commit foul crimes. Others are focused solely on enriching themselves, even at the expense of their neighbors. And some have an inkling of the Truth, but are, as yet, unable to live it.

"These men cherish a religious feeling in their hearts, a flame that should be fanned, so that it may grow big and bright. No matter that they are temporarily attached to their lanterns. That attachment will eventually pass. What is important is that they be encouraged in their holy sentiments. For now, they are concentrating on the tiny wicks, but, in future, they will turn their attention to the Great Light of the Absolute."

Walk and Talk

They eventually reached the cave and Theo immediately fell down into a deep sleep. No dreams came to disturb his rest. In the morning, he noticed that the Master was outside, and went to join him.

The two began to walk. The scenery in the soft morning light was breathtaking. Broad sheets of tender light, spaced maybe a quarter mile apart, angled at forty-five degrees over the sides of the distant mountains. They looked to Theo like landing strips onto which celestial beings would soon cruise down. A lake beneath them shone with the perfect turquoise color of an unblemished gemstone. The shadowed portions of the mountains seemed like sleeping beasts, not yet ready to rouse themselves for the day. A chine of low hills zigzagged through the middle of the visible space. Threads of soft cloud interlaced against the background of baby-blue sky.

"When you look at such great beauty, Master, you wonder how people come to suffer as much as they do."

They sat down, the teacher on a large rock and his student at his feet on the ground. "All human problems result from breaking universal law. Another way to define Realization is to say that it is the inability to ever go wrong. The Realized move in accord with natural law, because they are established in it. The Absolute is the home of Truth, the foundation of righteousness, and the basis of right action."

"So an Enlightened Being cannot do wrong?"

"No, it is impossible. To the unenlightened, it may seem as if someone like Shivaji commits a sin, violates a Brahmin rule, say, but no rules of the relative world constrain One who is beyond the relative. People once said of him, 'Look! He cannot be a true Saint, for he has grown angry at his disciple.' Now, that disciple no doubt needed to be scolded at that moment so that he might further his own development. Shivaji did not lose his temper. He possessed no 'mind' to contain emotions like anger. But he did spontaneously perform actions

155

required by the environment. And in this case, he had to lash out at the bad behavior of his student. There was never a question of his Peace being overshadowed by this display. Compare it to that of an actor who, at a moment's notice, can display any emotion you ask of him. Only, in the case of the Realized, nothing is faked. The necessary behavior arises, is displayed, and disappears without ever disturbing the inner Peace of the Saint."

"That's really interesting! So a normal person seeing a Saint display emotion likens it to his own emotions, when, in reality, it is something else entirely."

"One might even say that the Saint's entire living experience is such an actor's performance. None of it is real to him. Neither the body, the mind, nor the outside world is 'real' in the profound sense in which he understands that word. As we have discussed, his senses are *aware* of the world, but he sees Pure Consciousness as its essence. The essence is Real; the film playing upon it is not.

"Imagine a frozen lake with holes of various sizes in it. The water under the ice is Pure Consciousness. The ice is maya. Each hole is a human body and each pool of water in the hole is a human soul. When the ice melts, when ignorance disappears, the small pool of water rejoins the vast lake, which it was never truly separate from. The Realized see only the lake; the ignorant see only the ice. That is the difference."

"But to get back to Shivaji's emotional display..."

"The Absolute can create any appearance. It has, after all, created the appearance of all this." And the Saint motioned to the mountains and sky. Shivaji responded to his disciple's needs as the ocean rises into a wave when called to do so by the wind. Everyone expects the 'Shivajis' they see to be constantly meditating with a blissful smile on their face. But prarabdha karma, as you will recall, remains with the Enlightened as long as they have a physical body. Some Saints have been noticeably grumpy; some have cried at the loss of a close disciple.

156

It is not for the seekers to judge those who have already arrived at the goal."

"Please tell me about samskaras, Guruji. I know that they are impressions of past action stored in the causal body."

"Every action, every thought creates a subtle impression. Those which are done with full intention produce samskaras. These are, indeed, stored in the causal body, and are unconscious. A samskara gives someone a tendency in a certain direction. Similar attracts similar: so when a situation arises that is akin to the samskara, it gets activated. Someone sees a person who looks like his old school teacher, who used to punish him, and immediately feels dislike for the man. Another fellow hears about a certain dish, which his mother used to prepare deliciously, and he straightaway has a craving for that food.

"From samskaras come desires; from desires, thoughts; and from thoughts, actions. Actions then further deepen the impression of the samsara, and the cycle repeats. Once the impression is worn deep, a vasana, or deep groove of habit, is created, which leads to habitual behavior very difficult to stop."

"So, Master, you are describing a negative reinforcement cycle, right?"

"Name doesn't matter. In fact, the vasanas can be positive or negative. You yourself have a strong positive vasana to exist in Pure Consciousness. One wants to weaken the vasanas, to starve the mind, which is nothing but a collection of thoughts, desires, aversions, feelings, and habits."

"How does one do this?"

"By meditating, by reading the sacred books. Experience and knowledge are both important. Knowledge helps one understand the experience, and experience proves the value of the knowledge. When one settles down into Pure Consciousness, the mind does not exist.

157

Thoughts are not there. Emerging from meditation, one's intellect is stronger. One can resist the temptations presented by negative vasanas. One can more easily choose to love rather than hate. One begins to find sattvic, positive, activities more pleasing. This is the process of spiritual growth."

"So desires are really the problem, right?"

"Desires are defects of the mind. Without defects, the mind is not a problem. A Realized One like Shivaji can discuss the details of the Upanishads as well as the greatest scholar. The mind then is not different from the Absolute: information is presented as necessary."

"But you mentioned my own habit of desiring Enlightenment as a good thing."

"The single desire of ignorance that is useful is that one: the desire to find Pure Consciousness and remain Forever in It. But most desires, and their opposite sides, aversions, cause problems by facilitating the cycle spoken of before."

The Saint stood up and led them back to the cave.

An Opened Door

The following morning, the guru told his disciple that he should close his eyes and meditate. Theo did so without question. For a few minutes, he simply felt himself settling down to the quiet state he regularly experienced in his meditations. Thoughts tapered off and faded away. An echo of Silence filled his awareness.

Then something unexpected and strange happened. The Saint was sitting across from the meditator and staring at him with those eyes like pieces of stars. But mine are closed, Theo thought. How can this be? The Master, as he locked "eyes" with his student, also connected to his soul. Theo thought of it afterward as a sort of fuel-docking between two aircraft. He felt completely exposed to this psychic searching by the guru. His most deeply buried secrets came sheepishly out of hiding. All his greatest fears trembled visibly. The actions which he most regretted now appeared before the dock of spiritual justice.

But all this passed quickly. Then a wonderful sense of inner cleansing flowed over him. He felt as if his insides had been polished bright by a shower of purifying light. Smiling at the corniness of the phrase, he considered himself a "new man." But this man did not now consist of a body and a mind. It was fashioned completely from Consciousness and through its veins coursed Bliss.

Theo no longer saw the Master, but knew that they remained somehow connected. The seeker's essence began to stretch out, expanding further and further into space. He saw the moon and the sun get absorbed into his Self. Thousands and thousands of stars flashed bright as they became One with Him. Vast numbers of souls, floating in the ether of different cosmic regions, melted into Him.

Throughout this marvelous happening, Theo had no sense of "experiencing" it. No central core existed. No command center controlled or even observed the process. No captain steered this stellar ship. Words, of course, could not do it any sort of justice. All

159

that Theo could later say to himself was that the small "he" had disappeared, leaving in his place an anonymous vast It, which had nothing whatsoever to do with Theo Reyesin, but which, at the same time, constituted the pith and quintessence of what "Theo" truly was.

Despite the appearance and swallowing of celestial bodies and souls, despite blazing stars and effulgent spirits, a profound Silence characterized Theo's voyage. All was as deeply quiet as the farthest reaches of outer space. And this great Silence was infused with Bliss so intense as to be almost unbearable. The Bliss possessed an energy that seemed to want to explode whatever subtle envelope inside of which all this was happening.

At some point, nothing further entered into Him. He was Alone, Illimitable, Forever, and Blissful. Peace such as he had never imagined possible graced this vastness of his Awareness.

The next day he awoke, not remembering anything other than this last conception of perfect Peace.

The Return

Theo's experience had proved too intense to process for the time being. Dozens of questions would arise, but for now, he was glad to simply bask in the wake of his cosmic sojourn.

They left the cave for unknown parts, the Saint telling his student that he not need bring any warm clothing. They hiked for several hours through the fresh air and past the soothing sights of the alpine Himalayas. The area through which they walked was covered in spruce and fir trees, which scented the air with a pungent, invigorating perfume. Two equal-sized buttes rose up in front of the hikers. The tops of these structures were thickly covered in evergreen trees.

At midday, they stopped by a stream, whose pellucid waters purled like a natural lullaby. The Saint did not eat, satisfying himself with a cup of the fresh water flowing at their side. But Theo took two rice balls out of his pack and bit into them slowly, with appreciation, as though they were the creation of the world's greatest chef. He had found these balls next to his sleeping bag when he awoke the day after his cosmic travels.

After finishing his meal, the seeker cleaned up the area in preparation for departure. But something in the attitude and attentiveness of his Master told him that they would not be leaving straightaway. He heard the faintest rustle off to his left. Then his arms erupted in gooseflesh and the hair on the nape of his neck stood up. Under a tree not ten feet away sat...Shivaji!

The great Being was surrounded by flames of light, light so bright that Theo had to lower his eyes for a moment before he could again look upon the figure before him. This was no apparition. Shivaji sat there cross-legged in the fullness of his fleshed body. Theo noticed where the sun lit up a portion of his face and where shadow darkened the rest. He could see the recently deceased man breathing slowly in and out.

Theo's Master addressed the visitor. "I see that you have taken flesh again, Shivaji. The so-called world is better for it." The visitant did not reply, only nodding his head in acknowledgment of the compliment.

"My young student here must be amazed to see you like this, in the body again." One look at Theo caused them both to laugh. The prediction was too true. The pilgrim looked aghast.

Shivaji spoke. As he did so, the flames surrounding his form palpitated in rhythm with his words. "Nothing is dead. All is alive, vibrating, and intelligent. Look around."

Theo did so and was astonished to see that the grass, the trees, even the buttes and mountains did, indeed, throb with life force and glow with subtle luminance. The speaker continued. "Eternal, all-encompassing Bliss surrounds even the smallest particle of creation. Death is an illusion."

The seeker turned his head toward the buttes. From the thickly clustered evergreens emanated cascades of what looked like silver foam, bubbles of glinting argent. From the buttes themselves flowed huge sails of the same frothy, frosted silver. He lowered his eyes to the grass near his feet, and watched as the blades breathed in and out, in ever-so-shallow respirations. The stream fairly danced with vitality, revealing a subtle "waterway" above it, which traced its course and movement in flashing dots of brilliant light.

When he returned his gaze to Shivaji, Theo could not find him. Scanning the landscape, he finally located the Holy One: on top of one of the buttes! The buttes sat at a quarter mile's distance and rose up sheer at least 500 feet. In an instant, the Saint redivivus had positioned himself atop one of the trees on the butte, on its peak, like a finial on a cathedral. Then, mesmerizingly, he began to levitate, rising from the apex and coming to a stop in midair! He sat cross-legged and looked no different than he had while sitting close to Theo a few minutes earlier.

162

Theo blinked several times, wondering if his eyes were playing tricks on him. When he opened them again, Shivaji no longer floated in the distant air. The seeker looked at his Master for a hint, but he seemed not to have noticed that anything at all unusual had occurred. Then Theo turned his head left, and....there was Shivaji, under the same tree as before!

The pilgrim had an inspiration to offer the magical Saint a flower, as one often did to holy men. But only one flower lay in sight, and it had been dead for some time. Theo looked at Shivaji and the Saint returned his gaze. A second glance at the flower: it now stood up proudly, fully alive, colorfully bright, and emitting dancing motes of vital energy. The student dug around its roots and pulled up the flower with all of them still attached. He knelt before Shivaji and presented his offering.

"Even for flowers there is no such thing as death," the Holy One said, first taking the flower into his hand and then gently placing it back into the soil. The second he let it go, the petals tripled in size, the stem rose half again as high as it had been, and a charming perfume filled the air around the flower.

When Theo finally stopped staring at the magical flower, he saw that Shivaji had disappeared from under the tree. Scouring the vista, the seeker noticed his small form at least a mile away, walking rapidly in the direction of his lotus pond.

"Save all your many questions for later; right now, simply muse upon Shivaji's words. Consider their meaning and consequences. See how they might apply to you in your search for the Absolute."

The Saint then began to walk back the way they had come, with his disciple, busy picking up his water can and pack, and giving a last look at the burgeoning flower, hurrying to catch up.

A Slew of Questions

The next morning, back at the cave, something unexpected happened. When Theo awoke, he heard a low murmuring outside and went to investigate. A group of ten people, mostly men, but including a couple of women, had gathered outside the entrance to the cave. The disciple's appearance momentarily quieted the visitors. They looked sheepish and hesitant to speak. Theo realized that most of them knew no English. But, finally, one tall, thin fellow, who was better dressed than the others, stepped forward.

"Namaste."

"Namaste," Theo replied.

"We like to see gurudeva. If possible."

"Just a moment." The student reentered the cave and acquainted his Master with the situation. The latter immediately stood up and walked out to the people.

The group sunk to its knees and prostrated before the Realized One.

"Blessings to you, everyone. Tell me your wishes."

The tall man acted as spokesperson. "The stream runs high, gurudeva. See!" he pointed to the sky, where dark clouds were approaching from the northeast. "Tonight, maybe a flood. Houses near the stream would go. Big flood."

"I see. You worry that if the stream crests, the houses near the banks will be lost. That is a concern, indeed."

"You will come?"

"I will come tonight, and we will watch the stream together."

The grateful villagers bowed and made the namaste gesture, expressing thanks in their native tongue. They then departed for their homes, to make preparations against the waters.

"It's a serious problem. Ever year, when the flood comes, many homes are lost. The people are poor and it's hard for them to build new ones. So they worry, having little faith in Providence." And he smiled.

In the evening, the main path having still not being cleared of debris, the two descended on a forest trail to the village. The tall man, who was a sort of sarpanch, or mayor, welcomed them into his house, providing water with which they could wash themselves, cool fruit juice, nuts, and flowers for the guru. After half an hour of such hospitable services, most of the village accompanied the two newcomers down to the banks of the stream.

The situation was grave. The water had reached the upper limits of the banks, and further rain would send it forcefully racing out toward the dozen or so huts that sat not ten yards from the water. By now the sky had the appearance of an immense bruise. Black and dark blue clouds hung poised directly over the village. Their bellies distended with moisture, the clouds threatened to dump huge amounts of rain on the already filled-to-capacity stream. Villagers in the nearest huts hurried to carry food supplies and precious fragile possessions to the homes of friends and relatives on higher ground.

As the group stood by the stream, the sky opened wide its sluices. Fat drops of rain poured down as if from overturned buckets, drenching the people, the ground, and the trees. One could actually see the level of the stream rise, as the deluge swelled it. Women began to moan, cows, to moo, and children to cry. A few men gave hurried last-minute instructions to their sons, "Get the beds into the loft!", and "Keep digging that trench! The deeper the better." But most of them seemed resigned to yet another year of disaster.

The water, dark and noisy, was just at the point of cresting the stream's banks. A few loud prayers were sent up to Indra, the god responsible for storms, but most of the sad-visaged men could only shake their heads. At the moment when the flood topped the bank,

165

when catastrophe appeared imminent, a tremendous shout was heard. The shout thundered louder than the fulminating heavens. It shook the very ground on which they stood, carrying within it some omnipotent power, like that a god might wield.

And the water stopped moving! Rain continued to pour into the stream, and everyone could see that over its opposite bank the flood was inundating the forest, but on this, the inhabited side, the water ceased to advance.

At first, the villagers were too stunned to make sense of the event. They simply stared, jaws dropped, eyes wide, at the arrested water. But then someone spoke the word "miracle," and all eyes turned to the Saint. He stood just where he had been all along, neither smiling nor showing any other emotion. His stature was not large, but his presence, as always, dwarfed that of all those around him.

Theo realized that the godlike shout they had heard had come from his Master. The holy man had literally commanded the waters to stop, and they *had* stopped.

After ten minutes of continued rain, seeing that the flood did not move any closer to their houses, the villagers let out ecstatic cheers and threw themselves into the mud at the guru's feet. They had, they said, been doubly blessed: with the salvation of their homes and with the observation of a genuine miracle. Invitations to dinner came from every direction.

The Saint chose the poorest man amongst the villagers as his host for the evening. The mayor and those whose cows and rice bins were more numerous and deeper than others' objected, pretending that they did not wish to burden the poor man with the load of hospitality. But the gurudeva politely shook them off and, with Theo following, allowed the penurious fellow to take him home.

The laborer's hut barely had enough room to hold his family of six and the two visitors, but everyone managed to find seating. His wife,

166

who appeared on the verge of starvation, so visible were her bones, was utterly flustered by the responsibility of hosting the guru. Neighbors shouted in through the windows with offers of savory dishes, but the Saint gestured to his host that he would prefer to partake of the man's simpler food.

After half an hour, the wife and her three daughters appeared, carrying a modest-sized earthenware bowl of rice and a small platter of steamed vegetables. One of the girls offered the illustrious guest a hoary, chipped tea cup filled with spices.

Now there were eight people to be fed, and all the excitement surrounding the flood and the miracle had roused the family's hunger. The mother kept making surreptitious gestures to her children and husband to refrain from eating, so that the guru and his disciple might satisfy themselves. Guests were, after all, honored as gods in India. But when it became obvious that the man intended to stint himself and his family, the holy man overruled the division of food.

Handing back his filled leaf-plate, he said, "Let us reverse the normal order of things and first serve the children and then the hosts," he said. His word had, of course, to be taken as law, so the mother dutifully doled out rice and veggies for her husband and children, and, finally, at the insistence of the guru, for herself. After every spoonful, she expected to see the depressing bottoms of platter and bowl, but she never did see them. Shocked, her hand froze in midair. After a chiding word from her spouse, she recommenced her dishing-out and managed to pile a substantial amount of food on both the Saint's and the disciple's leaves.

"Very delicious! Especially with this turmeric and coriander that Lakshmi was so kind to offer us." The sloe-eyed teenager's face flushed red as a tomato at these words of praise from the miracle-worker, obviously, she had not heard many over the course of her life.

"Indeed," added Theo, in his coarse Hindi, "very good!"

167

Everyone but the Saint, who never consumed much, ate and ate and ate, and still the platter and bowl remained full. When they had reached their limit, the hostess collected the leaves and carried the platter and bowl to the back of the one-room hut.

"You will have some left over for tomorrow," the Saint pleasantly suggested.

The father now prostrated, having a difficult time finding room to do so, and his children followed his example. "I have no words for what has happened here, great guru. I only wish that we could offer his holiness some dessert. But..." he opened up his palms to indicate dearth.

"I believe your wife has something tucked away, which you didn't know about," said the holy man.

There followed a loud exclamation of surprise from the dark recesses at the back of the hut. The wife called her daughters. After ten minutes, the women reappeared with the same earthenware bowl, this time filled with that toothsome delicacy rasmalai: a dessert made from ricotta cheese and thickened milk and spiced with cardamom.

The family had never before tasted this treat. And it would have warmed the heart of even the Scroogiest Scrooge to hear them oohing and aahing as they inhaled the pudding. The children, not easily impressed by holy figures, became instantly loyal fans of the Saint the moment they tasted the rasmalai.

The family obviously had no room in the hut for the guests to sleep, so the Master acceded to the persistent requests of the mayor to spend the night at his larger house. During the time before the family retired to bed, the entire village paraded through the house making obeisances before the Saint, placing flowers on a tray placed near him, and, in several cases, offering small fruits and leaves filled with spices. They had all heard about the cornucopian miracles of the dinner and

168

were eager to show their appreciation for his having saved their village from flood.

The mayor wished to go to great lengths in his welcome of the Gurudeva, but that simple Being refused a fancy bed, preferring to sit in Silence half the night, as he usually did, and then lie down on a simple mat to rest his body, his awareness remaining completely alert throughout the night.

The next morning, to the acclaiming hails of the residents, with the children scurrying in his wake, the Saint and Theo departed the village for their cave.

Just a Beggar?

On the way back, the two men came upon a beggar, dressed in worn-out and soiled cloth, his hair tangled and dirty, and his face dusty and smirched. He sat on the ground, among thorny bushes, with a crinkled leaf, intended for contributions, at his feet. Theo was surprised to see the Saint sink to his knees and offer the namaste greeting to the old-timer.

"Blessings to you, holy brother," he said, "on this morning that rests so perfect in God's own hand."

The beggar mumbled something back to his greeter and pointed to the leaf. "I have not even a single rupee to offer you, child of God, but let me wander into these woods and see what I can find that might be suitable as a gift." And off he walked.

Theo was surprised to hear the old beggar speak to him in good English. "You wonder how he could have produced that food in the village."

Trying but failing to suppress his astonishment, Theo nodded his head.

"The scriptures say that those who habitually speak the Truth possess the power to materialize their words."

"I know that he speaks only Truth."

"And you, who wish to find your way to Self, *you* must speak it only, too."

"Thank you for your guidance, sir." Theo was still torn between his feeling that this man was nothing more than a wandering beggar and an intuition that he might be something else entirely.

"I can see that you continue to resist what is being shown to you. You allow logic to interfere with your intuition. The quickest path to Enlightenment is complete surrender. Surrender everything to God. And Guru is God."

Theo understood exactly what this wise "beggar" was telling him. Even just moments before, the seeker's mind had been telling him to disregard this fellow's advice: how could a beggar know anything? logic asked him.

"You have already been instructed regarding book knowledge. It can do nothing to reveal your Self to you. Real knowledge is forgetting everything *except* the Self. Yet, you insist on understanding precisely how each miraculous event occurs, as if such information mattered in the least."

The teacher-beggar pointed to a dead bird under the bush beside him. He picked it up, and the bird shivered. He stroked it, and the bird slightly ruffled its feathers. He blew air into its beak, and the bird began to hop about on his hand. The reviver looked at Theo, who knew that he was supposed to simply accept this feat, but could not manage to do so.

Then the man covered the bird with both hands. When he opened them, a gorgeous, bright-pink butterfly was revealed. These were like the tricks of a master magician, the difference being that in this situation they were not tricks. Lifting up his hand, the magus encouraged the butterfly to test its wings, which it successfully did, fluttering off into the clear morning air.

At this moment, the Saint reappeared. His hands were pressed together. "I could only find this," he said, sinking down and extending his arms toward the beggar. When he opened his hand, a gorgeous, bright-pink butterfly was exposed. It hopped from his hands to those of the intended recipient.

"Just the offering I find most welcome!" the man said. Closing his hands over the butterfly, he quickly opened them to reveal the formerly dead bird. He lifted it up on his palm, and, with a slight motion, encouraged it to fly away, which it did.

"We must be heading back now, holy brother. We have had been honored to have your darshan."

Theo bowed and held his palms together. ""I am humbled to have received your advice, sir."

In an instant, the beggar became just that once again, the air of wisdom that had recently enveloped him disappearing like a melted mist. And the two travelers moved on down the path.

After allowing a few minutes of respectful silence, Theo could not resist speaking. "You spoke of 'darshan,' Master, which, if I understand the term correctly, is used in the presence of a great Being."

The Saint chuckled. "And you don't consider a simple beggar to be 'great,' right?"

"I know that he is not a simple beggar. You wouldn't believe what he did while you were away." Again, Theo immediately realized that he was making the mistake of assuming the Master did not know things that he most certainly did know.

"With birds and butterflies?"

"Sorry, Master. But do those tricks make him a Saint?"

"What you perceived as a beggar is actually one of the Himalayas' greatest Beings. Indrananda has dwelt in these mountains for countless years, rarely appearing to anyone. When he does make himself visible, it is always in some guise like that of the beggar. He enjoys teaching those still on the path. And I would not be at all surprised if he taught you a thing or two."

"Mainly he reminded me of what you yourself have taught me, Master. He spoke a lot about Truth."

The Saint made no reply to these words.

Philosophy

The following day, the rain continued, so they stayed inside the cave. After Theo's morning meditation, characterized, as it always was when he sat in the presence of the Master, by profound Silence and periods of breathtaking Bliss, they began to discuss Vedantic philosophy.

"You are clear on all the basics, I know, but, if you have any remaining questions, this is a good time to ask them."

"Why is it that we seek Enlightenment, Master? If we are buried under heavy loads of ignorance, which obscure the Absolute, which is our genuine Self, what prompts us to search?"

"You have come from Bliss and part of you remembers that. And so you search, some in effective ways and others in wrong directions, for what you have lost."

"Won't it take forever to get rid of all my bad karma, Guruji? It has built up for lifetimes, after all."

"Who tells you that you must do so? All that is required for Realization is the understanding of Who you really Are. One can never empty a dark room of its darkness. One simply brings a light to accomplish this. Focus on the Light, not on the darkness. Meditate and keep meditating. Put your thoughts on positive matters. Assist others as best you can. Live a clean life. Pure Consciousness is like an all-powerful magnet. As you come closer to It, It pulls you in irresistibly.

"The more often you experience It, the more easily you remain with It. The progress towards Realization speeds up as one near the goal."

"So Enlightenment can be achieved before all my karma is exhausted?"

"Become the Self and then ask me this question."

"Back to that old question about the unreality of the external world, Master. Most people would laugh out loud if we said it wasn't real."

"And I have explained to you that the 'unreality' we are talking about does not mean that if you step on a sharp rock, you will not injure your foot. The holy texts explain that what is ultimately *real* is Everlasting and does not change. All things in the material universe are finite and ever-changing. Only the Absolute is Eternal, Infinite, and Never-Changing.

"What the rishis mean by 'reality' is this substratum of everything in the universe, the Self. A Realized Being looks around and sees nothing but the Self. Of course he notices the mountains and the clouds, but they are revealed in their essence as Pure Consciousness. If you put a crystal in front of a colored paper, the clear stone appears to share the paper's color. You would swear that it is red and not transparent. Remove the paper, and its clarity is easily seen.

"Ignorance colors our view of the world by modifying the Absolute with conceptions of name and form. One in ignorance sees a mountain and nothing of the Absolute. A Realized Being sees the Absolute over which is superimposed a "mountain," a name and a form that attempt to separate it from what it really Is."

Theo mulled these ideas over for a few minutes before speaking again. "And by meditating long enough, one carries the Absolute over into the waking state, and sees the mountain as Absolute?"

"The more agitated the mind, the stronger the sense of the 'reality' of the world. Conversely, the quieter the mind, the more powerful one's awareness of the Absolute."

"And this ties in to your teachings about desire, too."

"Yes, when the mind is weak and careless the winds of sense objects easily carry it away. Meditation is deep rest, remember. Fatigue is the cause of mistakes. One cannot forget the concept of 'body' when the body is so tired that it cries out for sleep. And the Self is forgetfulness

174

of the idea of 'body.' The Self reminds one that It is all, that the body, mind, and ego are artificial constructions, built up and maintained by ignorance."

"What, then, is the purpose of the material world, Master?"

"The world, as your poet rightly said, is merely a stage, a stage on which an individual's prarabdha karma plays itself out."

"Because one thinks he is a body in a world."

"Just so. One forgets that he is an actor and actually *becomes* the role he is playing. The teaching is to remember that one is *not* this role, but something far greater: the Self."

"But the action of the play helps one toward the goal?"

"Those karmas that are blocking Awareness must be played out. Positive karmas that are facilitating Awareness help push one in the right direction. But the entire play depends on avidya, ignorance. The theatrical play is an illusion, and so is this worldly one that consumes the attention of billions of people. Don't add fuel to the fire that illuminates this spectacle. Resist the process of desiring objects and results. Live simply; eat lightly."

Theo could not resist: "We sure are doing that!"

"Put out the fire so that the spectacle constantly grows dimmer. The Light of the Self will increase as one does so, until, eventually, there is nothing perceived *but* that Light."

"Seekers are always so worried about what they should do, Master. How much should they meditate? What diet should they follow?"

"Don't worry about what to *do*, but how to *be*."

"But they're tied together, right?"

"Everything, every single thing: karma, the external world, decisions, desires, all of it is the activity of the power of Consciousness. Simply meditate and find Pure Consciousness, then all these questions will answer themselves."

Evening had come and a gesture from his Teacher told Theo that it was time for him to follow that advice and meditate. He closed his eyes and immediately sank deep.

Alone in the Mountains

"Today you will visit a holy man I know. He lives in a cave some distance from here. Don't take anything with you. I want you to find him without using directions."

Theo was stunned. How could he find a single man in these vast mountains? Furthermore, how would he survive without a canteen of water and a supply of food? "I shouldn't take anything at all?"

"Nothing. You lack faith, and must exercise it like a muscle until it becomes strong. This little trip will help you do so."

"What is the man's name?"

"That is of no consequence."

Theo's frustration mounted. "I'm meant to find an unnamed man in a vast mountain range without the use of any supplies?"

"Yes."

When he was about to leave the cave, the Saint said, "Consult your intuition. It will not fail you."

And so Theo began to walk in the direction that, for some reason, appealed to him. The morning was fresh and lovely, packed with the delightful scents of herbs and flowers, filled with the pleasant sounds of nest-building forest thrushes and perky, striped squirrels. The seeker forgot his frustration as he admired the cloud shadows moving across the mountain faces.

Once he managed to let go of the discomfort of not knowing what he was doing, a lifelong pattern of getting very uncomfortable in unpredictable situations, Theo enjoyed himself thoroughly. There was a wild freedom in setting out to who-knows-where to see who-knows-whom. After all, the Saint undoubtedly had a plan that could be relied on to produce whatever result was destined to occur.

Whenever he had to make a choice regarding direction, the seeker simply went whichever way struck him as best, allowing intuition to guide him. After about four hours of walking, he arrived at a most unusual spot: a flat, circular space surrounded on four sides by immense boulders at least twenty feet in height. The sun being directly overhead, he was blinded as he attempted to see the tops of these great blocks of granite. He could detect no way out of this circle except for the path that had brought him to it.

Then something extraordinary occurred. The blazing sun over his head, though uncovered by clouds, suddenly dimmed. The reduction of brightness allowed Theo to make out the tops of the boulders. On one of them sat a yogi ablaze in light. At first, the light prevented the seeker from making out any details of the man, if such indeed he was. Its effulgence spread out several feet all around the body. But gradually, once his eyes adjusted, the watcher was able to clearly observe the stranger's form. The face and torso were extremely pale and hairless, but long, straight hair hung down behind the yogi's shoulders. His eyes were closed and his lips pursed. He sat on a deerskin.

So this was the man I was supposed to meet! Theo knew. But what will happen next? I have no way to reach him up there on that rock.

As Theo watched, the yogi began to rise into the air. Celestial beings appeared in worshipful attitudes, standing slightly away from the Being, as if in awe of him. The body floated out and down, eventually settling on a small rock several yards from where Theo stood. The rock had not been there before. Just before the yogi landed, the deerskin also appeared out of nowhere.

The pilgrim sank to his knees and prostrated before this perfect Being. When he rose, the yogi's eyes were open and looking not *at* but *through* him. His gaze had the effect of twin lasers of Bliss: they penetrated Theo to the core, causing every molecule of his body and every particle of his soul to sing with joy.

His mind instantly stopped functioning. All sense of his persona, the small "Theo" that he considered himself to be, disappeared. He became One with the mountains and the sky and all else that lay beyond them.

Now the Being began to communicate with him, but not in words. His thoughts entered directly into Theo's awareness. "You have wondered about karma. Know that the fires of knowledge reduce karma to ashes."

And Theo responded with thoughts. "Yes, Great One, I had worried about escaping from the world of ignorance, which I realize is only a delusion."

"Samsara, the world of suffering you refer to, means flowing with the phenomenal tides. A soul caught up in samsara is like a shell carried endlessly here and there by the recurrent waves of the ocean. This artificial world is nothing but an extension of your destiny. So long as you believe that you are a separate individual, a small body with a small mind, then you will play out this destiny.

"Just as dreams are based on the experiences of the waking state, so waking consciousness is rooted in the experiences of past lives. Your desires from those lives become the desires of this life. Your fears in those lives play out as the fears of this one."

Theo became aware of a disturbance in the air. He saw a sort of buzzing of light-dots next to the yogi. Then the Saint appeared, sitting cross-legged quite close to him. Pressing his hands together in respectful greeting, the Saint bowed from the waist and spoke. "What a great honor you have bestowed on us, Babaji." Babaji did not reply, but met the eyes of the Master straight on. His gaze, which had all along been distant and almost stern, now softened. The two great Beings looked at one another for several seconds. Then Babaji once more rose up into the air, again angels flocked around Him. After he settled on the boulder's top, the sun came out once more, blinding Theo's eyes.

After the dancing red dots had disappeared from his vision, he looked for the Saint, who was nowhere to be found. He realized that the visit with Babaji had ended. So, offering respect to Him, the pilgrim backed away to the path by which he had entered this space. Turning round, he headed back toward the cave.

Timeless Sages

Once he reached the cave, Theo, exhausted after the long trek and from the excitement of what he had seen, collapsed onto his sleeping bag, not even making it inside. He slept late into the morning the next day. When he awoke, he saw that the Saint was not present. After meditating, an invariable habit, he went outside to look for the holy man.

After some time, he found the Master seated by a stream, which sparkled like a myriad of diamonds under the almost vertical rays of the sun. The gentle flow of the water served as a relaxing musical score for the peaceful scene.

"Master, who *is* Babaji?"

The Saint continued to stare out into the distance, almost as if he were seeing the great yogi in its clear air. "He is one of the Great Beings who reside in the Himalayas, only revealing themselves on rare occasions to special people. You should be greatly honored to have met him."

"I know that the honor is due solely to you, Master. For only with your involvement would I ever have had the chance to meet such a Being. Thank you."

"What impressed you most about him?"

"Other than the levitations accompanied by choirs of angels?" Theo chuckled. But he quickly gathered himself. "He told me that the world we see around us is only an extension of our destiny. It's like we have to build the stage appropriate for the play we are about to produce. That stuck with me."

"Anything else?"

"He said that the fires of knowledge reduce karma to ashes."

"And from both of these teachings, what did you conclude?"

Theo raked his chin with his fingers and stared up at the pristine vault of the sky for a few seconds. "I guess that we should gain knowledge and thus burn down the world as we know it."

"It is the karma that is burnt, like a cooked seed that can no longer grow into a plant. The world was never real to begin with, so there is no need to burn it down. The light beam of Consciousness is like that of the theater projector: it shines through the ego, product of one's karmas, and projects a colorful world on the blank screen. Realization is simply coming to see the screen as Real and the dancing images as mere excitations on that screen."

"But will there still be a 'me' to watch the movie then, Master?"

"Mind and ego are illusions. The 'I' thought identifies with the body and imagines that it is an individual person. This illusion has been perpetuated throughout so many lifetimes that it has become firmly ingrained. But once it is shaken off, the 'I' thought no longer views Itself as a separate, limited body/mind/ego, but as an Infinite, Unlimited Self, unattached to a body.

"The transcendence of one's individuality *is* Realization of the Absolute. One doesn't need to *find* anything other than one's true nature. One doesn't need to go anywhere or do anything. The Self is always with you; it is your innermost essence. One only has to separate out the false 'self' from the true 'Self.'

"Easier said than done, Guruji."

After some time, Theo spoke again. "Master, you said that there were other Great Beings in these mountains."

"Yes, and it may happen that you will meet them someday. But now I want you to prepare yourself for tomorrow. Tomorrow, you will spend twenty-four hours by yourself outside."

"Outside the cave?"

"No, outside in a special place I will show you. After your meditation, eat something and go to bed, so that you will be well rested."

"What will I do all that time outside, Master?"

"You will see as the hours unfold. It is a necessary part of your training that you spend this time alone."

So Theo meditated, ate, and climbed into his sleeping bag. The Saint sat by the low fire, eyes closed and legs crossed.

Solitary Refinement

The next morning, the Saint led his pupil to a spot about an hour's walk from the cave. The quiet nook in the vast mountains seemed perfect for what Theo imagined as a sort of Native American vision quest.

The mountains rose sheer behind the spot, their sides covered with thick evergreen growth. Shorter, more lightly colored trees formed a border around it. A square, flat rock roughly eight feet square occupied the middle of the space. Smaller ones of various sizes lay here and there, looking not as though they had randomly fallen, but as though they had been carefully placed in their locations. All these rocks had the palest of gray hues. They looked almost white.

The Saint told Theo that he should meditate here as he always did, and that if he felt like meditating more often than normal, should feel free to do so. Besides that, his only instruction was to look around him and think about what Babaji and Shivaji and Anandaji had said. The Saint then left him.

The spot turned out to be preternaturally quiet. Theo heard no birds and saw no squirrels or other animals in the trees and bushes. No wind blew through the branches. There was only a profound silence, something like what one would expect in a deep, subterranean cavern.

After walking around the area and noticing its features, the seeker decided to lie down and rest for a while. So he stretched out on the bare rock and closed his eyes. His first thoughts centered on the fact that the Master had forbidden him to bring any possessions to this place. He carried no sleeping bag, no canteen, no knife, and no compass. He now worried how he would survive the cold night.

But, for some reason, the rock felt comfortable against his back. He noticed a subtle fragrance in the air: not a floral perfume, nothing so strong, but just a hint of something very pure. Then his mind began

184

to drift back over the conversations of the three Saints whom his Master had asked him to reflect on.

Anandaji, he recalled, had spoken about the past and future all being rolled up into the present. He had explained how thoughts were actual energy forms moving through the air. And, unforgettably, he had shown him, simply by tapping on his chest, all those marvelous visions.

Shivaji really hadn't talked about anything. If he had conveyed a "lesson," it was that one can control the body simply by the application of one's mind. He had dematerialized his own by means of a yogic technique of inner fire.

Babaji's instructions were fresh in Theo's mind; he had just reiterated them to his Master: karma and knowledge and the world: all as an expression of destiny.

He began to mull over these ideas. There is no time. The body is unreal and can be made to disappear. Wonderful celestial places and beings exist beyond the normal human's range of vision. This world I see is the playhouse of my karma, which knowledge can burn away. Then I will see only Pure Consciousness, with the worldly objects floating flimsy over Its Infinite extent.

The tumblers of the safe of knowledge were now falling into place, so that the bolt might be thrown. The pieces of knowledge no longer stood apart as discrete bits, but coalesced into a great assembled puzzle. His mind lit up, almost as if a switch had been flicked and a bright bulb turned on. All was silent inside; all was quiet outside. His sense of having a body disappeared.

Theo had the very strange idea that the place itself was somehow instructing him. As he lay there, stretched out on the flat rock, information that could not be expressed in words, ideas that could not be explained with reason, entered his soul. He felt like a patient on an operating table lying quietly while invisible surgeons worked to heal his deepest wounds.

Subtle energetic knots in his spinal area warmed up under the invisible scalpels of these doctors, before dissolving completely. Washes of hot liquid spread out over his abdomen, causing the tightness there to relax. Needles poked into microscopic spaces along the nape of his neck, enlivening nerves. A laser of intense heat aimed at the right side of his chest released an immense reservoir of love.

It was dark before he opened his eyes to marvel at the stars above him. A sort of dragon of dull lilac color wound its way up through the central vista of the sky. Behind and to the side of the dragon flamed molten golds borrowed from the setting sun. Stars of varying brightness, some bluish, others silver, still others white, crammed the sky to its limit. Never, never before had he seen so many stars! It was as though they wished to witness some spectacle on earth and so had pressed together in a serried mass leaving not a tittle of space between them.

Theo felt magic in the air of this blessed spot. He stood up and began to walk carefully around it. The starlight provided just enough illumination for him to do so safely. Rocks thrust themselves up before him, but always in time to avoid collision. He noticed that the temperature remained moderate, even though the sun had set.

After exploring the place for half an hour or so, Theo came to a spot where two rocks abutted each other to form a low opening. An intuition as strong as a verbal command told him to crawl through this opening. He crawled in the dirt for twenty yards or so before finding a cavern filled with speleothems, mostly stalagmites crystalline, pink, and blue. A perfectly circular pool, its waters the tenderest of baby blues, occupied the middle of the cavern. Along the walls were semicircular niches, and inside each of the six niches sat Beings.

These Beings appeared at the same time to be both physical and spiritual entities. Their heads and shapes were human, but their glowing translucent effulgence was anything but. All were straight and tall; all wore lengthy beards and long hair; and all had the most perfectly pure faces imaginable.

Theo remained utterly still at the entrance to the cavern. If one took the atmosphere of an 800-year-old cathedral and raised it to the tenth power one might have an idea of the vibrations that filled this sacred sanctuary. Unevenly shaped light-forms regularly floated across the space and up toward and out of its roof. Silver lights the size of fireflies danced in choruses here and there. An invisible energy so strong that it quickened one's soul permeated every inch of the room.

The Beings sat cross-legged and rigidly straight. Their eyes remained closed. No expression showed on their faces. Theo could not determine if they were bodies or spirits, for they seemed too radiant for the former and too tangible for the latter. He hesitated to move, sensing that any noise or disturbance would violate the sanctity of the space.

Theo turned his gaze to the Being nearest him. As he watched this Great Soul, a scene enacted itself above the pool in the cave's center. In a makeshift bed located in an impoverished hut, a little girl suffered miserably. Her face had broken out into pustules; beads of sweat dotted her forehead; her small form writhed under a handmade blanket. It was clear to Theo that she stood on the verge of death.

Then the Being he had just been looking at appeared at the bedside. None of the adults gathered around the sick girl noticed the Being. But the child *did* notice Him. She stared hard at his eyes, which bathed her in the balm of loving compassion. She implored him silently to stop the pain, to release her from the suffering body. The Being stretched out his hand and made a slow pass over the tiny body of the girl. Her visage instantly changed. From suffering it changed to contentment. Her limbs stopped flailing and relaxed. The moisture on her brow dried. And, unbelievably, the pustules visibly began to dry and shrink, until, after a few minutes, they were no longer to be seen.

The parents and the village "doctor" stared at one another in amazement. The mother felt her daughter's forehead and let out a huge cry of gratitude. Her husband sank to his knees and raised his pressed palms to heaven. The doctor could only shake his head and bend it to the side, as if asking himself how he could possibly have been so mistaken.

Then the scene dissolved, going from the realest "real" to nothing in an instant. Theo looked over at the Being, who sat just where he had always been, reposing motionless in perfect peace.

A stunningly clear thought came to him, in answer to a question that had perplexed him for decades: faith matters! The parents and the little girl's doctor lacked true faith. But she possessed it in abundance, and drew to her dying bedside the miracle-worker who pulled her back from the clutches of the dark-visaged Yama, god of death.

The seeker turned his gaze first to another of the Beings, and then to the baby-blue pool. Again, a scene of perfect verisimilitude rose above the still water. First, there appeared a delectably beautiful girl of about twenty years, whose face spread out toils of seductiveness and whose body lured one irretrievably in. She combined the innocent allure of the maiden with the sexual toothsomeness of the woman. Theo recognized her as his adolescent fantasy, the girl-woman he had chased down endless hallways of his imagination, never catching her, always being an instant too late to hold her in his arms.

Now she looked directly at him with invitation in her eyes. "Make up for lost time" she seemed to say. "What matters age, when you can enjoy me now?"

188

But Theo had traveled too far down a different road to be susceptible to the fantasy's allure. He remained calm and the beauty disappeared in an instant.

This vision, too, had a powerful message for the seeker. Throughout his life he had wanted women and never really had them. The fantasies he had entertained since adolescence, of seductive waifs who would recognize his poetic soul for what it truly was, had lingered in the subterranean depths of his mind. And now they had emerged from imagination to clear propinquity: he had seen her alive and beckoning. And yet he had not been moved to reach out to her.

Theo directed his attention to the third of the Beings, and then to the baby-blue pool. Before him stood a man, erect and proud, who was orating eloquently to a large crowd of people. The speaker's words were inaudible, but obviously made a great impression on his listeners. Many jumped up and down with enthusiasm. Some rushed forward, attempting to climb onto the platform where he stood. Everyone was madly applauding. Mothers held babies up in the air so that they might catch a glimpse of this luminary, this wonder among men.

After the conclusion of his speech, the orator accepted the embraces of gathered dignitaries; his hand was repeatedly shaken and his back patted. Clearly, he had achieved wonderful success with these illustrious authorities. And his face showed that he saw and understood all this, understood that he was a star shining brightly among duller bodies. The man radiated confidence and assurance, knowing how great he was.

Theo took this lesson to heart. Having never believed that his worth was appreciated by others, he had, as a young man, longed for fame and recognition. As a middle-aged one, he had pretended humility while actually delighting in whatever applause came his way. But, throughout his life, there had persisted the nagging bother that he had brought gifts to the world, which it failed to appreciate.

Seeing the speaker basking in approbation dissolved whatever fascination remained in Theo for fame and recognition. There was something so cheap, so tawdry about playing to a crowd and gaining their whistles and applause. It all seemed completely empty now. And so he let it go.

The pilgrim now glanced at the fourth of the Beings, and then over at the baby-blue pool. Above it, a sadhu was walking along a trail in the mountains. His surroundings were rocky and barren of vegetation. The path on which he walked barefoot was strewn with sharp stones. Strong rays of the sun beat down on the wanderer. He carried only a danda, or staff, and a watering can. No home, hut, or traveler's hostel appeared on the horizon. No tree offered shade from the blistering sun. No birds flew by. No flowers scented the air. But Theo could hear the sadhu chanting the name of God, and could see that he remained blissfully happy, despite the bleak scene through which he passed. Who knew when he might find food or fresh water? Who could tell when he might meet another wanderer or a hospitable family? But none of that made any difference to the man. He spoke to God and smiled.

Now Theo had always been a soul apart, a black sheep in a herd of white. He had not simply heard a different drummer in his life, he had listened to another orchestra altogether. What had fascinated his peers had failed to interest him. The things he cared about, the visions and poems and bliss, never entered the minds of those he knew. But always he had cherished a desire deep down to have an intimate friend, at least one person with whom he could say anything, share any hope, express any doubt, without fear of being misunderstood or, worse, mocked for doing so. And he recalled the profound loneliness that had settled on him one evening when he listened to the singer's words, "And if you go, no one may follow. That path is for your steps alone." At that moment, he had realized that life is, by definition, a solitary voyage. But, deep inside, the faint wish had lingered: what if he could meet a kindred soul?

190

Seeing the sadhu's self-sufficient contentment burnt that faint remaining seed of desire. Theo knew that no one would ever come to keep his innermost thoughts company. But he could rest in peace, while still in the body, by living in the vastness of his interior Space.

The seeker sought out the fifth of the Beings, and then slowly moved his gaze to the baby-blue pool. Over its surface, yet another scene played out. A fakir, or magician, was engaged in the performance of remarkable feats. Out of thin air, he materialized a bellowing bull elephant. And then, with a wave of his hand, the fakir reduced this great beast to the size of a squirrel. He then produced an exact copy of himself, located it in the center of a ring, and caused its form to levitate. After the magician spoke some strange words, his floating doppelganger first became transparent, so that one could see the clouds behind him, and then dissolved into a dozen miniature forms of himself. It was all extremely fascinating. One wondered how the thaumaturge had ever managed to pull off such tricks.

The seeker immediately understood the message intended for him. Ever since childhood, he had been fascinated by the idea of superhuman powers. Most children outgrow this fantasy, but for him it had lingered. After years and years spent in meditation, he regularly asked himself, "When will something extraordinary occur?" He didn't want the powers so that he could show them off. He wanted them as proof that all his dedication to the spiritual life had yielded dividends, had produced some tangible benefit. But never had he enjoyed even the slightest spiritual marvel. Never had he lifted up off the ground or manifested a ripe mango. Miracles were not in his repertoire.

But now, by observing the fakir, he understood the shallowness of tricks and magic. Even had the "miracles" been real, what good would they have done? They would have inspired observers to pursue magical powers rather than Enlightenment, and the Master had told him all about the consequences of that mistake. And thus the buried desire to perform great feats withered and died in Theo's soul.

191

Only one Being remained for Theo to look at and now he did so; and then, immediately, turned his eyes toward the baby-blue pool. Hovering over that tender blue water were all six of the Beings. Whereas, when he had gazed upon them in their wall niches, the Beings had seemed identical, all Wisdom and Profound Peace and Perfect Contentment, now Theo noticed the uniqueness of each.

One showed a more ascetic face, which might have been rendered gaunt by austerities performed. A second projected a force and power that could have burned holes through the solid rock surrounding them all. A third revealed a childlike delight, something like what a boy frolicking through a spring meadow might display. A fourth sent out ripples of love, like an ocean constantly pouring forth waves upon the shore. A fifth could have been a starless night, so vast and peaceful did he seem. And the sixth appeared to contain within Himself all the wisdom that the world could ever know.

Then something very surprising happened. The faces of all the Beings began to switch from one body to another. At first, this happened slowly, but then, the pace sped up. Soon, they shifted rapidly, one head being now on one end and, a moment later, at the other. After several minutes, another change occurred: all the heads became identical. And this identical head possessed none of the characteristics of the Beings previously noted. Then the forms of the Beings grayed out to such a degree that they could no longer be distinguished from the background of rock. Then the Beings turned baby-blue and tilted back until they merged with the surface of the pool.

Theo looked over at the niches in the cave wall. All six Beings, now showing their individual peculiarities, occupied their respective spaces. But a glance at the pool showed them to be floating above it, all grayed-out and utterly identical.

In a flash, the scene reverted to what it had been before Theo's last vision. The undifferentiated Beings sat where they always had been, and the baby-blue pool contained nothing but water.

The seeker contemplated the message in this experience. He had always feared, deep down inside himself, that Enlightenment would destroy 'Theo Reyesin,' the person he had always known himself to be. If one merged into the Absolute, as, according to the Master and the holy texts, a Realized Being did, then one ceased to exist as a distinct entity. One would *Be* Everything, but by that Everything one's former identity had been wholly swallowed.

For years, he had sought to wrap his mind around this paradox of becoming who one really was by, in fact, disappearing as one had always known oneself to be. He had assured himself that such a change must be eminently desirable, as Saints waxed rapturous about it, but something about cutting the ties with the little self terrified Theo. The descriptions of Enlightenment made it seem as if one turned into something akin to Infinite Outer Space: a Vast, Eternal, Existence that knew nothing about what it had once been.

Pondering the recent vision, Theo got hold of its intent. The Beings were showing him, in various ways, that what he took to be their individuality was only a guise, a mask worn over the underlying Truth of Oneness. The masks could be easily interchanged and it made no difference. Unique appearances could exist side by side with Universal Uniformity. The Enlightened could *seem* like distinct people, as the Saint did to Theo, while actually Being Absolute, Undifferentiated, Pure Consciousness.

Tranquility settled over Theo's soul. He had finally made peace with his only doubt about the worth of Enlightenment, now seeing that the Bliss he had enjoyed during respites of Transcendence would be perpetually extended if he were to attain Realization. Who would miss the struggles and doubt of the small self, once One had come to Be

193

the Great Self? No wonder the Masters spoke so enthusiastically about the value of this rare attainment.

Theo now knew that the time had come for him to withdraw from the cavern. He prostrated before the Wise Beings and said silent thanks in his heart for the wisdom they had shown him. And then he crawled back out of the cave into the crepuscular half-light.

The sun would soon rise. Theo realized that he had spent an entire night in the cavern. What had seemed to take mere minutes had obviously spanned hours. He mounted the tallest rock on the small ledge where the Saint had left him and looked out. Oh, what a scene!

Clouds extended out to the horizon, rising and falling in gentle undulations like ocean waves on a day of light breezes. They hid, by their obscurity, the variable features of the valleys and hills that lay beneath them. The not-yet-visible sun sent out sentinel rays, gigantic, golden, cylindrical spotlights pointed at five directions of the firmament. These precursor beams turned the semicircular rim of Himalayan mountains into nondescript black silhouettes. The overall effect was of rendering the features of earth, which normally so fascinate people, blank, and transforming the stunning Himalayas into nothing more than backdrop for the scene about to be enacted.

A few moments later, a small lower lip of mountain on the horizon got doused with flame-yellow luminance. Eight more beams, these so yellow as to almost appear orange, now radiated out from that lip. Then the crown of the sun's head rose above the flame color, shining with that unbearable white that *is* the blinding sun. Soon, the entire round star rested on the tiny pedestal of that far mountain lip. The ocean of clouds changed color, becoming a soft pigeon blue. Stray clouds to the left of the sun were sprayed the pink of cotton candy. Forward of the mountain lip, the cloud waves melted into electroluminescence, deliquesced into fire-water, and transmuted into liquescent gas.

Now the sun so dominated the scene that nothing else even existed. It shone massive, all-powerful, vivifying, and spectacular. It was all there was, and yet it was not there, for, when one looked directly at it, the sun seemed not to exist, but to break up into trillions of minute photons racing out in every direction.

And as he stood, rapt, lost in the cosmic grandeur that was the sunrise, Theo understood its message. Pure Consciousness, like the rising sun, obliterated the details, and drastically diminished the importance of the everyday world. When the Absolute rose, everything else ceased to be of consequence. When that blinding Light shone, no shadowy object could possibly compete for One's attention.

Reunion

Theo turned away from the sunrise and saw his Master seated on a nearby rock. He, too, seemed to be watching the bravura of the newborn star. For a moment, the Saint looked as he usually did. But, after a few seconds, the disciple saw his Teacher transform into...the sun!

No longer could he make out any form whatsoever. Instead, there blazed the brightness of a red-giant star. Oddly, the brilliance of the light did not hurt Theo's eyes. He was able to stare at this new "sun" without ill effects. In it swirled millions of pulsations of luminous energy. In fact, the star reminded him of a gigantic dance of infinitesimal pulses, a great swirling jota, that Spanish folk dance performed in triple time. This sun looked just like the one that the seeker had just watched rising. He had to resist an urge to turn his head to make sure Apollo continued to sit in his sky.

From this proximate star, Theo felt a radiance of Absolute Peace and Utter Bliss. Its light soothed and tranquilized him. Its effulgence welcomed him, beckoning him in, prompting him to forget all else and merge with this orb of Perfect Being. He could only stand there, transfixed, awestruck by what he was experiencing.

And then the vision ended, and the Saint regained his wonted form. But no sparkle of hint showed in his eyes. He continued to look straight ahead, just as he had been before becoming the Sun.

"And how have you enjoyed your stay here?"

"Oh, Master! Where can I begin? What is freshest in my mind is what I just watched." Theo waited for an opening, but one did not come. "I mean seeing you in your full radiance, like a sun."

"Tell me what you discovered about this place."

"I discovered the cavern and the six Beings. And from each of them I learned a certain lesson, something important that I needed to know."

"And your final fear?"

"They taught me about that, too, Guruji. I have always been afraid of losing 'myself' if I merged into the Absolute. It seemed like drowning, like forgetting the single most important thing you ever needed to remember. But the Beings taught me that Enlightenment does not allow for any regrets. The Bliss of Pure Consciousness leaves no room for a sense of loss. The small ego is an illusion, a sort of selling-oneself-short, which has to go. And so that last fear left me."

"Good, good."

"May I ask who those Beings are, Master?"

"They are six Eternal Ones. They maintain their bodies by absorbing elements directly from the air. That is their form of 'eating.' They have mastery of all siddhis. They can easily become invisible, move to any place in the universe, travel instantaneously, all those things. They are a reservoir of Wisdom for the human race, preserving the knowledge of the Rishis even in this ignorant age in which we live. You are fortunate to have been allowed to see them."

They stood up and began the walk back toward the cave. Neither spoke. Theo had a great deal to think about. What the past twenty-four hours had shown him!

I Wonder Why?

That night Theo felt the urge to ask his Master some questions that he still had about ignorance and Enlightenment.

"Master, there is so much suffering in the world. Everywhere one turns there are wars and killings, diseases and injuries, heartbreaks and loneliness. Why must people go through all this pain, when Enlightenment is their natural state?"

"Bliss is only in the Infinite, and sorrow is only in the finite. Because avidya, ignorance, obscures the Infinite, people believe themselves to be bodies, mind, and egos, when, in truth, these are all delusions. They are actually nothing but Pure Consciousness. But karma has built up over innumerable lifetimes, one cannot say where it all began, and this karma is intimately tied in with desire and aversion. Someone loves something, and grows attached to it. And he hates something else, and develops a strong repulsion to it. These tendencies play out in future actions. He seeks to gain more of what he desires and to fly away from what he despises. The cycle is thus set, and the habits engendered by it perpetuate the man's ignorance."

"And suffering is just an inevitable part of that ignorance?"

"Suffering plays a role in spiritual evolution. It reminds people to seek Spirit. One always hears about the mother praying hardest when her daughter is sick, or the businessman who began to recite the name of the Lord when his fortune was threatened. Overwhelming sorrow shows the sufferer that the only way out is through the Spirit. The Bliss of the Self never abandons you, no matter what is happening in the external world. The Peace of Pure Consciousness is always there inside, even if the battle is raging all around one's body. Suffering should not be viewed as solely negative. If everything were to proceed smoothly in life, most people would never even bother to pursue Enlightenment."

"The misery reminds them that there must be something better."

198

"Yes, something that provides a complete break from all the pain and sadness of life in the body. Who wants to put up with the illness and grief and, eventually, death that come inevitably with corporal existence? Everyone has had flashes of Perfect Peace, and they are drawn back toward it whenever the pain of daily life grows too hard to bear."

"So, Guruji, the paradox is that the pursuit of true happiness is accelerated by the experience of misery."

"Best not to think of it as one unreal experience being better than another. They are all necessary and occur strictly according to the karma of the individual. But you asked why people must go through suffering, and the answer is that it, too, serves an evolutionary purpose. It is harder for a millionaire to get interested in spirituality than for a poor laborer. The former has been taught that he has access to all the best sources of happiness, while the latter knows that he has very little of that precious substance."

"Is that why the Bible says it is hard for a rich man to get to heaven?"

"Yes. The rich think only of gaining more wealth. They are convinced that in money lies happiness. The father may rarely see his children because he is so busy making more money. The mother may give her child to someone else to care for, so that she can enjoy the money she possesses. Where is the time for or interest in meditating? Where is the suffering that might prompt an inward look into the soul?"

"Be careful what you wish for?"

"Indeed. If you place all your hopes for happiness in external things, you will never be blessed with the Bliss of Pure Consciousness. One who does not have all this gold and all these houses and cars, one who struggles and suffers to get by, is more likely to turn toward the Self in search of what they yearn for."

"The rich seem so selfish, Master. Think of all the good they could do for others if they wished to."

"'Concern yourself with your own progress. Thinking about the faults of others only soils oneself."

Theo felt chastened and took several minutes before speaking again. When he did so, he asked, "I was also wondering about prarabdha karma, Master. You have talked about it as the karma that is already in progress before a Realized Being gains Realization. You said that Anandaji would keep his body so long as his prarabdha remained." He glanced at the Teacher, who was looking into space. "My question is why such a Being should no longer be affected by this karma."

"The Enlightened One does not see himself as a body or mind; therefore, the prarabdha has no delivery location for its effects. This has been discussed already. Others may see a 'body' that gets sick, because of this karma, but the Enlightened One perceives no connection between that form and Himself. He is the Absolute, while the body, which others think of as 'his,' is strictly relative.

"Even before Realization, the more one turns the mind toward the Self, the less susceptible one is to prarabdha karma. One begins to transcend one's destiny as one gets close to Realization."

Theo wondered: "Because one is less convinced of one's identity with the ego and the body?"

"Yes, the more familiar one becomes with the Self, the less one identifies with the body and mind. And they are the 'address' for the karmic delivery. Remember that kama, desire, and karma, action, lead directly to objective consciousness. Desire prompts one to take action. Action and desire both require a world of separate subject and object. The actor believes that some 'thing' lies 'out there,' and proceeds to go get it. This is why the texts encourage the seeker to diminish desires

200

and spend as much time as possible looking inward rather than externally. What one practices becomes a habit, after all."

"And the knowledge of the texts is important, for you have said that knowledge and experience go hand in hand."

"The material of life is woven from the woof of devotion and the weft of knowledge. Without devotion, one will never persist in the search to find one's True Self. And without knowledge, one will know neither how to go about this search nor what to make of what one finds on its path."

"I have a question about reincarnation, Master." The Saint did not look pleased.

"Pay attention to this life and ask about the next one if it comes."

Theo looked sheepish, but persisted. "If you would indulge me, Guruji, just to ease my curiosity. I was wondering how the soul actually gets a new body."

"The soul takes fine particles of the gross elements with it as it passes out of the body. The organs—remember that the organs are actually subtle, not the gross ones like nose and mouth—also travel with the soul. Together, these enable the soul to bring with it the seeds of the new body it will require, in order to continue to work out its karma."

"And the parents' contribution to the new soul?"

"The prana, or life breath, in the egg and sperm guide the development of the fetus according to the karma it has carried with it into the new lifetime. But why do you continue to think about matters that have nothing to do with your own evolution? Enlightenment is not a course at school, in which one needs to memorize facts and key examples. It would be better for you to spend your time in meditation or in reading the holy texts. Being caught up in the mind perpetuates the delusion that One *is* mind. But mind is..." He paused pregnantly.

"Nothing but a collection of thoughts. If the thoughts die, so does the mind."

"So by continuing to encourage thinking..."

"I am keeping the mind alive and strong. I see, Master, I do see."

More Questions

The next morning, following his meditation, Theo left the cave and found his Master seated on a rock above the stream that ran close to the cave. That day, the water barely moved at all: one had to look carefully to note the slow progress of a twig borne on its surface, destined for the great Ganges and eventually the Bay of Bengal. The water had the color of an aquamarine gemstone, that tranquilizing grayish turquoise shade which harmonized so perfectly with the whitish gray of the rocks and stones lining the banks.

A numinous air surrounded the Saint. Theo felt that anything gross would constitute a disturbance of the atmosphere of grace emanating from his Teacher. He sat down at his feet as quietly as possible. Neither of them spoke for a long time.

Finally, the rajasic energy that remained within the student prompted him, albeit in the softest of voice, to break the silence. "Master, you have told me about the dangers of attachment, and yet you have praised the power of love. I am confused. Isn't attachment the very essence of love?"

"Attachment leads to bondage and love, to freedom. Attachment causes possessiveness. One wants to control the objects or persons one is attached to. This is easy to see in jealousy between husband and wife or in greed concerning one's material possessions. Such efforts to control lead to tension with others and mental disturbance. One becomes selfish and the cycle turns vicious."

"I see all that, Guruji, but how does one square it with love?"

"Love is not selfish. Selfish love is not really love, but infatuation. Infatuation produces misery. One is all the time worrying about losing the person or object one is attached to. Love yields peace and harmony. Genuine love does not require anything from the beloved. On the contrary, it accepts them for who they are and works to help them become all they might be.

"Love is natural to One who Exists in the Self. The Self is All Love. Everyone the Self deals with, everything It touches, receives Love spontaneously, just as one gets wet touching water. There need be no effort. The Love is just there to be shared with all. As detachment increases, so does love for God. Maya is itself rooted in attachment. All are connected: break attachments to get beyond maya. Get beyond maya to find the Self. Find the Self to discover All-Encompassing Love."

Theo responded. "And someone who is not acting from the level of the Self will not be able to freely give such Love?"

"Correct. If the mind is involved, then attachment creeps in. The mind, remember, only works in a dualistic world: *here* you are and *there* is the person or thing you desire. With the separation inherent in duality arises the need to possess and hold. That *is* attachment."

"So you are saying, Master, that personal love is not for the Enlightened."

"For the Enlightened there is no 'person,' so how can there be 'personal' anything? You are not that body and that ego. You are the Infinite Self. Once you realize that Truth, where is the person to be found to initiate personal love?"

"So, it's more of a generalized Love for everything."

"There are no 'things.' There is only Pure Consciousness. Once the Love that is the Self is known, then what you call 'everything' gets subsumed within it. You are making the mistake of considering the situation of the Enlightened from the perspective of the ignorant."

"Sorry, I *was* doing that. I forgot that to the Realized what appears to others as the background of Silence has become the foreground; what were separate 'things' are then only ripples on the stream of Pure Consciousness."

"Since All is One, the question of loving some but not others cannot arise. Love exists for the Realized as the ground state of All

204

that He sees. The Ocean remains the Ocean whether its surface shows waves or not."

Theo continued his questioning. "But if one is unattached how can one care about anything? I have seen you care about the villagers and their homes, Master."

"Non-attachment does not mean indifference. The Enlightened Being will spontaneously assist those in need, however and whenever it is appropriate. He does not have to be attached to those he helps. In fact, non-attachment will make his efforts vastly more successful, as they will come from the Source of all the laws of nature, the Self. Remember that you attain Freedom by mastering your desires, not by fleeing your duties. One does not need to renounce *action*, but only the *fruit* of action."

"You mean that one can still work in the world, so long as one does not become caught up in the results of one's work."

"Yes, see the work, do the work, stay out of the misery. Humility is very important. The ego is an immense obstacle to be overcome. If one swells up, thinking, 'Look what I have accomplished!' the benefit of the deed is lost. Perform righteous action automatically, without reflecting that it is 'you' who are doing it. After all, it is not."

It was lunchtime, so Theo went off into the bushes nearby and picked some blackberries, which he brought back and offered to his teacher on a leaf-plate. They remained quiet for a while.

"At first I thought that the experience in the cavern with the Eternal Ones had gotten rid of my final fear of losing myself in Enlightenment. But now I wonder if there are not other fears lurking deep inside my soul."

"Fear is the greatest foe. From fear comes danger. You have heard the comments about fear, that it is possible only when one thinks himself separate and apart from others, when there a subject-object world is imagined. Develop a comfort level with Being, and that sense of separation will gradually dissolve. Once it leaves, it takes fear with it."

"And that is one of the most difficult things to imagine, Master: being able to see no separation between oneself and others. I get glimpses of it, certainly, during meditation sometimes, but it's hard to conceive of experiencing that with my eyes open."

The Saint pointed to the stream. "What do you see there?"

"A lovely, slow-moving stream."

"And there?"

"The Himalayan range."

"Look again."

Theo turned his eyes back to the aquamarine stream. But, to his astonishment, the water had turned into a fluent curve of Light. Not sunlight. Not moonlight. But Light! Light supernal! This Light was what he often saw surrounding the body of his Teacher. It belonged to another, better world, not to this terrestrial one. In it lay Bliss and Peace. It moved without moving. It sang without breaking Its own Silence.

Then he switched his gaze to the far mountains. And they, too, were nothing but Light. Like the stream, they had the shape of mountains, but, also like the stream, they pulsed with nothing but vital Light. They seemed to breathe Light. They shimmered in the soft radiance of this Light.

Theo, having been transported to a place of pure Spirit, looked all around him, where there had formerly been trees and bushes, rock, stones, and boulders. All now gleamed with Light! Heavy boulders looked as weightless as dust. Thick trees appeared as if they might, at any moment, simply float away. And then he caught sight of a thrush. The bird was singing with joyous celebration. Theo felt an uprush of supreme tenderness. The bird was the most precious creature in the

206

world; its song, the most beautiful. Its breast swelled with expanding Light. Its throat gurgled with vibrational Light. Its feathers ruffled with twitching Light.

As Theo observed this wonderful new world, he got a glimpse of Enlightenment. Enlightenment, he now saw, was *literally* a state of Light, rapturous, tenderest Light! It was a state of mergence with other creatures and objects, such that one felt at One with them all. Above all, It was an Awareness of the Unity of everything: nothing was separate, nothing apart.

Streamside Once More

The following day, the two men were again seated by the stream. The water looked just as it had before. Neither had the mountains changed in the least.

"Is it still so hard to conceive of the absence of separation of knower and known?" asked the Saint, a faint smile on his face.

"How can I ever thank you, Guruji, for such an experience, in fact, for all that you have done for me throughout my life? No, my doubt got dissolved in Light. I could never have imagined such an experience had you not blessed me with it."

"But you *still* have questions. You are the most curious soul I have ever come across."

"I read about chakras. I know that they are subtle energy centers. But I can't figure out whether they are really metaphors or actual things."

"Think what you are about! Again, you focus on the body, which is, as you as you have been repeatedly shown, nothing but the Self. You have read that, in order to be Realized, one needs to coax the kundalini up the spine/sushumna to the thousand-petaled lotus at the top of the skull. After all you have learned, does it seem correct to you that Enlightenment is to be gained by working on the level of the body?"

"No, sir."

"The Self is Everything. It is in 'you' all the time. Where is the need to go seeking it? The body is a creation of the mind, which, in turn, is nothing but thoughts churned up by samskaras, the impressions of your past karma. When you come to exist in the Self, all sorts of changes may happen to the body. Energy may rise. Visions may be seen. Sounds may be heard. Perfumes may be smelled. But

You will not care. For You will be established in Unchanging Pure Consciousness."

"I only wondered about the chakras out of general curiosity."

"To satisfy it, you will understand that they work on the physical, physiological, energetic, mental, and spiritual levels. Depending on the degree to which a soul has evolved spiritually, its chakras are open in one place or another and to varying degrees. Spiritual evolution carries the soul up from having as one's primary concern bodily survival, on to sexual fascination, and a focus on the use of power in relation to the world. Love, creativity, communication, intuition, and, finally, Enlightenment follow."

"But, as you implied, this is not a purely sequential process."

"No, one may, for instance, have a relatively open heart, while still dealing with survival fears. But so long as there are blockages, what have been previously discussed as vasanas, those ingrained tendencies people have, then Realization does not come."

"But I shouldn't be concerned with chakras."

"Forget the body entirely. Other than feeding it with light and healthy food, giving it sufficient rest, and curing it if it falls sick, one should ignore the body. Meditate and trust to nature to alter the body as it sees fit."

"The other question I had related to astrology, Guruji. I have heard you say that everything that happens in one's life is destined to happen exactly as it does. Astrology maintains that this is true, and that the arrangement of stars and planets at the time of one's birth indicates this destiny. But logic argues against this position."

"Again, nothing with which you need be concerned. But if you *must* know, astrology is a channel through which karmic energy flows. There are innumerable metaphors for describing the condition of a soul as it enters each lifetime. Astrology is one of these. By meditating, one transcends the material influence altogether. Then, the 'stars' cannot affect one. Remember, karma cannot be delivered when the recipient has left his last known address in the body."

"But the body is always there, Master. The Realized One may not relate to it as his own, but it is still *there*. He wouldn't be living without it, right?"

The Saint stretched out his arm and lightly touched Theo on the chest, in the area of the heart. Instantaneously, the disciple was aware of his heart stopping! He could "hear" it not beating, and the absence of sound terrified him. Instinctively, he felt for his pulse, at wrist and neck, and found none. He directed a pleading look at his Teacher, but He was calmly looking out toward the distant mountains.

The fear passed as quickly as it had come. Theo closed his eyes and sank into deep meditation. There was only Stillness and Peace.

After some time, he opened his eyes. His heart was still not beating. The Master turned and touched his chest again, and the precious pump began, once more, to do its work.

Theo mused on what this lesson meant. He had just been arguing that the body was essential to life, when the Saint stopped his heart. So the Teacher must have wished to show him that Life went on, no matter what the body was, or in this case was *not*, doing. But how had he managed to stay conscious, even stay alive, without a functioning heart? He could only attribute this event to another of his Master's miracles. Surely, he had been meant to see that Spirit, not body, was all that truly mattered.

As they walked back toward the cave, the Saint asked him, "Are you still filled with questions?"

Theo took a moment to consider the matter. "No, Guruji, I can honestly say I am not. You have thoroughly explained spiritual matters, and even been kind enough to indulge me regarding questions that were a little off the topic. I feel confident now that my understanding is complete."

"Let's test it then. What are You?"

"I am nothing but Pure Consciousness."

"And what is your body and mind?"

"My body is a production of my mind, which, in turn, is nothing but thoughts and feelings."

"And what is the world?"

"The world is a projection of my karma, a play of maya, the deceiver. It is the waves on the Ocean of Being.,"

"What keeps one from Realizing the Self?"

"The Self is always Present as one's innermost Reality, one's True Identity, but the delusion of the ego prompts the individual to consider himself limited and separate from the world. He comes to believe in a knower, himself; a process of knowing, through his senses and mind; and an object to be known, outside of himself."

"And what will One Be after all this useless paraphernalia is junked?"

"The Self, pure and simple. One will sit at home in the Absolute, at One with everything."

And so the lesson ended.

Inward

For the next week, Theo was instructed by his Master to spend day and night meditating. He would close his eyes and spend two hours in profound Silence, and then open them once again. They would eat their simple meals, still delivered mysteriously in the night by the locals, take short walks, and exchange a few remarks about trivial matters such as the weather or the cloudscape.

The Saint taught his student a new mantra, one that, he explained, had been given to Him by His Teacher, and told him to use it in all future meditations.

It struck Theo that the Master, who had always looked more like Spirit than body, was daily moving further in the direction of Spirit. His bodily outline looked vaguer somehow; his beard, more like a cloud than a cluster of hair; and his face, something like a vision or a dream. Theo asked himself if he might be imagining all this. After all, the Saint moved about with the same facility as he always had, and his energy was still abundant. But yet He seemed different.

The long meditation sessions had an effect on the disciple. More and more easily, he slipped into the deep Silence of Self and rested There without the disturbance of thoughts or feelings. The Master's aura had always been conducive to such settling, but now Theo found that he had reached a new stage of concentration, one characterized by a sort of rock-solid steadiness and deep, oceanic Calmness.

And when he emerged from these long sessions, the world looked different. It was difficult for him to put the feeling into words, but the difference had something to do with perceiving the Stillness behind nature's movement. The trees branches might be shivering in the wind, but he noticed their steady attachment to the trunk. The squirrels might be darting here and there, but he remarked their motionlessness. The sky might be filled with drifting blimps of cumulus, but he observed the calm black heavens across which they sailed.

He carried over some of what he experienced in meditation into waking consciousness. There was still a clear distinction between the two, of course, but the latter now partook of many of the characteristics of the former. The "world" seemed more intimate, less "out there" and more "in here." It revealed its inner depth, its inner ataraxia or quietude, its inner joy. The great "background" of the world began to move forward and assert itself. The noise and changes, the colors and varieties, though still apparent, now seemed less important than what lay behind them.

Theo wondered if all these changes were only the temporary effect of prolonged mediation, akin to what he had experienced earlier in life during his teacher-training sessions. But intuition told him "no." This was different, more fundamental. Whereas, formerly, he had left transcendence behind in his meditations when he ventured forth into the world, now he was carrying it *with* him into the world, and finding that world steeped in the Beauty of Inner Space.

His interactions with the Master had changed too. The Saint spoke less often and spent far more time in Silence, eyes closed. Theo believed that, having gotten all his questions answered, he was likely now seen by the Teacher as requiring less direct training than he formerly had. And the student knew that the time the two spent in Silent communion was even more efficacious for his spiritual evolution than explicit teaching. Silence, after all, as the Saint had often showed him, *was* the lesson.

Everything moved in a new direction, a pristine and austere one. Theo felt as though, for him, the world of Spirit had now overtaken that of substance. He had begun to join his Master in the dwelling of the Consciousness-Universe. It all seemed a bit weird to him. The ingrained patterns of many lifetimes are not easy to change. The habit of identifying as a body is not simply broken. The seeker noticed himself passing from one world to another, almost as if he were stepping across a fairy-tale threshold into a magical kingdom where all the accepted rules no longer applied.

During his long meditations, Theo experienced huge uprushes of gratitude to his Teacher. What love the Saint had shown him by watching over his progress all through the years! What care he had demonstrated, calling the American across the ocean so that he might find his way to this cave! Teachers like him had nothing to gain from what they did for their disciples. They were already Enlightened. But they acted out of a sweet and almost maternal love. They protected their spiritual charges as diligently as a good mother did her vulnerable toddler. The nourishment they provided was wisdom, more truly essential than even the food cooked by the mother. They tolerated the whims and disobediences of their students with the patience and forgiving heart of a caressing parent.

Theo realized now the value of all that the Saint had done for him. Without his guidance, the path to the goal would have been incomparably longer and more painful. Souls living in ignorance suffer. They suffer in birth and in infancy, from sickness and infatuation, from aspirations and failures, from dreams unrealized and realized dreams that never measure up to expectations. Such souls are always either subtly or overtly seeking Bliss, but never finding it, for they look outside of themselves, to the illusory world, where nothing truly worthwhile is ever to be found.

Death came for those in ignorance and then the same struggling life began again, the cycle repeating thousands and thousands of times. How many heartbreaks, how much torturous pain, how many fractured aspirations would have to be endlessly suffered before Realization came to free the soul?

And the chances that one would find a Teacher such as he enjoyed to guide one through the maze were next to nil. Yes, he was a lucky man! Destiny required this good fortune, he reminded himself. He must have done much good in other lifetimes to merit such a mentor. But just deserts or not, Theo thanked the Saint from the depths of his heart for all that he had done for him.

A quiet hint of intuition told the seeker that an important phase of his teaching was now ending. Maybe the Saint would send him home. Or possibly he would require him to head off and find a cave of his own to continue his inner exploration. But something major was about to occur. He sensed that much.

Important Words

After several weeks of these intense and lengthy meditations, Theo was surprised one morning to see the Saint rise and lead him out to their favorite place on the banks of the aquamarine stream.

"You have learned much since coming here. Your curiosity has been subdued. It is obvious that you are comfortable spending much of your time in meditation. How are these sessions going?"

"Very well, Master. I find that whereas formerly I could only sit in Absolute Silence for short periods, now I remain there for long ones. No doubt your close presence has this effect."

"And the outside world?"

Theo glanced around him at the burbling stream, the spindrift clouds, and the rustling trees. "It has changed, too. The outer world seems now to have more of the quality of the inner. Its Silence is more audible; its Infinite expanse, more visible. The Absolute is starting to shine out from behind the relative."

"But you still think of yourself as separate from it?"

"Yes, I have to admit that while there is a closeness, I do not yet feel that Oneness with the world that you have talked about so eloquently. I do feel more intimate with it, as though I know we share a deep affinity, but I can't honestly say that I am One with it."

The Saint remained Silent.

"And what do you need to do to bridge that gap?"

"Meditate more?" The Saint remained Silent. "Just allow Pure Consciousness to seep into my awareness. I think it will gradually happen over time as I continue to meditate." Theo took his teacher's Silence as implicit agreement.

Finally, the Master asked, "Any fears remaining?"

Theo paused to examine himself closely. He wanted this answer to be completely honest. "No fears, Guruji. I think my biggest one was losing myself in the Absolute. And the Great Beings helped me get rid of that one. I no longer fear damage or sickness in the body, which used to scare me. I lost my fear of death a long time ago, when I came to understand reincarnation. So, I would say none of that is left."

"What will you do with the remainder of your life?"

This question surprised Theo. The Teacher did not normally ask him such personal questions. "I really don't know, other than do everything possible to attain Enlightenment. That will be my sole focus, naturally. But how I will spend the hours of the day not consumed by meditation, I don't know."

"Trust your intuition."

"Yes, I am sure it and You will always guide me."

"Don't rely on anyone other than your Self. The more you live in the Self, the more dependable your intuition will be. Aligned with the laws of nature, you will spontaneously do what is right in every situation."

Theo began to get concerned. The Master's tone carried in it something of farewell. The Holy Being stared at the distant mountains, almost as if he himself were out there, far away. What Theo had been noticing for some time, the fading out of the physical sense of the Teacher, now looked quite pronounced. His body seemed made of gauze or cotton fibers. His beard blended into the air around it. And his aura of shimmering light spread wider than the student had ever seen it.

For the first time ever, the Saint, continuing to stare out into space, spoke to him with personal affection. "You have been a spiritual son to me. I adopted you long ago, in another place, at another time. It has been my mission to watch over your growth, so that you might attain Freedom as soon as you possibly could.

217

"You have pleased me. It is good that you came here and that you have followed instructions, not only from me, but from the others you met. Since you know that we are not bodies, you are also aware that I can never be lost to you. Where can One go, when One is Everywhere?"

Theo wanted to speak, to thank his Master, to explain how much he still had to learn. But he never got the chance. At that moment, the Saint's body rose off the rock on which it had been seated and floated out over the water. It turned to face Theo. The right hand rose up, palm forward, in valediction. And slowly, but steadily, the body dissolved into sparkles of brilliant Light, until, finally, there was nothing left.

What Now?

Everything had happened so fast that Theo could not even begin to make sense of it all. His Master had given no explicit warning about leaving the body. Yes, Theo had noticed the progressively less physical nature of the Saint, but that alone had not been enough to prepare him for the shock of losing him entirely.

But the moment he heard that phrase in his head, he reminded himself of the Master's last words, "I can never be lost to you. Where can One go, when One is Everywhere?" Intellectually knowing this was not, however, the same as making peace with it emotionally. The Teacher had been everything to him: his instructor, his guide, and his example. What would he do now?

Theo recalled the Saint asking him that question. And he had responded that he would seek Enlightenment. But that goal was great, and the steps to be taken to reach it were unknown. No, he couldn't really say that. He knew that the goal required steadfast meditation, pure living, light eating, and reading of the holy texts. Associating with the Realized was vital as well. Yet one could do most of these things anywhere in the world.

And he had his children to think about. True, they were adults now and busy leading their own lives, but he could still play a role, albeit a small one, in their lives. Would he ever be able to attain the great goal if he returned to the hyper-speed craziness that characterized modern American society? Wouldn't he serve his children best by progressing as far down the path as he could, even if such progress required him to live on the other side of the world?

These and related questions occupied Theo as he made his way back to the cave. The cave was utterly filled with the blissful spiritual presence of the Saint who no longer occupied it. In his honor, the seeker sat down and began to meditate, using the mantra the Master had lately given him. He remembered that the mantra had been given to the Master by his own Guru.

When he finally opened his eyes again, Theo was stunned. The sound of the mantra reverberated through the cave. The walls, floor, and ceiling of the space were reciting the mantra out loud. Dumb nature had been given a voice!

Meditation had, as it always did, clarified Theo's mind. He decided to remain in the cave until a plan presented itself. His first question regarded food: would the locals continue to supply him with goat's milk and chickpeas, now that the Saint was no longer there? He didn't worry, though, trusting that whatever was meant to be *would* be.

When he emerged from his morning meditation ritual the next day, and exited the cave, Theo was pleased to see that the milk and gram sat near the entrance, just as they always did. He whispered a silent prayer of thanksgiving to the generous villagers, who, by now, certainly knew what had happened by the stream.

As he slowly walked down toward it, Theo looked around him at the glorious Himalayan morning. A tiny bushchat bird, whose ruffled head made it seem as if its owner had just risen from bed, sat atop a dead tree stem, like an architectural finial. Slanting sun beams, the breadth of giant tree trunks, highlighted portions of the mountains to his left. Distant mountains possessed that otherworldly look one often sees in Maxfield Parrish paintings. A nearby hill covered in brown lichens resembled the head of a gargantuan buffalo.

Although he noticed all these particularities, Theo mainly sensed the Oneness that underlay them. It seemed as if some of the spiritual power of the Saint had been transferred to him after the Great Being had left His body. For a knob controlling the vibrational background of Spirit had now been turned way up. The scenery tingled with Spiritual energy and shivered with Spiritual vitality. He could see the canvas behind the painting of these lovely scenes of nature. The

Absolute's hand could be perceived as It held the creation balanced on Its palm.

Theo thought of it all as a sort of cosmic trick. Yes, the world appearance was there; one could plainly see it. But no, the appearance was not the Reality. Behind the painting rested the great canvas, the Infinite Being of which all nature was merely an apparent perturbation.

Ideas began to come to him full-formed, almost as though he were not "thinking" them, but simply "knowing" them. The first was that the Saint had remained in his body, probably longer than he otherwise might have, in order to lead his student as far as possible down the path to Realization. The Master had methodically introduced him to Anandaji Shivaji, Babaji, and the Great Beings so that he could learn from them the lessons they had to teach.

The second idea was that the Holy One wished him to remain, at least for some time, in the cave where they had spent time together. Theo somehow understood that such residence would serve as a sort of spiritual wake for the Saint, while simultaneously allowing the seeker to bask in his radiance, which continued to brighten the cave.

The last idea Theo had was that he would need to stay in the Himalayas for an indefinite period of time, if not until his physical death. He realized that the natural beauty of the mountains was matched by their spiritual purity. Many reclusive Saints had lived and continued to live here. Whether he sat in their bodily presence or not, he partook of their spiritual communion simply by being in this sacred region.

Theo was surprised that he did not feel a greater sense of loss at the absence of his Teacher's corporal presence. But he knew that this equanimity was a consequence of two facts: one, he had matured spiritually into great steadiness; emotions hardly ever jolted him now; and two, the Saint, as he himself had explained, could never really "go" anywhere. He *was* Consciousness, not a sliver of Consciousness, not a portion of Consciousness, but Consciousness Itself. Therefore, in truth, he remained just where he had always been. The physical shell had value when dealing with those in ignorance, who misunderstood what the Realized truly were, but it had far less significance for anyone approaching the correct understanding of the Truth.

Theo now questioned himself regarding his daily regimen. The Master had not laid down a set plan for him; rather, he had indicated that he ought to trust his intuition. So he decided to continue as he had been: eating the donated food, meditating for prolonged periods several times a day, taking walks by the stream and in the woods, and doing yoga exercises to keep his body fit.

He had brought with him *Yoga Vashistha*, one of the best of the holy texts, which he would read from daily, in an attempt to use its wisdom as a substitute for that of the oral instructions he had been in the habit of receiving from his Teacher.

Beyond this plan, he foresaw nothing. Nature and destiny would provide for him as they saw fit.

Solitary Unconfinement

And so daily life proceeded, much as it had when the Saint had sat in the special spot Theo now considered sacrosanct. He would rise and do his yogic asanas, perform his pranayama, or breathing exercises, and then begin to meditate. Usually, his morning session would extend to about two hours. Once done meditating, he would leave the cave and always be grateful and pleased to see the jug of goat's milk and the bowl of chickpeas tucked under its protective ledge. Then he would sit outside to enjoy his light but nourishing breakfast.

Theo liked to take a long walk after this meal. He would set out in one direction or another, it made no difference which, and glory in the beauty of the Himalayas. He would marvel at the rich scent of the cypress trees and at the browns and purples of the granite rock faces. Sometimes he saw pheasants blue as the sky above and often he watched as lizards darted across the trail and thrushes and exotically colored butterflies flitted from branch to branch and bush to bush.

Twice he encountered some of the villagers whom he had met during the crisis of the flood. They were leading their mountain ponies, whose harness bells sang gaily to the morning, along the narrow path leading from their village to the neighboring one. Monsoon season was approaching, and landslides would render travel dangerous, so the villagers were stocking up on the few necessities their scant money and barterable goods would buy.

Theo had picked up a fair amount of Hindi, which allowed the villagers shyly to commiserate with him over the loss of his Guru. They were obviously curious if he would immediately return to his homeland, and were surprised, to say the least, when he informed them that he planned to stay on indefinitely. They then painted a bleak picture of cave life during the monsoon season.

"No one will be able to deliver your food!"

"You will catch a fever if you get soaked and then sleep in that cold cave!"

"If you attempt to go out in the monsoon, you will be swept off the mountain like that" and the fellow snapped his fingers.

The seeker listened politely and acknowledged all their concerns. But he also made it clear that his mind could not be changed. He was determined to say and survive as best he could.

But their fears about being able to reach the cave to deliver him food did impress Theo. One day he went down to the village and purchased some grains, dried vegetables, and dried fruits that would tide him over in the event of an emergency. As he did so, he asked himself if, by doing this, he was distrusting the support of nature his Master had so often emphasized. Most likely he was, but then he was not yet Realized, and could not count on the same bounty from nature that someone like his Teacher could.

At the same time, he also acquired a couple of large, heavy tarps. The village men had explained to him that the rain of the monsoons was one thing, but the winds associated with them quite another. If he did not effectively block off the opening to the cave, they said, the wind would blow so much rain into it as to make it unlivable.

And he acted just in time, for the rains began two days later. Theo had never experienced a monsoon, so he was unprepared for its incessancy and volume. There would be stretches of hours during which an ocean seemed to be in the process of being emptied on the mountains. Then the massive volume of rain would decrease, and a moderate but steady fall would last for half a day. Breaks would come, when the thick blankets of nimbostratus temporarily separated, and the sky would remain dim in gray or rust colors. But, before long, the duvets of sodden clouds would regather and begin to drop their loads on the rocks, trees, bushes, and grasses of the Himalayas.

Theo had stored a load of firewood and kindling in the cave, but knew that it would not last him for more than a week. During a letup in the downpour, he would have to seek new fuel, bring it back to the protected cave, and dry it out near the fire. The tarps worked well. He had placed them one behind the other as a double protection, securing them at their corners with heavy rocks. When the winds rose, as they did several times during that first week, the canvas flapped and puckered; the seeker wondered whether it would hold against such forceful gusts. Luckily, the cave had a leeward orientation, so it did not have to face the full brunt of the mountain winds. But the tarpaulins shivered so energetically that Theo sent up a silent prayer to the Saint that they might hold. Otherwise, the wind would drive in the rain, douse the fire, wet the food and supplies, and reduce the floor of the cave to a quagmire.

The food deliveries became intermittent. But Theo was filled with gratitude whenever they did arrive. Imagine, he thought, the devotion of villagers to risk their lives coming up here in this weather, for someone they had not even known four months earlier.

He tried to use his wood sparingly, in order to eke it out. His meditations grew longer and, hence, deeper. By remaining in meditation, he generated internal warmth that allowed him to go longer without a fire.

Every night he would hear the landslides gargling from near and far. Small ones sounded like children throwing gravel; large ones like the demolition of some great medieval cathedral. Outside the cave, the paths had disappeared under layers of mud, wrenched-off twigs and branches, and whole bushes. The flanks of the mountains shone slick and sleek. Small waterfalls appeared where none had existed before. Old waterfalls transformed into torrents. The stream crested its banks, and turned the surrounding area into a lagoon. The water in the stream raced furiously forward, threatening anyone unlucky enough to fall into it with quick death.

The various creatures of the forest had gone to roost and were nowhere to be seen. The cypresses, oaks, and firs steadily dripped water to the ground. Puddles abounded. Every rock surface, being wet and often coated with slippery mud, proved dangerous to stand on. Theo found himself walking like a frail old man: planting each foot carefully, and testing it before moving the other.

The skies presented an ever-changing panorama of cloud. Muscled comic-book monsters of grayish-blue would rise up over a ridge. Cat-headed monstrosities in lighter lupine blue floated over to challenge them. Schools of swordfish clouds swam horizontally across the firmament. Crocodile shapes opened their toothed jaws to swallow some wispy ones. Once there appeared a tripartite cloud whose bottom third, empurpled, resembled a shark; whose middle third, pearl-gray, looked like a Greek acanthus leaf; and whose upper third, meringue-colored, shone like twin icebergs caught by the glare of the noontime rays.

The sky seemed to be constantly at war now. Its cannon would thunder and its rifle fire crack. Ranks of nebular vehicles raced forward; explosions flashed all around them. Armies would meet and clash and then the welkin would be left with the detritus of battle: shreds of cloud, immense bruises, disabled tanks, and torn forests. Fury would flare and later subside. Skirmishes would be countered and neutralized. Torrential downpours would drown the fight to a halt. Brief amnesties would end in renewed carnage. White flags waved surrender, but the enemy ignored them and surged violently forward.

Theo had found a protected spot, under a ledge of rock, where he could observe all this firmamental madness without getting drenched. He marveled at the creative powers and magnificent forces of nature. Then, during a respite in the fight, he would step carefully back into the womb of his cave and begin another long session of meditation.

An Experience

At the end of the second week of the monsoon, Theo sat deep in the Silence of the Absolute when something extraordinary occurred. Something told him to open his eyes and he did. In the back of the cave stood an angel, an angel very much like what angels were supposed to be. This one stood as high as the cave, at least eight feet, and shimmered with an ever-so-soft blue-filament sort of light. The angel had what appeared to be wings, but Theo could not be sure, for they were folded in close to his torso. No hands or limbs of any sort were visible. His face shone with love and even, Theo hesitated to think it, devotion.

The seeker thought that the angel must have come for the Saint, not knowing that he no longer possessed a body. The celestial being emanated a gentle vibration of tenderness and protection. "Or maybe it is my guardian angel," the seeker thought.

Theo expected that some psychic message would be exchanged between them, but nothing was transmitted. The angel seemed content to simply hover in the corner radiating benign waves. And, for his part, the seeker could think of nothing to "send" to the angel. He had gotten so used to Silence that even crisp thoughts struck him as too much mental noise. So the beings contemplated each other, both happy to share communion.

Theo closed his eyes once more and sank deep into the Absolute. Later, he opened them. Lining the walls of the cave, pressed closely together like pedestrians waiting for the light to change, were dozens of angels. They shared many qualities—having as their constitution a sort of fuzzy gauze of light, bearing wings, showing indistinct features—but each differed slightly from the next. Several were clearly female, something in their faces showed it; some were taller and some shorter; and they gleamed with subtly different colors: palest silver, light bluish, and delicate gold.

Theo noticed, with great surprise, that he could "see" the angels behind him, in all their detail, without turning his head. This group of angels sent forth the same aura of compassion and care that he had noticed in the first one to arrive. And the effect of their collective emanations was strong. Theo felt embraced by goodness.

He now again wondered about the reason for this visitation. He knew that it could not be meant for him. Genuine humility prevented him from thinking such a purpose possible.

After a few minutes, developments proved him right. On the sacred spot where the Saint had always sat, an ancient-looking Sage appeared. He was a most marvelous-looking Being. Dolichofacial, his long face was paired with an even longer and equally narrow white beard. His hair was gathered in a knot atop his head and held in place by a wooden stick. Wearing the ochre robes of a Brahmin, the Sage had a long string of beads hanging from his neck

Theo instantly prostrated before this Visitor. When he rose, he noticed that all the angels had sunk to their knees. The Sage at first appeared to wear a severe mien. But the longer Theo examined him, the more this impression changed to one of beneficent wisdom. Clearly, the Sage was not One to be joked with, but He also looked as though He would render assistance to anyone who might ever need it.

The Sage communicated nothing. But after a few minutes of profound Silence, a blazed of Light expanded out from his form to encompass the entire cave. So bright was this Light that Theo could see nothing else. The Light erased the angels and the roof and the walls. Nothing existed except the Light.

When the Light finally pulled back and dimmed, the Sage had disappeared.

A few minutes passed. Suddenly, another Being occupied the Saint's place. This One had an almost-Chinese face. He, too, wore his hair, brown to the degree of almost being black, tied up atop his head.

A bright yellow garment covered the lower half of his body, while his chest remained bare. Twin necklaces of rudraksha adorned his neck, and smaller ones his wrists and upper arms. The Being's beard was rectangular and dark, and his eyebrows, thick.

Again, without even intending to, Theo found himself prone before this Rishi. And the angels, too, again sank to a kneeling position.

Sounds began to fill the air. The Rishi remained mute, his mouth did not open, but mantras, sacred sounds from the Vedas, echoed off the rock walls of the cave. Theo could not make them out. They resembled Sanskrit, must have been Sanskrit, he realized, but were, at the same time, different than the language he had seen in books. The mantras contained such power that Theo could feel both his soul and his body changing under their influence. They had none of the rubberiness of modern words. Instead, they penetrated and acted, as if they were spiritual scalpels designed to perform precise operations on the patient.

The Rishi lifted his hand in blessing. From the palm flowed wave after wave of beneficent energy. Theo felt lighter, more joyful, and more peaceful as the hand sent forth its tangible blessings.

Then the Rishi transformed Himself into a single mass of brilliant golden Light. The Light possessed the exact shape that the "man" had. It lasted for half a minute or so. Then it dissolved into millions of golden pinpoints, and the Rishi was gone.

A total of eight Great Beings presented themselves to Theo and his angelic chorus. His intuition told him that these Souls had been residents of the cave from time immemorial. One had likely left it for the next and so on through the ages. His own Guru was the latest in the lineage of Enlightened Beings who had lived here. But then he felt embarrassment wash over him. What then was *he* doing in the cave? On considering the matter, he decided that not every resident here would have been a Rishi or Saint. There must have been times when a student or sadhu still seeking the Truth had taken refuge in this comfortable spot.

After the last Being had faded away, so did the angels who had come to see them. Alone again, Theo looked around the space. Nothing *physical* had changed, but the atmosphere had gotten stimulated and stirred. A liveliness of purity filled the room. Theo felt that anything practical that he might now do would constitute a profanation. How could one eat three feet away from where a genuine Rishi had just sat? How could one light a fire that would have singed the feet of an angel? So he chose to close his eyes and take comfort in Inner Silence.

Remembrance

The visit from the Saints and angels spurred Theo on toward greater dedication to the goal. He spent more and more time in meditation, hoping to purify himself sufficiently to merit his residence. He did not, in the least, wish to defile it by any worldly or impure thoughts.

One evening as he sat by the fire in deep Peace, recollections began to appear in his mind. He saw himself in southern India, in a temple by a river, working as the assistant of the temple's priest. And this priest was none other than his own Master! Although his face and body differed from the ones Theo knew, there was no disputing the identity of this revered soul.

The temple held an almost palpable air of divinity. Prayers were recited there twenty-four hours a day; aratis, ceremonies in which the light from camphor-soaked wicks was waved toward images of the gods, were held nightly; pujas, elaborate thanksgiving rituals, were regularly performed.

Theo saw himself busy in his tasks around the temple. The priest under whom he worked was strict with him, even hard on him, but the assistant could tell that this roughness arose from genuine love and affection. The priest was held in high esteem by the temple's worshippers, for he was not simply a Brahmin executing his responsibilities, he was a holy man acting in the role of a priest.

The seeker, in his vision, saw himself sitting beneath the priest as people came to him for assistance with their problems. Women yearned for sons; farmers needed rain; businessmen sought advantage; and the sick desired recovery. To each supplicant, the priest offered appropriate and beneficial advice. Even if the advice was not pleasing to its recipient, its purport was for his or her ultimate good. Sometimes, the assistant would watch as what he knew to be a miracle occurred.

One day, a crippled girl nearing marriage age came to the priest with a sad look on her face. None of the village boys would look at her, despite the comeliness of her face and the modesty of her manners, because of her lameness. She did not explicitly ask to be healed, but simply laid out her predicament. Her father had made it clear that her fate would be a harsh one if she remained in his house as she aged.

The priest simply told her that everything would work out. As she hobbled away, the assistant wondered what that prediction meant. But once she reached the door of the temple, the girl sprang up into the air, and then began to spin round and round in an excited, improvisational dance. She fell on her knees and prostrated toward the priest before running home as fast as her new legs could carry her.

But, generally, the priest simply dispensed advice to his supplicants. He would remind them to deal fairly with one another in business; to honor their spouses as gods and goddesses incarnate; to contribute their share to charity; to refrain from forbidden foods and inebriating drink. Only those with a predilection for spirituality would he counsel to meditate and read deeply in the scriptures. These few souls he took under his wing, telling them inspirational stories, and elucidating difficult sections of the *Bhagavad Gita* for them.

The priest had set up a rigorous curriculum for his coadjutor. "Theo" read holy books morning and evening and meditated thrice daily. And he assisted his superior in all the temple ceremonies, basking in the man's aura of purity and wisdom. Rarely did the priest praise his helper. Far more commonly, he scolded him for lapses, for frivolity or paying too much attention to a certain young woman, and lectured him for his tendency to mentally wander off while meditating.

"Meditation is not an excuse to go woolgathering!" he thundered. And his assistant wondered how the man knew he was doing precisely that. "Meditation is for settling the mind, not treating it to delectable morsels of fantasy. See that you stop your thinking and come to

232

experience Brahman, for it is in Brahman that all questions are answered and all desires fulfilled."

Theo knew that, in all things spiritual, he was a relative beginner compared to his superior. These subjects attracted and delighted him, but he was not yet ready to say goodbye to the beautiful world, the world of field games and river sport and lovely girls and tasty food. No matter how many times his instructor informed him that one did not "give up" the world on the spiritual path, but only invested that world with its true worth, Theo did not, in his heart, believe him. He had seen the sadhus wandering in the forests, begging for food, looking dirty and disheveled. He had read the scriptures, which stated the requirements of chastity and abandonment of desires for worldly pleasures, and they frightened him. In essence, he had one foot in each of two worlds. He yearned to be holy like his teacher, but he delighted in the simple sense pleasures that fascinate most young people. The priest knew all this, of course, and did his best to encourage the former by not absolutely forbidding the latter. The boy could best be moved by nudging him back toward the right path rather than jerking him away from the wrong one.

This vision ended and others followed. Theo was being treated to a series of films depicting former lives in which he had been tutored and mentored by the Saint. Most of them had been lived in India, but one remarkable life had been spent as a Native American. The Saint had been the medicine man in a tribe of Yaquis located in the Southwest of what later became the United States. Theo observed, in this vision, fascinating scenes of magic and incantation, events reminiscent of those he had read about in Carlos Castaneda's books.

When Theo finally opened his eyes again, it seemed that no time had passed. But then he noticed that the fire had long grown cold. Walking outside, he saw two day's worth of food and drink sitting under the rock ledge. He then realized that he must have spent a full day reliving his previous existences.

The weather had broken and the sun made an appearance. Badly needing to stretch his cramped legs, Theo headed off to the stream, where some of the best times with his Master had been spent. As he gazed out over the water, which today had given up its aquamarine for a glinting quicksilver, he pondered the long dedication of the teacher to his pupil's evolution. The Master has watched over me lifetime after lifetime, he told himself. He guided me from the wildest tribal rascal to whatever I am today. A sense of awe and humility washed over him. What love he had been given! And by what a truly generous Soul!

The Teachings Sink In

Theo had barely made it back to the cave when the skies opened up again and the landscape turned into something out of the Noah's Ark story. The seeker built up the fire and closed his eyes to meditate.

Rather than calming down, sinking into Pure Consciousness and basking in its Joy, as he usually did, Theo found himself in a condition of maximum intellectual clarity. The many teachings of his Master and the scriptures came into his mind and he perused each of them carefully.

He first considered what had been one of his biggest confusions over the years: how the world actually looked to an Enlightened Being. Now he was able to answer the question from his own direct experience. Of late, the Absolute had pushed further and further forward in his perceptions. He saw the material world, no doubt, but he saw it as a perturbation of the Absolute. The great Light of the Absolute now shone out of rocks and bushes, trees and streams. Everything was interconnected; nothing separate. A single Breath of Life held the entire world together. And now Theo could hear It breathe in the tiniest insect and in the most magnificent constellation.

Finally, he could understand how the Realized moved through the everyday world while actually experiencing something quite different from what other people saw.

It also became abundantly clear to him that gurus and books of wisdom advised seekers to turn their attention away from the outside world for more than the obvious reason of finding Pure Consciousness within themselves. Such an inward orientation lessened the extent to which one fed the addictions of the senses. Desires from past impressions lead to thoughts, which, in turn, proceed to actions and thus to further karma. Allowing one's thoughts to center on pleasures and aversions in the outer world deepens these past impressions. If the material world is a grand projection produced by the ego, then watching the show with great interest only serves to reinforce its apparent reality.

After all, everyone believes that the show is real. The drama on the television screen of the world has been fully internalized by people everywhere. Nothing is easier than to simply go along with the crowd.

But now Theo appreciated that the duality of the experiencer and the experienced, of subject and object, amounted to the most all-powerful of addictions. And the more one indulged it, the stronger the habit became. By meditating, deep and long, the Realized defeated this almost indomitable foe, and abandoned the delusion that they were separate islands of body, mind, and ego, realizing instead that They were at One with Everything in the universe. Not metaphorically at One, but actually, fundamentally at One.

As these clear thoughts continued to shine forth in his mind, Theo remembered all his earlier curiosity, the endless questions he had plagued his Master with: chakras and astrology and a host of other conceptual matters. Now he could see that, when the mind is strong and Pure Consciousness remains hidden behind it, the so-called "monkey brain" jumps from one branch of knowledge to another, never satisfied to remain long in place.

Theo understood now why the Guru had shown impatience with all these questions: their answers did nothing to advance his soul down the path toward Enlightenment. They were children's games, with the matter of Realization being ultimately serious. The seeker could now see that, with time in the body being short, a Teacher would always wish his student to dedicate himself fully to the work that would most quickly take him to the goal.

Many of the subtleties of the Master's teachings gleamed perspicuous now. Theo could grasp how superpowers might be available to someone who resided securely in the Absolute. For the Absolute was an Ocean of All Possibilities, out of which arose the marvels of the multiform universe. Just as scientists, when they reached ever-subtler levels of physical creation, gained access to extraordinary energies, as the nuclear discoveries had proved, so the Enlightened, when they retook possession of the Their true nature in the Absolute, also had ready to hand mind-boggling powers.

But all these topics, which had earlier fascinated him, now struck Theo as vapid. The mind loved to frolic, to keep its body and ego amused, so that it could continue to reign as the overlord of the soul. The mind, however, was of no importance to him now. He no longer wished to indulge its caprices and short attention span. Information that was important for him to know would appear naturally without effort on his part. And the Silence of non-thinking brought him infinitely more joy than thinking ever had.

Higher Ground

The monsoon ended in September. Theo had now been in India for five months. That period had passed neither quickly nor slowly; somehow, time did not factor into his memory of it.

The pilgrim realized that he was meant to move on, up higher in the mountains, to discover a cave of his own, to find his way forward on the inner path without the invisible but tangible support of all the Realized who had once lived in this cave.

He chose to journey onward just as he had come here, without much planning, trusting to his intuition and to nature to guide him where he ought to be. The villagers, from whom he gathered a few foodstuffs, expressed deep sadness at his departure. They told him that everyone felt more secure when there was "a holy man in the cave." Now Theo did not, by any means, consider himself as such, but not wanting to disabuse them of their notion, he simply smiled at their kind words. They asked him where he would go, and he could only point to the higher reaches of the mountains and say, "Further up, up there."

His Western background showed in his preparations. Theo was not going to climb into those inhospitable regions with only a deerskin and a water pot. Jettisoning the equipment that experience had shown to be unnecessary, the seeker made sure that everything he *would* need got stuffed into the big backpack. Not having room for both, he did manage to strap one of the tarps to the pack. The canvas had so successfully blocked the monsoon wind and rain that he considered it invaluable.

And so, on a clear morning in September, with a dozen villagers present to send him off, Theo departed the cave where he had learned so very, very much indeed. As, turning round on the path, he waved goodbye to the locals, the seeker understood that another important chapter in his life was about to begin.

238

The temperature, while not winterlike, must have been around fifty degrees Fahrenheit. A slight headwind pushed against the trekker's forward progress, and he interpreted it as a sign that hard spiritual slogging lay ahead.

After climbing all day, Theo had reached an altitude of 12,000 feet. His body felt comfortable, for he had been acclimating to these heights over a prolonged period. Not finding a cave, he set up the tarp and his tent in a sheltered nook that seemed to have been scooped out of the mountainside just for his comfort. And he slept very well that night.

The snow had not yet come, but Theo knew that he would witness its arrival if he were still here in a month's time. The topography at this height differed markedly from that near the Saint's cave. Grass grew underfoot and hardy bushes and herbs could be spotted here and there. But one's overwhelming impression was of rock: rock, rock, and nothing but rock. The mountain faces resembled dried-out chocolate chunks, their colors ranging from buff to nougat to buffalo hide. Everything about them whispered, "This is not a place for human beings." These mountains were the hard and sharp-edged, dry and uncompromising. They existed in themselves and offered not even a hint of invitation to potential visitors. Those who came here only came to get away from the teeming life in the valleys down below.

Theo decided to keep climbing. His idea was to reach the 14,000-foot level, as he had at Gomukh, that otherworldly lithic wonder, which was the source of the holy Ganges. Something told him he needed to be physically higher than he had ever been, so that he might successfully continue his spiritual pursuits.

It took him three days to attain that height, but, on the fourth, he found himself overlooking a sapphirine-blue lake, into which emptied a waterfall in the shape of a Greek lyre. Mocha-hued rocks atop and at the side formed the frame of the instrument, and narrow white filaments of water, its strings. The natural composition of this scene was ultimately tasteful: the dark brown rocks set off the gleaming waters, and the white waters contrasted wonderfully with the dark blue of the lake.

The moment he saw this place, Theo knew that he was meant to stay here. Whether or not it offered a cave, he would have to see. But the access to fresh water was crucial, and the sound of the waterfall and the appearance of the tranquil lake suited him well.

As he roamed the area in search of a cave, Theo breathed more quickly than was his wont. He had forgotten how very thin air felt, and the high altitude here soon reminded him what an absence of oxygen meant to the human body. But he knew that he would grow used to the air, so he simply slowed down his pace and took short rest periods whenever he needed them.

Late in the afternoon, when the wind had begun to pick up and the temperature to drop, he felt drawn to a spot near the place where the waterfall met the lake. He could not see any indication of a cave, but he went closer to explore the place nevertheless.

Here again, as at the plateau where he had encountered the Great Beings, the seeker discovered a not-obvious entrance to what he hoped would prove a cave. A mound of stones stood in front of a flattish rock face. These stones looked as if they had been put their intentionally, for the mound tapered toward the top, so that the whole thing formed a pyramid. It would take work, work made harder by oxygen deprivation, to disassemble this mount, but Theo decided to do so. He painstakingly moved stone after stone, until he had reduced the mound to a height he could step over.

Behind the remaining rocks he found some sinewy bushes. Parting these with some effort, he got behind them and discovered an opening barely bigger than his own circumference. He took out a flashlight and crawled through the opening.

Here was, indeed, a cave. Not a spacious one such as that which he had shared with his Master, but a cave nonetheless. No other creatures could he see. The cave was dry, and a small cavity in its floor indicated that someone had lived here before; for it was obviously a fire pit. The dimensions of the space were no more than ten by ten by eight. But he could stand without hindrance, and there was plenty of room for his backpack and the water and fuel he would need to survive. Theo pressed his hands together in gratitude to his Master, to whom he attributed all blessings such as this discovery.

Settling In

The remainder of the rock mound served to protect the cave from the winds, which grew strong during the night. Even the bushes, Theo realized, would be of use to keep animals away and to prevent snow from blocking the entrance during the winter. The orientation of the cave was ideal as well: it faced west, while the prevailing winds blew from the east.

What surprised Theo most in the cave was finding, in its far back corner, a small stack of dried wood. This wood, which seemed very old indeed, would get him through the first night, and provide him time to look for new fuel the following day. Again he whispered silent thanks to his Teacher.

His first meditation that night convinced the pilgrim that this cave had certainly been used by others of more advanced spiritual state than he. It was almost as if a hugely powerful magnet pulled him down deeper than he had ever gone. If Spirit might be compared to matter, he conceived of himself as being pulled into the very center of the earth, far down into its rocky bowels, way down into the ultimately silent spaces, where humans rarely ventured.

The atmosphere possessed an austerity conducive to spiritual search. The cold purified one's mind. The rocks blocked out the vibrations of the world. The vast silence aligned one with the Self.

After meditating, he ate from the dried food he had in his pack, and drank from the canteen he always carried with him. By the normal rules of human existence, he ought to have felt supremely lonely up here, close to the very top of the world. But, on the contrary, his mood soared. Nowhere else, he was convinced, would he have been able to concentrate so completely on the task at hand: establishing himself in Pure Consciousness, as his Master had taught him to do.

242

The next day, Theo emerged from the cave to reconnoiter his new home. Never had he seen a place so bereft of living things. Yes, ferns and lichens did grow here. Indeed, he did find a small growth of cedar trees about a quarter mile from the cave. But he had seen no birds as yet, no butterflies, not even any scurrying rodents on the ground. Rocks completely dominated the landscape: rocks formed mountainsides; rocks bordered the lake; rocks lay everywhere on the ground. Had it not been for the lake and the waterfall, he might have thought that he had been transported to the moon.

Finding the trees was a great blessing, for, without them, he would probably not have been able to survive the cold, especially the cold that was coming as autumn approached. Theo carried as much wood as he could hold back to his sanctuary. Even mild exercise such as wood-carrying tested one's endurance in this zone of attenuated air.

The lake fascinated him. He tasted its water and found it to be delicious, almost too cold to drink, but delicious. The color of the water changed as one approached or distanced oneself from it. From a hundred yards away, its blue was that of a sapphire ring of the highest quality. On its banks, that color changed to porcelain blue or, sometimes, cerulean. Clouds reflected on its surface like strange gossamer fish slowly finning by. The pellucid water allowed him to see far down into what was obviously a very deep lake. He made out fish lazily finning their way through the icy waters. And some willowy plants could be seen in the shallower spots near the shore.

And the waterfall delighted the seeker even more than the lake into which it emptied with such a roar and splash. The angle of its descent must have been 80 degrees, so the ice-cold water pounded down into the narrow reservoir below it with the force of mighty pistons smashing against the bottoms of their cylinders. Cold spray shot out from both side of the falls. Near it, one's hearing got utterly overwhelmed by the furious explosions of the water's impact on the waiting rocks.

From fifty yards' distance, the threads of the waterfall looked discrete, individual, unique. Theo mulled over the image of the lyre. It pleased him to think that each of these streams represented a specific string on the musical instrument of the falls. Nature had strung them on their rocky frame to make the music, which, given some separation, he could now enjoy. For he only needed these few yards to *hear* the waterfall as it was meant to be heard. Now it played its incessant downpour in such a soothing manner that it could have lulled even the meanest grump to passivity. It crackled like crushed foil; it poured like monsoon rains; and it vibrated like a nervous kitten.

Theo made the effort necessary to leave this beauty and return to his hide-in from the world. After another long meditation, he read from the *Brahma Sutras* and performed his yogic asanas.

He already felt thoroughly at home here. A committee of recluses might have prepared this abode for him as friendly neighbors welcome a newcomer with casseroles and offers of tool loans. The cave seemed to have been swept clean of cobwebs and superfluous dirt. (And, by now, Theo knew that such excess was possible even in a dirt-floored cave.) The load of wood he had found still gave him pause: how long had it lain there?

The weather appeared to be getting colder all the time. Today was several degrees colder than yesterday. He guessed that the first snow would come in October. And he wondered what else he should do to prepare for its arrival.

Astonishingly, when Theo went to hang the tarp at the entrance to the cave, he found four crevices precisely where he needed them to be to secure the corners of the canvas. He had some nails in his pack, which he used to firmly attach the top of the tarp to the rock of the cave walls. He weighed down the bottom corners with heavy rocks. As he had previously, Theo left some slack in the material, so that the tarp would not rigidly take on the full force of the winds.

He moved his possessions to the rear of the space, so that if moisture of any kind did find its way in, they should be protected. From herbs and juniper that he found growing in a sheltered spot a few hundred yards away, he fashioned some primitive dhoop, which he planned to use for both lighting and incense. Exerting all his energy, the pilgrim made repeated trips to the cedar grove to stock up on precious wood. He did not wish to found himself snowbound in the cave and lacking fuel for the fire.

After several days of work, he looked around his new home and found it to be acceptable: clean, protected from wind, rain, and snow; containing fuel; and, more important than any of these, vibrating with a rich spiritual energy.

Changes

Whether it was due to the thin air of the place or its profound spiritual power—Theo couldn't tell which—he began to feel different. The sense of being in the body, which everyone is used to having, that feeling of the muscles tightening, the blood flowing, and the skin itching, had weakened in him to the point where he hardly knew he *had* a body. Even when he exited the cave and faced the elements, the seeker did not immediately become aware of physical sensations, as he had all his life. The body seemed to have withdrawn itself, pulled back from his awareness, so that it no longer stood front and center. In the foreground spread his consciousness, the almost tangible essence of himself that now continued its outward spread to encompass his environment. He felt as if he were living in a great bubble of frictionless gas that possessed an intoxicating quality.

It was a good thing, too, this losing focus on body consciousness at this time, for the weather grew progressively colder. Even though the cave was on the mountain's leeward side, the wind still shot out in blasts that had the effect of a cold-scalding. The sky clouded up more often, a harbinger of snow. Another benefit of his dimness of body-sense was loss of appetite. The depleted air at 14,000 feet greatly diminished one's hunger. Theo now had no one bringing him daily rations. He depended on the supplies he had carried up with him from his Master's cave. And, since he had not found anything in the vicinity edible by a vegetarian, he would need to eke these out for as long as he remained here. So, he was glad to have lost much of his taste for food. He wondered if the waterfall would freeze solid during the winter, whether the lake would turn to ice. Those two were his only companions now, and he felt close to them, almost as if they were brothers in Spirit.

Then one day, while out on his walk around the lake, Theo heard a weird, gurgling cry and looked left to see a gull smoothly winging its way over the surface of the water. The gull had a brown head resembling a rodent's snout. The brown enveloped the front part of the bird's face, but separated cleanly, as if it were a mask, from the white feathers on the neck. The gull sported a long, narrow, rubious beak, pearl-gray side and black tail feathers, and feet matching its beak. Theo raked the horizon for other birds, but saw none. The lone gull passed over the lake and the waterfall and on to who knows where.

If the gull had caught sight of the seeker, she would have seen a man very different than the one who had first come to India six months before. Theo was now twenty pounds lighter; he had allowed his beard to grow, and the unkempt gray-brown hair covered his cheeks and extended three inches down from his chin. His eyes were visibly brighter now than they had been before. Their green irises had something of cat's-eye marbles in them now. His face was thinner, and his hair reached to the bottom of his neck. But, despite this loss of weight, the man looked healthy, sinewy, and strong in his leanness.

That night, as he sat by the low fire, Theo began to think about his Teacher. He had called him to India. And he had introduced him to wondrous Holy Men. He had explained the most complicated matters and answered the most difficult questions. His very presence had, without question, accelerated the spiritual development of his charge. But Theo wondered why the Master had left him with the job incomplete. Should he not have remained with him until Realization bloomed? Why had he been left to find his own way through the most difficult part of a seeker's journey: the final mile of the pilgrimage, when the ultimate barrier had to be broken through?

As soon as he posed the question, Theo understood that it was improper. The Master undoubtedly had a perfect plan for his development, and it would unfold as destiny required. Here again, he thought, was the mind causing trouble. Rather than trusting the Master, he was sitting around second-guessing his course of action. Theo's body physically shook, as he sought to rid himself of such doubts.

Inner Visions

Theo's meditations grew longer. He didn't *try* to meditate for longer periods; he simply felt no impulse to stop. And the quality of the sessions changed too. An austere isolation characterized them now. Although he did not think about them at the time, for he was beyond thought, later examination showed him that his soul had been sitting in a place as metaphorically far from the noisy world as one could ever get. He had found his way to the basement of Consciousness, where Silence and only Silence Existed.

Then one day the Silence yielded to inner visions. A goddess of rare beauty rose up before him exuding such seductiveness as he had never before encountered. Unlike the girl he had seen in the cave with the Great Beings, who corresponded to his adolescent fantasy, this woman was mature in every way. Long falls of serpentine black hair reached down nearly to her waist. Her breasts pressed out full against the fabric of her silk gown. Black arched brows surmounted even blacker eyes, from which a magnetic force shot forth. The lips of her small mouth beckoned.

The goddess communicated telepathically with the meditator. "Come with me," she cooed. "Come with me to heaven, where your every wish shall instantly come true." Her hand lifted, her tapered fingers, ringed and with their nails flashing brightly red, bent back and stretched forth to pull him to her. For the first time in a long while, Theo felt his genitalia coming to life. The goddess had succeeded in awakening his desire. How delightful it would be to follow her, to spend his time in heaven, beyond the tests and strains of earthly life!

But, then, in an instant, he perceived her differently, as a temptress to a fall, a great fall, from the realm of Pure Spirituality to that of erotic pleasure. He willed her away, and she receded from his inner eye, growing steadily fainter until she had disappeared completely.

248

The next day brought a similar experience. Established deep in Silence, Theo found himself surrounded by powerful-looking magicians. These men, like the goddess, communicated with him psychically. "You are a great soul, my friend," said the first to speak, "and worthy of magnificent powers. Come with us and you will learn the secrets of the universe. You will be able to produce mountains of gold and lakes of diamonds by the wave of your hand. Nothing will lie beyond your reach. You will reign as the master of this world."

But these procurers in the employ of power held far less attraction for Theo than the goddess had. His Master's warnings about special powers had made him especially wary of such temptations. And, in his life, he had never been one to show off and seek the admiration of the crowd. He dismissed the magicians with a single flick of his intellectual switch.

On the third day, again while he rested serenely in his own Nature, a handsome recluse appeared before his mind's eye. The man possessed some of the ever-youthful appeal of Babaji, who had graced Theo with an appearance that one day months earlier. He, too, had long dark hair and an epicene face, which one could not have called either masculine or feminine. This recluse shone bright, as Babaji had. And like that Great Being, he sat upon a deerskin.

"How foolish of those others to try to seduce you with the pleasures of the flesh or the powers of the common sorcerer. You are far too highly evolved a soul to be interested in such cheap offers. All that interests you is the development of your consciousness. You want nothing more than to follow in the steps of your Master and light the world with the torch of Realization."

Here the recluse paused to smile and slightly bow to the seeker, demonstrating subtly how great was his respect for the extent of his spiritual development. "Come with me to a sphere where only the most exalted Beings commune, in the purest of sacred atmospheres. There you will sit amongst the Saints who have broken through the final barrier and attained that to which all human beings ought to aspire. There you will bathe in the Knowledge of the Enlightened and hasten to the conclusion of your long journey by associating with the Wise, as the so wisely Scriptures advise us to do."

The recluse's words appealed to Theo. Nothing in his life had ever satisfied him more than the time he had spent in the cave with his Teacher. Imagine being in the presence of many Great Beings, all of whom radiated the high-frequency of Enlightenment. Such company would, as this man said, surely speed him on to the goal in the shortest possible amount of time.

Then Theo thought again. Why would he ever need to move to another plane of existence, to some celestial plane apparently, in order to evolve his consciousness? He recalled the holy books and their discussions of heaven as a place where wholesome souls reaped the fruits of their good karma while preparing to take yet another body. And he recollected that the human body was praised in both the scriptures and by the Master as being the ideal vehicle for the attainment of Enlightenment. He looked again at the recluse.

The visitor's face showed faint signs of urgency, of imploration. "Why hesitate, my friend? Only nod your head and we will travel in the blink of an eye to a world more beautiful than any you have ever imagined. Think of all those wise Souls with whom you shall communicate."

Theo caught that word "souls." The Realized did not have "souls." They had, by definition, ceased to identify themselves as distinct creatures. Their Awareness was Infinite and Eternal Being. That one false note alerted him to the sham that was being foisted on him by the recluse. He wished him gone—but the recluse did not disappear. So he looked him squarely in the eyes and waved his hand to indicate his dismissal. The previously imploring eyes gleamed momentarily with anger, but then the visitor could be seen no more.

White Silence

Three weeks after his arrival, the snow came. It came stealthily, in the night, while he slept. It dropped down silently, like those white-camouflaged WWII paratroopers, powerfully armed but barely noticeable. It sneaked up on the lone occupant of the cave, so that, when he awoke, its entrance was completely sealed off.

Having prepared for such a day, Theo was not in the least worried. The mound of stones kept most of the snow away from the antre; the sinewy bushes blocked much that got round the stones. But, despite these twin barriers, the clever powder had managed to block the small opening that served as Theo's only access to the outer world.

His preparations had included sharpening the trowel that had been part of his equipment since arriving in the country. The pilgrim had also thought to bring a long, thick, and sturdy stick into the cave. These two instruments would, he thought, enable him to dig his way out whenever the situation demanded such excavation.

When he was ready to exit the cave, Theo found that the snow was so light and loose that he could easily clear it away with his hands. The stones and bushes had served him well.

What a different world he discovered! One night of snowfall had utterly transformed his mountaintop. What had been gray and brown was now uniformly white. What had been sharp-edged was now smooth-faced. What had been moonlike now resembled the North Pole of one's childhood fantasies.

Only the waterfall and the lake remained as they had been. The strings of silvery water continued to cascade down the steep gradient of the falls, and the sapphirine surface of the lake stood out now like a giant blue gemstone in a perfectly contrasting setting of truly white gold. But everywhere else one saw only white. The piling of the snow reconfigured the topography of the place. So many jagged edges had been reshaped, overnight, into gentle undulations, which looked to

251

have been worked by a master sculptor on a grand scale. Stony stretches a hundred yards wide were now smoothly polished avenues of pristine white. Holes and depressions had been tastefully filled in. Irregularities of contour had been made to give way to a conformation of elegant design.

Theo hesitated to walk away from the cave's entrance. He did not wish to mar the perfection of the surface of frozen granules that stretched as far as his vision could reach. New fallen snow always had this same effect on him: it made him think of a fresh new earth, one where all mistakes and failures of the past were wiped away by the grand-scale sculpture of nature's hand. Such snow spoke of innocence and everything immaculate. It represented rebirth and higher life. Whenever he looked upon such stretches of fresh snow, Theo believed himself to be entering into a flawless new world.

Gazing over the prominence to his right, the seeker paused, covered his eyes with one hand, and stared hard. What *was* that? A short-horned sheep stood on the hill staring directly at him. Theo recognized it as a bharal, a so-called "blue" sheep indigenous to the Himalayas. The man felt an immediate sense of brotherhood with the bovid. Aside from that gull, this was the only creature the pilgrim had noticed since his arrival here.

The bharal was leaner in face and body than a sheep. Its fur was, indeed, a bluish-gray on top, and white both underneath and on its legs and tail. The sheep would have blended in perfectly had the snow not been spread so completely over the landscape. Its blue-gray would have matched the tones of the area's rocks. But now it stood out, and Theo hoped that no predator sat on a higher peak looking down at it with thoughts of a hearty meal.

The bharal showed no signs of moving on, keeping its eyes on Theo as long as he remained there. But standing motionless made him cold, so he decided to overcome his hesitation about despoiling the snow and venture forth.

Whenever he went out, he headed for the cypress grove so that he might replenish his stores of wood. Cypress was not an ideal fuel, for it burned too quickly, but, being a beggar, Theo could not afford to be choosy.

Walking through the deep snow made the normally strenuous exercise quite difficult. Although he had acclimated to the altitude here, there was never any pretending that one's body did not miss that good, rich oxygen of the lowlands. Now, as he methodically placed one boot in front of the other, sinking each time ten inches deep, Theo looked at the distant trees as at an oasis in a parching desert, something he would never actually manage to reach. But his honed willpower kicked in, and he simply kept putting one boot in front of the other until, after taking forty-five minutes to complete a ten minute walk, he arrived at the grove.

There he rested, inhaling deeply to pull into his lungs what oxygen the air offered. He leaned against a tree and noticed that the bharal stood in the same spot where he had previously seen it. And still it looked at him. He must wonder what this strange new creature is, the seeker thought. I hope he isn't worried that I might be a threat. Surely he sees that I roam here in peace.

After a quarter hour's rest, Theo took his armload of wood and made his way, even more slowly than he had come, back toward the cave.

Glimpsing the End

Theo built a fire and once again settled into meditation. He remained so long in his cross-legged position that, when he finally surfaced to waking consciousness, he had lost all sensation in the lower half of his body. Since he never used the watch buried somewhere in the nether reaches of his backpack, the seeker had no idea how long he had been in the Absolute. The fire, of course, had burnt out long before now.

The cave was darker than it normally was, so he assumed that night had come. But then an intuition warned him, and he went to the entrance and saw that it was again blocked by snow. Using his hands, he dug away the accumulation. When he had gotten it out of the way, however, he found something unexpected. A massive boulder closed off egress.

Theo reasoned that the big rock must have fallen down the cliff overlooking the cave sometime during the night, if, indeed, it *was* night. For the boulder allowed no light to enter the cave. Instantly, he was aware that this happenstance most certainly meant his death. For the tunnel out of the cave was so small that, even if he would have normally been able to move the boulder, he would not now be able to get any leverage on the obstacle. Since the rock pressed right up to the entrance, it would not only prevent him from getting out to find water, but also severely limit the amount of air coming in. Most likely suffocation and dehydration would battle it out to see which consumed him first.

The seeker had come far down his path, though, and this glimpse of imminent death did not even bother him. If such was destiny's plan, he would accept it. Maybe he was meant to sink deep into samadhi and never again emerge. Possibly, this was some sort of spiritual test to determine how attached he was to his corporal shell. Whatever the purpose of the boulder, Theo knew that he had to accept it and continue to perform his spiritual exercises just as he had been.

He chuckled inwardly at the thought of being entombed, for he had been claustrophobic all his life, and had always believed that the death of a spelunker trapped in a narrow passage would be the worst of all possible ends. Maybe this was a last fear he had to deal with. Who could tell?

His canteens held enough water to last him at least a week. He would meditate almost continuously. Such prolonged sessions would accomplish two purposes: one, the eking out of his water supply and, two, the acceleration of his spiritual growth. If he were indeed going out, he might as well get as far down the path as possible, in order to set himself up well for the next life.

And so began the most intense period of meditation Theo had ever experienced. His body metabolism slowed to the point where he needed hardly anything to eat. He sweated so little that his thirst diminished greatly. The darkness of the cave rendered the inner Light more dramatic by contrast.

After an indeterminate time, which he could only gauge by the small amount of water remaining in his last canteen, Theo realized that the end was near. Once he drank this last bit of water, he would survive only as long as the body could tolerate dehydration, maybe a week at the most. Yet he felt neither sadness nor fear. His trust in destiny and his Master had, by this time, ripened to perfection. Whatever was meant to be would be for the best.

So he sipped the water carefully, savoring it as an oenophile might have tasted a rare vintage wine. And when the canteen was empty, he screwed on its top and returned to meditation.

No sense of time existed for him now. Nor did he possess an awareness of body. All that he knew was the Bliss of the Absolute, which floated him in Its embrace as an adoring mother might her infant child in the calm waters near the ocean shore.

At some point in his meditation, however, a thought of diamantine clarity rose up in his mind. "You are meant to survive and continue your work!" was the message. Immediately afterward, his Consciousness spontaneously formed the subtlest of subtle desires: *this cave will open...*

A thunderous rumbling. The walls of the cave vibrated as if they had been made of paper rather than rock. The hard floor rippled like water. The world seemed to have lost its balance. Theo's body got moved this way and that. He had no control over his position. All this titanic shaking continued for what seemed like ten minutes, but was actually only thirty seconds. There was a second shudder of Gaia's shoulders, of far less magnitude than the first, and then a palpitation of the ground, something like a cat shivering.

When Theo finally opened his eyes—he had kept them shut all through the disturbance—he was forced to quickly close them again. They could not tolerate what they experienced: light! Light was glimmering palely in the cave; but even this pale light proved too much for the seeker's dark-accustomed eyes. Gradually, they got used to the light and he managed to keep them open.

The quake had moved the boulder. The entrance to the cave was once more free. Calmly and slowly, Theo picked up a canteen and crawled through the tunnel leading outside.

The snow had disappeared. Talus shaken from the mountainside above the cave lay thick to the right of its entrance. It looked as if a truck had emptied a full load of stones that stood a foot high and spread across a hundred square yards. Rocks, big, average, and small, rested in unusual positions, leaning against one another, resting on the edges of precipices, and clumped together higgledy-piggledy. Three long fissures in the earth, each about four inches deep, zigzagged across the ground leading toward the lake, like the scars left by traumatic injury.

256

Fine, particulate dust floated everywhere. Mother Nature might have just been shaking out her winter rugs. The lake no longer showed its rich blue color, being, instead, dirtied by brown sediment that must have risen from its bottom. But the waterfall had survived intact. Its stream-strings still played their tune, albeit they emptied into a now beclouded pool.

One might have imagined that Theo would look upon his "rebirth" to the world as characters from novels always do in such situations, with a feeling of deep gratitude and awe, with a sense that what he now experienced shone with a freshness and beauty it had never before possessed. But such was not the seeker's experience. He had spent too much time lately in the world within the world to grow rapturous over its rearranged rocks and seamed surface. Yes, the fresh air felt good in his lungs. Indeed, the water that he now drank, after letting the sediment settle in the canteen, gratefully moistened his throat. And, certainly, the Himalayas stood before him as beautiful as they had always been. But he now thoroughly understood that "death" was not only a matter of the body. Life spent in spiritual ignorance, in which one saw only its superficies, in which nothing lasted and nothing truly satisfied, represented a sort of death itself. True Life was that of the Realized, Life enjoyed in unadulterated Bliss, in changeless Peace, and infinite Knowledge. Theo sought only this Life and could not be satisfied with anything less.

Venturing Forth

It took Theo a week to recover his strength and regain the energy that the deprivation of food, water, and air had taken from him. At the end of that time, he had a strong intuition that he should venture forth into the mountains that surrounded the cave.

He decided to take only a bare minimum of his possessions: a canteen, the sleeping bag, and some dried fruit. He had not the slightest idea where he would go or what he would find when he got there. All he knew was that he *ought* to head into the nearby mountains.

Although there had been brief and light snowstorms over the past seven days, the snow had not stuck, so the ground was easily walked. His acclimation to the altitude was complete, and he hardly any longer noticed the thin air. But the lack of calories in his diet caused him to be more easily fatigued. The hiking proceeded at a slower pace than it had in months past. And he was climbing, not simply trekking on a level plain.

The first night he spent in the recess of a mountainside, behind a sheltering boulder. The night was cold, but the mummy bag protected him from its effects. On the second day, he reached a glacier, whose beauty would have won a cover from *National Geographic*.

The glacier, at least that portion of it visible to Theo, stretched for a quarter of a mile. It rose sheer to a height of about one hundred feet. Its base consisted of knobbled, low-relief ice; but, at its top, dozens of massive towers stretched toward the sky. Some of these towers resembled monoliths, others, oversized stalagmites. One of them looked like a shark's fin, two others, like the pointed teeth of a Megalodon. In fact, viewed all together, these towers might have been conceived as a set of the highly irregular teeth of a Titan's lower jaw.

What made this glacier worthy of wide notice, though, was not its structure, but its coloring. Because of its angle to the sun, the face of the glacier reflected the colors presented to it. It sat there, massive, flashing pure colors as though it were a giant prism. One portion of the ice gleamed in a very pale turquoise; another, shone pure azure. A section far to Theo's left sparkled, like the water of his old river, in gemmy aquamarine.

As the pilgrim came closer to the ice, he noticed that small pieces of it were veritable kaleidoscopes. In the facets of one chunk he found amber, baby blue, ultramarine, pale rose, violet, and leaf green.

Here, then, stood a marvelous jewel created by nature herself, apparently for her own delectation, since he must have been the only person to have seen it for months if not years.

Something magical about the glacier made Theo want to spend time near it. So he began methodically exploring the area, searching for a cave capable of sheltering him from what he knew would be a very cold night.

As it began to darken, the seeker found himself in front of a semicircular opening in the glacier face. Stalactite ice shapes, shaped like ancient dagger blades, depended from the crown of the arch. He slipped in between them and discovered a cave that could only have emerged from the powerful spell of a wizard.

Imagine a cave narrow and deep, about twenty feet high. The roof and walls of the cave are rounded knobs and ovoids reminiscent of dense clouds. Light penetrates through these rounded shapes sporadically, creating a feeling that one is in a half-subterranean and half-terrestrial world. The floor of the cave is an immaculate sheet of blue ice. The circular rocks above look like illuminated bombs raining down on one's head. In the far distance, the light entering from the roof shines much brighter than where one now stands, promising a glorious heaven in one's future. In the middle of the sheet ice nearby, sits a thick pile of what looks like frozen scree, stone shapes of ice that must have fallen from larger slabs above. And everything here is *blue*: steel blue, Prussian blue, Egyptian blue, and violet-blue. One expects gnomes here and sorcerers, airy goddesses of the Ice, and ghosts of lost warrior kings.

Theo stared at the cave in utter amazement. Once he had overcome his astonishment, the seeker began to examine the place from a practical point of view. Sleeping here would be COLD! He doubted that even the trusty mummy bag would serve to keep off the chill of solid ice. But, nevertheless, he knew that he *would* spend the night here. No other option existed, nor did he wish that one did.

Theo arranged his sleeping bag into the smallest possible compass, so that it was effectively four times its normal thickness. He then sat down on it and began to meditate. His session was, as usual, deep and quiet. And maybe it was his imagination that later invented it, but the Silence seemed to possess a frozen austerity quite suited to his physical environment.

He must have spent many hours in the Absolute, but he had no way of knowing. When he opened his eyes, the cave looked just as it had earlier: all shades of blue and whites, all shadows and bright gleams, all rondures and hillocks and swells. But a great difference existed now: all the blues and whites pulsed like light bulbs whose electrical source is unsteady. The pulsations came regularly, like intakes and exsufflations of breath. The cavern had turned into a vast living body of ice.

At first, Theo thought that his eyes were tricking him or that the flickerings were a consequence of his pupils adjusting to the strange semi-opaqueness of the place. But he soon saw that his organs were not at fault. The ice was living, breathing, pulsing.

It struck him as perfectly natural, after all. The Master had taught him that Pure Consciousness lay as the foundation of everything in the universe. In the largest sense, nothing was ever dead, and no one thing was ever more alive than another. Certainly Consciousness could be more readily seen in a human being than in a piece of ice, but, ultimately, both were Pure Consciousness and nothing else.

260

So he was simply observing the life-force, the prana, the Being of the ice-cave at a level closer to its reality than the eyes typically allowed one to see. And what a sight it was!

Only in science-fiction movies had he ever seen the likes of this cave, its eerie beauty and awesome coloration. Only in those films had special-effects technicians managed to create breathing structures such as the one in which he now sat. Theo thought that this place compounded the value of isolation with that of cold. Cold was more conducive to Spirituality than heat. Saints seemed more like ice sculptures, pure and frozen in Eternal Beauty, than like steam baths. Human ancestors had learned to drink from cold water sources, realizing that the warmer the water the greater the chance of contamination. This subterranean ice chamber struck him as ideal for the exploration of the depths of the Absolute.

His body had, by this point in his evolution, developed the ability to generate inner heat. The best *external* environment for Spirituality might have been cold, but his experience was that transcendence often produced a powerful *interior* fire.

Reunion

Theo spent that entire first night settled deep in Pure Consciousness. His concerns about being too cold in the ice-cave proved baseless. For whatever reason, his inner heat or the protection provided by invisible forces, he experienced not the slightest discomfort while meditating.

Toward dawn, his inner Silence gave way to a cavalcade of spiritual visitors, all of whom he had known in his present lifetime. The first visitor was his long-deceased grandmother Elsa, a tough, sturdy German woman who had lost her husband early in life during the early years of the Great Depression. Theo had, in his youth, enjoyed an oddly close-but-distant relationship with Elsa. He rarely saw her, and she was a taciturn woman, but they bonded during those times when he assisted her in the production of homemade doughnuts and noodles. Theirs was a silent affinity, where words of affection were never exchanged; but a sense of mutual understanding made interaction smooth and easy.

Elsa appeared just as he had remembered her in life: with her hair frizzed close to the scalp, her almost masculine jawline, and her no-nonsense aura. The only difference this time was that she wore a white dress rather than her former black ones. She stood ten feet away from Theo (at least as his inner eye measured things), and stared at him closely. His love flowed out to her unconstrained. She remained motionless and simply examined him. Then, possibly for the first time ever, she smiled upon her grandson. The smile was small and almost embarrassed at its own experience, but it was a smile nonetheless. And then she faded into the ether.

Immediately on her disappearance, Theo's father stood before him. He, too, was precisely as his son remembered him: the almost Italianate face, handsome and winning; the mostly bald head; the delicate, somewhat feminine mouth; and the dark brows. Here was the seeker's childhood hero, the man whom he constantly strove to impress, the charmer of ladies, the athlete capable of playing sports with boys twenty years his junior, the raconteur and wordsmith.

Theo had always been torn between admiration for and disgust of this man, his father. On the one hand, he possessed gifts aplenty, but, on the other, he had the morals of a junkyard dog. He had never truly "looked" at Theo, never really "known" him. And the one time in his life that the seeker had sought to make a deep connection between them, Keats had refused it, by joking off the foray.

Now he smiled his familiar, winsome smile at the pilgrim, reminding him of all that Scorpio charm that proved irresistible to men and women alike. And although Keats himself had never experienced a single spiritual moment, his son could tell that he now understood what had carried his offspring here, to this remote Himalayan ice cave.

Keats had lived for the pleasures of the flesh and the ebullient revelry to be enjoyed in bars with friends and pretty women, cards and beer. So his present juxtaposition with a ramrod-straight, bearded meditator ought to have amounted to a complete clash of values. But it did not. The father made his son understand that he appreciated what the boy's years of discipline had brought him to. His projected thoughts let Theo see that his father had always, deep inside, dreamt of the purity that he now saw before him. He himself had run, frightened, from even the faintest hint that such a realm of clean Being actually existed. He had run and lost himself in the fevers of sex and the hilarity of jokes and the backslapping of buddies. But now he let his son know that he appreciated and approved of his progress on the spiritual path.

Out of Theo's heart flowed forgiveness. He had never truly forgiven his father, but now he did. The man had terrified him with his temper and crushed him by ignoring his accomplishments, but now the time had come to let it all go. Waves of golden, tender Love emanated out from the soul of the son to that of the father. And then Keats was gone.

In an instant, his place had been taken by Grandma Nadine, a woman Theo had deeply loved throughout his life, until she had peacefully left her body in bed at the age of eighty-two. Nadine had led a life characterized by hardship and suffering. Her family had lost its fortune in the collapse of 1929; her lover had abandoned her after their elopement, while she was carrying his child at the age of sixteen. She had, by herself, raised a daughter in New York City during the worst years of the 1930s. Then she had married a bully who wanted nothing to do with her daughter, a man who shouted at her if his dinner was delayed, and who tried to farm her child out to relatives.

Theo had suffered, too, inwardly but equally painfully. And the two souls found each other and bonded. Some of his happiest childhood days had been those visiting her in Florida at the beach and when she brought him soothing milkshakes during stretches of illness. In later years, she had often taken him to lunch, when he was just out of college, working at his art, and penniless. They had cared for each other without any bounds or barriers. Theo thanked destiny for giving him such a grandmother.

Now here she stood, in the angelic equivalent of one of her colorful Florida muumuus. Her hair was still done in a "permanent," and the flaccid flesh under her chin and on her cheeks struck Theo as thoroughly lovable. From her eyes and mouth radiated the childlike love that had always characterized her.

These two had no unresolved business. They had honestly loved one another in life, and continued to do so now that one of them no longer existed in bodily flesh. Nadine was a woman of strong faith, not churchly faith, not faith memorized from a book or instilled by preachers, but *human* faith, the kind that prompts one to acts of self-sacrificing generosity and clear belief in the better times that lay ahead. She had been abandoned and abused, used and tricked, cheated on and stolen from. And yet she remained loving and tender, understanding, patient, and generous.

264

Although she had never followed any spiritual tradition, Nadine now smiled at her grandson as though she herself had long been a yogi. She could see what he was striving for, and she approved of his efforts. And she could see that he had made great progress in opening up his heart, which had long been buried beneath rock layers of fear and hurt. Everything radiating from this loving woman said, "I approve!"

For his part, Theo sent back to her laser beams of Pure Consciousness. He wanted her to meditate when she next came back to earth, from the heavenly plane where she now resided. Her soul had such purity that, once she got on it, the path to the goal would be short. For Love was the great Enlightener: It washed away ignorance in its floods; It burnt away confusion in its Sun. And Nadine consisted entirely of Love.

With her signature gentle nod of acceptance, Nadine slowly dissolved into the icy air.

A few moments passed, and then, almost hesitatingly, came the spirit of Elsa, his sister. Although named after her paternal grandmother, Elsa more closely resembled Nadine. In fact, if Nadine's soul had been purged of all memory of pain and trouble, Elsa's might have been the result.

She was a seer of fairies as a little girl, and a witness of angels as a young woman. She had been the one who coaxed Theo into signing up for meditation classes. She and three of her friends, all graced with celestial perception, had taken Theo and his logical male friends on picnics, complete with stuffed animals that the girls believed to be alive, attended by eight-foot-tall blue angels, and spiced with abundant laughter, joy, and merriment.

Elsa lived as if her feet did not touch the earth. All that was important for her existed in the heart, in Consciousness, and in the realms of heavenly beings. Then, one day, she found her husband dead in their bathroom. A heart attack had struck him down at forty.

And he left no savings and no life insurance. Elsa had two young daughters, and knew no trade from which she could earn a living. Thus began the unbearable stress that finally broke her mind. One day she, too, was found dead by a paramedic called to the house by worried neighbors.

Elsa and Theo had been alone together in the unhappy house of their childhood. Both were loners, so they never really came to know each other until their young adult years. Meditation brought them together. Elsa supported his aspirations as an artist, and drew up astrological charts and commentaries on them for his use and benefit. They grew close, especially after she bore her first child.

Theo could see that Elsa had been hesitant to come to this cave. For an instant, he wondered why. But then the answer flashed: she worried that he might judge her for the mental collapse after her husband's death. Nothing could be further from the truth!

She appeared as he had last seen her: a bit heavy of "body," blue eyes immaculately bright, and mouth almost imperceptibly smiling. She wore white, but white in the style of the loose dresses she had long preferred. It took only one look for her worry to disappear. The two souls connected immediately and at the deepest possible level. Elsa was a highly evolved soul, who had sought out meditation as a twelve-year-old girl in a small Midwestern town, who had spent her entire lifetime seeking the Truth and spreading her Love. If anyone could appreciate what Theo was doing in this surrealistic ice cave it was Elsa.

They stretched their hands out toward each other. Though the hands did not touch, the intent made it seem as though they did. The brother sent out to her all his compassion and tenderness. He expressed through thought his deep gratitude for her having gotten him on the path this time around. He showed her how sorry he was that she had had to leave her body while sick and alone in a cold Iowa attic. Receiving this welcome energy, Elsa brightened up and showed more of her wonted childlike joy.

266

She praised his dedication in coming to India so late in life. Her thoughts indicated approval of his isolation amidst the soaring Himalayas and in the company of invisible Saints. She wished that she had been able to join him here, but hers was a different plan.

They could not easily bear to break off their reunion, so she lingered and they basked in one another's aura. But, finally, an irresistible call came, and Elsa began to float away. She did not dissolve, but faded back into a deep space lit by an otherworldly glow. They both smiled; and then she was gone.

Icing the Soul

After the parade of visitations from people he had lost during his lifetime, Theo sank once again into the pristine, icy Silence of the Absolute. For an unknown length of time, he remained with his eyes closed. He did not open them to drink water or to eat food. Nor did he adjust his position on the quartered sleeping back. He simply sat.

What was actually happening to Theo at this time was the overpowering of the body-sense by Pure Consciousness. Bodily urges ceased to have importance, and, somehow, the body stopped needing the food and water it normally demanded. The Bliss of the Absolute utterly dominated his attention. It surrounded him, composed him, suffused him, and *was* him. Nothing else existed; nothing else could be conceived of.

When he finally did open his eyes, Theo saw the same ice cave he had seen before; but now it looked different. The cave was the same in terms of outward appearance, but it had lost its sense of tangibility. It struck him more as an "image" of an ice cave than as a "real" one. The image sort of flickered, like the reel of a very old movie; it had no depth, only surface. There was something "tentative" about what he saw, something momentary, something evanescent.

Theo didn't think about what he was experiencing. The long immersion in Being had partially frozen his mind. That's what Being did, after all, and what it was meant to do: stop the functioning of the mind. To a modern person such a result sounds terrifying, like insanity. But the yogis of India understood that Enlightenment arose at the precise moment when the mind completely ceased to function.

Such cessation did not mean that a Realized Being could not perform perfectly well, even brilliantly, in matters normally thought to require a highly functioning "mind." It did mean that the "monkey mind," which darts from one idea to the next, which constantly dredges up memories, which constantly looks forward in time, and which constantly attaches itself to desirable objects and seeks to repel undesirable ones, disappeared. The functions of what would normally be called a "mind" were now taken over by the spontaneous arising of words and actions appropriate to the occasion.

Thus, since mulling over the new way his Consciousness presented the ice cave served no evolutionary purpose, Theo did not engage in it. In earlier times, he would have wondered what the changed perception meant, speculated on its benefit, and imagined what great progress it indicated for him. And all that thinking would have amounted to wasted energy, a distraction from simply Being, as he was now.

Knowing that his time in the ice cave had come to an end, the recluse picked up his few possessions and departed. The exterior of the glacier still showed its kaleidoscopic facets, but all their colors looked like so many gemstones protected by thick plate glass. The immediacy of experience had left him. He was no longer an active participant in perception. The percept remained, but he had withdrawn his own involvement in the process of perceiving.

Theo, out in the open in the wide space of the glacier, up in the high elevations of the Himalaya Mountains, no longer comprehended objects as external to himself. It seemed to him as though his Awareness was a gigantic bubble inside of which fit everything he observed. The separation between himself as the observer and the perceived object as the observed no longer existed. His soul had expanded to such dimensions that it was capable of holding the whole world within its sphere.

A thermometer and an anemometer would have told Theo that the temperature hovered around the zero-degree mark, and that the easterly winds blew at thirty miles an hour. But his body, wrapped only in a coat, felt no discomfort. The fire of the inner heat had been set blazing, and the ingle now burned bright.

He had no plan, but simply kept walking forward, noticing the blues and gray-blues of the mountains looming up all around him.

Had he been musing, which he was not, he would have remarked the twin bands of glacier slanting down a mountainside to his right. They showed the texture of roughly broken glass shards and possessed the coloring of a twilight sky. In the area a quarter mile ahead of him, lay an expanse of pyramidal ice clusters tourmaline-blue in hue. Fingers, arms, wings, and bodies of spectral white climbed up into recessed areas and crevices of the mountains above the twin glaciers.

The highest peaks had been rounded off smoothly by deep falls of snow. Some resembled waves rising toward the oncoming shore. Others looked like cyclonic cloud masses as seen from outer space. And the uppermost one might have been an A-shaped temple painted in the white of purity by its loyal congregation

Theo walked alone in a world where human beings ought really not to have been. For this world belonged to the elements of rock and ice, snow and wind, sky and peak. But since he no longer truly identified himself as a human, he walked on, without a thought in the world.

Any normal person observing him would have feared for the man's life. After all, he was not appropriately dressed for the increasingly bitter cold, had no idea where shelter might be found, and lacked any plan for reaching a destination. But Theo was not perturbed in the least. He just continued to march forward, quietly absorbed in the cocoon of Being that now enveloped him.

As the afternoon advanced, and the wind increased in force and frigidity, he stopped and looked around. No thought came, "You should seek shelter," but he observed his surroundings nevertheless. He stood in a perfectly circular space covered in snow about six inches deep. Walls of rock rose straight up all around him. But directly ahead was a narrow opening in the rock, something like the entryway through which gladiators marched into the Coliseum. At the edge of the opening stood an extremely tall Being. The angel, or whatever it might have been, extended to a height of twenty feet. It possessed no discernible human features, only a body of soft, silverish light. Theo understood that he was meant to follow this Being.

The passage through which they walked was remarkable. Its walls, of perfectly smooth granite, stretched higher than the eye could see. And its floor, made of the same granite as the walls, was barren of snow. And, oddly, this floor felt warm, as if it had been placed directly above a massive underground fire.

The two walked for some time. Theo showed no curiosity about what was happening; he simply accepted it and went along as he was intended to. Eventually, they reached another circular space, like the first one, whence he had entered the passage, but larger and devoid of snow. No roof covered this round space; yet, the sky could not be seen above it. And it had no walls: it looked like an oversized communion wafer floating in space.

Theo sat down and crossed his legs in the full lotus position. The tall Being was now nowhere to be seen. The yogi's eyes naturally closed and he sank deep within the Self. At some point, he was prompted to open them again. On the far side of the circle sat a God, whom Theo recognized as Ishvara, the Creator of the Universe.

One could see that the God's form was like that of a human, that the shape of his face could have been that of an Indian gentleman. But little else conveyed an impression of a human being. Ishvara's face and body consisted entirely of colored light. His face was an oval of soft white light. Set in it were large eyes of the deepest black. Violaceous swirls indicated the folds of his loose garment. A scarf of aqua light draped over his left shoulder and onto his right arm. An aura of gentle luminance radiated out from the body of the God in threads and waves of pink and sky blue and ultramarine.

The yogi prostrated before Ishvara and did not rise. Eventually, a quiet but authoritative intuition summoned him to an upright position. Theo did not reflect on what he was experiencing, but an all-knowing observer would have remarked that the effect of Ishvara's energy on

271

the man was profound. He had been greatly changed by that of his Master and the other Realized Beings whose company he had been honored to share. But the magnitude of the emanations passing through him from the other side of this circle proved tectonic. He was blasted into a million pieces; solid residues buried deep in his soul were exploded as if by nitroglycerine charges. His soul got stretched and pulled, palpated and massaged, twisted and bent. Had he been considering his experience, Theo would have seriously wondered if he would live to remember it. For these energetic assaults threatened the very nature of his soul.

Ishvara did not telepathically talk with him as the other Enlightened Beings had. No thoughts passed between them. The observer previously mentioned would have concluded that the God was beyond human communications. But Theo did manage to express one thought to Ishvara: "Please show me who you are."

Then, as the yogi looked into the very deep black holes of the God's eyes, he was sucked straight into them as if by some immensely powerful force. And then he beheld a brightness such as he had never conceived possible, as if a million noon suns were blazing at full potency. The Light gave way to a vision of unlimited galaxies, billions of clusters of twinkling stars stretching out into an infinite distance. The galaxies disappeared and in their place appeared billions of people of every size and shape and color, people hurrying about their business, people dying in their beds, people suffering in their pains, babies crying, children playing, lovers cooing. Everywhere the yogi looked, there were people and more people and still more people.

Then the people left the scene, and the heavens appeared in their place. He witnessed myriads of spirits savoring the subtle pleasures of their celestial abodes. Angels floated past him to the sweet sounds of flute music. Archangels wrapped great wings around the angels in their charge. The perfume of Love scented the air.

272

The heavens gave way to the hells. Dark souls battled in their greed and anger. Sharp words cut the smoky air. Tension permeated every crevice of the polluted space. These souls hated and fought, argued and ranted, struggled and connived. All distrusted the others. Plots and schemes were constantly laid and set.

And the hells faded and there was....Light! Not the overwhelming light of the million suns, but a gracious, tender Light that lapped one's heart and cuddled one's soul. This soft Light reached high and stretched low. It extended left and it spread right. It so filled space that there was room for nothing else. And then the vision ended.

The yogi sat once again across the circle from the God Ishvara. But now the colors that had formerly surrounded him changed. Immense concentric circles of stars, an image out of a Hubble Telescope photograph, floated above his left shoulder. A series of Saints, radiant in their spiritual beauty, passed by his right arm. Out of his navel appeared fields of flowers petaled in scarlet and snow and royal blue and vast ranges of colossal mountains, and oceans rising in waves as tall as ramparts.

All these stellar and spiritual bodies, all this flora, and all these peaks and billows were of the same essence as the God Himself. They flowed out of His Light and consisted of nothing but that Light.

Suddenly, Theo saw himself in the spot where Ishvara had been. And all the Light that had formed the God now formed Him. And then the God was there and then it was Theo. The figures kept reversing one after another. Finally, Ishvara became a uniform mass of blinding Light. And then he was gone.

Theo sat in Silence with his eyes closed. Nothing of what had just passed rose up before his inner eye. All that he knew and all that concerned him was this Silence of Pure Being. Time was forgotten. Space was unconceived. Nothing was Everything. There was only the Absolute and it sufficed.

Higher Still

When he finally did open his eyes, the recluse found his body in a tiny enclosure of rocks, out among the exquisite Himalayas, under the brilliance of the morning sun. Nothing around him suggested the snowless circle; there wasn't a hint of a narrow passage, just this circle of rocks, which served to buffer the chill winds of the high mountains.

He felt thirsty and looked around. The canteen was there, so he drank. As to hunger, he felt none, even though he could not have said when he last ate. The cold air and the wind that managed to sneak in between the rocks, bit his face, but the yogi felt warm inside.

Finally, faintly, a vestige of his mind showed itself. He smiled at the recollection of Ishvara. And he directed a silent prayer of gratitude to his Master, who had, without doubt, gifted him with this supreme vision. Arjuna had experienced a similar vision in the *Bhagavad Gita*, with Krishna as his benefactor. The seeker understood that he had been placed in precious company and felt grateful, indeed.

He stood up and surveyed the landscape. What he saw all around him would have reminded few human beings of the earth with which they were familiar. The crescent shape of the most distant mountains seemed to comprise hundreds of guttering candles of colossal proportions. Just as such candles form bizarre, baroque, vertical encrustations, so these mountainsides bore weird melted shapes, as if they had been made of wax and had become distorted under the heat of the sun. Or they might have reminded an observer of one of those completely seamed and deeply wrinkled, parchment-skinned faces sometimes seen on very old people who have toiled outside all their lives. A child would have wished to run her hand over the contours of these mountainsides, for they would have felt like so many ridges and nodules to a sufficiently gigantic palm.

In the middle-ground, three perfectly smooth declivities might have been ski runs. Their snow ought to have made them white, but these inclined planes picked up some of the midnight blue of the cliffs nearby. Two of these cliffs, whose rough texture and jagged edges recalled extinct volcanoes, formed a lane down which ran a cadet-blue "river" of pyramidal ice-shapes, each roughly three feet high.

Close to the yogi reared steep walls of black rock reminiscent of sharp-edged coal chunks magnified one thousandfold.

No caves nor natural alcoves could be seen. If the earth might be described as sometimes wild, this place was the wildest imaginable. But the walker did not worry about his situation or ponder the possibilities for improving it. Instead, he simply trusted in destiny, and continued to move forward toward those rugose mountains in the far distance.

The simple act of walking here proved arduous. The ground, rather than being flat, consisted of an endless stretch of sharp-pointed rocks and pieces of ice. Theo had to move carefully so that he did not lose his balance and strike his head on one of these spikes. And the ice was slick, and that slickness also presented challenges at every step.

He finally felt hungry and thought of sitting down to eat. But where could he find a smooth place on which to sit? Glancing down, he noticed a flat rock of exactly the size required. He hadn't seen it before; it seemed to have appeared out of nowhere.

As he chewed his dried fruit and sipped some water, the recluse gazed about. The weird, extra-planetary scene still presented itself, but, as before, in that shallow, façadelike way in which he had seen things since the Ishvara episode. A typical person would never have imagined that these colossal walls of rock could possibly be viewed as flimsy, but so he now viewed them. He could make out all the details, as the other viewer would have, but these elevated masses still struck him as mere overlays. Pulsing through them, revealing Itself as their true nature, was Consciousness. Consciousness was at play here, as it was everywhere. Only now he could see it with his outer as well as his inner eye. The vast lithic world that surrounded him was actually only a configuration of his own Self, the Absolute that underlay the entire universe and all that it contained.

Refreshed, he stood up and continued his trek toward those melted mountainsides in the far distance. The going was slow: each step required precise foot placement. Theo did not think about what he was doing, but he automatically advanced slowly and with exquisitely balanced body.

Night fell and he looked around for a place to spend the externally dark hours. As fate would have it, he stood next to an outcropping of rocks having that now familiar pyramidal shape. The rocks stood four feet high and, if he positioned himself correctly, the yogi could stretch out at their bases and gain protection from the nighttime winds.

He would normally have meditated now, but the exertion of climbing through such difficult terrain, combined with the ever-thinner air, had tired his body considerably. So he stretched out and passed into his new form of sleep.

This sleep had none of the obliviousness of regular human sleep. Theo remained aware and alert all through its duration. Its purpose was solely the refreshment of the physical shell. His mind now barely functioned, and, doing so little work, did not require cessation of awareness to rejuvenate itself.

So his body slept while his Awareness continued. He did not cogitate; he did not plan or muse or remember or conjecture. He simply remained Aware, joyful and peaceful in his own Consciousness.

Someone learned in the teachings of Vedanta would have described the seeker's condition as that of the Witness. The Witness is the Silent Awareness that lives in human beings, ignorant and Enlightened, twenty-four hours a day. It is the Witness that informs the awakening sleeper that she has "rested deeply." For while one's thoughts may be stilled during deep sleep, one's Awareness is not.

One's Consciousness Witnesses the inert state of mind and body and reports back that the sleep was, indeed, deep.

Theo had begun to live aspects of the state of the Realized, despite not yet having attained the Goal. Quieting the mind like this, being able to spend long periods without thinking, served as a milestone for progress on the path. Isolation, long periods of deep meditation, the influence of the Holy Men he had spent time with, and his already advanced state of evolution had combined to bring him to this point. And it was with a happy heart that he observed his own Consciousness throughout that long and very cold night.

Before Dawn

Darkness still prevailed, but Theo was upright and deep in the Self at the commencement of Brahmamuhurtha, that period ninety minutes before sunrise, which yogis understand as the ideal time to meditate. Ayurvedic medicine states that the body contains three energies or doshas that regularly circulate in it and govern physiological activity. One is predominant in any of six four-hour cycles. Vata, the dosha related to air and space, rules the body from 2 a.m. until 6 a.m. It is then that one is able to proceed deepest in meditation.

When he finally opened his eyes, they beheld not a world, but an exquisite dream of beauty. The entire space before him was covered by a gently undulating mass of cloud. The cloud billow presented itself in cerise and raspberry, sobered rose and livid purple. At its summit, where it thinned, the rose and purple gave way to shell pink and peach. And tiny, thin, wispy fragments of cloud, quite high up, had their white tinged ever so faintly by pink dye.

The predawn light had combined with the early-morning fog to completely blot out mountains that were the largest features on the face of the earth. A painter would have imagined herself at the edge of not a wine-*dark* sea, but one showing the more delicate hue of a sweet rosé. It was a sea of rose water, a vast bath of fragile petals, in which the painterly eye could bask and refresh itself for further labors.

But the yogi did not contemplate this marvelous scene with the vision of an artist. He saw its beauty, but that beauty did not invoke his emotions or disturb his hard-won steadiness of mind. And this roseate ocean respired with the sweet breath of Consciousness as did everything that now came into his Awareness.

As the dazzling wafer of the sun appeared over the rim of the eastern range, its circumference spoked with flares of various lengths and brightness, shooting a 200,000-candlepower spotlight straight at the yogi, the cloud cover dissolved as if it had never existed, revealing the mountains on the western side. These were the ones that resembled melted candles. They now shone as huge pieces of pink chocolate from which many bites had been taken. The shadows on their far and nearest edges so cut off the highest and lowest points of the mountains that their entire visible shape could be seen as an immense Norse warrior, long shaggy hair hanging down his chest, every muscle and tendon detailed, and his arm bent to strike.

Such glorious natural beauty would have been hard for almost anyone to resist. It was as if the Himalayas existed to serve as the ultimate test for those seekers determined to rise above any and all attachments to which a human being might be susceptible. Theo saw the gnawed pink chocolate; he saw the muscled Norse warrior; but neither of them mattered to him in the least. The one thing that did matter was the vibrant Being radiating out of those mountains, shining inside of and pouring down out of that sun, the Being that constituted Him, the world, and everything in it, from the smallest gnat to the most unimaginably large supergalaxy. And Being was what he saw.

Through the expanding pink aura of the mountains walked the parka-clad seeker. The spotlight followed him, lighting up the way for his feet, as they positioned themselves carefully to avoid sharp apexes and ankle-threatening holes. No wind blew, so the stillness of the high-altitude morning spread vast and deep. Theo had no plan other than to keep moving forward, onward to those highest peaks in the very far distance.

A rational observer would have tugged at the sleeve of the man's coat and asked, "Why do you wish to go up there? You will only find death. Most human bodies cannot survive such elevations without the benefit of extra oxygen. And what will you do at that summit once you arrive?" But no such reasoner existed. And the trekker failed to ask himself such questions. These days he relied solely on his intuition to guide him, and his intuition told him to push on, ever higher, until he attained the zenith of these holy mountains.

279

As he walked, the yogi had the strange sensation of moving within himself: it was as though he were stretched out and constantly passing into his own Self. None of the traditional subject-object dichotomy pertained to him any longer. There was no "him" trekking through a separate and distinct "world." Rather, there was simply a vast sea of Consciousness made to ripple by the apparent motion of a body.

It had been a very long time since Theo had interacted with other people. Not since he had left the Master's cave and said goodbye and thank you to the villagers had he had even a glimpse of another human being. Yet he felt no loneliness; the company of the Absolute was all the company one ever needed.

His metabolism had greatly slowed by this point. He needed little nourishment, which was fortunate, for he carried the scantiest supply of food. Water was readily available in the form of melted snow, so the trekker had no concerns on that score. His boots showed severe signs of wear. The functional brain alerted him about their condition. Would they even make it to the summit? The question was quite reasonable. But not once did Theo debate or ponder his next move. He functioned on a sort of autopilot now, the body simply moved and did what it was required to do, without any intentional guidance from the mind.

Seeing a shadow on the ground before him, the walker looked up. Circling several hundred feet over his head was a golden eagle. Its crown and neck feathers were blackish-brown and edged in tawny gold. The bird's thighs, tail, and shoulders were distinctly rough-brown, and its wings were mottled with yellowish-white.

The yogi did not ponder the significance of seeing this bird, which traditionally symbolizes the connection with Spirit, and endows its viewer with the courage to move forward to a meeting with the power inherent in Spirit. But he did smile at seeing a fellow creature here in this endless expanse of rocks and snow.

280

The eagle began to perform dextrorotatory circles around the man, flying slowly, and always to the right, and keeping up with his progress. A shaman would have made much of this appearance and circumgyration by the ruler of the bird kingdom. He would have seen a tutelary guide sent to lead the traveler to his goal in the world of souls. But Theo gave not even the briefest thought to such ideas, simply rejoicing in the appearance of this graceful, gold-trimmed creature gliding in that thin air near the top of the world.

At some point the eagle stopped circling and set out in an eastern direction. But it never flew out of sight. In fact, it several times returned to the hiker as though to indicate that he should follow it. And so he did.

The going was very slow now. Theo had been climbing for days, and the oxygen in the air had progressively thinned. The ground offered little in the way of smooth surfaces, consisting instead of jagged salients, uneven rocks, and surprising holes. The weather had gotten colder and, at times, the wind blasted out from the east like an icy laser.

Slow or not, the seeker kept moving, watching where the eagle flew, and doing his best to follow its path forward. He did not wonder where the bird was leading him, nor did he imagine what might await him when he arrived there. He simply allowed the body to automatically proceed as it wished to, under no intentional guidance from its inhabitant.

Where the Eagle Lands

Several hours later, when the sun had already sunk below the western range, Theo reached an area of graupel-covered rocks whose even undulations looked like ocean waves or a herd of sleeping seals. The consistency of these ridged waves gave them the illusion of motion.

The eagle had alighted on a higher pile of rocks in the near distance. Early twilight rendered the wavy rocks in the more shadowed areas lotus, and their lighter counterparts, butterfly blue. At the far end of the stony "surf" rose a flattened pyramid of ice whose blue hue, though close to cerulean, was actually that unique color seen only in blue icebergs. This mound, which stood fifteen feet high, appeared to be made of gel. It had the uniform consistency of that substance, and its color did not at all seem to belong to things terrestrial.

Theo immediately climbed to its top and sat down. The cold of the ice proved so extreme that his body instantly numbed. Nevertheless, he closed his eyes and allowed his awareness to bask in the Bliss of the Absolute.

Then he found himself above the earth, looking down at the Himalayas. The eagle floated off to his right. The blue ice mound looked, from this height, like a lustrous gem set in the rusticated metal of the wavy rocks. From it came a throbbing energy: it must have been endowed with a supernatural essence that caused it to possess immense power and unique appearance. Maybe, an observer would have mused, it had landed on the earth from some other planet.

Theo passed through space easily. He saw the magnificent crescent of this portion of the Himalayas, the thread of the Ganges, and the plains below them. In front of him floated the moon, softly luminous, pocked, and homey. And behind this satellite rock spread an infinity of stars, some glowing blue and some white, some flashing silver and some radiant in soft red. He had always wanted to fly, but now that he could, the yogi took no satisfaction in the feat. Being up here, above the planet, was no different from being down there upon it, for the Absolute permeated both and everything else besides.

In an instant, he found himself on an astral plane, where he watched, as a participant, the heavenly scene he had previously witnessed as a guest of Ishvara. Now he floated beside the spirits, who acknowledged him with a gentle nod or a delicate smile. What he noticed most here was the utter absence of anything earthy. These souls had no appetites, no corporal bodies, no physical senses. They enjoyed the fruits of their previous good deeds and enjoyed delights of the soul: tranquility, peacefulness, cooperation, joy, and love. They neither sought anything nor resisted anything, but simply accepted with gratitude what came their way.

These, the yogi realized, were the good souls who had lived upstanding lives on earth, but had never made efforts to seek Enlightenment or transcend their earthly condition. Their good karma exhausted, they would return to the planet to work off the bad. It might be in the next life, or it might be many lives in the future, but, at some point, each would turn inward and develop Pure Consciousness. And then would commence their determined march to the great goal.

With the snap of some invisible finger, Theo was transported to the hell of demons. This, too, he had watched from a distance in his vision with Ishvara. But now he stood amongst these miserable souls. His Awareness perceived their ferocious energies as an attack on Its tranquility. And that attack proved hard to resist. Bombs of invective exploded all around him. Missiles of hatred blew up nearby. Souls grappled ferociously right before his eyes. The very air stank with deceit and treachery. The place was like the crime scene of a mass murder. Everywhere he turned came some new noxious vibration.

Although he sought to remain steady in his Self, the banging and poking and tearing directed at him as a newcomer here ruffled his Peace. The thought came to him that he was clearly not yet fully established in Pure Consciousness, since these forces of darkness were able to pull him away from it. To his Calmness, they opposed rancor; against his Peace, they sent war; and contrary to his Bliss, they leveled hatred. While their chaos and cacophony failed to elicit negative feelings in his soul, they did succeed in tinting the perfection of his Silence.

Theo opened his eyes and found himself back on that amazing "blue ice" pyramid. The golden eagle had lit on the same spot it had occupied before.

For the first time in a while, the seeker explored his experience. The reason for his doing so was also the subject of his investigation: the hellish souls had rattled him! They had not managed to overset him completely, but they had certainly blurred the clear Awareness he had grown used to enjoying. Why was this? he asked himself. He ought to have been able to see Oneness even in the grim divisions of hell. Nothing, no matter how much it reeked of tamasic energy, should have succeeded in shaking his steadiness. All that he could conclude was that his path lay still before him. He had some distance to travel, till he should reach that peak from which no force, no matter how negative its charge, would be able to move him.

And so he stood up, and left that gel-like mound, and continued toward those far peaks, whose summits must have been the wicks of their guttered candles.

The Robed Back

The eagle had disappeared. Apparently, its mission had been accomplished in that Dantean flight through the welkin and the other worlds. So Theo continued his pilgrimage to the heights without another creature in sight.

As the afternoon ended, the landscape got bathed in a light of gold more precious than any king's treasury. The rough ground to his immediate right gleamed like piles of strewn nuggets. The higher hills above this ground resembled bars of gold warped under great heat. A stretch of glacial ice could have been an auric platter capable of carrying a banquet fit for gods.

A poet might have imagined one of these gods pouring a valley-sized bucket of golden paint over this entire section of the Himalayas. For every inch of it, every peak, hill, glacier, rock field, and crevice was sparkling, brilliant gold.

The trekker saw this sight and kept moving on. For as marvelous as its beauty was, he knew Perfect Beauty in Infinite Being. He saw the gold shimmering from the rocks, but more impressive to him by far was the faintly rippled waves of Consciousness that permeated the rocks, the gold, and the sky. Superficial beauty could no longer capture him; Infinite Beauty was all that truly mattered.

Progress got harder and harder with every step he took. No amount of acclimation could prepare the body for the attenuated air at this altitude. And the cold numbed the limbs, making walking as difficult as performing ballet in steel-toed boots. The wind blew constantly now, and it entered into one's body regardless of all the intervening layers of clothing.

The sun had set and night was approaching. Theo looked around for some shelter, any shelter, from the dangerous weather. He saw neither a cave nor a recess in the mountain where he might hide from the elements.

But then he noticed a robed figure ahead of him on the ice. There was no mistaking it: the form was that of his Master. Instantly, he followed it.

The white robe turned past a corner of rock and stopped about fifty yards ahead of the seeker, who could still see him only from behind. At first, Theo could not detect anything useful. But then he looked closer and noticed that a bulge in the side of the mountain offered the narrowest of slit openings in the side facing inward. Dropping his backpack, he got down on his knees and squeezed through the slim space. He found himself inside what amounted to an igloo made of stone. The floor of the igloo spread smooth, clean, and dry. No signs of habitation could be seen.

Theo exited to fetch his backpack and looked around for the Master, who was nowhere to be found. The disciple whispered a heartfelt "thank you" to the Saint before crawling back in to the welcome protection of the stone hut.

He wished he had a fire. Looking left, he saw a small pile of seasoned wood, which he knew had not been there five minutes before. And he once again prayed his gratitude. After lighting the fire, Theo huddled next to it, as close as could safely get, and wallowed in its warmth. His body seemed literally to defrost beside the grateful flames of that small fire. Cold had worked its way into his very bones, and now the heat winkled it out of them quite effectively.

The Bliss he constantly experienced got stirred by the appearance of his Master. Flat Joy, now enlivened, washed over him in waves. The Master had kept his eye on him! The Saint was traveling with him on this journey to the ultimate heights. A sensation of being a child enwrapped in its mother's arms warmed the pilgrim as much as the snapping fire, with all its wildly dancing oranges and blues.

That night's sleep proved a godsend. The terrain, air, and weather of the high Himalayas had left their impression on the trekker. Eating little and constantly exposed to the cold and the winds, Theo's body had weakened markedly. A night of warmth and shelter had come just in time to stave off illness or worse.

He must have slept the clock around. When he opened his eyes, the fire was nothing more than frigid ashes. His Consciousness had not changed, but his body felt greatly refreshed. The burden of fatigue and weakness had been thrown off. He found some dried food and ate it in slow bites, slaking his thirst from the canteen.

Instinct told him that he should stay here for a short while, in order to recruit his energy and strengthen his body. He wished that he had access to more firewood. Only a glance was needed to show him a surprising new stack of dried wood in the same spot where he had found the first one.

He could hear the banshee wails of the east wind as it whipped across the glacier, growing colder with every mile of ice it passed over. The wind shrieked high and then moaned low; it sawed in quick cuts and it growled in low threats. Had there been anything other than rocks and ice here, the tempest would have picked it up and carried it away. But the rocks simply withstood the onslaught, and the ice, at most, gave a thin peeling of its crust up to the greedy gale.

No man would have been able to withstand these blasts. Theo had found shelter at precisely the right time; otherwise, he would certainly have been lifted off his feet and sent like a propelled bullet straight into the nearest rock face standing in the wind's path.

A normal man would now have felt that ever-so-reassuring sensation of being protected from the storm busy unleashing its fury outside. But the seeker had no such comforting thought. Oh, he was grateful for the shelter, no doubt about that, but he no longer called up the ancient thoughts grooved into humanity's deep memory by two hundred thousand years of battles for survival. Constant meditation had erased most all of his vasanas, the canalized impressions that guide most people's behavior. He now acted spontaneously, by the inspiration of Pure Consciousness, freed from the toils of endless repetition of learned responses.

But though Theo did not spend time musing on his condition, an onlooker would have easily understood the predicament he had narrowly escaped. He had walked on the razor's edge the previous day. The storm would have devoured him, but the intercession of the Saint, and his creation of the rock-shelter, pulled the pilgrim out of its jaws at the last possible moment.

As Theo reposed in meditation, the observer might have noted the dramatic contrast between the peaceful Silence inside both the hut and the man and the violent cacophony of the elements outside. The seeker floated in Oceanic Bliss; the blasts of the hurricane tore at the earth like gigantic, demonic claws.

Time completely disappeared for the lone soul in the stone hut. He ate a lit, drank some water, and sat by the fire, relishing the vital power that it brought into his muscles. But mainly he meditated or slept with a Witnessing Eye always open.

The storm showed no signs of abating; it was as if a huge gate had been flung open, allowing the icy gusts of Boreas, the god of the frozen winds, to rush unhindered across the wide Himalayas. Theo did not venture outside. If he had, he would have seen airborne chaos: snow lifted from the ground and churned up and down, round and round in the air; pieces of ice and small stones hurtling like flung weapons toward invisible foes; mattresses of fog ripped and shredded into fluff and then swallowed by the gale. The mountains were largely hidden from sight by the snow-laden winds. Boulders that would normally have looked immovable appeared ready to topple under the incessant and powerful fulminations from the northeast. The ground itself seemed to surrender, breaking up into chunks and flakes, which got sucked into the vortex of the storm.

But through it all, the lone seeker basked in the warming glow of the Absolute.

The Storm Departs

Theo didn't know, but it was a week after he had entered the shelter before the storm finally ended. Although there had been few troops and little equipment on the battlefield, it still showed signs of the war that had passed over it. Rocky debris, new to the area, had been scattered all over the ice. Twigs and cones that must have been carried many miles littered the snow. Some places had been swept clear of snow and others showed deep drifts piled up by the winds.

The yogi ventured out to test his newfound strength. And he smiled at the welcome sight of the highest peaks, which stared down at him like elders awaiting his respectful visit. His body felt good, felt strong. Rest, warmth, and some nourishment had done wonders for it. He knew that he was now capable of continuing his pilgrimage.

After gathering his few possessions and strapping on the backpack, Theo bowed to the hut, for, like a good Samaritan, it had welcomed him into its home at his hour of greatest need. At the same time, he said a silent prayer to his Master, whose gift he knew the hut to be.

An experienced climber would have known that the summits toward which the seeker moved stretched two thousand feet above his present location. That expert would have doubted the wisdom of a man of Theo's age attempting such a climb, at this season, with limited equipment. But no expert stood there to warn Theo off. Not even the golden eagle showed up to guide his steps ever higher. The pilgrim was on his own; but, in his present view of the world, his "own" included all that he saw and even everything that lay beyond his sight.

Slowly and carefully he made his way higher. An accident could be fatal, so he watched where he put his feet and how he spent his energy. The Saint, he knew, was watching over, guiding, and protecting him. Destiny would unfurl itself just as it was meant to. No mistakes were possible. But part of destiny was acting in an optimal manner, performing right action at every step, so he took all necessary precautions to maintain his safety.

The weather grew mild, at least as mild as it could get at this height, in this place, at this season. One might have said that it was like a petulant child who had thrown a long-lasting temper tantrum, but now lay placid in its bed. Theo did not have to force his way through headwinds, nor pull his boots out of drifts as he progressed toward the peaks. The sun shone clear and bright, lighting the path before him and faintly warming his cheeks.

He had gotten so far that he could actually see, directly in front of him, the peak that he aspired to reach. It wasn't a v-shaped summit or really one especially noteworthy for its appearance. But something about it had attracted the seeker for many weeks.

The mountaintop was rounded and covered in smoothly spread snow. Approaching it stretched three wide and winding paths of level snow. Below it, on both sides, lay mamillary protuberances of similar shape. A poet might have conceived of this area as a reclining goddess with swollen and snowy breasts exposed.

This part of the mountains differed from the others surrounding it, which pointed arrowheads and tridents and clawed paws toward the overarching sky. Those others seemed masculine, but this one, welcomingly feminine. While the others threatened, this one beckoned; where they promised war, she offered peace.

But quite a distance still separated the pilgrim from his goal. The ground continued to jut upward in thousands of spiky stones, all ice-encrusted and slippery. Steep hills intervened between him and those three wide lanes, which looked so welcoming to one whose footwear had been torn by the obstacles met over many miles of climbing.

Even an experienced climber could have been excused for shaking his head and muttering a curse at the trials continually laid before him. Theo had no experience as a mountaineer, but he neither spoke harsh words nor gesticulated impatiently in regards to his situation. He had come far, and he still had a ways to go. He had survived, by the grace of the Master, what a less fortunate hiker would not have survived. He had grown in Consciousness and deepened his Awareness of the Bliss that is life. And so he would move on, regardless of what might obstruct his path.

The seeker made slow progress now, slower than he had ever made before. Breathing was a great effort. Fatigue made his legs heavy as iron bars. And the cold slowed the movement of every muscle he used to walk.

Thus, sunset arrived and he still stood far from those welcoming, smooth roads. Thick bolsters of cloud had moved in, almost completely obscuring the view in front of him. Only the soft rondure of the summit could now be seen. The clouds showed pleasing shades of carnation pink, cherry blossom, and grayish magenta. The poet would have conceived of the reclining goddess now nestling under a comforter, decorated in many shades of pink, to warm herself during the frozen night. The sun's last rays carried sufficient brightness to paint the areas where the deity's thighs might have been a warm creamy color containing an ever-so-slight hint of pink.

Theo looked around to see if there was any sort of protected place where he might shelter for the night. But there was none. The best he could do was a relatively flat space not much bigger than his body, set all around by the sharp rocks over which he had been trudging all that livelong day.

His functional brain told him that, even inside the mummy sleeping bag, exposure to the night's weather might prove fatal. But having no other options, he accepted the one he did have. Piling up some flat stones, to keep his body away from the frozen ground, he stretched out on them and slid into the padded bag.

Contrary to weather science, the mildness of the day grew still warmer that night. The moon seemed to have taken on the role of the

291

sun, its normally passive beams somehow warming the icy rocks beneath them. And maybe a protective web was spun around the sleeper by unseen powers desirous of guaranteeing his welfare. Whatever the cause, he survived the night, with nothing more than soreness and stiff joints to show for his eight hours of exposure to the Himalayan night.

On getting up—for he spent all his nights fully Awake these days—Theo once again said a silent prayer to his Master for the assistance he knew must have been provided him to produce this miracle. He sipped some water, put snow into his canteen, and packed up his bag. And then he was off toward the maternal peak that called him on.

Anyone who had omniscient knowledge of Theo before he had come to India and now that he had been here for months would not have been able to connect the two men. His present internal experience of the world had virtually nothing in common with what it had been in the United States. As he walked now, the body that carried him did not seem to belong to him at all. In fact, it did not really appear to even exist. The rocks and clouds and sky and peak that shone before his eyes, no longer possessed the indubitable "reality" that they had in the past. Now, objects in the world showed themselves as mere conformations of the Consciousness that underlay everything. And the objects were not external to Theo, but part of his very Self, as Real to him as the Awareness that revealed them.

The ups and downs that had, in the past, lifted and depressed his mood were gone, giving way before the ocean of Peace that had flooded his Being. Nor did he spend time thinking of the past or imagining the future. Ram Dass's "be here now" recommendation had become the seeker's living reality. Whereas, in America, he had dipped into the Inner Truth occasionally, during meditation or quiet moments, that Inner World now utterly dominated his Awareness. The omniscient knower would have thought that Theo had thoroughly transformed himself in a relatively short period of time.

292

But such is the nature of spiritual evolution. One works for decades noting little progress. But then, one day, the drill of discipline finally bores completely through the rocky wall of ignorance, and the Light shines through. It may only be a single Ray, but it shines bright nevertheless.

Theo had spent lifetimes on the path to Enlightenment. He had yearned for it as a small child. And he had engaged in spiritual exercises all his adult life. When the Saint called him to India, it was in acknowledgement of how far the seeker's soul had advanced. And now the summit lay before him.

Towards the Peak

The blessing of the more temperate weather continued to grace the climber. The harsh winds had died down and the temperature stayed at a level higher than it ought to have been at this season. The reclining goddess, the poet would have said, must have welcomed her devotee's approach.

By midmorning, Theo had reached the bottom of the first smooth "lane" leading up to the summit. But he discovered that perspective had shortened the real distances and distorted the perspectives here. The flat route he had imagined actually wound round several times. And though it had looked, from a distance, to be not far from the summit, it turned out to be several miles away.

Since he had no timetable, however, none of this made any difference. His boots enjoyed the smoother terrain, and it proved both less dangerous and less fatiguing than walking on sharp stones.

A sensitive observer might have remarked on the appropriateness of this smooth white pathway to the peak, as a sort of immaculate carpet spread out to welcome the pilgrim moving toward his final destination. But Theo had no similar thought, simply remaining in the Silence which now permeated and encompassed him at all times.

As he neared the end of the first major stretch of the white way, the seeker glanced up at a rock face whose form was that of a concave hexagon: a five-sided wall whose bottom was indented in the middle. This wall stood out because no snow whatsoever stuck to it. Its color was ensign blue, and several of its facets were remarkable for being almost perfectly flat.

Theo stopped to observe it. Rock faces in these parts almost invariably showed jagged eruptions, broken ledges, or sharp angles. He had not yet come across a uniformly smooth face like this. It would not normally have attracted as much of his attention as it did. But some quality of this rock wall pulled on his soul.

294

As he stared at it, Theo lost all awareness of everything around him but the wall. First, he saw it as a quietly vibrating blue monolith. Then the blue solidity softened into a sort of loose mesh of blue-white energy. And finally everything "blue" and "wall-like" faded away, revealing the interior of that section of the mountain.

And, inside it, he saw dozens of golden Beings. He could tell that they were Yogis, for they wore ochre or white robes, long hair, and extended beards. Some of them moved around inside the mountain, just as if they were walking along a clear stream, as the Master had been wont to do. Others remained seated in meditation. The seeker noticed that there were little caves inside the interior walls of the mountain face. Sometimes a Golden Being would emerge from such a cave and stand at its entrance, as though in contemplation of the wonderful scene playing out around Him or Her.

The air inside this space was dotted with microscopic specks of soft, golden light. These dots formed themselves into streams and flowed up and down, left and right, washing the great cavern with their luminance.

Such thrilling blessedness emanated from this sight! These Beings, Theo thought, must have been great Rishis or latter-day Enlightened Ones, who had chosen to remain in the Himalayas, possibly in order to radiate benevolence to the earthly world.

The Saint had certainly led him to a holy mountain. Who could ever have imagined that it would be filled with invisible Beings living the life of the Enlightened, near the summit home of the mountain goddess?

Theo relaxed his gaze and the vision ended. Once more the ensign-blue wall stood before him as a smooth rock face vibrating with the energy of the Absolute. A well-read observer might have compared the inside of this wondrous mountainside with the treasures found in Ali Baba's cave, its gold and jewels here represented by Purity and Bliss. But no such observer could be found. And Theo merely uttered a silent word of thanks to his Master for the blessing of this vision.

Only when the yogi had put some distance between himself and the smooth mountainside did he notice that it was one of the two smaller breast shapes that he had made out while staring at the mountain from a great distance.

Time had passed and the sun was again sinking beneath the range of peaks to the west. Theo examined his immediate environment in search of shelter. The scene offered him even less protection than that of the previous night; for there were not even any pointed stones to block the wind or any flat stones to distance himself from the cold snow. Without other recourse, he decided to simply wrap himself in the sleeping bag and meditate through the night.

Just after the sun had set, the sky above him, lit by a nearly full moon, presented a strangely beautiful sight: tangerine-colored clouds wound in whorls in the near heavens. They possessed the shape of those helical constellations one sees in astronomical photographs. The space between these spiraling clouds was pigmented in a washed-out aquamarine. Sparkling from the bracelets of the tangerine clouds were diamonds made of stars. And these diamonds flashed in the open space like gemstones that had fallen off the bracelet. The sky was putting on a fine show, indeed, though Theo failed to go off in raptures about it, as a poet might have done. Instead, he closed his eyes and settling into Silence.

Transportation

After an indeterminate period of time, something prompted the meditator to open his eyes. To his surprise—for this development did indeed surprise him—Theo found himself seated in the interior of the mountain where he had earlier observed the golden Beings. The scene was just as he had envisioned it before. The same golden stream of specks glided through the air, spreading Bliss. The Beings stood or walked, sat in meditation or stood in contemplation, as they had in his vision.

None of them noticed his presence. It was as if he were invisible. For his part, Theo utterly surrendered to the atmosphere in this hidden-from-the-world space. It reminded him of the aura of that other cave in which he had, months ago, seen the six Beings in their niches. But those Beings had preserved some aspect of materiality about them; they had seemed to be both human and divine. These golden Beings were devoid of any trace of physicality. An observer might have described their forms as being loosely woven of Light beams.

The atmosphere here consisted in Purity and Bliss far superior to that which he had witnessed in his trip to the heavens. That all-knowing observer might have speculated that the air here was supercharged with the Consciousness of so many Enlightened Beings brought together in one place, that their individual Energy was exponentially increased by their proximity to one another. Theo was quite aware that this company of Realized Beings had created a spiritual space unique in his experience. It was not the Silence of personal Transcendence, but a liveliness of Being that thrilled one to the core. Here was the fun and innocence of childhood play, the infinite possibilities of youthful imagination, and the sheer delight in existence of the enraptured poet. But these delightful feelings were no longer based in ignorance and destined to be short-lived; they existed in Enlightenment and would never cease.

This inner mountain paradise made of the dreams of humankind a Reality. As he sat in his corner, Theo felt the repeated plashing of waves of Joy, which washed through his Being. His body seemed extremely light, as if it would lift off from the ground at any moment. He could not help smiling, for no apparent reason.

This was Life as it was meant to be lived: Life from which the cull and dross has been separated and discarded; Life wherein all that is worth cherishing shines bright and all that is unworthy of belonging disappears. This, the poet might have remarked, was heaven on earth!

An intuition told Theo that he remained invisible to the golden Beings because his journey to the summit had not yet been completed. He remained an outlier. But, undoubtedly due to the grace of the Master, he had been transported here so that he might witness the possibilities of Life on earth as lived by Realized Beings, and for the more practical purposed of keeping his body safe from the mortal threats of the nocturnal Himalayas.

The seeker did not need to close his eyes that night. The energy pervading the cavern refreshed his body more deeply than sleep ever could have. And he did not want to miss even a moment of the scene constantly unfolding before him. It wasn't that the Beings took any unusual actions or performed any unusual feats; they did neither. But watching them gave one an indescribable satisfaction. They shone with Perfection, and Perfection is supremely worthy of notice.

The Beings did not communicate with each other, so far as Theo could tell. Each was fulfilled and in need of nothing, not even a word or a gesture from anyone else. Still, without speaking, all of them sent forth soothing mists of love that refreshed and enlivened everything they came into contact with. One had the feeling, in this space, that everything positive that could ever be imagined might come to fruition in the very next moment. A rich sense of "all possibilities" enriched the air. Joy beyond any one had ever conceived possible could be tickled into existence by the mere movement of an eye or lift of a finger.

The intuition came to the pilgrim that these golden Beings served as protectors of Life on earth, as the positive force that would constrain the immense evils that plagued humanity. They were, in essence, the gold reserve that guaranteed the value of life for the billions who lived on the planet amidst the dreadful sufferings brought about by ignorance. They functioned as the safety net preventing the worst catastrophes from every occurring.

Theo would have been glad to remain in this joyful cavern forever had he not known that he could not possibly be a full participant in its Life until he had attained the summit himself.

Back in the Snow

Morning came to the mountain, and Theo saw that his body sat once again in the precise spot it had occupied the night before, when he had first closed his eyes to meditate. The still invisible sun had already worked its magic on the clouds overhead. They looked like pieces of rock broken off from a lava flow. Their dark edges atop gradually gave way to cinnabar, strawberry, flamingo, and flame yellow. Stray cloudlets closest to the horizon, candescent and luminiferous, seemed to have caught fire from the sun. A column of pale violet mist drained down from the far right side of the sky, spreading violaceous fog over the top of the peaks in that area. One singular cloud just to the side of that column looked like a cinder that had burst open to reveal a chrome-yellow flame burning brightly in its center.

The mountain flanks gleamed like polished coal. The snow spread out on this the second lane approaching the summit had its white tinted with the most delicate of pale purples. This was the scene in which the seeker now found himself.

The weather continued mild, a blessing not to be taken lightly by one subject to the vicissitudes of the high Himalayas. Theo packed up his folded sleeping bag, drank from his canteen, whose snow somehow always remained in liquid form, no matter the outside temperature, and chewed several pieces of his dried fruit.

He stood now at the start of the second straight avenue leading to the goddess on high. What he had not been able to notice from a distance now became apparent: this straight stretch inclined steeply. It was shorter than the first one, but it must have angled up at least thirty-degrees. No matter. He checked his gear, took a quick look at his boots, and began to walk.

Strangely, the night without sleep had actually refreshed rather than tired his body. So rich was the energy projected by the golden Beings that it had vivified and enlivened the muscles he now so greatly needed. The fact that he was able to continue climbing, at this altitude, on the meager diet that sustained him, would have amazed a physiologist. Obviously, he was drawing on some sort of energy more subtle than that provided by food.

Four hours of steady climbing brought him to a bend in the lane, one which he had not expected. Yet again, perspective had played tricks on him. It turned out that this second snow road was not one continuous path, but two, angled obtusely vis-à-vis each other. When Theo examined the new leg of the road, it gave him pause.

This second stretch inclined not at thirty degrees, as the first one had, but at forty-five. This would be the most challenging of all the trek-legs he had completed since arriving in India.

At least the path was unlittered by sharp stones and boulders one had to surmount. And the snow was no more than six inches deep; greater depth would have significantly increased the difficulty of the climb.

Like any goddess worthy of reverence, the reclining one atop this mountain proved not easy to approach. If one wished to pay his respects to her, to bend his knee and acknowledge her beauty, one first had to establish his worth. The knightly test now challenging the seeker was this steep climb up the second avenue of snow.

Theo had none of these ideas, of course. He simply assessed the task at hand and set off to accomplish it. First, he changed his climbing style: bending forward at the waist, shortening his strides, and lifting his knees higher at every step. Gravity was the opponent in this duel, so he matched its force as best he could.

Above him, attenuated clouds that looked like body-surfing angels let their wings get blown up and back by the oncoming winds. A lentil-shaped mass blocked the sun, causing its rays to spread out into distinct spotlights, of varying intensities, focused on certain areas of the mountains. The unclouded portions of the sky showed color shades ranging from pale turquoise, to cobalt, to Peking blue.

The temperature had dropped a few degrees; nevertheless, Theo had to constantly wipe sweat from his brow. His breathing was labored. It seemed impossible to satisfy the needs of his lungs for oxygen. If the goddess wanted to see her admirer panting upon his arrival, the elements all combined to fulfill her wish.

Unlike most climbers, Theo never turned to see how far he had come. Nor did he stare up at the end of the lane, hoping for its approach. Instead, he focused completely on each step that he took, maintaining the optimum posture, breathing regularly, and making sure that sweat did not get underneath his shirt, where, later, such moisture could make him colder than he needed to be.

An artist might have been inspired by this scene of a frail man making his way up an immense and steep mountainside. It did, after all, rather effectively sum up the challenge of accomplishing great things in life. A person might appear small when set against a gigantic mountain; he might look weak when compared to its massive strength. But the soul of the striver made up the difference. Theo would gladly have left his body dead on that mountainside if the only other choice had been to abandon his search for the Goal. The Spirit will always win in these contests with the elements.

Several times during the climb up the second lane Theo needed to stop and rest. Gazing around him, he took in the profound beauty of the Himalayas. The snow on the ground glittered like the lively dance of a million fairies. Fog had settled into an elbow of the mountains and resembled a vast field of billowed snow lifted from the earth and planted in the sky. Rock faces of ebony black randomly shot out lasers of white light as sunbeams caught their facets. Above it all, the goddess reclined in her curvaceous ease, a spiritual odalisque challenging the heavens and defying all earthly mortals.

As evening shadows began to spread, the seeker found himself at the end of the second lane, on a narrow chine of rock barely three feet wide. This backbone ran for a quarter mile or so, connecting, at its termination, with the third avenue leading up to the summit.

Theo looked left and right. From this straitened bridge, the drop was straight down at least 500 feet. One had to wonder if the night winds, should they pick up, might roll a human body over the edge to oblivion. The pilgrim calculated all the variables in an instant, and realized that, if he found a depression of any sort, he would be safe here for the night.

Walking forward a few yards, he came across precisely what he needed: a body-length trench about a foot deep in the exact middle of the ridge. This recess would serve two important purposes: protecting him from the weather and preventing him from literally being blown off the mountain.

Although his body craved rest, it was still too early to sleep. He sat down to meditate. The sunset reduced the mountains to stencil outlines. The glowing white orb of the earth-star was surrounded by a halo of primrose yellow. Long brushstrokes of cloud angled up from the south toward the north. Nectarine, peach, and apricots ripened in these streamers of cloud. Faint and delicate dying rays languished like weak gestures over the horizon's hills.

Theo closed his eyes to meditate.

The Mother Mountain

Theo had eventually given in to his body's craving for the horizontal position, and lain down in the narrow trench. A hyacinth-blue dragon, complete with gaping, fanged jaws and clawed feet, extended directly overhead, many miles up into the sky. Stars on its body glittered like spangled scales. The sky seemed to be snowing stars; they covered it as if frozen in mid-fall toward the earth. The brightest ones, scattered from east to west, and from north to south, formed a sort of grid, into which all the thousands of others fit.

The moon must have been out, though it was not within his range of view, for the mountains did not appear black and deep asleep, but gray and slumbering lightly. The world showed a twilight effect; it might have been watching and waiting for some dramatic development it didn't want to miss.

Theo shut his eyes and found himself in the deep Silence that served as his constant home. He could feel his body immediately begin the work of repairing itself from the day's exertions. Thousands of small operations were underway all through his organism. Tight places now relaxed; overexerted ones began to twitch; chemicals released from strained muscles triggered pain receptors; blood flowed to these muscles in larger amounts, causing them to swell; and some unknown physiological process seemed to wash the fatigue out of his limbs, so that it could be safely carried away.

The seeker Witnessed this whole process as if it had nothing whatsoever to do with Him. He was Vast and Peaceful, no matter whether this damaged carcass tried to pretend otherwise.

Despite his being below the surface of the ground, Theo sorely felt the night's bitter cold and wind. The mummy bag might end up housing an actual mummy; it could go either way. Theo found escape from his bodily sensations in the Absolute, which, of course, remained utterly unaffected by the low temperature of the Himalayan night.

The pilgrim began to experience something unusual. His Consciousness felt caressed, enfolded, and cherished by some great power of Love. What had been flat now became curved. What had been sterile now became fecund. The immense Ocean of the Absolute was now stirred and stimulated. The Love that was always immanent in It now came to life.

Theo knew the feeling of being held by a Divine Mother, of being cherished by her Eternal Love. She rocked him in her vast arms, and pressed him close to her bottomless breast. She promised him unending Devotion and infinite Benevolence. She sang him lullabies whose music was that of the spheres, whose lyrics were those of the heavens. Caressed by Her, he felt immaculate and forever safe.

A poet might have understood that Theo was, that night, being protected by the reclining Goddess Herself. He might have realized that She saw the danger faced by the One who sought Her, and came to his rescue with her tenderness. This artist might have said that her immense, rocky arms were all that saved the seeker on that cold and blustery night in the high mountains.

Theo tried to move his limbs, but they refused the command. When he finally was able to unzip the sleeping bag, he saw not the sky but snow. It had come down during the night and buried him.

Methodically, he began to scoop the snow off to the sides of the trench. It took him fifteen minutes to completely extricate himself. A scientist might have said that this snow-insulation kept him alive during the frigid night.

Once out, he had to dig in the snow to find his backpack and canteen. After some time, he succeeded in locating them. Now Theo looked about. The narrow backbone ridge stretched in front of him, white and immaculate like a young girl's confirmation-dress ribbon. The snow was not deep, but had covered, with a light, bright encrustation, many of the salient rocks and stony crevices that had formerly been dark. The undulations at the top of the mountain looked the same. Many of the boulders and steepest facades showed no effect from the snow, their angles having protected them from its settling.

The landscape looked as though it had been scrubbed perfectly clean. Every rock and stone gleamed. The snowy integument sparkled. The sky, devoid of clouds, looked like a vast lake of cobalt-blue water. Maybe this was what the slumbering mountains had been awaiting, this pristine morning of shining, smiling beauty.

Theo could not immediately set off. His body had been put, by the night's traumatic cold, into a sort of semi-comatose state. Not only did it lack energy, it continued to refuse commands to move. It might have been a solid block of ice, so little did it act like a regular human body.

The seeker closed his eyes and waited for the faint sunlight of the morning to thaw him out a bit. After half an hour, he managed to move his arms sufficiently to take some food out of his pack. Eating the food and drinking some water helped bring the recreant body back under his command.

But still he did not dare go forward. The ridge was narrow, and he knew that his balance was not sufficiently established to allow him to safely progress down it. So he stayed where he was and waited for his muscles to regain their wonted responsiveness and his corporal balance to again show itself as functional.

At midday, he set off. When he reached the end of the rocky backbone, and arrived at the third lane, which led to the summit, he was surprised yet again. This avenue was straight alright, but not level, as it had seemed to be from a distance. Instead, it resembled a greatly magnified black-diamond ski run, whose moguls proved to be taller than he was.

A creative philosopher observing the situation might have remarked that the Goddess had set her most difficult test as the final one. For this mountainside lane was angled at thirty-five degrees and offered the very thinnest of oxygen-poor air. Add in the effort required to surmount the man-sized moguls, and one faced a formidable challenge indeed.

The Third Avenue

As he prepared himself to begin the last leg up to the abode of the reclining goddess, Theo wondered whether or not his body could accomplish the task. These months in India had immeasurably deepened his spiritual vitality, expanded his Consciousness in ways that he could never have imagined possible, but, conversely, they had sapped the energies of his physical shell. His pilgrimage, the long trek that had finally brought him to this divine mountain, had been like an immensely fatiguing decathlon, tiring, straining, weakening, and draining his body day by day.

He had been deprived of oxygen and sufficient food, had slept in hard and cold places, had climbed steep mountains and crossed jagged stone-and-ice sheets. He had faced sickness, and weariness so deep it seemed to ache in his very bones. He had been cut and bruised, rained and snowed on, and nearly frozen to death. And all of it had taken a toll on his haggard and emaciated body.

Now, as he examined the angle and contours of this third avenue up the mountain, the seeker asked himself whether his body could overcome the challenge, or would simply fall down in the snow, never to rise again.

Any attachment to his body had long since dissolved, of course. But the pilgrim understood that he required it not only to summit the mountain but also, and far more importantly, to continue his search for Enlightenment.

But Theo trusted his Master, who, he knew, was constantly watching over him, so he summoned all his energy and began the climb.

Progress was extremely slow. His legs no longer felt like they were made of muscle; rather, they seemed like brittle sticks capable of cracking and splitting at any moment. On the first big mogul, he had to get down on all fours, like an infant first learning to how to move, and crawl up the snow-covered boulder. His lungs gave him so much trouble that he found it necessary to stop moving every twenty-five yards or so.

Once he got to the top of that first mogul, he saw that the topography of the avenue was even more threatening than he had understood it to be. What had looked, from a distance, like relatively smooth undulations were now each seen to be irregular small hills. This lane to the top was not even close to being a straight way; it was more of a series of individual battles that had to be fought in order to reach the next one waiting.

A different climber would have gotten frustrated and angry with this discovery. Theo did not. All he thought was that these new challenges would prove the ultimate test of his collapsing body.

Luckily, the wind had abated and the temperature remained at a bearable level. But his boots were in a sad state: pieces of the uppers, torn by sharp stones, flapped loose. The soles were gouged and cracked. The laces had broken and been tied back together many times. His face was sunburnt and his lips chapped. Every once in a while, his left knee gave signals that it was on the verge of dislocation. Sharp pain near his tail bone made certain movements difficult.

His clothes and body were falling apart, but Theo's Awareness remained pristine. The knotted boot laces floated in the Ocean of Tranquility and the ripped parka sleeve gleamed with the Light of the Absolute.

Essentially, the question became this: could the indomitable Spirit *will* the collapsing body to the top of the goddess's mountain? Theo kept moving forward, making little bits of progress, pausing to get as much oxygen as possible into his lungs and to rest his weary muscles.

One of the moguls looked completely unmanageable. It rose at a seventy-five-degree angle and was completely covered by frozen snow. Theo walked to both sides of the lane to see if another path existed, but one side led to a cliff and the other to a drop-off that would have been more difficult to ascend than the mogul itself.

He reached into his pack for some food and came out with an old, dusty energy bar he had totally forgotten about. Then he stood in front of the obstacle and examined it carefully. This close observation showed him that the uneven surface of the boulder provided finger and footholds. If he was diligent and skillful, it might be possible to climb *over* the rock in the same way that a mountaineer climbed *up* the side of a mountain.

All he could do was try. So try he did. It was necessary to first dig the snow out of these small recesses so that his hands and feet would be able to use them to their full extent. This excavation got more difficult the higher he climbed, for his strength was sapped by the ascension, and his body had to struggle to maintain its balance on the uneven surfaces.

After fifteen minutes of climbing, he was within a few feet of the top. Suddenly, every last bit of his energy disappeared. He felt like he could not lift a finger, let alone a leg or arm. And if he could not *climb*, why then he must *fall*. And a fall would mean his head striking jagged surfaces lower down on the boulder.

Theo was, as usual, acting automatically, relying on the intuitions springing into Consciousness from the needs of the time. Resting did not promise recovery; the fatigue was too complete. Going back down would be similarly impossible. He silently whispered a prayer of gratitude to his Master. *He* would assume control in this precarious situation.

The instant the prayer was complete, the seeker felt an uprush of energy through his body. Extending his arm, he found a chink in the boulder just big enough for his three fingers. Three more steps took him to the top of the rock, where he sat down, panting and exhausted, but consciously grateful to the Master.

After having endured what Theo had endured, not just now but over months spent inside caves in primitive conditions, most people would have suffered some sort of collapse. They would have sunk into despair, lamenting that they would never attain their goal, or they might have gotten furious, shaking their fist at the sky and shouting every epithet and bit of profanity in their vocabulary at unseen but malevolent powers. Not only did the seeker *not* behave in this way, he actually spent the next half hour thankfully acknowledging both his Teacher and the other Beings who had helped him get this far in his journey.

For he now constantly lived in a realm few people can even imagine: that of All Possibilities. Nothing could ever *possibly* go wrong in this world of his. Everything that happened, happened for a purpose, and a life-enriching purpose at that. Each test that he was put through was a necessary one. Every obstacle that he had to overcome was an inevitable one. The journey from spiritual ignorance to Enlightenment could not possibly be an easy one; otherwise, most of humanity would be enjoying the Bliss of Realization rather than suffering through the misery of ignorance.

Living every moment as if it were, as indeed it truly was, Forever, he never projected himself into the future, to a place further up this avenue, or to the next difficult mogul. Each step he took, he took in a Changeless Eternity, and nothing could pull him out of that residence in Pure Consciousness.

Theo was certainly aware of his bodily condition. He did not pretend to feel strong and healthy, stout and energetic. But the body would get along as best it could. All he could do was feed and water it and give it an opportunity for sleep at night.

The thirty minutes refreshed him sufficiently to allow the trek to continue. He slid down a relatively smooth section of the back of the boulder and regained flat ground. Then, once more, the process of putting one foot in front of the other began.

311

Further Along the Avenue

Theo successfully surmounted two more moguls before the sun started to set. The days were growing shorter at this season, thus reducing the hours available for climbing.

A gigantic mass of cumulus cloud hung poised over the reclining goddess. The cloud had the shape of a stretched out giant, whose brow was flushed with excitement and whose hips were inflamed with yellow fire. The groin of the giant, positioned directly over the goddess's hips, burned hot red. A poet would have imagined that two deities from a Greek myth were about to engage in celestial hierogamy. Theo noticed the smoldering hues of the mountain summit and the fiery shape of the cloud above it, but his main concern was shelter.

The best idea he could come up with was nestling in the lee of the mogul he had just made it over. He decided that he would spend the night sitting up, for his instincts told him that lying down might well prove fatal. So he climbed into his mummy sleeping bag and pressed as far as possible into an indentation in the big rock. Only the Master would be able to assure his survival for yet another night in this frigid weather near the very top of the world.

That night the weather took a serious turn for the worse. The wind blasted the summit and Theo's sheltering boulder lay directly in its path. The temperature dropped ten degrees.

The seeker sank into deep meditation and loss contact with his body soon after entering it. In the morning, an observer would have noticed an upright body squeezed into a crevice of a large boulder. And the body did not move.

Only a physician would have been able to accurately describe Theo's physical condition that morning. Anyone could have guessed that he suffered from hypothermia after spending the whole night exposed to the assault of the Himalayan cold. But he never moved while meditating, so the observer who knew about his habits could not have been sure whether he was alive or dead.

The sun rose that morning with a sort of anemic lethargy. It seemed to have to drag itself above the horizon. Its wan ochre, dandelion, and butterscotch yellows looked depressed. The distant stretch of mountains remained black. Even the sea of high fog that extended from east to west could not manage more than the palest of violet hues.

Still, Theo did not move. It was just as the sun made its full appearance on the horizon that a shape of brilliant light settled around the meditator. The shape most closely resembled a large pair of wings, but exactly what it was no one could have told. The light compressed itself around the seated human. It faded and then brightened numerous times, looking something like a fire that had been partially doused and then refueled. In a final flaring moment, the light exploded like a fireball. And then it disappeared.

Ten minutes later, Theo began to move slightly. First his fingers shivered; then his arms twitched; and, finally, his eyelids began to flutter. Life had come back into his body. Something had revivified him. Something had sucked out the cold from his physical shell and breathed vital warmth back into it. He was alive.

It took more than an hour for the seeker to fully return to life. It would have required a doctor to say whether he had completed that most difficult of round-trip legs, from death to life. But there was no mistaking the fact that now he *was* alive.

Gradually, he regained control over his limbs. His hands made tiny little gestures; his nose crinkled; he worked his lips. Only when he had assumed command over his torso and head did he contemplate the use of his legs. Standing up loomed as a terrific challenge.

When he did succeed in rising, Theo felt unsteady on his legs. His sense of equilibrium had left him. The legs did not any longer want to work in tandem. It took half an hour for him to be able to take a step.

As he prepared to move forward, Theo had no thoughts about what had happened overnight. Had he checked back to his experience at the time, he would have found that nothing had changed, even when that last connection to the body snapped. His Awareness continued to be the same, all that night, as it had been the previous day and as it continued to be today.

Consciousness was one thing, but the body another. There was no ignoring the fact that the physical mechanism he depended on to reach the summit had died and come back to life. Even now it felt as if it had one foot in death and the other in life. The sensations it passed to his Awareness were indescribable, at least in precise terms. They were of vagueness and disconnection, of coldness and stoppage. Despite his having gotten the systems working again, the body seemed not to consider itself totally alive.

But the seeker knew that time was as short as the day, so he began to advance up the third avenue. When he reached the next mogul, not as intimidating as the last one, but still substantial, he stopped. The body would never be able to climb over this obstacle. That much was certain. He trudged to each side looking for a way around the boulder. On its right lay the narrowest of thin strips of earth: about three inches of snow-covered rock, below which fell an abyss five hundred feet deep.

Theo realized that his balance at this time was unsteady. And it was obvious that teetering either way would result in a fatal fall onto the rocks below. Yet, no other options presented themselves.

Having no remaining fear of death, his nerves did not complicate the challenge. He chose to wear his backpack rather than throw it forward; if he did not make it across, and had to turn back, he would need the sleeping bag to survive. The pilgrim examined the snow on the thin strip of ground carefully. Then he started forward.

Astonishingly, his movements were automatic and correct. He remained upright and placed each foot securely before moving the other one. Five minutes later, he stood on the far side of the mogul.

Progress that day was slow indeed. If he had been weak before the "death" experience, he was now outspent and foredone. In a similar situation, a normal person would have found their mental condition in correspondence with their physical one. Tiredness would have meant depression. Theo, on the other hand, knew no change in his Awareness, despite the thoroughly worn-down condition of his body. But that body, at its best, could barely maintain a slow walking pace. The old enemies, thin air and enervation, guaranteed that the machinery would never get out of its grinding first gear.

By the close of the day, Theo had made it to the end of the third avenue. He fully expected to see the summit just above him. But perspective had, yet again, put upon him. Rather than the reclining goddess, the seeker observed two wide plateaus of level snow, which, being below the level of the third avenue, had remained invisible.

Thoroughly spent, he decided to wait until the next day to venture onto the first of these broad fields. The thought came to him to dig a snow fort in which he might manage to survive the night's cold. His energy being at its nadir, an observer might reasonably have wondered whether or not the climber could actually manage such an excavation. Without a second thought, he began to dig in the side of a small rise, planning to uncover enough of its interior to shelter his body.

As he dug, the sun attempted to cheer him on by washing the distant range with a pigment of frozen fire: a cool, dampened admixture of pale yellow and pale rose. Then the star sought to amuse him by multiplying, creating a flattened twin just above itself, so that the horizon seemed to offer up a double-yoked egg. Livid isles of cloud floated untethered, and the upper atmosphere turned slightly green.

The digging took hours. Snow had a greater power of resistance than Theo's hands did power of attack. But he kept at it, tossing little pile after little pile to the side, using his feet as shovels, and wielding a small stone that he found nearby. By around midnight, he had scraped out a hole big enough to fit himself into. He climbed into the sleeping bag and then pulled snow in front of the opening to block out the wind. By the time he had finished working, the digger had a reasonable facsimile of a snow cave around his body.

The work had raised his body temperature, which proved a blessing. Now he would see if that higher temperature, partly preserved by the mummy bag, could withstand the onslaught of the Himalayan night.

As Theo meditated that night, he had a strange experience. The six Beings from the cave with niches, whom he had watched in that night of initiation the Master had set up for him, now appeared close to him, sitting in a circle, their niches still behind them. They pressed quite close to his body, forming a tight circle around him. The Beings looked just as they had before, partly human and partly divine, with long hair and beards and faces of the ultimate purity.

The seeker dissolved into the syrupy Absolute that was enlivened by the presence of these divine Beings. He later had no recollection of the experience other than one of the most delightful Bliss.

Morning Comes

Theo did not emerge from the snow cave until the morning sun was high in the heavens. He had no doubt whatsoever that the Beings had, by their close proximity, kept him alive that night. Without them, even the enclosure and the sleeping bag would not have sufficed to preserve his life. But, despite their assistance, his vis vitae, or vital force, had ebbed near the danger point. Only the higher temperature brought by the sunlight succeeded in pulling the climber out of his snow cocoon.

As he chewed on the last piece of his dried fruit, Theo realized that his food supplies were running as low as his energy levels. There was, of course, nothing edible to be found at this height in the mountains. But he knew that the Master would always look after him, no matter how dire his predicament might seem to a reasonable observer; for it had been his Teacher who had sent the Beings to shield him from the frigid night weather.

It took an effort to get his pack onto his back, but he managed to do so. And then the trek continued. One step after another, always watching out for hidden holes that might twist an ankle and for sharp stones that might cut a boot. At least there were no more moguls in sight. The snow stretched out flat ahead of him. His footprints in the powder looked like alien hieroglyphics.

The day seemed to elongate unnaturally. The precious hours of sunshine, during which the pilgrim had to make his progress for the day, lingered, almost as if they had been bespelled to move more slowly than they were meant to. Theo made it over both broad fields of snow before the sun began its glorious ritual of saying goodbye to the earth. The reclining goddess's head was only a few hundred yards higher. If his body could make it through another night, why then he would actually meet her on the following day.

Never before had Theo faced the shelter challenge that he faced that night; for he stood on a small plateau, flat as a frozen lake and certainly as cold as one. No rocks offered themselves as safeguards. He lacked the energy to dig a cave, and the snow was not deep enough to let him do so even had he been able to. This flat space was completely open to the Himalayan winds. Even the most tested of mountaineers would have felt depressed by this predicament. But the seeker trusted both his destiny and his Master and felt no worries.

As the sun sank, the cloud masses overhead came to resemble a vast lake of boiling lava. Great boulders of scoria, purplish-black in color, had been thrown to the sides of the lake. The central mouth of the volcano had eructated broad rivers and thin streams of molten yellow in all directions. Hot liquid threatened gray rocks, ready to melt them into oblivion. The hot edge of the lava colored the entire lower sky warm peach. Snippets of cloud looked like cerise islands fringed in liquid fire. A poet might have felt warmed by this vision of fire in the sky. Theo took in its beauty, but saw behind it That which was the sine qua non of all beauty, the Absolute.

He turned in every direction to see if he could find anything at all to help his body make it through the night. But he saw everywhere nothing but snow. The thought came to him: This will be my last night in this body. But he instantly recognized it for the vestige of ignorance that it was. The Master had brought him to this mountain for a reason; and the reason was that he should reach its summit. The Saint would never abandon him so close to the goal.

Practically, however, he could think of nothing more to do than climb into his mummy bag and turn his body away from the prevailing easterly wind. He would enter the meditative state and trust to the unlimited powers of his Guru.

The sun disappeared and the night grew cold. Theo lost contact with his body, and remained deep in the Silence of Pure Consciousness. Suddenly, his inner vision exploded with Light. He

318

opened his eyes and saw, directly across from him, Babaji! The hairless face and torso, the long hair, and the deerskin were just as they had been during that first wonderful meeting, when the Great Being had levitated off the boulder in the company of worshipful angels.

Babaji once again sat in a blaze of Light. And once more Theo had the impression that this Great Master maintained only the faintest connection with the earth and all material things. This time Babaji did not communicate with the disciple telepathically; he had no intellectual message to convey. But what he did do mattered much more than any words could possibly have. A warm cocoon of Love enwrapped Theo. He felt himself to be floating in a veritable heaven of tranquility. Peace, divine Peace, permeated every cell of his body and every interstice of his soul. He was left with no experience of the physical form. But he did experience the perfect wonder of Enlightened Contentment.

He had lost sight of Babaji under the influence of the flotational cocoon that enveloped him. When he finally did open his eyes, the Great Being was no longer to be seen. But morning had come, and Theo's body was thoroughly alive.

Peaking

Babaji had somehow reinvigorated Theo's body. Its wonted deep fatigue was gone; its joints felt looser and better lubricated; its muscles no longer ached. And the time spent with the Great Being had stirred and enlivened the Pure Consciousness in which the seeker lived at all times. He was in ideal shape to summit the torso of, and come face-to-face with, the reclining goddess.

The final few hundred yards of climbing had to be done at a steep degree of incline. Theo could only progress a yard or so before having to stop for rest. Finally, in the late afternoon, sweating profusely and nearly numb from exhaustion, he stepped onto the summit of the mountain.

Immediately, he sank to his knees and spoke silent words of thanks to his Master. He also expressed his gratitude to Babaji and the six Beings who had helped him survive those two frigid nights. And he spoke lovingly to the reclining goddess on whose outstretched form he now knelt.

The atmosphere of the summit differed from anything Theo had as yet encountered in India. The very ground itself, though formed of solid rock, exhaled the perfume of fertility. The slabs of granite over which he walked pulsed with that profound energy that could, with a mere flinch, crack wide open the earth itself. Above everything, the summit breathed forth the Spirit of life, the creative, nurturing Soul that inspirited both animate and inanimate creation.

As he explored the top of the mountain, toward which his tired feet had been so long moving, the seeker made a discovery: three-quarters of the way down the "body" of the goddess was a perfectly smooth-sided and deep hollow, a sort of earthly foramen so finely fashioned that it looked to be a work of art. The snow had piled up in shreds edging the circumference of the sunken sanctuary. The pilgrim thought that this natural opening in the earth might be an ideal place to shelter from the inevitable darkness and cold of the coming night.

As he wandered from spot to spot on this highest of high locations, Theo once more experienced that feeling he had known in the presence of Babaji, of being enfolded in the warm cotton robes of Love and penetrated by the calming motes of Peace. Only this time, the Love and the Peace revealed a more intimate character and engrossed him with a charm of a deep richness he had not imagined possible. The mountain summit seemed to be entrancing, thrilling, and delighting him, but not at all in a grossly physical way. The spell being woven around him was of Cosmic Tenderness. It was almost as if the solicitude of all the world's mothers had been united in the atmosphere being constantly exhaled from the pores of this mountain summit.

As Theo stood looking out over the panorama spread before him: the range of the Himalayas encircling the summit, the plateaus leading up to it, the three long avenues, the further valleys and lower hills, a sweet syrup of happiness dripped slowly down from his mouth into his torso and lower limbs. The sun was now descending behind the farthest peaks. A band of horizontal cloud resting above those peaks turned pure rose, presenting a ribbon of color that would have thrilled a painter's heart. Above this ribbon rested three bunny-shapes of cumulus, which the sun had colored primary yellow. And the vault of the western sky was uniformly washed in the most delicate tint of crocus lavender.

The great world rested in Peace. The natural elements moved in Bliss. The universe showed itself to be an immense work of art whose quality no hand could ever improve.

Theo climbed down into the opening in the earth, thinking that he would spend the night there protected by its invaginating walls. He discovered that the bottom of the hole was covered in soft, finely sifted

321

earth. He would meditate here with the night stars glinting down their benison upon him.

What a joy that sheathing burrow turned out to be! Possibly due to volcanic activity within the mountain, the place stayed warm during the night. The soft seat proved a welcome relief to the cold stones on which the seeker had so often sat. The high walls completely blocked out the wind. Theo settled into his meditation.

Sometime in the night, he felt compelled to open his eyes. Before him sat the Goddess. She was not simply a "reclining goddess," but *the* Goddess, Shakti Herself. As Theo contemplated the Goddess, he felt overpowered by her Cosmic Energy. In her shone the heat of not merely a unitary sun, but of all the stars combined. From her radiated the heat not of a single lava flow, but of all volcanoes combined. About her spread the love not of a solitary wife, but of every wife, mother, and lover who had ever existed. Her beauty was not that of a woman but of Women. Her charm could not be constrained by a personality; it encompassed all Being. In her lay that ultimate paradox: Infinite Potential unmanifested. One got the idea that she could have, with a swipe of her hand, spread new galaxies across the heavens; but her hand stayed still. Her smile could have caused the demons in hell themselves to grin; but her lips remained straight. Her eyes might have burnt a channel clear through the core of the planet; but she held them in check.

Theo quickly realized his bad form and bowed deeply, and remained low, in front of the Goddess. He had, at first, been too astonished by the sight of Her to remember his manners. He did not straighten up until the thought came to him that doing so would be acceptable. The Goddess kept transforming before his eyes. One moment she was white; the next she turned pink and then red. She held a lotus flower; then, the same hand held a staff. A lion peeked out from behind her. No, it was a perfectly white cow. A snake crawled up her arm, only to turn into the prongs of a trident.

Although he had not thought of it, Theo was now in the presence of the consort and essential partner of the God he had previously met, Shiva. Shiva shone as the Silent Absolute, and Shakti danced as the Living Energy of that same Pure Consciousness. Without Her, He could produce nothing. Hers was the animating force of life, its current and power, its well of living water and its cave of desires. Shiva showed the universe, but Shakti created it. Hers was the fecund vitality flowing in every cell, vein, and body of the magnificent cosmos.

Theo's experience with Shakti was the perfect converse of that he had known with Shiva. If He was passive, She was active. If He silently displayed, She noisily created. If He demonstrated potential, She made that potential come to life. His energy was that of the stern father; hers that of the adoring mother.

And the seeker knew now an entirely different Divinity. Ensconced in this deep hole, this omphalos of the world, he enjoyed the liveliness of the sacred, its dance and song, its tender and dulcifluous currents, its bright colors and euphonious sounds. The Absolute lay all around him, but It was enlivened now, bubbling with energetic impulses, frothing with pink bubbles of happiness.

Whereas Shiva had shown the pilgrim heavens and hells, galaxies and constellations, his partner revealed meadows of vast extent, covered in profusions of pastel-hued blooms; oceans teeming with gleaming fishes and porous sponges, clawed crustaceans and mammals the size of space shuttles; and skies whose clouds and lights wrote poems capable of breaking hearts. Shakti conjured spinning houris, dark-maned and sloe-eyed; handsome warriors galloping on sleek steeds; diademed princesses, upper arms coruscant with gems; silk-clad maharajas mounted on caparisoned elephants; showers of exploding meteors; geysers of spurting volcanoes; and lightning storms that looked like intricate lace electrified.

And throughout this entire display of exquisite beauty ran a deep current of Love. Shakti loved her Creation, loved it as a Cosmic Mother should. The flowers and lobsters, rapids and precipices, thunders and rumbles were Her children at play in the vast nursery of the universe. She delighted in their antics and encouraged their mischief. She took pleasure in their frivolities and solaced their sufferings. Her great eye missed nothing that was occurring in the cosmos: She saw everything and approved it all.

Let Shiva sit, silent in deep contemplation. She would dance, and by her dance enliven the very molecules of the most deeply buried rocks in the Himalayas. She would jump, and by her jump lift the heavens above to new heights. She would spin, and by her spin twirl the planets, constellations, and galaxies in their own revolutions. Shakti was the young wife tugging her sedate husband by the hand, pulling him out into the spangled morning to frolic in the redolent gardens and steal kisses in the shadowed woods.

Although Theo thought none of this, still, he knew it all.

In the Womb of the Goddess

When the morning came, Shakti was gone. Theo opened his eyes only to see an earthen wall where her bright form had been. The soft, pearly light of dawn played delicately above the opening in his deep hole.

Theo saw the world afresh that morning. The Goddess had enlivened his Consciousness such that the flat Absolute, in which he normally moved, now pulsed with energy and liveliness. For the first time in a long while, he began to examine his situation. He knew that he had progressed quite far on the path toward the goal of Enlightenment. Pure Consciousness was his home and the "external" world now appeared as a mere configuration of that Consciousness. But he also realized that he had not yet *arrived*. Some ineffable, ultimately subtle barrier still separated him from the final breakthrough.

He asked himself what he could do to achieve it. Intuition told him to remain here, atop the Sacred Mountain, and continue his meditation routine. The Master, he felt sure, would guide him as to any new direction he should take. Practically, he was nearly out of food. And nothing edible grew on this high summit. Water was not a problem, as snow abounded here. His body felt much stronger and more vital after the encounter with Shakti. Some of her vast energy must have penetrated deep into his body.

Theo also reflected on all the amazing experiences he had had since finding the Saint: meeting Shivaji, Anandaji, Babaji, the Great Beings in the niches, Ishvara, and now Shakti. The Master had generously showered rich moments on his undeserving disciple. And what would the future bring?

The seeker remained in that deep enclosure for seven days straight. Meditation blended into waking Consciousness so smoothly that he

325

would not have been able to tell one from the other. And he had many unusual experiences: the Goddess appeared before him and performed her thrilling cosmic dance, drawing him to Her, so that he stood in for Shiva as it were; She took him to a vast garden in which aromatic gardenias blended their perfumes with those of erect sandalwood trees and drooping racemes of lilac, in which fawns danced in graceful ballets, in which lovers upheld their joined hands to frame the globular moon; She set the planets spinning ever faster and then slowed them to a stop with the extended palm of her hand; She opened up the earth to reveal the slowly spreading rock of its mantle, the hot liquid of its outer, and the scalding solidity of its inner core; She let him see inside massive oaks, so that he could watch the phloem feeding the rest of the tree, the cambium cell layer responsible for its growth, the sapwood carrying water to all its parts, and the dead but ultra-strong heartwood.

The Goddess introduced him to the normally invisible creatures of the astral world, and he delighted in the frolics of the fairies and the worshipful glidings of the winged angels. She took him to the depths of the sea so that he might observe the strange bioluminescent squid, supergiant amphipods, and eerie snailfish. Everywhere Shakti appeared, life forms swayed and moved in greeting. Never had Theo suspected that so very much of the invisible world was actually teeming with life.

At the end of seven days, the seeker emerged from his womb and stood atop the sacred mountain, looking out over the magnificent panorama of the Himalayas. The white-hatted peaks sparkled under the morning sunshine. The wispy clouds looked as though they were straining to stay above the heaven-piercing pinnacles. The chiaroscuro of the black rock faces set against their white counterparts implied epic contrast. The shimmering sun smiled its approval of all over which it reigned.

Theo saw the Absolute everywhere he looked. But the Goddess had brought Divinity to the Infinite Consciousness; she had allowed him to understand that not just the depth but the surface of life twinkled with sacred energy. The world was alive to him now as it had never before been.

But as the seeker looked out over that awe-inspiring scene, he realized that despite all the progress he had made over the past months, despite the coaching and guidance from his Master and all the others, despite the visions of Shiva and the tutelage of Shakti, he had not yet attained his goal of complete Enlightenment. Something held him back. Some tiny knot somewhere within his soul prevented him from merging completely with the Absolute, never again to stand apart from it. The problem was that he had no idea either what this small fault was or how he should go about correcting it.

That evening, as sat atop the Goddess's mountain watching the sunset, he noticed that the near mountains lay shadowed in dull white and gray, while the far range glowed in fiery shades: ochraceous, primrose, and persimmon. That far range was where his destiny called him. He yearned to glow with the fires of Perfect Realization.

His eyes naturally closed. Before him stood the Master, smiling and benevolent. Without words, he conveyed to his student that he approved of all the great distance he had traveled, on foot and in spirit. Without speaking, he communicated his understanding of the disciple's poignant predicament: that of being so close to the goal, but not yet there. Without gestures, he showed Theo that his blessing was upon him now and always.

Transported

When Theo opened his eyes, he found himself back in the Master's cave. Everything was just as it had been months before: the dhoori burned low in the center of the space; the aromatic dhoop sticks provided some light and sweet fragrance; the blankets were neatly stacked as they always were; the water can sat in its usual place; and the photograph of the Master's Guru leaned against the far wall.

The Saint had somehow transported him from that distant summit to this cave where he had first heard the living words of Enlightenment from a Realized Master. But the Master himself was not here. Theo understood that he had been brought back to the home of his Teacher so that the holy vibrations of the Saint and all his predecessors would surround him as he attempted to attain that highest of all summits: Perfect Enlightenment.

He closed his eyes and sank into the now lively Absolute. Time did not pass for the meditator, although, outside the cave, the sun rose and sank and the moon changed phases, although the earth spun and rotated and the creatures slept and woke.

He was very close now, but some subtle knot, some connected thread still tied Theo ever so faintly to a sense of individuality. He stood on the brink of the great leap into Infinity, but something ever so tenuous held him on the ledge. He would feel the Great Ocean of Being about to sweep him away forever, but then it ebbed before engulfing him. Nothing had ever seemed so hard to him as this abandonment to Impersonal Consciousness. All the lives lived in egoic delusion, all the years spent in the roles of a persona tugged on him. The mind and ego would not die before expending every resource at their disposal.

Images of tantalizing beauties danced before his inner eye. Fantasies of fame and wealth shone clear as day. His children pleaded

328

with him not to abandon them. All the memories that brought him greatest pleasure flooded into his awareness.

And he would refuse to grab hold of these temptations, continuing with his meditation, preserving his Consciousness of the Absolute. Yet, STILL the release would not come. The mind would not let go once final time.

At last he opened his eyes and rose from his seat. After leaving the cave, he walked down to the Master's stream and sat listening to the purling water silvered and asparkle under the influence of the soft rays radiating down from the immense full moon overhead. As he sat there quietly, Theo heard a soft rustle, whose sound he recognized. The Master had occupied a place by his side. The disciple bowed his head and pressed his palms together in gratitude for this gift. He felt the rich waves of Love washing over him from the Guide who had, for so long, *watched* over him. Such perfect Peace and such innocent Bliss shone in His face.

The Saint leaned close and whispered something in Theo's ear.

And the world was a vision of Light!

Thank you for reading!

If you enjoyed this book, it would help me spread the word of Enlightenment if you could write a review of it on Amazon. Having reviews helps people who are deciding whether to purchase the book make a decision. Reviews are not easy to get, so if you could take a few minutes to write one, I would be greatly obliged.